SAMUEL GRIFFIN

SEEKER

The Sentinel Archives
Part One

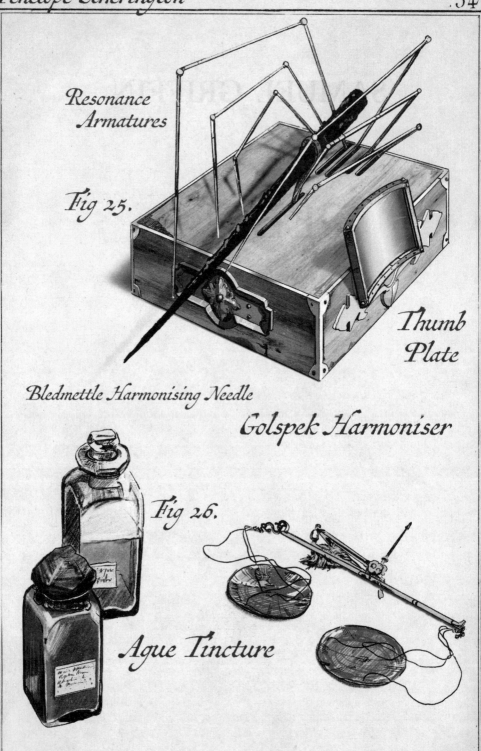

Resonance
Armatures

Fig 25.

Thumb
Plate

Bledmettle Harmonising Needle

Golspek Harmoniser

Fig 26.

Ague Tincture

GOLSPEK HARMONISER

SAMUEL GRIFFIN

SEEKER

The Sentinel Archives
Part One

Panthe Press

Panthe Press
www.panthe-press.co.uk

This hardback edition published 2024

3 5 7 8 4 2 1 6 9 10

A catalogue record for this book
is available from the British Library

UK Hardback Edition: ISBN 978 1 8380212 2 1
Worldwide Ebook Edition ISBN: 97818380212 7 6
US Hardback Edition ISBN: 97818380212 3 8

Edited by Rebecca Sweeney
Cover Design by Panthe Press
Cover Illustrations by Warmtail
Chapter & Device Art by Jonas of Stardust

Set in Adobe Caslon Pro by Panthe Press, Glasgow,
Lanarkshire, Scotland

Printed and bound in Great Britain by CPI

*To Cathy, who carried me halfway there, and to Becky,
who took me the rest of the way.*

Ken, Nina, Roy, Mary, I wish you could see this...

WHAT EARLY READERS
ARE SAYING

'This is a new flintlock fantasy that I devoured in only a couple days... this has a chance to become one of, if not the best flintlock fantasy out there.'

'Fantastical threads running throughout the tale surrounded by real, living imaging. Thoroughly enjoyed the story and a terrific crescendo to finish.'

'I loved the magic and fantasy.'

'What a great book!'

'I absolutely loved the lore and world building, it felt like slowly peeling back many gossamer layers of an intricate universe. If you're looking for a unique and complex story, check out Seeker!'

'...found the whole book to be utterly entrancing.'

'I love the unique lore that Griffin has created...'

'Seeker by Samuel Griffin is such a unique debut book that is laced with equal parts magic and fantasy...'

'I found myself immersed into a captivating tale of mystery set in the Regency era...'

'...a wonderful fantasy tale set in the Regency era with a good measure of magic thrown in too!'

'There is an ever-present strangeness that lingered as I read...'

'...if you're looking for incredible, descriptive writing? This is a must-pick-up book for you!'

'This is a truly wonderful book and I look forward to seeing what comes next!'

'I hope this book gets the hype it really deserves...'

-NetGalley pre-release reviewers

"Of this, sir, I am certain: that which we have held to be the stuff of magic, shall yield to our investigation and the keenness of our reason, as have all other facets of the natural world."

Private Petition from Marquis Lark to Freeman Hawkins, General Secretary of the Consort Perpetual

The Year Three, in the Fifth Hundred of the Signing of the Great Concord of Westerbrook

Part One

UNREASONABLE ACQUISITIONS

Chapter One

A PREPARATORY SCHOOL FOR ORPHANED WAR GIRLS

Since the sickening revelation my actions may be irreversible, I have been scouring the library for anything that might soothe my mind. Such that I might gain some understanding of what has befallen me. What I have done.

I have found, in a book so old the letters are much faded, an ancient mantra used throughout the ages. It seems it may be useful for those in my unusual situation, though I cannot be certain.

Regardless, I have memorised it. In the small hope it might offer me some protection. For I know not what else to do.

I will always remember the day I was bought. Which may be of little surprise, for who could expect to forget such a thing? And I shall tell of it, for I believe I have earned that right.

The month was twomoon's rise; the year four, the fifth hundred since the signing of the Great Concord of Westerbrook; the place the Preparatory School for Orphaned War Girls within the Protectorate of Quom.

One may imagine that such a day would be momentous. And it undoubtedly was, if we are to exclusively regard its effect upon myself and my situation, at the least.

1

Yet, in many ways it was rather ordinary; it was not a day of explosive colour or action or violence or magic. No, such things would come later. Instead, it was a day full of the mundane little bothers which plagued all the other days I had known, and would plague many more thereafter.

I remember, for example, there being a small stone in my tattered shoe which I, for some reason, chose not to remove. I recall that my hair did not respond to my fretful ministrations in any satisfactory manner, but that I tried for too many moments to tame it, regardless. For such were the habits of presentation in which I had been ruthlessly schooled. I did so, hidden away for as long as I dared before resigning myself to clipping it up as neatly as I could manage, as was the mode of that place.

I recall, too, the quality of the afternoon air: sweltering, and oppressive, even by the muggy standards of Quom. The day had a constitution as thick as soup, sapping the power to think, or work, or do much of anything at all. To add insult to this considerable injury, my threadbare, overwashed, many-times mended shift and my undergarments were stuck to me in all the places that were most unfortunate.

I was called out of our morning's tiring study by Mistress Jenkinson and left amidst gasps and mutterings; there was but one reason the governess would fetch a girl herself. A keen jolt of fear recast my sluggish musings as feverish worries. The governess explained the situation to me in a clipped tone that matched the sharp rap of her heel upon the floor: the free gentleman who had come to purchase me was not the sort one would keep waiting. We would be leaving that very afternoon.

Then she left me sitting in a rather pretty but uncomfortable chair, to attend a final meeting with the stranger. Though one point was made most plain to me before she departed. The terms of my indentured servitude were clear and fair. Many of my peers would be frightfully fortunate to sit in my position and I should consider myself incredibly grateful.

I shall record here only what was painfully true: I was *not*.

I shall record something else here, too: I was, in this matter as in many other things, a somewhat wilful child. Though one considered somewhat strange in her proclivities by those whose duty it was to administer my rudimentary education and guardianship.

Which was to say that I possessed a meticulous, obsessive nature which frustrated my superiors. Patterns, and order, were the balm for my mind. I tried to administer this structure to my surroundings in excess. Tallies and systems and rhymes and categorisations did I devise, games and metrics and monikers. Private little things, that were mine alone. All for the passing quiet that they provided to me. It would not be a stretch to say that these were my true friends, truer than any I knew in that place in all of fifteen years.

It took a long time, their conversation. I stared out the window, to the sight I had studied all my life whenever I was called to the governess' chambers for discipline, which was rather frequently, or for commendation, which was not. Were the option open to me, I would have continued my reading, for the calming measure such an act had on my mood. Instead, I nipped the skin of my thigh between my forefinger and thumb, and nibbled my lip. Safe in the knowledge that the rule which had so mercilessly watched over me, and should chide me strongly for these inelegant habits of mine, was very nearly over. Though what might replace it I did not know.

I wondered where I might be taken, thinking of the tales the girls often whispered to one another. Those which seemed likely: a terrorising mistress on the tea plantations, in far away Kalchetti; a simple clerk in some rural part of Quom; housekeeper to a crazed minor landowner intolerable to his own family. Those which seemed — or, at least, I hoped to be — less likely: a bawdy house moll, in the Concord; a lone picker of tabac in some arid, shelterless field; nursemaid in a sick house for weeping pox, typhus, or some other grim and as yet unknown malady.

With neither materials nor opportunity to entertain myself, I turned instead to the effect of my earlier privations. I was frightfully hungry, my stomach clenching painfully at periodic intervals. One of the younger girls had been sent to fetch me for lunch and I had been happy for the opportunity to leave the stiff chair. But when the lunch matron had walked down the row of expectant young ladies, I had refused the offered food as a final act of rebellion against the place. An act which won nothing more than a sad little shake of the head, her lips pressed firmly into a line, before her businesslike resumption of the afternoon's duty. The familiar clang of the tureen and the wet splat of a single ladle of watery pease upon pewter for the next girl marked the end of her regard.

Once we had been dismissed from the meal, I dashed to our shared rooms to attend to my final preparations, lest I have to leave my few things behind. The other girls had tittered and hissed at me, and Jrusinda's terrorising hand had leapt out to prod me with a quill.

I had ignored the offending appendage with the regal indifference of a queen. Or so, at least, I fancied, despite the prickling heat that burnt across my cheeks as I knelt down to gather my meagre possessions. Before I strode away, forever, with all the decorum I could muster.

No word, or glance, did I offer any of them.

Today I am equipped with the knowledge that my future was to be far greater, more exciting, and more disturbing than anything so simple as my young imagination could then conjure. Indeed, looking back, my forecast was positively quaint. I ask myself a question often, and it is this: if I had understood all that was to befall me, would I have run, that day, or exulted?

I find I do not know.

I continued to sulk silently as the end of the afternoon drew near and still I sat outside the governess' chambers, my collection of paltry possessions at my feet. And, just as I had begun to believe that perhaps this day was not the day I should be bought after all, that I might not leave, nor find a new life, came the moment that the door swung open with a familiar creak. For here he was, he who had bought me and would take me away to who knew where.

In the doorway stood a man, as I had expected, though he was older than I had imagined upon hearing his approaching footsteps. His eyes, somewhat bloodshot, were brown and deep. His gaze was curious, almost apologetic, as he considered me. He wore a linen shirt of moderate quality, white, and breeches of the same, in black. His hands seemed very large, despite the fact he was tall.

He was the type of person you could not imagine had ever been young. As if he had instead simply come into being one day, lined and wrinkled and bent as he was, moles and all. There was something undeniably solid about him that put to mind the gnarled old cedar tree nestled in the scree of the gardens of the school. That had grown longer than anyone could remember, having been planted, perhaps, by the folk who founded the colony many, many years ago.

I kept my eyes lowered, unsure if I was expected — or permitted — to speak. Until softly, though without any great intonation, he said,

"Shay?" When I nodded, he smiled, showing me long teeth. "Good. I am Ridley. Ridley Fassinger. You are to come with me and I hope we shall get along well. I believe you have been informed of... our agreement?"

He reached out one of his large hands, and clutched it above the leather bag he had placed upon the floor. He did this three times before drawing it back into himself, in what I surmised in that moment was a particular habit of his. Then he massaged them together, nodding to himself and this business upon which he must attend.

Despite the long time I had waited, my eyes were alive in those moments, and I latched onto every detail of his appearance. I noticed those hands were calloused and well used, so too that his nails were clipped, though not fastidiously, and very clean. Who was he, this man who would buy me, and where did he wish to take me? I remembered suddenly the stories the girls told one another; a final raking glance confirmed no marriage ink below his earlobe.

As if capable of understanding my thoughts, he chose that very moment to speak once more.

"Well," he said. "We must be underway. No doubt you've questions. I'm afraid those must wait for now. A long journey we have ahead of us." He extended his hand to me. "But I shall say this. If you can find it within yourself to trust me, you shall find me reasonable. I will always be fair with you. On this you have my word."

When I did not reply, he asked, softly, searchingly, as if to a babe or a simpleton, "Well, now. What do you think to that?"

I managed a stiff little nod of my head, and I grasped his hand in mine. It was reassuringly warm and dry, despite the oppressive heat.

Now he did permit himself to take up his bag, and surprised me by stepping past me to take up mine. The scent of cloves and camphor, unknown to me at the time, came with him, sharp and astringent.

Then he turned and walked out without another word, his long stride eating up the bare floorboards. After a moment's hesitation, I rose to follow, trotting slightly on stiff legs to keep up. And we were out the door of the mistress' corridor, then out the main door of the school, and gone.

The strangest thing is that I cannot recall whether I looked back. I like to think that I did not.

***

We were to depart the Protectorate of Quom within two days whence I was purchased, and we spent the intervening time acquiring me a small number of garments. Any details pertaining to my future were limited, and to be expanded upon at our arrival. The clothes we obtained were simple: two shifts, stays, petticoats, skirts, and nightcap. They provided little clue as to my destiny.

Then began a long, interminable voyage of exhaustion and confusion, and now I did experience new colours, and sights, and sounds. Though a vicious bout of tropical fever struck me and many of our fellow passengers in the first week of our month-long journey, and from that point did not let up, causing the greatest embarrassment and discomfort.

This terrible truth was compounded by a lifelong terror of excessive heights, and a questionable constitution for physical excess. For while the ship and the water were entirely new to me, the familiar lurch in my stomach as I made my way up the slick, slimy gangway in all of its narrow horror was, of a certainty, no such stranger. Heights had always been my deepest torment, wherever I encountered them.

The motion of the ship coupled with the feeling of being so very, very high up made me so unsteady and nauseated that I scarcely dare speak. I could not admire the construction of the vessel as I had wished, nor could I enjoy the novelty of my first ever voyage, across the Whispering Sea. My first trip of any reasonable distance, to tell the entire truth.

I had known a brief desire to speak with the pretty ladies in the fine clothing who I saw when we were boarding. But this desire was soon driven out of me by my dreadful ailment.

Indeed, my anxiety, shortly followed by the sickness many of the passengers succumbed to, almost trumped my not inconsiderable trepidation on the subject of my new life. I was unable to get the measure of this man who had bought me, learning only that he was a surgeon, by trade. Perhaps mercifully, he failed to press me for conversation, merely offering me water and several kerchiefs, which I ruined far beyond recovery.

Other than these short interactions, I saw very little of Fassigner, spending much of the voyage upon my bed in a cramped cabin I shared with five other women, more than half of us sick as horses. I remember very little of my first time upon a ship, beyond the painful cramps, my awful dizziness and a growing resentment for being subjected to this harrowing ordeal.

***

The first thing I remember with some clarity is being led through the dingy streets of the city that was to be my new home upon our eventual arrival. I was far from well, but the cool air refreshed my clammy skin as we left the wretched ship to walk, at last, on blessedly solid ground.

Leaning heavily on Ridley's slim, strong arm, I was half-carried, half-dragged through the night, buffeted by relentless wind and rain. Between the squalls, shouts and cries reached me, from stallkeeps and hawkers leaning upon their hand carts. Cries that further tormented my tender head but also excited some distant part of me, the part that wondered at a life so different from that to which I was accustomed.

"Oysters and ale! Four for twopence!"

"Fair baked apple dumplings!"

"Lemons, twelve pence a peck!"

Ridley pulled me to a halt beside the most magnificent of buildings, a colossal construction in the Fellrinthian styling of the ancients, the great steps of the entranceway held up by the most impressive columns. Vicious rain and howling wind drove at us, bracing and disorientating in equal measure.

"Talk o' the town! On the up again, unlike to be stopped! Youngest Grent admitted to the Great House Counsel. Hard to doubt their favour, now!" A young man, barely more than a boy, stood beside a tall stack of papers, calling out into the street. He wore a dark arrangement of clothing that, worn by another, might look quite smart but was far too large for his slim frame and short stature. He chattered good-naturedly to everyone who took a broadside from him in exchange for a coin.

The gleaming stone of the construction shone brightly even in the night, such was the array of lamps installed around the building upon wrought iron. My insensible state could not prevent me from recognising the beguiling charm of the place and that curious part of my mind rose once more, somewhere beyond my discomfort and bewilderment.

Ridley bade me wait, the chilly air plucking incessantly at my garments, as he approached one of the carts and exchanged some words with the man. There was a familiarity between them, tainted with a slight tension. Ridley asked after the man's daughter. The fellow touched his hand to his forelock, his eyes studiously avoiding me as he answered. Finally, with a cough and a wave, the exchange was complete. With a paper-wrapped parcel tucked beneath one arm, Ridley guided me a much shorter distance to what was to be my new home.

Within, the darkness was almost absolute, though a fire burned low in the hearth at the far end of the room. There was no sign of a maid or housekeeper — indeed, the clutter apparent in the gloom suggested no such person existed — but something steamed in an iron above the coals, and the room's fragrance was rich with the earthy scent of bubbling grains.

Ridley placed the package from the vendor onto a clean but otherwise disarrayed table, and busied himself with two pewter tankards while I tried my utmost not to fade to sleep upon my feet. He pushed a steaming one containing a soothing, hot spiced tonic into my hand and told me firmly to drink up. I complied quickly and without complaint.

Once I had finished, Ridley told me it was time for us both to retire. When he waved absentmindedly at the closed door to his own bed chamber I froze, but he was already bustling past me. A small room was presented to me and I shall describe it here as I perceived it that first night: a blackened fireplace crouched quietly in a dank corner; condensation crowded the cramped panes of the undressed window, chill and foreboding as the night's darkness beyond; a threadbare rug, singed slightly at the edge closest to the hearth, was the only decoration; the furniture, a bed and dresser, were mismatching and old but seemed of a sufficiently stout quality.

In many ways this rough little room was far finer than that to which I was accustomed. For it possessed one virtue that my previous situation had lacked: it was deemed to be mine, and mine alone. I was struck then, with the emotion of the moment. For much as my new situation terrified me, I realised that I had never had such a thing. The prospect of solitude, of *privacy*. A place to which I might retreat. The misery of the voyage fell away and my heart soared at the prospect.

I sat down heavily on the simple bed frame, with the thought that I should discuss the arrival of our trunk. Yet before I could unclasp my damp shoe buckles, I fell headlong into a deep and fevered slumber.

9

Chapter Two

LOG BOARDS & TRAVERSE TABLES

*Fivedock the city was known as, and with those five docks I would soon
become familiar during the enactment of my varied duties. Not least the
acquisition and negotiation of navigational charts and arrangements and
shipments from the many offices with which my unknown benefactors did
business.*

*No coastal city was my new home, however. Instead, she was fed by the
fat, dirty river that wallowed so wide and lazy through her never-sleeping
centre. And fed well she was.*

*Well enough to trade twenty-eight thousand, four hundred and
fifty-two Concordian drams per year in war time, and forty-two thousand,
seven hundred and three in peace. Or so I read one sodden morning in a
pilfered Gazette, my fingers stiff and numb with the chill of the early hours.*

*But for all the city was named, talked of and cursed for her five docks,
scarcely a one could handle the great mercantile and naval colossi. And so,
more often than not, these vessels were unloaded in the channel itself. A
channel so thick with the thousand-ton burthen merchantmen of the three
great trade companies, and the lightermen buzzing around them like a
swarm of water-striders, that a spritely youth could hop, skip and jump from
one bank to the other, were he so minded.*

And I might find myself pushing through the crowds of the Slips. Past the street children lounging on the railings, their dirty heels nonchalantly tapping their behinds, with keen eyes ever watchful for the first sight of the returning merchantmen. Whereupon they would burst away like a flock of birds in a sudden cacophony of excitement and action, into the bosom of the Slips. Through legs and around arms and down the grubby alleys they would run, three streets back into the coffee houses of Popham's Place. The prize to the fastest urchin a Concordian half-penny or two for the sighting.

Or I might sweep past the warehouse men, and the eager buyers with their well-thumbed chop books, who had perhaps even keener eyes than those intrepid and numerous youths. Their eyes watching for bundles of Kalchetti tea, or Pomorian clove barrels, or giant cinnamon bundles from Quom, dragged up the river stairs from the lightermen by porters with savage billhooks.

'Fivedock,' from The Worldly Journal and Commonplace Book of Shay Bluefaltlow. The Year Seven, Five Hundred Since the Signing of the Great Concord of Westerbrook

I awoke in the depths of the night to the sound of rustling. My head swung with disorientation, my tongue felt thick in my mouth. There was a brisk chill in the air, something I was scarcely used to. I instinctively grasped towards the threadbare sheet tangled around my lower limbs, sorely tempted to pull it around myself and roll back over. Instead, with a little shake of my head, I forced myself to sit up.

The eerie silence of the earliest hours settled upon me, stirring within me a careful respect. With nothing but the regular tick and tock of a timepiece outside my chamber for company, I sat for the longest moment. It felt strange to know that this place would be my home. I patted the simple wooden frame, dared myself to clear my throat, and peered into the darkness.

It was at this very moment I heard the sound again, the rustling. Part of me wished to stand, and part of me wished to flinch back. And then it came once more, louder this time. I forced myself onto still-wavering legs to pursue it.

My damp shoes were nowhere to be seen; I was as light upon my stockinged feet as it is possible to be, my skirt whispering against the cold floorboards. I hitched and held my breath, straining my hearing as hard as I possibly could. I rested my palm against the splintered oakgrain of the doorframe. There was nothing.

I ever so slowly lowered my eye to the darkness of the door crack, and peered through. Still nothing, but the sudden chill of a draught upon my cheeks. Then, just as I turned my head away, there it was. A sudden rustling and a flash of movement from the corner of my gaze.

This time I did not hesitate; I bravely flung the door open, and padded out into the cluttered main room. As I had ascertained when I arrived, every surface was covered in surgical implements, jars, bottles, books, writing materials and other papers of my new master's trade. The paper package Ridley had bought was sprung open on the table; inside were a number of empty oyster shells.

As in my own modest room, the furniture was sturdy but well-used, and from a quick perusal I gained the distinct impression that this was not its first home. By the door, our trunk squatted; I had been so deeply asleep I had not heard it arrive.

A loose floorboard creaked under my weight. I picked my path carefully, standing up on the tips of my toes, as I closed the distance to a hallway where I had seen the figure disappear. Then suddenly I was upon my bounty.

It was a small boy. In the time it had taken me to come upon him, he had somehow burrowed himself into the dank corner, upon the floorboards. To say that this was the last thing I expected to see would be an understatement. I clutched my hands together and let out a small squeal of surprise, despite myself. To this outburst he, curiously, gave no mind at all.

12

In the dull lamplight, I could tell that one of his wide cheeks was smudged with soot. Apart from a short pair of sailcloth breeches, his legs were bare and very small. They were crossed beneath him, his pink and white soles staring up, wiggling at me cheerily. In his hands was a piece of twine, worked into a cat's cradle, and he moved his lips soundlessly as he inspected his game with such intensity that I might not have been there at all.

I crouched low, and gently spoke to him. Without so much as a glance in my direction, he rose abruptly to his feet, and scuttled through a door to some unseen part of my new abode. I decided I should pursue him no further that night. I wondered if there might be others lurking here, too. But no, the place was not so large as that, surely! I realised the child must have been the one to bank the fire and heat the water we'd taken upon arrival earlier that night. I thought it a strange arrangement.

As I turned to return to my own bedroom, I caught sight of my missing shoes; the sodden things had been neatly lined up beside the dying fire, alongside their buckles, next to a very small, very scuffed pair.

***

The morning after my arrival, tentatively breaking my fast on dry bread and sliced apple, I kept out a keen eye for my midnight apparition. To which I won a few passing glances, but nothing more.

"Ah," the surgeon said when I asked about the child. "So you have met my other charge. Peck is his name. You'll have time aplenty to become acquainted with one another. But for now we have much more important business to attend to."

Once I had cleaned away the grime of our voyage and my sickness from myself with gloriously hot water and dressed in clean, if crumpled, clothes from our trunk, the situation — or some of it, at least — was explained to me.

Everything had been arranged, I was assured. By whom remained, however, one of many mysteries to me. That did not matter, for the moment, Ridley assured me; if I worked hard, I should do well. If I did not, I should not. My base needs would be attended to; I would not want for food, clothing or employment. Unreasonable questions or the broaching of unserious subjects, on the other hand, would be met with the dullest regard. Patience would serve me well.

Within the array of subjects deemed unreasonable dwelt the identity of the mysterious benefactors. While any details regarding their identities were closely guarded, there was one thing the man was more than happy to share with me: I was not to be idle. My education would be first inspected and evaluated, then augmented wherever it was lacking. This was a responsibility he took most seriously, and I was expected to follow suit.

The days that followed permitted me to learn more of my surroundings for I began to recover from the terrible sickness, and was sent on a range of basic duties; collecting Ridley's letters from the penny mail office or visiting the grain exchange for oatmeal and pease.

I did not much enjoy these sojourns, finding the city cold and cruel. It was a truly massive place, and I had lived all my life, as far as I could remember, in one building, rarely venturing further than the bottom of the grounds.

To make matters worse, for several consecutive days a gaggle of children took to following me and pelting me with pebbles, base slurs that were unknown to me riding their lips, but whose foul intent I had no difficulty grasping. Fivedock was vast and I was terrified of becoming lost forever among the winding alleys, and the crescents, the places of industry, and the warehouses.

I quickly found myself unhappy in my new situation. I did not much like the idea of having a benefactor, or several, nor was I happy not to know their motives. For in my imagination lived a variety of dreadful possibilities.

Indeed, being both stubborn and wilful, I promised myself I should repay their entire endeavour with any malice that might have been intended in its delivery. With material interest for insults rendered. And I was positive that insults were indeed being rendered, of that one can be certain.

With a surety which I believe is only present in one very young, I made up my mind to escape the situation as soon as possible. Ridley seemed kind, yes; I had a room of my very own, that was a luxury beyond anything I had imagined. But the uncertainty of my situation and the idea that these people I did not know should retain control of my future for ever more? Well. That was unacceptable. Further, I could not imagine how the place could ever feel like a home to me.

But, alas; I digress. All this was to say that — until I organised my escape, of course — four mornings each week were to be devoted to the rather considerable task of bettering my mind. I had received an education in Quom, it was true, albeit of a certain, brittle quality. Dishearteningly, this was not deemed to be sufficient.

So I would find myself seated at a corner of the very old, scarred table in the main room of our shared lodgings, to pursue further enlightenment on a number of subjects. I was first questioned relentlessly on the areas of my previous study, and on my proficiency in each branch of knowledge. To which I gained the unmistakable sensation that I was severely lacking in most every field. As we had been instructed at length to match the likely requirements of any potential master, this left me somewhat bewildered. This was not at all what I had expected. A fact compounded by my disorientation at the complete alteration of my circumstance. A new city; a new guardian; a new set of baffling subjects. It was, in total, all too much.

As promised, the holes in my capacities we set to patching. I studied the fundamentals of mathematics, the minutiae of logic and reason, as well as the bewildering Fellrinthian languages of the ancients. Not to speak of anatomy and astronomy, natural philosophy and history. Dancing and manner were not, Ridley acknowledged, particular strengths of his. But he produced a number of dusty old books on these learned topics, the once-thick leather of their bindings rubbed smooth in patches from frequent thumbing, and together we worked our way through a dreary quantity of tasks.

15

Yet that was not all. As the good surgeon had, prior to his medical attainment, once served as a navigator aboard a small sloop, he informed me he was to be entrusted with my instruction in the art of navigation. While he never expressly said so, I gained the unmistakable impression that those who held power over me wished this to be given precedence. A fact which initially rendered within me an obstinate will to neglect the subject entirely.

But the topic was not to be avoided. So it was that I was admonished for my sloppy trigonometry, and praised for my tidy arithmetic, chastised for my clumsy cartography, and lauded for my neat and developing hand. Subtractions, additions, and logarithms were the things of my days; Gunter scales, sextants and point compasses the items of my new pursuit. Formulas and fractions became the stuff of my dreams.

I came to understand the principles of latitude and longitude, and could complete traverse tables and log boards with some measure of capability. That the measured metre of such study was of the particular flavour I favoured, I did not share; I was loath to allow myself to be comforted by the absorbing work and insisted that it was tiresome and boring, instead.

After the frightful experience crossing the Whispering Sea — not to mention my lifelong fear of heights — I was more than terrified of the practical necessities required to put my new knowledge into practice. Certainly, I never wished to board such a vessel again. And yet… I could not deny that, somewhere deep within me, dwelled a hunger to at least dream of a time I might be freed from such fears.

I will now allow myself to admit that there was pleasure to be had in many of the learnings I undertook. Some late evenings in those sodden, chilly days, Ridley and I paced the fat cobblestones of the armoury quarter. And, with our necks craned and arms aloft, I would recount the primary stars as well as hum the rhymes of the lunar reckoning; the complex dance of the three moons by which the Concord calendar composed itself. Gussi, Ra, and Aises.

At first I wondered at the absence of Peck from these outings, so captivated was he by the stars burning bright above the crack of a skylight in the garret. Only to find the child huddled upon the hearth when we returned; and for all my efforts to coax from him conversation or acknowledgement, he gave scarcely a sign of interest.

Instead he busied himself with the many chores that were his responsibility. He was often found upon his knees scrubbing the hearth, or upon his toes with bellows and log, and he sat on the tiniest stool and buffed potatoes with a great exuberance, or applied a regiment of order to Ridley's abundance of papers with his clever little fingers. Errands that involved crossing the threshold, however, were to be undertaken only by Ridley or myself.

This was a puzzle to me, and one to which I craved a resolution. Yet I was too shy to push the questions that might provide an answer — if I could even piece together what they might be. So instead, I quietly wondered about the boy, in the scarce moments I was not entirely consumed with my own tasks.

The surgeon was an enthusiastic tutor, and quick to offer encouragement. Quite despite myself and my earlier affirmed ploy to flee just as soon as I was able, I came to enjoy his company. Perhaps it was simply that he offered me a measure of limited warmth; mayhaps I should have reacted so to any who treated me without cruelty. For it was certainly true that the singularity with which I felt my isolation and immersion in a completely new situation had struck me with great force. Perhaps all I needed was a friend. In any case, it was a strange relationship and one to which I clung as desperately as an orphaned kitten to a bare and adopted chest.

Between my studies I retreated to my room, which was blissfully peaceful but also rather lonely. Or, in the hours that were permitted to me, I might tentatively wander the city I had been so suddenly brought to. That, too, felt like a lonely endeavour.

Our lodgings were located in the theatre district — on Biltern Road, near Durrot Row — at a busy intersection, deep in the heart of the Concordian capital city of Fivedock. There was something enchanting about this particular district, despite my initial distaste for the clamour and bustle of city life. This — and the whole city, truly — was in such a state of agitation and business compared to the only places I had any experience of, that it was difficult to assess my feelings on the matter in those first heady days of my new life. It felt strange and exciting and horrible.

And, while I had never particularly favoured the relentless and muggy heat of Quom, I found the changeable weather bewildering; one moment dark rain clouds crowded the sky, the next the sun was glancing off the many puddles of the street, quite blindingly.

The plays and operas held within the theatres themselves intrigued me, however. Though they were things I had only vaguely heard of, they were something I had found greatly appealing for all the days I had lived. Once, a travelling troupe of performers had attended the school to purchase two girls, and the lead madame had spoken to a gaggle of us, for several hours. Her tales had transported me entirely to another place. To such a degree that the other girls had despatched to me a most merciless and relentless teasing in the days afterwards. They were looking for *interesting* appearing girls but the distinctive mark upon my face made me, perhaps, too interesting for their purposes.

I wandered, wide eyed, from task to task, and place to place, feeling very much an outsider in the strange new place. Not more than a few moments walk from Ridley's lodgings was the most stunningly beautiful park. Wellspring Gardens. It made the garden of the school seem like a dry scrub of land by comparison. The frequent rain encouraged fat, fragrant blossoms and bright, cheerful wildlife, where under long lingering sun a broad array of fine patrons promenaded beneath resplendent parasols, or in glinting curricles or phaetons or chaise and four. And yet, if one were to step out in the other direction, it did not take long to come upon the thickly packed backstreets of the Fleshmarket, the Draper's Ward and the Slips.

The good surgeon was a busy man and, as with much, it often fell to me to assist in the necessary research his position demanded. And if that were not sufficient responsibility, I assisted him in the transcription of his medical notes, too.

In the evening I was set to read the dense journals of any number of learned men and women. Some acquired that very day. Rare were the subjects which were restricted to me; the man felt it his duty to keep abreast of many such topics. Which, by extension, meant it became my duty to keep abreast of them. But not only this. For some unseen master seemed keen indeed that I enjoy every advantage open to me, if I was to be shaped into an individual of quality and substance upon their watch.

Work and diligence were the qualities that would carry the day. No matter one's distaste or limited ability for the tasks. If Ridley's own life had taught him anything, it was this. His own station had not come easily to him, he confided in me; he was a practical man, but learning, I soon found, was not a natural mastery and he often diligently studied alongside me in the subjects with which he was least familiar.

The man was also something of a reluctant naturalist, and so anatomy of man and beast were often my reading fellows. Though clearly capable within his own domain, he did not strike me as excessively sharp; I never quite acquired the impression that he derived much pleasure from his own studies. Yet this did not stay his hand. Indeed, quite the opposite proved to be the case; for Ridley, education was an obligation for a man of his position.

The way he had won for himself an advantageous position in life was through the application of rigorous study and obstinate determination. Oftentimes, he referred to his own masters and teachers, such individuals to whom he attributed a great degree of respect. One gained the unmistakable sensation that their methods had become his methods, and were not to be questioned.

He assured me he would normally spend a great number of hours studying the journals, as he had been taught, and if it was good enough for him, it was good enough for me. The sharpening of my intellect and reason was bound to follow such an exercise.

19

He was, at that time, extremely busy. He regularly taught classes at the Surgeon's Hall on the outskirts of the city and he was one of a scant handful of practitioners of those arts who the poorer citizens could afford to employ. I later came to suspect that he often worked for little or no money. Three afternoons per week, he was to assist at the Foundling Hospital. And as such, besides my other duties, it fell to me to support him with his research.

Sometimes I was to attend the circulating library, where I would compare the current catalogue with a list he had prepared for me of materials he wished to peruse. If I could find any of these, I was promised his favour. Each week I was to rise early, and go down to the coffee houses upon Exchange Way, to acquire a broadside, and the news.

While I did not enjoy the interruption to my sleep, I did favour the bustle of the coffee shop, where every kind of person could be found: merchants and stockmen whispering excitedly of coming interests; dandies and sharps arguing about where the best tailor or wine or bread might be found in the city; artists and wordsmiths and barristers and storekeepers, all blathering and laughing and quaffing the restorative beverage of growing repute.

I found I myself quickly developed a taste for the rich, hot drink that was so very popular. Upon which decadence I went so far as to guiltily spend a reasonable portion of the small stipend Ridley assured me was for whatever personal victuals I deemed fit.

In this way my first few weeks in Fivedock passed; studying, exploring, learning and dreaming of a way to escape.

Chapter Three

SLEEK OF KEEL
& TRUE OF GUN

I have committed myself to sharing my own findings so that others may learn from them. And the good surgeon believes it to be an exercise which will fortify my education, even if my eyes alone are ever to see the material. He believes the regular application of ink to paper organises one's thoughts.

What's more, he assures me such a task will be essential in advancing my situation with my unknown benefactors. Even now, I am told, they watch and take note. I admit to being somewhat self-conscious at the prospect, but he will brook no argument on it. I am to study, and I am to study hard.

And so, I begin. Looking over the sheer volume of material before me, I expect I shall be learning for quite some time. It is daunting, but also exciting. Seldom, when in Quom, would I have fancied access to such reserves of knowledge. Sometimes, I imagine showing it all to my younger self. It is a pleasing thought.

From The Worldly Journal and Commonplace Book of Shay Bluefaltlow the Year Six, Five Hundred Since the Signing of the Great Concord of Westerbrook

So the weeks passed, and Ridley started to pay a little less attention to me. He became increasingly distracted; I overheard him one morning muttering to himself about something that sounded rather grave.

"It'll be me who's held to account, if we come into trouble. I don't doubt that," he murmured as I listened on, my ear to the door. He spoke as if to a friend, though he was quite alone. I had discovered, just that morning, a nasty curse scrawled upon the wall outside our lodgings. When I had told him of the incident, he had tried to reassure me by passing off the thing as nonsense. But I saw in his eyes he was uneasy and I misliked Fivedock as much as ever.

After a fortnight or so, seemingly convinced I was settled enough, Ridley began to disappear early each morning for the deliverance of his duties as a surgeon, or so he told me.

Yet I was unconvinced by his explanation. It did not take much time for me to acquire enough gumption to follow him, curious about this man who had bought me and where else it was he went, and what it was he did. And so I follow him I did, all the way to a busy cluster of tea houses on Binder's Way.

I peeked through the frosted glass panel of the establishment he had entered, wiping away the cool condensation with the side of my gloved hand. Little thought did I give to the sodden chill that seeped through the fabric to my skin, nor to the school children who giggled and guffawed as they passed — though, these, mercifully, were not the terrors who had pelted me with stones, I found I was still an amusing sight to them.

I suspected my unique facial markings drew them; not only was I used to receiving curious glances, but I had also long realised that physical difference drew ire. My eyes darted across those seated within and my attention was drawn to one table in particular; the patrons were well lit by the golden glow of lamplight.

Somehow, I was certain they discussed me.

It was indeed Ridley I could see, with three companions: two women and a man. Though I struggled to make out their faces and character exactly, there was enough for me to form an impression. The man and one of the women held a military aspect, and serious bearing. The third, the other woman, was very well set out, and clearly of significant station. All three were deep in conversation together. The more severe-looking of the women leaned across the table to make some point, leaning an arm against the table. As I looked on, my master raised his arm and gesticulated, I imagined to defend his own position.

I longed to watch them longer, to understand who these people could be, as they did not seem, to me, to be either foundlings or in need of surgical attention. Yet, alas, it was at that exact moment that the proprietor stepped from the doorway, cleared his throat noisily, and glared at me. I hurried away with more questions than I had held when I set out that morning.

The next morning, near noon, Ridley interrupted me during the interminable task of sweeping and scrubbing the main hearth.

"I have another duty for you, a most important one," he said, smiling as he settled down into his old armchair. "When you have finished your more base chores, you will deliver a packet for me. It is important that you do so promptly. You must not dally. This shall be a test of your manner and bearing. Is this a thing you think you can do for me?"

"Of course," I said, with barely a moment's reflection. As much for my curiosity, and my earlier fear that I had been discovered in my subterfuge, than for any other reason. Though I was keen to gain any advantage that might aid me in my escape, sensing that good behaviour would afford me such an opportunity far better than obstinance.

And so it was that one of my principal duties became, henceforth, to deliver weekly a packet of papers to the offices of the courts and civil duty, near the Rose Palace. I was not privy to the contents of these letters. The only clue as to their content was the clear H marked cleanly upon each, which I carefully studied as I performed the task.

I could not say why, but I was certain that the contents of this package held information pertaining to my own future, and the strange occurrences around us. The glance I made one day, as Ridley bound the documents tightly with twine, only reinforced my belief. I endeavoured to discover what this was about from what I read in that brief moment:

> *By palatial and parliamentary prerogative, on behalf of the Concord of the Houses*

***

Despite living in entirely new and fascinating place quite at odds with the quiet life of discipline I had known, my recent situation remained intolerable to me nonetheless. I felt the place unsafe and it seemed to me time to take my future into my own hands. I must escape as soon as was feasible.

I had plotted, and I had waited until the most opportune moment to act presented itself to me. I felt trapped, as might an animal who had spent its life in a cage before being released for one delicious moment, only to find itself transferred to another, unfamiliar enclosure, and locked up once more. That my cage in Fivedock was moderate and contained some scant comforts mattered not: I longed for freedom, whatever the cost.

Now I had tasted liberty, I craved more. There was a large world out there, and I intended to discover it. My extended persecution seemed assured.

Still. I was loath to put to action a plan with so little knowledge of everything around me; it sat uneasily with me. I made as careful designs as I could manage, in the small measure of time that was my own. And the people who I met — shipping officers and teahouse patrons, dock porters and post office clerks — I did my best to survey for any hint they might assist me. With very little luck in that regard, such that I began to fear I might never find a person suited to the task.

It was, of course, widely known that the Great House Navy was hard pushed to keep open the mercantile sea channels which guaranteed the nation's considerable vigour. The Kalchetti embargo was partially successful, as the meandering proxy war between the two powers sparked and spluttered. The main trade post was lost; the strait of Monkey's Folly was contested; a small number of harbours in the colonies had been completely blockaded.

With a commensurate press on the demand of those ships which could squeeze through what was available which was considerable. In short, there was far too much brandy to pass through the funnel, with the result of spillage and rancour.

This knowledge any fool knew, or would shortly be told were they to spend any time about the endlessly enchanting stores in the Draper's Ward, the pungent coffee rooms down Exchange Way, or the damp markets of the Slips. And if you were not told, you could witness it with your own eyes in the increased press of folk within the city, or the rising price of grain and fruit. That I was, therefore, not the only individual keen to gain such passage created a somewhat considerable problem for my endeavour.

To alleviate this challenge to the nation's fortunes, the palace and the three chambers had legislated that civilian traffic was to be limited to those with particular need or station. With the result that no one should pass through who did not have a stamp from at least one authority. This, then, would be my first challenge.

The comings and goings of the ships I meticulously noted within my journal and commonplace book. With which, through innocent questioning of Ridley and careful interrogation of those attending the shipping yards, I was able to make a guess at several essential details: the likely available berths; the general cost of such a thing; the availability and difficulty of acquiring it.

When the opportunity presented itself at the end of a day's work and study, I carefully slipped away the shipping charts and almanacks while Ridley was busying himself with his supplies; these I copied out in my careful hand in my bedchamber at night. To this I supplemented the possible destinations in a number of tables, and to those I appended my thoughts on each. The advantageous outcomes, or the detrimental. My preferences and the realities, as well as I could guess them.

In another table I tallied the costs, and the potential remedies for returning them. For this information I had little to go on but hearsay and speculation. That this was so speculative I did not allow to deter me, though I knew frustration at its limitation. Instead I set my teeth to the challenge.

The small snippets of information I could innocently acquire from my tutor, I readily did. Whether from gently steering the conversation, or eavesdropping upon his discussions. I tried to think back on what I had heard the old governess mention as rates in servitude in the Principalities and the other territories of the Trader's Plenty. Yet I struggled to recall. And scolded myself for not having taken notice of her reckoning on the issue. Even if the truth of the estimation had been altered by the passage of time and the measure of leagues, it should better serve to guide the judgement on the accuracy and assumptions of my expectations than no model at all.

But, eventually, enough time had passed that I believed it was time to act. I had gathered an amount of information sufficient to embolden me and, with what seemed no choice, I waited for an opportunity to put the plan into motion.

***

Still, despite my planning, I could not put the young boy — Peck — out of my mind, nor feel anything but great sympathy for his plight. I had tried, unsuccessfully, to find time to speak with him. I set myself the task of acquiring him a gift; something I might offer him, to show I was a friend. Something he might like. I ran that morning to the palace, clear in my mind that by acting so I should win the time necessary to get him a little something.

I took the bundle from the cart seller, and wandered over to the railing overlooking the river Lire. With the blustery wind tugging at my cloak, I clasped one hand around the cool cast iron — the other shielding my eyes from the sun's glare — leant out, and stared at the great merchantman *Plentiful Bounty* of the Murmesseril Trade Company.

I traced my gaze along the lines of the huge brute, considering the ship in the light of my most recent and enlightening studies. I took in her great hull, from mizzenmast to stern, which had been recently — perhaps that very day — scrubbed clean of barnacles in the buzzing harbour, and fair gleamed in the sunlight. I counted out her gunports — seventy-four — and I was making an approximate guess of her tunnage when my reverie was interrupted by a voice at my shoulder.

"Fifty-two across the keel. Sits lower in the water than any of her sisters. Can't fire those forty-six pounders, when fully victualled," said the dry voice. "Faster and truer in a fight, though, mark my words."

"She's beautiful," I said, quite despite myself, turning on my heel.

A man nodded to me. "She is that! We don't build many like them, no more. Not as many as we should."

He was a sinewy fellow, all angles and bones. He had a strong brow, and large, expressive eyes. His skin was moderately pale, as was common in Concord men. His hair was barely managed, and receding.

Stubbornness lived in the set of his mouth, and seriousness in his manner. His clothing was simple: breeches of the old style as well worn as he, and a top coat of peculiar cut and provenance, blue and purple. Yet when he talked of merchantmen and frigates or hulls and keels and tunnage, as he did now for several moments, his eyes came alive. Such that it seemed they invited one in. And it was quite impossible to ignore the call.

He did not tell me his name, then, but I did come to know it in time. He was Edgar Bamcroft, Master Shipwright and Navy Surveyor to the Sea Lords and the combined Great Houses of the fair nation in which I now resided. Had I known who he was I should have been, perhaps, too shy to speak freely to him. As it was, I found his pride in the vessel charming and recognised the pleasure he felt at finding an audience appreciative of his knowledge.

And I stood listening to him right there, that cool morning, clean forgetting the time, or the sense of urgency for my task.

When he made a point he found to be particularly pleasing, which happened frequently, he liked to flick his forefinger against his knee. Just as I was beginning to relax more into enjoying his company, he very suddenly, with as little prelude as that to which he had inserted himself into my affairs, was gone.

When an assorted bunch of dockmen passed us, he disappeared among them; I wished I had learned his name, or where he worked, for I felt strongly that I would have liked to meet with him again.

Then I spotted him, raising his hand to wave at me from a distance as he fell in with his fellows. Leaving me standing where I was, baffled and embarrassed and more hungry for warm company than ever. Despondent, I hurried back to our abode and my chore.

***

I rushed into our rooms, invigorated with my interaction. I saw the little boy as soon as I entered the main room. He was sitting in the centre of the floor, scrubbing brush in hand. It was clear he had vigorously deployed this tool upon the spotted old oaken boards of the floor, judging by the soapy trail he had left in his wake. To his side was an incredibly well-used bucket, brass bracings long ago dulled with use, staves long swollen, filled with grotty water. I coughed into my fist. The boy stared into the fire, seemingly waiting for the kettle to boil.

"I've brought these for you," I said at last, once the considerable awkwardness of my situation had built to a terrible head. A fact worsened by his complete and stupefying ignorance of my presence. A behaviour that increasingly seemed to me as his wont. Though I lingered for several moments, hoping that obstinance might win the day. It did not.

I left the oysters on the table by the fire and hurried immediately back to my chamber, forcing the door with my shoulder when it jammed in the frame.

I threw myself on my bed and buried my face into my pillow; for no matter what, I would not permit a child less than half my age to hear my sobs. But cry I did, for in Quom though my peers were cruel and unkind, they had at least addressed me. The truth was that this snub felt far more hurtful. Why a child in a seemingly not dissimilar position from my own would shun me so was beyond my understanding and it compounded my loneliness greatly.

Many hours later, once I was sure both Ridley and the boy were both abed, I crept my way through the hall in search of water for my tear-stained face. The package remained where I had left it, though it was now full of empty shells.

On the paper, scrawled roughly in charcoal, was a flame. It took me a moment to decipher the message but I laughed aloud when at last I did. On the hearth, beside what was left of the fire, sat a tankard of tea.

Chapter Four

A HEARTFELT PETITION

Traces of the Seekers are to be found in many of the most ancient records. Sometimes they are mentioned alongside the Sentinels. Other times they are found alone. Their presence in our historical texts is so sporadic and they appear in such a wide variety of guises cascading throughout the many intervening years from when we assume they walked the land, that some — nay, many — doubt their very existence.

Are they creatures, these Seekers? Or were they men, or perhaps gods? Who the Ul peoples name 'Urickanth', I suspect to be the ones we call Seekers; the bas-reliefs upon the crumbling palace of Bodsprun, the same. What is undoubtedly true is that there are traces of their presence and their influence in nearly every culture, in every place where written or visual history exists. The scattered nature of the records does not throw me aside as it has many others. Nor do the many contradictions and confusing discrepancies.

No. Instead, I say that these disagreements serve as further proof of their existence and significance. It is precisely because these accountings are so disparate that I feel they must hold merit. The famed city of Drakratha, for example, has now been proven to exist, after all. And within both mysteries lay answers so desperately sought.

Penelope Etherington, Archivist to the Great Houses of the Concord,
under the Treaty of Hawksbay
The Year Fifty Two, Four Hundred Since the Signing

I pressed Ridley once more for information about the boy and he seemed surprised by my questions.

"Well, he… the child is deaf and he is mute," He explained to me one evening, through a haze of pipe smoke, raising his eyes just above his broadside. This shocked me. I had never met such a person.

"I know he favours books. He always seems to have his head in one. I thought… I might like to buy him a new one. But does he… can he…?"

"Read? Why yes. Although he came to it a little late, perhaps, he proved an excellent student. Very determined."

"Is that how you… speak with him? Writing?"

"Well, sometimes, though not often. We speak to one another through gesture rather than words."

"Might you show me how?"

While Ridley never explicitly refused my request — in fact, he seemed quite charmed by the notion — he seemed reluctant to add another task onto his already long, arduous days. I desperately wished to take the child out to choose his own book but this request was flatly refused. I looked through the small and battered collection the boy already owned and brought him something I thought might suit. From that moment on, Peck seemed as concerned about my happiness as I felt for his and I was determined to learn how to converse with him. With our guardian's help or without.

The truth was that I required friendship. For all the good surgeon's best efforts, he could not deliver me all that I needed. And while I had made some progress in endearing myself to Peck — and, truthfully, he never seemed to resent my sudden appearance in his life and home, a testament to his innate goodness — I could not bring myself to confide in a child, even one more adept at running a small household than most people I had met.

31

In short, I craved, increasingly hungrily, the company of my own peers. Despite my promise to myself that I would soon leave Fivedock, companionship felt as essential to my survival as raindrops to a sprouting sapling. I began to dream up ways in which I might deliver satisfaction to this particular craving.

Everywhere I went my eyes roved over the activities of the young men and women of the city. I soon learned that, within the season, the grand theatres and assembly rooms of Durrot Row filled the wide avenues with a great deluge of Concordians, Grand Republicans, those from the principalities, and others from more distant lands. I must confess I was drawn greatly to the clamour, like a magpie to a shiny bauble. For the great deliverance of colour and spectacle was, though daunting, of such remove to what I was used or, in truth, had ever imagined that it bewitched me.

Some nights, when a fit of bravery overtook me, I found myself weaving between sedans to penetrate closer to the bustle. Whereupon I might brush past the heaving team of a coach and four, to crouch behind their carriage, all so I might catch a glimpse of the mode set, or those preparing to fill the theatre pit. One such frequently observed being the drunken old parliamentarian in his many caped greatcoat, nose and cheeks rosy with coarse broken blood vessels, his scent of sweet sherry carrying on the chill spring breeze. Who, with hoarse throat, raised his cane to gesticulate garrulously to his scowling dowager companion. He attended, it seemed to me, every occasion I happened to witness. He never seemed to recognise me, despite my distinctive appearance, so in his cups was he.

For I had a curious birthmark that made me somewhat memorable. It covered more than half of my torso, peeked out from under the lace of my sleeve onto my hand, and ran up my neck to crawl across my right cheek. It was serpentine, from a certain angle. The clean lines and particular shape of the blemish appeared entirely man made in its imprint, as if a postmaster had punched his stamp upon my flesh with the freshest of inks. It had been a source of constant teasing in my youth; though I often quite forgot it was there at all, I was unused to seeing so many perfect strangers and found myself blushing each time folk peered at me with curiosity.

Quite like I found myself entranced by the perfectly beautiful blueblood with the exquisitely dressed hair and flashing whalebone fan, who reached out her half-gloved hand so daintily to her footman when stepping from her phaeton, and elicited such excited murmurs from all gathered. After wondering long who it was I had witnessed, I at last resorted to filching Ridley's broadside, *The Newdock Statesman*, long before he had finished perusing it. And lying terribly to him that I had not seen it when he cursed and searched for it.

My deceit bore fruit. I discovered that the object of my intense interest was one Felicity Hapeworth-Arksthrotle, of the most distinguished Arksthrotle line; her uncle was an important member of the parliamentary houses and held considerable influence. Where he went, men were said to follow.

I made mumbling excuses when, occasionally, I was accosted and questioned for my voyeuristic proclivities by no small measure of stern footmen, and hurried away, face burning with shame. For I knew not then they most probably took me for a pickpocket, and must have regarded my longing for company as avarice of an entirely different kind.

I learned I could discover much about the performances of the night by whispering shyly with the bill handlers, and collecting a number of bills to stow away in my room. As rich a cache of which to moon over by the dull glow of candlelight as I could ever desire, put to tireless use when I finally retired from another day's bone-wearying chores. Where my exhausted mind, somehow, found a fresh flush of endeavour at their sight. Some nights I fell asleep still clutching a bill, my hand beneath the worn sacking of my pillow.

Within my mind these scenes took on great colour and richness, and they grew to impossible brightness and scale. I dreamt of attending those plays and operas, and of a tight group of new friends who attended them with me. In one such dream, I proudly signed vowels for a subscription box of the first rank, and so won lasting favour and no small measure of jealousy amongst my new, burgeoning circle of companions. In another, I became the greatest confidante of Felicity Hapeworth-Arksthrotle herself. We travelled together, everywhere: to the fabled gardens of the Rose Palace; the races at Goldsops; even abroad aboard the great flagship, the *Indomitable Spirit*, where I impressed her with my burgeoning knowledge of naval matters.

And those dreams were not restricted to my nighttime fervours, but also furnished me with ample escape from the more dreary assignments of my day. More than once I received stern admonishment from Ridley.

"You are vacant as a mooncalf, today. What has gotten into you? Come along, now! Attend properly to your arithmetic, you have missed a complete row." Tapping his scarred finger upon the ragpaper of the folio beneath my hand.

Just as I began to think that perhaps spending at least a little while in Fivedock might not be such a terrible thing, the harsh reality of life in the city presented itself to me in no uncertain terms. One miserable afternoon I was set about mercilessly by the youngsters who had taken to following me. So much so that I began to question my earlier dismissal of their attentions as childish curiosity. I was chased and then I was tripped, wicked laughter echoing around me. Finally they took to kicking and beating my face, and anywhere that they saw as sensitive, as I writhed on the cobblestones and lashed out to try and strike back, with little success.

They ceased their attack only when a set of dockworkers came upon us, and called out to their master. In my embarrassment, it took me a moment to recognise their man they'd called as the Bamcroft fellow from the day not long passed.

Once I had assured him I was not badly hurt beyond a few scuffs and scrapes, he offered me a drink of cool water to quench my thirst. To my thanks he told me I should save them for another time, and that if I ever fancied to talk on ships and other matters, I should visit him at the drydocks, near the Slips, where he plied his trade. I would be, he assured me with a wink, most welcome; the conversation of his fellow men being somewhat lacking.

***

Two mornings passed where I presumed I might act, but shrank away from the opportunity. My nights watching the theatre folk had further emboldened my plan, and I had rather taken the fancy that I should escape to become a dancer, or an actress — even a billhandler might suffice, for a time. So long as I was away from this wretched situation.

For several days I sat at my work, eyeing Ridley's empty desk with hunger for action but not the gumption. I was going over and over my plan in my head on my way back from the coffee house when I came across two of the girls from the street gang.

The taller of the two swiped out a dull little blade from her sleeve, as they both backed me into an abandoned doorway, down a dingy set of stairs. It was the other girl who spoke. The short one with long straggles of matted hair, and a smudge or dirt smeared across her cheek.

"You'll be stuck propa next time you're seen round 'ere. This ain't the place for ya," she had leered at me, malice dancing in her eyes and bearing.

My mind was more than set. I should either escape, or take some form of weapon and attempt to face them down, however that should go.

My plan then was simple: in some small moment available to me, I should use Ridley's supplies to pen a letter to the one acquaintance I had made who might be in a position to oblige me: Bamcroft. Who, I fervently prayed, might recall and feel moved to help me. The foolscap of paper would be easy enough to pilfer, I knew, though not the other things.

When I learned Ridley was to visit the Surgeon's Hall the next morning before attending someone's abode — and that I should not expect him home until lunch time or later — I knew the time, at last, had come.

He left after breakfasting on gruel and strong tea, his case in hand. I watched from the window, telling myself I could begin as soon as he was quite out of sight. Then I spread the large foolscap out on the table, careful to smooth the edges as I had seen Ridley do. I dipped my quill in ink and, painstakingly, began to write. All the while wishing, with a wry smile, I had attended to my lessons in Quom a little better. My best efforts, I told myself, should have to suffice.

> *I hope, sir, that you will consider my heartfelt petition with the seriousness with which it has been penned. I recall your kindness to me, and thank you most sincerely. I write to you at some risk to myself and, I am sorry to say, perhaps to you, though I fervently pray this is not the case.*
>
> *As you are the only person in this entire city known to me who has any connections, I am entirely at your mercy. I am trapped here, at the behest of unknown persons referred only as 'benefactors.' To what eventual end has not been revealed to me. Ridley, my guardian and supervisor, is not unkind to me, though I am held here against my will. I believe my benefactors may be powerful, and so I request that you do not intervene directly with them, for both our sakes.*
>
> *My proposed solution is to acquire passage to one of the principalities. I believe I may purchase a berth upon a merchantman bound for the colonies in the spring, for a somewhat reasonable fee of thirteen Concordian drams.*
>
> *Therefore, I require your assistance in two manners. Firstly, to grant me the stamp of your office, which will be required for any passage. The second is for a loan of the sum required.*
>
> *I would propose to repay you with material interest once I arrive at my destination, whereby I intend to enter into employment until any debts to you are paid, in full.*

I understand this to be a significant request upon your kindness. For this I can only apologise, and pray I might win your forgiveness in the fullness of time.

Yours in Desperation and Ever Your Grateful Servant,

Shay Bluefaltlow

I tapped my feet impatiently as I waited for the ink to dry; powder would make a mess I may not have the time to address. I folded the quarto as I had been taught long ago and pulled out the deep drawer upon Ridley's desk, which squealed abominably. I rifled through the disorder, picking up and inspecting sealing wax and other writing implements.

First, I considered wafers; for Ridley was least likely to notice their lack. But no, that wouldn't do. The difference between my own and my recipient's station was considerable and offence was the last thing I wished to cause. It should hardly signify if he failed to open the damnable thing.

With a frown I acceded I should have to risk a little more. Well. I pulled out another drawer, and with dull thuds and clinks, rifled quickly through the contents, all the while trying to memorise the configuration, so I might replace it in another few moments.

I pushed aside a bundle of rags, several bottles of ink, and an assortment of well-used pencils and quills. A notched and scored knife distracted me before I found what I had been searching for. With a nibble of my lip, I plucked up a heavy, velvety crimson wax stick. I knew Ridley favoured it for formal correspondence, for he often complained about its considerable cost.

With my other hand I found a black stick. No. That would not do at all, though clearly marking my missive for mourning may certainly force my prospective patron to open it!

I thrust the red wax into the candle flame before I could change my mind and twisted it impatiently. A pungent coil of mace-scented smoke rose to my nostrils. My eyes watered as I awkwardly dripped the wax onto the folded letter with nothing like the neatness that felt so natural to me.

I winced as an unsightly splatter of wax marred the corner of my missive. In any other situation, I should recast it most carefully, cost or discomfort be damned. And indeed, despite the clear foolishness of such a sentiment in the present predicament, that was where my instincts were leading me.

My hands absentmindedly grasped out for fresh paper when, with a heavy thunk, and a thud, the old walnut case clock clanged and bonged the hour. Which startled me so that I lurched backwards in my surprise and, with a bitten-off curse, sent the inkwell and blotter careening across the desk. I scrabbled for an oil cloth and dabbed at the rotten mess ineffectually.

It was at that moment that I looked up and locked eyes with Peck. I did not know what to do; my hands froze in place. What could I tell him? His curious little face took in all I was doing as he tilted his head to the side and smiled at me.

With an excess of caution, I slowly continued to pack away the items. Not for a moment removing my eyes from the boy and desperately wondering whether he understood what I had been doing.

I damned myself for failing to confirm that he was occupied. And it was time and time for me to be gone. Muttering under my breath all the while, I took a moment to clean the mess I'd made. An ordeal which seemed to go on and on, but I stayed the strong urges to simply dash away, no matter how they tormented me.

In my imagination, Ridley was at this moment arriving at the building. His key about to enter the lock. I strained my hearing for the hint of any sound, every sensation heightened. The slightest thing seemed deafening. Yet with the day's light falling to a dusky amber, it was finally done. All but the wax stick. It sat, half still in the candle flame where I had left it. With a wince and a little yelp, I enveloped it within my palm, and wiped off any excess with one quick swipe. Then I stuffed what remained into my pocket.

Better to take the entire thing and have it presumed missing than leave the obvious evidence of my subterfuge. I was certain he should notice. I would, of a certainty, be questioned on its whereabouts, but I should have to worry about that when the problem presented itself.

I glanced down at the letter in my hand and gave it a little pat. It scarcely seemed sufficient, and suddenly very foolish. What a silly little scheme this was. Regardless, I raised my fist to my lips and blew into it. It should have to answer.

***

With my head down, I hurried through the thoroughfare towards the penny mail office. When I looked up, it was to notice a young man across the street who seemed focused upon me. His hand was raised in gesture; and much to my dismay, our eyes locked together.

I realised, with alarm, it was the enthusiastic young chap I had shared a handful of discussions with at the shipping offices on Bishop's Row. Fenton, I recalled after a moment. I knew I would not be able to feign ignorance, nor hurry on with a nod or a wave. I would have to stop and converse with him.

I resisted the urge to look around for a clock. I forced upon my face a look of composure which I certainly did not feel. I attempted to mimic the relaxed demeanour of his posture as I approached, very nearly tripping over my own feet.

"Damn terrible day of it," he said, though his generous features suggested he felt otherwise. It seemed to me that an exuberant energy threatened to seize control of his actions at any moment, in the manner of the most energetic of puppies. "Don't you think?"

"Oh, isn't it?" I agreed, doing my best to stop myself from counting the moments I had remaining to me under my breath, a habit I have used to soothe myself since I first learned my numbers.

"Well. Let us get out of it, shall we? I'll take you down to Bows, get you a cup of the good, hot stuff. We'll see it passes in comfort."

My concern for the time quite surpassed any fear of being rude. I found I was shaking my head rather violently, readying myself to run. The look of genuine hurt on his face was all that stopped me darting away down the street, faster than a fox from the hunt.

I racked my mind for a suitable excuse. "Oh but if only I could! I'm on... well, an errand which is... time sensitive! And I must hurry. But... but, thank you. For the invitation. Or, rather, for the... thank you."

My discomposure, which should usually cause me nothing but problems, seemed in this case instead to ease the rejection somewhat, for he laughed easily. And leant in, with a conspiratorial air. As if we were fellows cut from a similar cloth.

"Some other time, then, perhaps? Say, where might I find you? Are your lodgings nearby...?"

This little gambit flustered me even more. And I must say, despite my other pressing concerns, quite warmed me to his character.

"I... Oh, I would very much like to! Pray let us talk the next we are both at the offices, and we.... we could... make the arrangements."

Thus it was that I submitted my letter in time to return home, ready to discover if my ruse had been uncovered.

Chapter Five

SIGNS & SIGNALS

The hand can be every bit as deft as the tongue in the realm of understanding. Indeed. The fingers can communicate as much, or as little. The controlling factor, as ever, lies with the capacities of the practitioner.

Medley's Almanack of Communication for the Deaf, Dumb, Crippled,
and Insane

I flashed my hand up, and chopped it down quickly, in the way we had developed between ourselves. Once I'd realised the boy was deaf, we had quickly established a shy friendship which had only deepened over the passing seasons.

Finished, the argument was finished; I would acquire what he wanted, somehow.

One day. Yes. As soon as I am able. Under the bridge.

We should get our hands on enough blackpowder, though I did not know, yet, how. But I should find a way to do it, and soon, even though the prospect quite frightened me. Ridley Fassinger be damned.

Peck sat, cross-legged, on the backhouse roof of the Baker Street gunsmiths. I, on the other hand, leant somewhat anxiously from the safety of the window, my arms resting on the damp and splintered frame.

From this vantage, I did my very best not to peer too much down into the street. The bangs and clangs of the very serious, and also — to Peck, at least — somewhat exciting, business of the gunsmith's made their way to us periodically. As did the scents: turpentine, charcoal, steaming metal. Occasionally, vibrations passed through the roof tiles and rattled down our arms and legs.

Peck nodded up at me, a wild little smile tugging at his lips. He had won, and well he knew it. He raised his arm, and pointed to Hangman's Bridge, and now it was my turn to nod. To which I added another flurry of hand signals.

I could, perhaps, understand Ridley's desire to disallow him the powder. I could also understand Peck's fascination. Ridley's mithering and downright tyrannical limitations on the boy's freedom I accepted with less grace. For I could see little reason for such control of a child who, though young and adventurous, was no wilder than any his age, and who performed his chores with diligence and very little complaint.

The dense blizzard that had caked every surface in the past month, thick as bunched Murmesseril silk, crunchy as a fresh biscuit, was one morning simply gone. Instead now the days broke bright and true — the sun's glare blinding from the dew's wetness upon the cobbles and muck. I allowed myself to take this as an omen of my coming luck. For I had little else to indicate my fate; though many days had passed, I had, as yet, heard nothing regarding my most desperately despatched missive.

Three vagrants, blind on ruin, slipped about in the filth in the yard below us. Until the gunsmith's 'prentice came out with a broom, as wiry as he, and shooed them away, stabbing his spear in their direction long after they had scattered.

Our hand signals were a functional method of sharing our thoughts and our repertoire had steadily grown with our regular practice. The first few, rudimentary signs I had learnt watching old Fassinger and the boy;

others Ridley had irritably taught me when I badgered him. Finally, we had supplemented and expanded this basic parlance to allow us to more clearly express ourselves, such that we could understand the spirit of our meaning. In the days since I had submitted my missive, I had come to realise that, when I came to leave, I would greatly miss the mischievous young fellow. I wished there was some way to take him with me.

I had found many of the signals we used to make ourselves understood in an old book I purchased from the Slips, with my small stipend. For while Ridley had a number of books and was dutiful in his studies when he felt it behoved him, it seemed his knowledge of hand signals and the like had been derived from a more practical instruction.

So it was that we combined the improvised efforts we mimed to one another with the dependable selection he and Ridley shared. While we peeled the week's potatoes together, flicking dirty water at each other, or as we waged a losing battle with the lodging's appearance, him sweeping cold ashes from the big blackened hearth in the morning, while I wiped and polished the desks, or tidied away Ridley's seemingly endless quantity of surgeon's oddity, in all their gruesome quality.

On the rooftop, Peck brought two apples from the loose flannel pockets upon his well-worn breeches, and proffered one to me as he came to sit before me upon the old sill. I was thinking again how I would miss the boy as I took a big bite, when I noticed a woman approaching with a brisk stride. I wiped the sweet juices from my lower lip.

Perhaps it was she who had been with Ridley what now seemed an age ago when I followed him to the tea house? I could not say for certain. Though what I could say, without any doubt, was that she headed straight for our lodgings.

***

Three days after I had promised the boy I should find him blackpowder, Ridley leaned forward in his seat, and frowned at me over his desk. Then he scowled down at the letter in his grasp. My stomach lurched sickeningly as the totality of my new truth became fully apparent to me; my handwriting was, of course, abundantly clear upon the missive, as was a splodge of wax. My secret had, somehow, been discovered. With a barely audible crack of paper, he gently opened the leaf with his index finger, and worked his lips while he silently read it to himself. The gentle drumming of the rain, present these last three nights, continued on.

I was given a moment to more fully take in his appearance. The billowing linen sleeves of his shirt were yellowed with the day's work, not to mention spotted with blood. Dark patches of sweat had dried under his arms. A further indicator of the strenuousness of the day was gifted to me with a quick appraisal of his face. His expressive brown eyes were tired and bloodshot, as though he had slept poorly, which I knew was often the case. He had not neatened his whiskers that morn, a habit forgotten only in the most fraught of circumstances. And so grey stubble hairs sat upright as little soldiers upon the leathery old skin of his chin.

I swallowed down a sudden flush of guilt. The hair upon his head was still damp, as was the leather of his battered boots and the fabric of his breeches. I was myself also drenched, drenched enough to shiver.

I swung my head away from his regard, nibbling my lip. His medicine chest sat open upon the table, as shabby and tired as he, dinky bottles half-filled. There was camphor essence and castor oil and laudanum. The leather roll of his surgical implements had been hastily dropped to the floor, where it had unwound enough for a bone saw and a wicked-looking clamp to peek out in the dull firelight.

"When we first met I asked you to place your trust in me," he said. "To which I promised that I would, in return, always be fair with you."

He stood briefly, plucked up the poker from the hearth, and jammed at the coals of the fire he had just set in his frustration. A great waft of heat and charred applewood scent swept into me, cutting through the damp chill of the evening, for which I should normally have been most grateful; this night

I found the wash of heat uncomfortable. Perhaps because I already bore a heat deep within me, that which was carried by my conscience. A wave of prickling itches ran along my skin.

Ridley returned and with a weary sigh, dropped heavily into the battered chair by the fire.

"Now, tell me. Have I been fair with you?"

"I, I—" I began.

"I said: have I been fair with you?"

"You have, yes," I muttered. The words poured out quietly, my voice quavering and breaking on them.

"I believe I have kept my part of our bargain. Which is why this is all the more disappointing."

I did not know what to say to him and, like a coward, I averted my gaze from his. But even with my gaze so averted I could still feel the anger coming off him in waves. Yet it was the coldness of it, the icy certainty of his fury, his very disappointment that stung me more than if he had ranted and raved. I almost wished that he would rant and rave, even throw something. That would be better, I was certain.

"Moreover, I believe that I have been *kind* to you, Shay Bluefaltlow. I have taken you into my home. I have made myself available to you, always. I have done my best to teach you. Have I not?"

He was, I suddenly realised, the only person who had ever taken an interest in me. He had cared for me, cared for me beyond providing a bed, and a roof, and a share of his grains and his meat and his bread; he had never once complained of the expense, or the press upon his time. Favoured topics, both, amongst the reluctant guardians of the preparatory school in Quom.

He had remembered the foods I favoured, and not just this, but more. That I was afraid of heights, and enjoyed numbers and order. He'd patiently taught me subjects that I found difficult, long after any teacher I had previously known would have given up. Every word he spoke was true, and I knew it completely.

He had offered me much, much that he did not have to. He had been kind, perhaps much kinder than he needed to be. His role in my situation he was himself likely blameless for. And yet I had never separated the two, the mystery of my situation and his care for me.

"But still you persist with this obsession with your benefactors. You plot and you scheme. I told you, once, that all would become clear in time. I told you that there were things in this world that are more important than our own selfish desires. I believed that I had succeeded in teaching you, at least, the very rudiments of what constitutes a person of character."

I must have looked somewhat stricken, for he paused then to allow me to speak. But words failed me.

"If this scheme of yours had… Well. Clearly, I was wrong. Clearly, I have failed."

He pushed his scarred fist to his lips, and noisily sighed. Then he massaged his bothersome knees, and elbows. Both of which had been much worse since the colder months had drawn in with such intractable certainty. I knew how much his joints troubled him. No matter what he might say to the contrary.

"And perhaps that error of judgement was entirely mine. It seems the archivist was right." He snatched up a mug of warm coffee, and threw back its contents hungrily.

"The who?" I said, daring, finally, to raise my lolling head.

"Oh, you'll find out soon enough. You wish for answers, eh? I shall provide them for you, young lady. And much more besides." And with that he thrust himself from his armchair, and loomed over me.

I looked up at him, and worked the dryness from my lips with my tongue. I wished to apologise, to say something to him about how grateful I was, truly. Anything to make amends. But the words would not come to me, and before I had uttered the beginnings of a sentence, he suddenly leaned forward to snatch up my wrist, his fingers digging in painfully, and stuffed my hurtful letter into my grasp.

Ridley reached his hand into the pocket of his breeches and deftly pulled out another letter — an old, brittle thing — and he held it reverently. I darted a concerned look at it. The paper was long yellowed, the creases deep, and if the faded ink upon it was the common tongue then I would mark myself surprised. He looked down at it, then with a grimace shook his head as if to work something loose. This he laid down on the first with a gentle, protracted pat. Finally he closed my fingers around them and stared relentlessly into my eyes. I longed to look away. To turn away from my own folly forever. But I did not, and it was not for any brave reason, instead the simple truth of my cowardice and fear. I was frozen to the spot.

"These, you will need. Do not open them or in any way interfere. But hold on to them dearly. You will know what to do with them when the time comes."

Part of me longed to know what the letter was. Another part to tuck them both somewhere they would never be found, or to tear them roughly into many pieces. So that we could go back to the way we had been before.

"Where are you taking me?" I said. I suddenly feared another voyage. And then I realised — with a start and much, much too late — that I would gladly undertake another awful month at sea to continue on in the manner I had begun in Fivedock. I had been so adamant that I must leave and now, I was being sent away. Away from Peck and Ridley and every other thing.

I could feel the tears welling up in my eyes, and I fought myself to hold on to them. They burst forth in a great torrent, regardless, and I wept openly in front of another person as I never had in my memory. I bubbled and I sniffled, hiccuped, and snorted like a pig.

Horrible imaginings filled my mind. I was certain that he must be taking me somewhere awful and surely I deserved it. Where exactly I could not say, though several terrible possibilities blossomed in cruel colour in my thoughts.

Suddenly, my small room in this little lodging seemed a paradise. I had been safe here. I had been fed — fed pleasant foods, the best the man could offer me, and not mere gruel. Had I not been offered the opportunity to learn? I had been bought, yes, but my time in the city had opened my eyes to just how lucky I had been.

Ridley offered no reply to my question or my tears. He rose and replaced the wet wool of his heavy tailcoat for a dry, well-worn one, which he shrugged his long arms into quickly, and with surprising dexterity. He tossed a clean handkerchief in my direction and said only,

"Let us do what we should, perhaps, have done many moons ago."

Chapter Six

A CURIOUS PROFESSION

The role of the perpetual consort of the Concord is still steeped in prestige and privilege, despite the fact the ruler has not, for many years now, ruled anywhere but in his own garden. Nor does he wear a crown, or sit upon a throne.

After the knives were drawn the night of the shattered vases, the great houses came together, and drew up the infamous Concord of Westerbrook. The throne was heavily neutered. It became nothing more, truly, than a ceremonial position. Power was instead to be handed to the already influential great houses, the aristocratic families who had themselves rent the nation apart. Those who wished no longer for the heavy hand of the crown to crush their capacity to profit.

As the great houses were ever mistrustful of one another, a balance was proposed. Major decisions would go through the parliamentary courts and counsels. The all important trading rights would be split up amongst the victors, and chaired by two members of those houses, in rotation.

The child who would have been king was thus spared. His descendants occupy the Rose Palace to this day, while the houses bicker on in parliament and ballroom, richer and more powerful and mendacious than ever.

Those who indulge in the society of the upper ten thousand, have ample opportunity to sight Elfron, Balferton, and Hector, the kin of the consort perpetual, Bathlow. Were you to meet them, the reports assure, you would find them as fine-mannered and ineffectual as their brother.

'The Consort Perpetual' from The Worldly Journal and Commonplace Book of Shay Bluefaltlow The Year Eight, Five Hundred Since the Signing of the Great Concord of Westerbrook

I found myself standing before a solid and ornately corniced door, having been led up a flight of stairs that was likewise grand. After we had passed through a large and, to my inexperienced eye, most impressive chamber.

This large room had been the very hive of activity; many folk applied themselves with serious and furious industry, with nary a moment for our business. The majority of this work occurred at three great tables that ran the length of the room, each well-polished to a rich gleam.

Some bent low, with slide rule and point compass in hand, over great diagrams of ships; others perused vast stacks of letters; others muttered together, deep in conversation, over the most detailed map I had ever set eyes upon. Each and all were smartly set out in white shirts and green wool coats, close fit in the navy style.

If I were not a bundle of nerves, I should have found it all quite fascinating, I shouldn't say. But I was, of course, and so my mind ran ahead of me, questions and worries tripping over one another. With no space for any consideration other than what I had done, and what it should mean to my future.

Ridley had hurried me across town. When I heard him briskly command the old jarvey, "To the Admiralty and Navy Offices, quick as you can," it offered as many questions as it answered.

We had clattered into a large courtyard, up to an imperious and incredibly imposing building, fashioned in the style of the ancients, with looming pillars, and a stout façade of precise geometric proportions, as was the dominant mode.

Upon several occasions I wished to apologise to him. Before I could work up the nerve, the man himself rapped neatly on the grand door, once, and put his ear to it. When a call of assent came from within, he turned the handle, and the heavy door swung open on well-oiled hinges. When I hesitated, I felt the palm of Ridley's big hand in the small of my back, and I stepped into the room.

This chamber was as grand as the one we had passed through on the ground floor and possessed a similar military aspect. Although it was smaller, and held only one occupant: a woman seated at a very great desk.

From this piece of furniture, and the objects arrayed upon it, I surmised I had been led to a study of some kind. The walls were wainscoted the colour of coffee, and a watery light filtered through the grand sash windows, imperious shutters latched back.

The occupant of the desk wore knee-length boots which had seen both shine and use, as well as tidy breeches. She bore each as easily as a second skin. The cut of the buckskin accentuated the not inconsiderable length of her legs, which were set akimbo as she leant forward to her work. The very top, gold-threaded button of a maroon waistcoat was rakishly undone. Her neckcloth, though clean and pressed, was folded more roughly than those of her counterparts within the room below.

A thick eye-glass with a green tint was grasped within her eye socket, and her other eye was closed as she squinted downwards. In clever hands she held a brass mechanical device of unknown provenance and a small silver tool I likewise did not recognise. This second she used to perform some action of repair upon the first. She did not raise her eyes from either as she spoke.

"Well then," she said. "Well then, indeed."

Now she raised a hand and flexed her fingers, her movements as measured and precise as the mechanics within her grasp. I watched closely, transfixed. I realised she had lost a finger, chopped bluntly above the knuckle, and that her remaining digits were mottled with a curious combination of colours and burns. These, I would later discover, were the mysterious inks of her unique profession, and the blackpowder scorches acquired in the defence of it. So, too, were the edges of her nostrils stained darkly in the most peculiar fashion. I found I could not take my eyes from them.

I suddenly recalled the letters that had earlier been pressed into my grasp. So I blinked quickly, and proffered them to her, as a nervous child to her schoolmaster upon her very first day of class.

She took them politely from me with a quick flash of a smile.

"Oh. Do sit down." She waved her hand at an imposingly sturdy chair upon the other side of the desk, all leather and dark wood and studs. She did not seek to hide her annoyance at being interrupted.

I did as I was instructed, dragging it across the floor with a dull rasp while she cracked the dark wax on the first missive, and unfolded it gently. She read it quickly, then tossed it onto the desk. The second she held more reverently. Finally she dropped it into a tray and nodded with satisfaction to herself. I realised my breath had caught, as I watched her.

"Introductions are regarded as appropriate at a time such as this." She leant back in her seat. "Very well. I am Penelope Etherington. You may name me Chief Archivist. Or Lieutenant Etherington. Either shall suffice. I know your name from this letter. Though, I knew it before, too."

I nodded, realising I was about to discover the answer to many of my questions. I leant forward hungrily.

"You wished to meet your benefactors. I am one such; the only one you need concern yourself with at the present moment." It was now that I considered her with fresh eyes. Was this the woman who had been meeting with Ridley that day, when Peck and I spotted her from the window?

"I am informed you have been asking questions? Most understandable in the circumstances. So. What is it that you wish to know, Shay, formerly of Quom, and now of Biltern Road?"

The sound of my own name rang out strangely in the room. And my attempt to match the brisk manner of my questioner was a poor one, as I choked out, "Why... why was I brought here?"

"You are in this city because I deemed that it would be so. You are also here because we decided that it should serve our purposes." To this I knew not what to say at all. I sat and slowly pondered her words. Suddenly my scheme seemed very foolish. "And so. I must tell you. That your wish will not be granted. But nor will things continue to be so... indefinite, for you. Instead you will serve a different purpose, here, with me."

She shuffled her papers then seemed to notice something, amongst the scattered objects of her very vast desk. Now she slid a small jar across the table to me. When I did nothing, she nodded towards it. "Go on."

I gulped and leant forward. The glass was thick and old and brown, and it was cold against my touch. Within was a strange substance, dark and ichorous, both glistening and robbing light in the most curious manner. I felt a queer thrill run through me, followed by a jolt of the purest fear — whose source I could not ascertain.

I dropped my hand suddenly and entirely without grace. The jar clattered on the desk. Lieutenant Etherington's hand leapt out, and caught it deftly. She set it back down gracefully.

I was still more than rattled from the day's surprises, and yet the reason for my oafish fumbling was not that. I glanced up, my fear and surprise no doubt apparent upon my constitution. I did not know what to say, and so I said nothing.

Yet she continued as if nothing untoward had occurred. "This substance is essential for the important business we do here. This is one the last samples we have. Very valuable. Very rare."

She paused and I took the opportunity to show I was not entirely stupid. "What is it?" I asked.

"The blood of one the last Sentinel's we sighted. Epthphilaas was his name. In our tongue. One hundred and twenty years gone." She looked reflective as she shut her eyes for a moment. "Do you know what a Sentinel is?"

"I have heard of them, but… I cannot say I truly know all that much about them, I must admit." I said to her, hoping the utterance should suffice, and please her. For it was the truth, I had heard stories of them. Who had not? Quom was not so far from the bled to have avoided that. I had studied the Great Quiet a little. Something about this woman — the Chief Archivist — made me want to prove myself to be at least competent, so I asked, "Do you… do you know what they are? Truly?"

"Indeed I do," she said, working the words slowly, deliberately, in her lips. "Behemoths as great as anything that has ever walked our realm. That is what," she said. "Noble creatures. Deadly. Terrifying. Do you know what else they are?"

I shook my head, mute.

"Something far bigger than your petty concerns." She waved towards my letter. "Have I made myself clear?"

I nodded glumly, transported momentarily back to the preparatory school and my frequent chastisements.

"Very good. Now." She clapped her hands together and her mood shifted. "A time has come to track them once more. Though, in truth, I never stopped. Perhaps it would be more accurate to say this: it is time for our masters, in all their invaluable wisdom, to pay due attention to that tracking. And, thus, a time has come for new blood to be tested. For the first time in many generations I have been permitted to break the old accords."

With the clap of her hands she seemed to have finished chastising me; she spoke to me now almost as a colleague. Her smile, though somewhat brittle, felt genuine.

"So. How would you feel about fulfilling that duty with me?"

"Fulfilling that duty?" I said, mimicking her words. My head was aspin with the sudden turn in conversation. I had expected to be punished, perhaps sent back to Quom. I had never been asked such a question in my life.

"Why, yes," she replied. "Following them, and keeping our archive, and all the other tasks we do here?" Her look was expectant.

"I don't understand." I said to her. "Why, of everyone you could… why ever me?"

"It is a great honour to be so chosen. Be under no doubt about that. I have needed an assistant for some time. I have craved one for much, much longer. Part of me believed I should die the only archivist in the Concord. But here we are."

I abandoned all hope of seeming sensible. My mouth gaped open.

"While I understand your curiosity… because I deem it so, should be sufficient. For now. It certainly was when I sat in your position. But I shall offer you a little more than that!" She gave a strange little laugh. "There are several reasons we chose you. We have followed your development fairly closely. You show aptitude and a sharp mind. The distant nature of your school meant we could take you without causing undue suspicion. Truthfully, the most important of our criteria is that you have no past. This is attractive to us. You are from a place where no one will miss your absence. So is this."

I was too shocked to be truly afraid. I simply stared.

"The truth is that by acting as we do — by taking you into our employ — we break a law that has held open warfare from the coast at bay for generations. Oh, and of course you possess some… qualities, also. That we may use to our advantage. For we did not choose entirely blindly. Tenacity the foremost amongst those we instructed our agents to seek."

I thought of all the possible futures we had imagined for ourselves in Quom. This was something beyond the realms of imagination.

"I do understand this is a difficult and strange position. A young woman, much like you now, once stood alone. So please. Do not assume I cannot understand how you feel. She was shown a rare kindness. She was given the opportunity to rise to a great responsibility. It was a singular opportunity, and a precious one. I owe those who provided it to me. Once, I made a promise to myself, that I should do the same for another when the time came. This closes an old, old, circle. I am the type of woman who pays her debts."

She inclined her head as if waiting for me to reply. When I did not speak, or move, she sighed.

"You, of course, may not view it as a boon. Yet there is much merit in the position. I will not lie to you, however. It will not be without considerable danger. Yet, it is a fact that your future prospects were undeniably poor. I offer you an improvement. In addition to these prospects, I offer you purpose and shape for your life. A dedication to something greater than yourself.

"I also offer to extend your life. If you survive." At this I nearly stood up and left, so ridiculous was the idea. But the archivist seemed perfectly serious.

"I understand that this is… well, I'm sure it's a lot for you to take in. Allow me to tell you a little of the… history, of this office. Of our origins."

She clasped her hands together on the desk and looked thoughtfully into her palms, as if she was reading from them.

"At one time, there were many who filled our role, chronicling the movements and activities of the Sentinels. Sentinels were…. while not exactly common, they were not the stuff of myth and legend they are today. All knew of them and of their immense power.

"When the Tripart Wars came to a close, agreements were made between the participants. The cost of peace, you understand? It is often the way. Back then it was feared the Sentinels may rise once again, or their power be used in battle. Our enemies were very… particular that that should not happen. All of the original and living archivists were to be removed. What was left of them, which was not much.

"They were to be held by the enemy, along with members of the ruling bodies of each nation, their lives forfeit were the agreement to fail. A single Sentinel archivist was permitted to stay in office in each nation."

She turned her thumb around and pointed it at her chest. "Which foolish young buck would fulfil such a role, eh? But the years passed, as they have a habit of doing, and the world forgot. The power our enemies feared ebbed away. Now, what was once the most patent and simple truth to every man, is nothing but half-remembered myth and legend. And here the old archivist sits, forgotten by all but those with the longest memories in the labyrinthine corridors of Palace and Parliament. A much-reduced station. Hobbled beyond all compare. Little more than an empty figure head, in truth. Until now. Now they remember us. Now, the Sentinels rise once more. It is our job to track them. To know them. To find out why."

"So that is why I have been brought here?"

"So that is why."

I tilted my head on its side to consider her once again. And the frightening words she had spoken. What she said could not hold the veracity of truth, surely. I studied her face again, in more detail, I performed the simple sum. It was… impossible. She gently placed down the mechanical device she had been working on with a soft thud, and leant forward to give me her full attention. She met my gaze directly, and it frightened me.

Her eyes were implacable in their consideration. I felt there was no hiding from them, that they could see anything within me, anything at all. Right there and then, I believe I conceived, very briefly, of the indomitable wisdom and power of one who has lived for such a period — though I would not truly conceive of it for many years — and it left me speechless. The futility of any subterfuge, the gap in our station and experience, it all combined to paralyse me almost entirely.

But eventually I managed, through some unimaginable force of will for which I am still entirely gratified, to surpass it and I did indeed move. And I surprised myself when I met her gaze and uttered the words which filled my mind.

"Surely, that cannot be…" I stammered. "You would be over two hundred years old."

"How very perceptive of you," she laughed. "Yes. That is true and it is a notable thing. Yet in some ways the other changes this duty brings are the more considerable. I should tell you not to think on it for now, but it would be a futile request. For our art — the art I would teach you — will change you, too. In curious ways."

There was very little I could think of to say to that. So strange was the concept, and I had not begun to understand its significance to me. So instead I intended to speak of something else. Something that was tormenting me, and filling me with questions and wonder as much as that most peculiar and intimidating truth.

"But I must beg your forgiveness. That, I am afraid, must be the limit of what I share with you on this matter." Here she spread her hands wide in mock supplication. "For now. At least. Time is not with us. Action is required. Oh, I wish I could spend a week and give you all the information you might desire, my child. Perhaps I will, in time. For today, I will make you this promise." Her eyes shone with something like excitement.

"If you will accept it from me. Serve me well, give me your trust, and I will do all I can to support any of your endeavours. As we learn together, I will share more. On this, you have my word and honour. Now. What say you to my proposition?"

Again, I did not know what to say, nor what to think. I was frightened, this was undoubtedly true. Yet I was also intrigued. I sensed truth from her; she was honest to her core.

I did wish to know more. To give myself over to her surety, to her undeniable power. For it attracted me, even then, in the innocence of that time. I understood that to say so much, to offer myself so easily, may be foolish. And there was so much I did not know.

"What will it entail?" I asked, this question bursting from me suddenly as the others had come slow. "This," I wrapped my thick tongue around the unfamiliar words, "this archiving…?"

She leant back and spoke softly, her eyes closing for a moment. "Ah. So much, and so little. Everything and nothing, all in synchronicity. The truth is we could expend a handful of lifetimes and you would not have acquired all that the old master archivists achieved. But we must move faster and so we shall.

"A wise workman uses the tools at his disposal, and does not mourn the ones lost to him. Surgeon Fassinger informs me you have a relatively sharp mind. And, with your little… indiscretion, it is clear you possess an intrepid spirit. Good. Bent appropriately, both will serve us well. I believe your regular education is advancing satisfactorily. You will need all of these things, and more.

"First, you will learn all there is to know about the great beings it is our duty to chronicle. You will learn their names and their history, their habits and their nature. For how else are you to track them with me?

"You will learn how to use the tools of our strange little trade. Then, you will learn how to deploy them upon both field and wave. I shall not lie to you. It is a difficult thing you will do. Sometimes, it may be painful. You will be tested in ways you might struggle to conceive of. But give yourself to me properly, expend all that you have and I promise you I shall carry you. I shall in turn offer you every pound and ounce of my own capacities. You will not be alone.

"I will teach you, too, how to defend yourself. Both from the many dangerous forces and creatures our profession must by its nature face, and from the in many ways much more dangerous people we may encounter.

"Now. There are a few details of our position it is important you understand. Our office is an ancient one and so it answers to three seats of ancient power. The seat of the king, though there is no king any longer, and so in that case we answer to the Rose Palace and the Consort Perpetual, and the three Chambers of Parliament. A fine nest of vipers."

She chuckled to herself. "So sometimes we answer and others we know when to keep our own counsel. Yet in time they will expect me to present you to them, and for that I apologise and you will require delicate preparation. We answer also to the academy, though this I believe you will find a less arduous responsibility. Finally, you may notice that we are within a naval office." She jabbed her finger up, down, then swept it in a circle around us. "So. Yes. We answer to the navy. Nominally and operationally, we are under their command most directly. In reality, we are somewhat independent. We are provided funds and offices and other needly things. But, for many years it has been a case we are more nuisance than boon. Better out of sight and out of mind, ey? Still, if you follow the path I would have you follow, you will earn, eventually, a naval rank. You will draw a small stipend. First as my assistant. Then one day perhaps as a Sentinel archivist's first."

It was all too much to take in. A bewildering assortment of strangeness. But I listened. I realised I had sat forward upon my seat. I wondered what else this might entail. Where might I live? As if she read my mind, she spoke.

"You may keep your current lodgings. It is a good arrangement, and keeps you out of sight.

"I will warn you. Within our society some hate us and would see us gone. Though we are not without allies. Soon, if you agree to join me, I shall introduce them to you. Alas, amongst the many dances I will teach you to dance, the dance of society is one it would be the greatest folly to neglect."

"Ridley," I said, in a sudden rush of realisation. "He knew of this, didn't he? My situation, that is, and your plans for me. He knew. He is... he is more than an agent."

"Yes. Very good!" She clapped her hands together and genuine merriment shone in her eyes. "Ridley is indeed an old ally. He has served beneath me, and served well. Though I consider him a friend, first and foremost."

"He lied to me." I said, suddenly sullen despite myself.

"Did he? I doubt he did so explicitly. And if he did, then you mustn't be too harsh on him. It hardly signifies. He was acting under my command. With your own profit in mind. We had to be certain we could proceed safely. We have enemies here, and they watch us ever closer. And when you took matters into your own hands... Well. We had little choice but to act."

I had the decency to drop my head at this revelation. For I understood suddenly just how much I had come to care for the man. It was beyond all dispute or reason. And because of this, I wasn't sure how I ought to feel. But I hardly had time to dwell on my feelings any further, for I was cut off from my reverie most abruptly.

"Well, I think that is enough for one evening. Don't you? There is much here for you to digest. Let me say though, I am pleased we are begun. If indeed we are…?" She raised a questioning eyebrow at me.

Then she leant over and plucked up a heavy little box which sat upon her desk. It was made of a tarnished, silvery metal, and upon its surface was the densest web of most peculiar and strange inscriptions.

I stole furtive glances at it, intermittently meeting the archivist's gaze. With a click she popped open the lid, and rummaged amongst the contents.

"Leave now, the saw-bones will be waiting for you downstairs. Think on all I have said; you have one week to make your decision. If you wish to join me, then take this," she said, pressing a small vial she plucked from the box into my palm. I squinted down at it dubiously. "I apologise for the flavour, and for any… unpleasant sensations. Eat well — to complete satiation — before you attempt to ingest it. You may gag.

"Some find it helpful to pinch their nostrils, others to brace the malodorous substance with a dash of strong liquor. Each student is unique, and no particular fashion ever gained dominance amongst the feted and once thronged ranks you are, perhaps, to join. In this, the choice is one for your own discretion."

"What will it do?" I whispered, hoarsely.

"Many things. The first time is a little different for every would-be archivist. It will bring on an ague, known as the archivist's ague. For a certainty, it will induce a deep, deep sleep, of many hours. Following which, you will know a vitality you have likely never experienced. It will also alter certain… faculties."

She held her index finger up before me like a composer, where it loomed menacingly, beside the hewn-off stump of its fellow, "But I give to you this

61

warning. If you do not wish to do this thing. Then you must decide. Do not take the tincture, nor experience the archivist's ague. I will not force it upon you. I will only have you by your own volition. You will have the freedom you crave. But it will be an empty freedom. For if you turn aside, I will not be able to protect you. I will not be able to back your situation. I will not be able to guide you. You will be cast adrift in the world, alone. A world more uncertain than it has, perhaps, ever been.

"Know that others are aware of the wheels we have set in motion. They are singularly dangerous and committed. They will not cease in their pursuit of any one of us. And that includes you. Indeed, they already pursue. They have simply been hidden from your view by a material and tireless effort on the part of those benefactors you would do without."

"And no." She held up her hand to wearily stop my protestation, "If you were to flee our company, such an act would not form an assurance of your safety. That is not the type of foe we are dealing with. Indeed. It should likely do the very opposite.

"I am sorry that you have been brought into this. Truly. Yet I offer as much as may be taken. And more."

To this I did not know what to say. We sat in a prolonged silence. Eventually, with a cough into my fist, I rose to leave.

"Wait!" she said.

At this moment she slid open a drawer below her desk. From within it she took out a small oblong of card, which she waved at me. "I feel somewhat obliged to ensure we get off on the right foot. All this business has been unfortunate. For all of us."

I sensed now an awkwardness from her that had been entirely absent until that point. "So. It has been brought to my attention that you harbour a penchant to sample the theatrical entertainments of Durrot Row."

I felt the rising heat of my cheeks colouring, as I realised what I had very childishly supposed to be my private dreaming had been anything but. I wondered if Ridley had found my stashed treasures? Or observed me when

I fancied myself a blueblood, pretended to confer with my new companions, or danced around the small room as if on stage. Oh. I wished so very much to flee. The shame was too much. Simply too much.

"Very good. I have acquired vouchers for the purpose." These she placed firmly against the table, with a little tap of assurance, before she slid them over to me.

"I can't say I've ever found much merit to the operas," she continued. "But I know many that do."

"Th-th-thank you," I muttered.

"Hardy offered you her box. Devilish useful that woman, in such regards. Her, you'll have chance to meet. But all in the fullness of time."

I nearly pressed her immediately for more. But something stayed my tongue.

"You may take these, whether you decide to join our office or not."

Gingerly I reached out for them and then hesitated, my eyes darting to the archivist. When she nodded kindly, I plucked them up. With a creak, I sat back heavily and without grace to the unyielding leather of the imposing chair. Then I allowed myself to inspect them closely.

Subscription Box 52, The Left Wing
Admittance is granted to the guests and chosen persons of the
subscription holder:

Her Grace The Duchess Esmerelda Hardy

The Boxes, Gallery & Pits open at 5:30pm
The performances begin at 6:30pm precisely

I held the slight bottle in one hand, and the vouchers in the other. I considered them both for quite some time.

Part Two

MALODOROUS PURPOSE

Chapter Seven

AN ARCHIVIST'S
IMPORTANT DUTIES

The field Golspek harmoniser is perhaps the most curious device I have ever had the displeasure of encountering. If one is happy to disregard its larger, immovable counterpart held within the archives, at least. In truth, both devices more than somewhat intimidate me.

And yet, as fortune would have it, I am to become much more familiar with it in the coming days. For all I would rather the steady dependence of arithmetic, which so better suits my capacity, operating the queer machine is something I must soon master.

The base of the device, a perfect cube of dull walnut, is no wider than my palm. The device itself is no taller than my hand from wrist to fingertip.

Spindly steel armatures jut from its body with the jaunty malice of the gangly-limbed, foul arachnid native to distant Karachi. The long central needle embraced by the armatures is itself fashioned of that most valuable and rare material, bledmettle. It is a black darker than night, darker even than the absence of night. It is curiously stippled, and distinctly rough. This you would discover if you were to accidentally rub the tip of your finger across its surface, though I would strongly advise against such an act, for the sensation is incredibly unpleasant. One learns to handle the device remarkably gently once that particular mistake has been committed.

In the correct employ of the tool, one places one's thumb upon a cold brass plate set at an angle to the device's eerie body. So one is then adequately equipped to detect a glimmer of the Sentinel odour harmonics sufficient to perform an archivist's important duty, when out in the field.

'Field Golspek Harmoniser,' The Worldly Journal and Commonplace
Book of Shay Bluefaltlow
The Year Nine, Five Hundred Since the Signing of the Great
Concord of Westerbrook

By the grace of the old gods — or, rather, by the grace of the mysterious benefactors I had so reviled and wished to flee from — I got my wish. We – Peck and I, for who else could I possibly take with me? — would attend the renowned theatre of Durrot Row.

Ridley hardly seemed pleased with the suggestion I take the boy with me into the evening's melee. But he finally agreed, after much extended nagging over the stretch of several days. Nonetheless, strict conditions were made clear: only if we returned straight to our abode afterwards, and only if Peck was incredibly well wrapped.

When he found an ashen footprint on the windowsill and took us to task for Peck's hijinks upon the roof, I thought he should very well forbid the entire thing. Now we felt ownership of something we much desired to retain, Peck and I found ourselves attending to our chores with a newfound and furious diligence. The window remained, for the time being, firmly closed.

An opera featuring Kitty Welphens, visiting for one week only from the Grand Republic was to be our introduction to theatre, on the dreariest spring night I had yet known.

And what a night it was. I was quite bewildered by the crowds, and knew not how to navigate them. Should we skirt the edges, or was pushing through acceptable? Should we acknowledge the other patrons with a nod, or perhaps some kind of greeting was more fitting?

It seemed almost entirely certain to me that we would be discovered as the urchins we, comparatively speaking, were, to be tossed forthwith into the street from whence we came. On the contrary, we were shown to a box of the very first rank, up a flight of stairs grander than anything I'd ever seen outside of the finest engravings.

And to be resident in a box, and not even the middle balcony, or the pit! Where we should most certainly belong, if we were to be anywhere at all. Why, it spoke to the connections and power of my new master; this notion fed my imagination, merrily stoking my fears for the reality of my coming days.

Who were these people, who now controlled my life? One might imagine that the combination of such a sobering truth, with the settling foreboding of the strange concoction I would now, that I had accepted this greatest of gifts, have to consume. But this was very much not the case. Instead, once the stirring orchestral movement filled my chest, I found I forgot myself entirely, too thrilled by the opulent new experience to dwell on any such concerns.

And yet I was shy. I felt almost entirely out of place in the finery of the box. Periodically, I ran my hand over the cheap cut of my garments. Or checked myself in the small, cracked looking glass I had smuggled in within my sleeve. Amongst those around us, the comparison seemed to me entirely displeasing. I knew the birthmark upon my neck and face destroyed what little chance I had at anonymity, a fact which served to add further concern.

Despite Fassinger's best efforts, having dressed Peck in his least-tattered breeches and shirt and spent time combing his fine, soft hair, the child's exuberant charm was quite unquenchable. While I fussed over the plainness of my dress and the fact I had nothing with which to dress my hair, such modesty, or self reflection, was not a problem for Peck, who might have been in our own lodgings, for all a hoot he gave about his appearance in the resplendent box.

The opera itself was entirely moving, though I spent just as many moments peeking at the other boxes as I did at the stage. I played a little game with myself, attempting to spot and name those of whom I had read in the fashion periodicals I had perused at the lending library, or in the broadsides of the coffee shop. So too the attendance of those I had for so many nights watched from afar.

I caught a glance of Arksthrotle, with a gentleman, as enchanting as she. I found I could not stay myself from tracing every line of his perfect face. Though the particular details were hidden by the low light. He spoke familiarly with an old fellow, one hand upon his shoulder. All three were laughing together at something. I leant up onto the tips of my toes to see what it was. To realise that a frail lady had dropped her cane, and seemed close to falling herself without it. I twisted my lips in distaste. Perhaps I had been mistaken, some detail missed. This was no thing to find amusing.

Peck had himself a thoroughly gay old time. So much so that I began to secretly hope that he might forgive me my earlier promise of blackpowder and mischief. To see him, now, sitting amidst the grandeur of the theatre box, rendered a ludicrous contrast with our adventurous plan.

He lay his cheek upon the thick varnish of the box's handrail, and closed his eyes. At first this very much puzzled me, and I nearly shook sense into him. Until I realised that it was so he might feel the thunderous harmonics of the music vibrating through the woodwork and into his very bones.

***

Hours later, my head was still full of the incredible sweep of the music. So much so that I hummed gently beneath my breath as I sat upon the edge of my bed frame and, with a single hesitation, touched the bottle the archivist had given me to my lips.

I had, as she had instructed, eaten most heartily upon our return and Peck had joined me gladly. We had shared several apples, a loaf of dark bread and an excessive amount of a sharp Watersley cheese, washed down with a scalding, savoury broth that we discovered bubbling away in the iron.

The archivist had neither lied nor exaggerated: the strange substance was truly foul, both in flavour and sensation. It seemed to coat my throat, so that it would not leave no matter how much water I took. As if it had been stained forever more. Still, once I had overcome an initial wave of nausea and the coughing fit I was certain would cause me to vomit, I pulled the cool fabric of my bed linens around me and awaited my fate.

***

I awoke late the next morning, having slept as deep and as long as I had been promised I might. And my work began.

Outside the light was almost blindingly bright. On my tongue, coffee tasted exceedingly strong. I was surprised that I found the change exciting. Yet this was only the start of it. And so began a bewildering set of incidents that would not let up for some time.

I soon found myself in the archivist's library at the admiralty, seated within a heavy and imposing chair, drawn close to a vast desk. Dizzyingly, uncountable books and books rose to a distant ceiling. Many of them priceless. Irreplaceable.

The cracked leather of the seat creaked gently as I leant forward to burrow my shoe tips through the weft of a top rug worn thin by the feet that had come before me, and after others; I felt these spectres of bygone scholars to be a great bustling mass, placed and dated who knew when. I could imagine the colours of the rug had once been vivid. Bountiful greens and bleeding reds, crystal blues and golden yellows had long fallen to dullness amidst the silence, as had everything else. Which felt entirely proper.

Ignoring the long dead with an apologetic, hollow little cough, I turned my attention to that which was immediately before me. Upon the richly varnished mahogany of the desk were a variety of items. By my elbow, a set of brass callipers and martial accoutrements; a flintlock pistol; a powder flask; a drawstring cloth bag sagging sadly open, lead shot peeking from within; a small ramrod.

Beyond this, several leather-bound books were scattered, delivering to me, despite their order, the impression that they had recently been consulted in great haste. What appeared to be a map of some variety was half unrolled, some indecipherable landmark encircled with a telescopic instrument.

The strong scent of a type of oil with which I was as equally unfamiliar reached my nostrils, and forced my eyes to water a little.

Chief Archivist Etherington loomed suddenly over my shoulder. She hefted a vast tome onto the desk before me with a dull thud, and waft of ancient air. Bound in metal and leather, the cover bore a dense lattice of iron artwork: strange creatures rippled and rose and fell and intertwined in an impossibly complex dance of exquisite craftsmanship. I both wished to reach out and touch it, and to recoil. Yet I did neither, instead merely staring, my mouth agape.

Etherington slid open a drawer, and drew out a small iron key. This she slipped into a tiny lock hidden within the mouth of one of the creatures, one indistinguishable from the rest of the strange menagerie, as far as I could see. With a gentle click the heavy cover fell open with the ease and heft of a well oiled yet incredibly substantial door.

Now the dusty scent of old paper rose to meet me. I felt the strange pull towards the volume once again, stronger now, strong enough that I allowed the urge to overpower my considerable fear. The pages were thick and dense and, in both depth and breadth, the match of my arm at full stretch. The archivist tossed a pair of kid gloves onto the desk before she pulled on her own. She tugged at the fingers in quick, practised movements as I fumbled with mine.

Then she turned the great pages with a reverent, sure hand and I greedily drank in every little detail, my breath hitching as I peered down. I had little experience with musical instruments but was familiar enough with musical notation for the harp, harpsichord, and lyre. Not enough to read or understand it, not quite, but certainly to recognise it. The markings on the pages beneath the archivist's gloved hands appeared like that, except there were peculiar differences.

Firstly, it ran out from the centre of the page rather than from left to right as I had previously known, curious as a spider's web. Secondly and thirdly, the symbols were entirely alien to me, and the metre was on the queerest scale. One which suggested vastness.

It was in this fashion that I was losing myself in a deepening reverie, my eyes searching and mind wheeling, when a question burst from my lips.

"Whatever is it?"

"Scent song notation," she whispered hoarsely. She drew her finger down the page and tapped a lengthy and particularly angry scrawl of symbols. "Each Sentinel has his own signature, as distinct as one's voice, or face. It is our honoured duty to record them for the benefit of our great state. This pattern appeared to match the known signature of Slinthril: one of the most imperious of the venerable ones. So recorded by the ancient archivists who preceded us, and kept here within the archive. Such that we may confirm the identity of the noble creature."

I turned and was startled to find the archivist's eyes locked on my own. They were bright and keen and wild.

"Silent for aeons. No longer." I broke her gaze and turned back to the impenetrable text. "One of your first tasks will be to fill these records," she continued, undisturbed by my hesitance. "But it is not a simple thing. First, you must learn to render the notation. I am given to understand that your language capabilities are excellent, which is a great asset to our endeavour. It is a task you will start immediately, and practise each day until you have gained a rudimentary proficiency. Enough that I can trust you with the real meat of our work. With current developments, we are most… pressed for time."

Just as I began to worry that a coherent reply was expected of me, she turned away. "Indeed. We will begin this very morning. The first duties I will give to you are of incredible importance," Etherington said to me. "You must proceed with an excess of caution. Do you understand me?

"One of your duties will be acting as my clerk, sending the letters of our good office to the people who require them." She moved around the desk so she was standing before me. "When you do so you must always use this." The archivist raised her hand, spreading her fingers to display a signet ring carved with similar beasts to those worked on the cover of the book. Then she pointed at a drawer in the desk. "This I keep here, when I am about my business away from the admiralty."

"Is it a seal? A…" I searched my memory for the word. "A signet?"

"Yes. Of a kind. This is a binding ring. Most ancient. Through its use our correspondents know a missive comes directly from us. You must guard it fiercely, when I am away."

Before I could ask about the binding, she went on, "You will have many such tasks. Yet the most honoured of your duties is, perhaps, this one: the notation and the representation of the office. For it is for this purpose from which the others all derive their need."

"Y-yes," I said, more because I felt it was expected of me than because I understood or agreed.

"The records you will manage we must maintain for the power of our good nation. The contract we follow, made upon a time by kings, binds us. So too does the ancient formulation we take bind us. Once with our word and twice with our blood."

I pondered the ominous nature of this pronouncement as I studied my hands. Bound us with our blood? How?

"Is this something I can trust from you?"

"It is." I said, after a long moment, for again it seemed expected of me. And I knew not what else to say. I swallowed, tentatively nodding my assent to the still open book. "Yes, it is." I spoke the words more firmly, jutting out my chin, perhaps to convince myself.

"But now, I have something else I must show you…"

***

I was taken to see the archives themselves: a set of rooms of impeccable, echoing quiet, located at the very top of the building. They were long rooms, and tall. I should have been pleased to know I would spend much of my time in the coming days there, though not that I might have to climb the high shelves.

And, oh! Those first days when I ventured into the archives.

A single, dull lantern, glass panes long stained black with grime and soot, was the only permitted illumination, the better to preserve the ancient samples and records.

With a little creak, the old iron hinges of the lamp would halt, as if in protest at its continued use, and, with a grunt and a press of force, suddenly give to swing open. Whereupon I would reach my quavering fingers within to press a lit taper to the wick and ignite a sudden flame.

No serving maid or naval clerk did Penelope permit to climb to that most secretive and precious of floors and so it was instead our duty — and, more accurately, mine — to maintain the quarters. If I close my eyes, I can almost taste the ocean aroma of the whale oil. And feel the cold press of glass upon my fingertips, so familiar, as the frame squeaks closed.

The lantern was heavy and old and it caused my shoulder to ache abominably. It was also difficult to wield alongside the quantities of equally precious recording I would invariably bear upon my person while trying to hold it steadily aloft. Though I dare not venture amongst the shelves without it. No. For it threw out a small but vital island of buttery light which seemed both entirely insufficient to the task and perfectly suited to it.

Regardless, I clung ever so closely to it whenever I dared to venture into the haunting archives, creeping in upon the tips of my boots, overfilled arms outstretched as far as I dared. To hurry to the location of my business, where I would place it reverently upon the tiles with a gentle clink, and try to stay always within the bounds of its scant illumination.

Never once did I forget to observe this law of my fancy. I even went so far as to climb back down from the ladder to adjust it a mere hand span, when I felt I had strayed worryingly far from its protection, before climbing up and up once more to continue the task at hand. As if having to contend with the height of the ladder was not more than enough of a challenge.

I had as yet kept my fear of heights a secret from my new master. And this caused a considerable problem. I had hidden a number of records in a dusty old drawer hidden in the depths, when I could not force myself to climb any higher than the tenth step to put them in their proper place. Promising myself I would work up the courage to mount to a sufficient height another time, soon, before the Chief Archivist noticed my aversion.

Located at the very end of the quiet corridor, the archives were a vast assemblage of apartments hidden behind lock and heavy key not once, but twice. Aged wood the colour of drinking chocolate covered nearly every surface. Wall to ceiling shelves, and the weight of the samples, or so I often allowed my wavering sensibility to suggest to me, gave the air a thick, foreboding quality, as if the colossal Sentinels themselves considered our actions and imparted their very essence to the place.

I felt like a trespasser, barely tolerated. The floor was tiled, and my furtive steps rang loudly throughout the hallowed space. As no natural light was permitted, there were no windows and the place was forever, to my mind, suspended in a timelessness I have only ever encountered in the archives.

Upon one wall was a vast section of drawers of varying sizes. Some were no larger than my hand, others ran the length of my arm, and a few more the length of my body. I estimated there were many hundreds of them, after I counted a column one day from floor to ceiling, my fingers lightly brushing against the hardwood of each drawer as I walked alongside them, my lips working silently so as not to lose count.

Tall, tall ladders set on casters rested against them periodically, and lurched upwards into the gloom and towards the cavernous ceiling. The old copper screeched gently when I nudged them. Brass plates were affixed to each drawer, plated with thick glass, beyond which the contents was indicated in careful Fellrinthian.

And throughout it all the unmistakable sense that I would not measure up to the assessment of my new and foreboding master lurked within me. That there would be found in time a way to out my true nature. It was in the little mistakes that I made, and the brusque scalds that fell upon me for my errors. Oh I did not doubt I could make a suitably decent worker, in charge of my own choices, in some other place.

But I began to wonder if I could ever be capable of becoming a Sentinel Archivist's First at all. Or if I even wished to.

Chapter Eight

MALODOROUS PURPOSE

It has been my latest task to study and elucidate the configuration of our state, and those that surround us, through their recent history.

The first and my new home, the Concord of the Houses, is one of the most prosperous nations upon the Whispering Coast. For, once the nation to which I now owe allegiance had stabilised from the internal strife that saw its formation into its current form, the great houses that are bound to rule it soon returned their attention to the bounties of the new lands to the far east and the south.

In the following years, three great trade companies were formed and expanded: that of Murmesseril, Kalchetti, and the Quom Protectorate.

Yet it is not the only nation with such proclivities: two other colonial empires compete with my new home. The nation of the Concord is buttressed in the temperate land mass by the Grand Republic and the Principality of Glisk. So it is that I must write what is clear to whoever lives in this place for any length of time.

All three have shared in a thick web of warfare, trade, culture, and history, for many a year. As incestious as the fabled royal family of Gombi.

And, as that family, the eyes of each are always jealousy considerate of the other, lest they lose advantage.

'The Nations of the Whispering Coast' from the Worldly Journal and
Commonplace Book of Shay Bluefaltlow
The Year Nine, Five Hundred Since the Signing of the Great Concord of
Westerbrook

I believe I will never grow used to the taste of the tincture one must ingest
to precipitate the archivist's ague. Countless uses have not made the stuff any
more palatable to me, and nor did the many days I assisted Chief Archivist
Etherington in attempting to reformulate the damnable concoction inure me
to its foul charm. The act was a thankless one, of foetid smokes which made
my eyes stream, of malodorous scents which offended my nostrils, and slimy
textures which caused me to squeal and gag in horror.

Every foul preparation imaginable went into their manufacture: pow-
dery orum and sticky amrot; stinking hartshorn and acrid bellweather.
Much of which was acquired - when the local apothecary, Jemima, could not
furnish us with what we needed - at great expense and difficulty from the
most unscrupulous traders choking the dockyards. Suffice to say, for all the ex-
perimentation, nothing we attempted answered in either taste or constitution.

Not that this should ever stay Etherington's drive on the matter. In fact
there was no matter she didn't give her full and sharp attention, no detail
of our work left unexamined. For if she drove me to exhaustion — and she
surely did — it was but half as hard as she drove herself.

It took a great effort to force myself to ingest the latest tincture we had
made, my eyes squeezed shut, my fists clenched. *Ready* to plunge my head
within the fat leather hood which hung, flaccid, from the large harmoniser,
and heavy as a blacksmith's apron. Or so I readily lied to myself, for I cannot
think that one could ever be truly ready for such a thing.

The hood was attached to the great apparatus braced imposingly upon
the stained floorboards of the highest attic of the archival offices. The use of
the dreaded contraption caused an aspect to befall me which left my senses
reeling. So that I could not distinguish one from another and they blended

together in the most sickening fashion. One where I became weaker than a mewling kitten, and my torso trembled as if from seizure.

A place too where sweat slicked my face and an icy pain burnt through my every surface in a sudden jolt that set my heart hammering an unpretty little beat, and inspired a deep and particular nausea that threatened to empty my stomach. A state where one's mind retreated from the small certainties of our usual mortal existence, such that there were many more senses, and less, and none. Or that is at least my impression, for I could never properly recall outside that most alien of experiences. As it slipped away so easily, almost as dreams do when one attempts to chase them.

To where I would find myself standing at the last, by the great contraption. The strange gloves, laced with shimmering metal fibre, drooping beside me hefty as jousting mitts to the measure of a great brute from the pits, rather than my feeble frame. These we used to slather the ichorous amplification substance upon a vast bledmettle needle that was longer than my arm, such that we could receive the odour harmonics sufficiently.

As I steadied the sense of myself with timid, doddering control I focused with a great effort. To taste and hear and smell, in some fashion, the odorous membrane of the scent music of the Sentinels. Scent music so rendered into a quality which we could somewhat sample, transcribe in strange notation and add to our great and ever-growing archive.

***

In the early days of working alongside Penelope I frequently wondered if I should mention to her the threats I'd received from the brutish youths who had so pursued me. In truth, I was a little ashamed to admit my concern to her, who seemed so very capable. Their blade, however, had been very real and I did not doubt their commitment to the cause they had set upon.

Soon, however, I found two of my problems remedied, of a fashion; my longing for a peer and ridding myself of my stubborn enemies. I made a friend.

The local apothecary, which I was given to frequent for the acquisition of supplies for both Fassinger and Etherington, was the domain of a young apothecary, who seemed always to be inside the store, no matter the hour: one Jemima Pincke.

I would later learn, from Fassinger and other chatter in the street and tea room and shipping office, that Jemima was one of twelve sisters, all brought to the Concord at once from distant Murmesseril as sick babes, with the ending of the falling pox. Miraculously, all had survived, they each ran apothecaries across the cities of the Whispering Coast, which were well famed as the best one might hope to visit.

Jemima always had time to make hearty conversation while she carefully took up a heavy glass bottle, and measured out the stinking hartshorn. Or when she leaned over and took my tick for Etherington's credit. I soon learned she was not only a friendly face but a fierce — and fiercely respected — young woman. When she heard my aggressors taunting me in the street outside her shop, she appeared in the door with a murderous look in her eye, shaking her fist and promising she would refuse the custom of every gang member and their kin, if they did not disperse immediately, and that she would further take the matter up with a name I did not recognise, but they clearly did, to judge from the startled glances and hissed exchanges they shared as they disappeared. From that moment on, I can only assume they regarded me as under her protection; for I was threatened by them no longer that year.

She was a stout thing, with full, reddened cheeks, and piercing glances, a person full of idle chatter, so unlike my own character that I was awfully drawn in. I was, in a word, enchanted. Enchanted with the idea of her, or of any friend. I began to pursue her, in my stilted manner. I made excuses to linger in the store, and pushed myself to ask her shy questions about the pungent and voluminous substances that were her trade, and then the city, and then, eventually, herself.

When it became clear to me that she returned my shy advances with a degree of genuine warmth, I was ecstatic. As the brisk wind of dusk forced me into the store one evening, she noted my weariness and asked me to wait while she closed up and apportioned out a particular blend of rose and camomile tea, which she informed me should almost certainly help me to sleep well. And that day I skipped all the way home.

As the season changed from piercing spring to warm summer, then from summer to a blustery autumn, we began to meet upon the rare occasion she could slip for an hour or two from her work, or she invited me to join her when she met with traders at the dockyard warehouses when a particular shipment had recently arrived to harbour.

Within her company, I felt a sense of levity and fun which had before been entirely lacking. She had a way of making me laugh no matter how miserable or heartsore I felt. Her own laugh was a booming, merry thing. She told me tales of renown from all the districts of Fivedock and showed me a baser side of life.

Finally the nights drew in with bitter relentlessness that quite shocked me; my breath misted before my eyes and my fingers were stiff with cold. My second Fivedock winter was even colder than the first, and was not rendered any more tolerable with my small experience. Now, with my small collection of bills, and from the vaulted Hangman's Bridge, she and I bought the sweetest gingerbread cake, all sticky yet fluffy and soft inside. Which was her very favourite treat, and came to be included amongst mine, too.

She took me to see the cockfights near the stinking fleshmarket, though I cannot say I cared for that sport at all, nor the enveloping atmosphere, the heat and the stink, and the claustrophobic aspect of the fighting pit. Where my heart hammered against my chest, and my palms grew sticky. And those around us shouted and bayed with such terrible ferocity it frightened me almost senseless. Here resided every variety of working man imaginable, and more besides. The types I had always been most strongly encouraged to avoid by those tiresome and insistent teachers whose liberal advice I had been cursed to abide by. One such man spoke with such vulgar intent that, when I asked Jemima the meaning of his words, she only blushed and refused to answer.

Still, I could not but agree that, despite being entirely at sixes and sevens, I knew a sense of exhilaration that followed me around the rest of that evening. So that my hand trembled slightly while I attended to my logwork, the green tea within my cup sloshing gently over the lip. My thoughts remained all aflutter, distracting me from my task and I struggled to sleep late into that night. Jemima taught me many of the parts of the city that I would not have discovered alone.

***

I hurried down the backstreet, glancing to either side of me. For I knew not yet that Jemima's efforts should last.

These last few days we had not taken any of the tincture, nor had I partaken in the laborious practice I must frequently in order to learn to capably scrawl out the scent song notation. Instead the lieutenant and I had worked on my simpler studies, and completed the more base tasks of the office; an endless array of oiling and maintenance of the various and curious contraptions that resided in the place. Followed by a brisk luncheon brought up to me by one of the low ranking clerks from below.

And yet, still my head swam and my hands periodically trembled. One thing was clear to me: my condition was not caused by the immediate effects of the tincture. This, it seemed, was a more vital malady, a fundamental weakness of the constitution. One that had dogged me all my days.

How could I become an archivist, or anything of any use, when I was so frail? It seemed an impossibility. As it stood, I should not be capable of passing the weakest test, never mind the strictest. A test meant for a child should best me.

Clearly, the position required someone quite unlike myself. Etherington was that sort of someone, possessing as she did the constitution of a bull. Well. I planned to fight it. I was nothing if not resourceful. I should come up with a solution.

As another wretched spell of dizziness clouded my vision, I reached my hand out to touch the stonework, but it was too late; my awareness swam away from me with a sickening lurch and all was darkness.

How many moments later I came awake, to peer upwards from where I'd fainted in the street, I cannot say. With a startle, I realised someone was watching over me. A man.

His entire face, all bar his eyes, was hidden behind the wrap of material. He was crouched down on his haunches, and he picked at his nails absently as he watched me. I noticed now he had a tattoo upon his hand, smudged, dark ink disappearing up his sleeve depicting letters I could not decipher, upside down as I was. He leaned over, and our eyes locked together. He was close enough that I could taste his scent: sour wine, rotting teeth, stale sweat.

I saw malice in his eyes. And power. I was so suddenly frightened that I gasped aloud. My mind urged me to stand, to get away, but I did not. Instead I surprised myself when I barked out at him,

"Act quickly, if you are to act, or back away. Or I shall end you, sir," I was suddenly sick of my tormentors, any tormentor.

For another moment he met my gaze, levelly, and a great smile curved his lips. He laughed out, loud and merry. Then he turned and strode away, with the confident lope of a prowling, feral beast, leaving me in my crumpled heap, my eyes wide and my thoughts coming in rapid, thrilling and broken bursts.

I dragged myself, finally, to my feet, brushing off my garments as best I could manage. The loud fracas of the streets, the tail end of the Festival of Dust, carried merrily on as it had all that day.

I could not tell Penelope of my fainting fits, especially not now they seemed to becoming more rather than less frequent. My weakness would see me turned away from her office, from Ridley's home, to who knew where. It was becoming abundantly clear to me that I would fail at this thing, unless by some miracle of the old gods I could overcome my own nature.

Whether I should tell her, or anyone, of the strange man was another concern.

Chapter Nine

ARCHIVAL RESPONSIBILITY

Who were the Seekers, and what mysteries do they hide?
Now there, is a very fine question. A very fine question, indeed.

Henidrick's Account of the Ancient Peoples

In the archive, I forced myself higher up the ladder, my jaw clenched tightly, as another wave of nausea washed over me. Below me, far below, was the small pool of lamplight. I dare not look down to it, but instead gazed directly ahead at the rows and rows of dark drawers, each containing a veritable trove of valuables.

I had still continued to abstain from consuming the tincture, so as to be best prepared to tackle my humiliating indisposition. Regardless, my weakness showed. I closed my eyes, and sucked in a great slow gasp. I forced myself to count under my breath, while I hung from the ladder, motionless. I tried not to consider falling or how high I was.

I grasped the artefact so tightly my knuckles were white. Etherington reckoned the object was dated to the twenty sixth century of the old Kalchetti calendar, long before the forming of the Concord. She had been pursuing it for more than a hundred years. It required the most careful of handling, and had to be stored within a dedicated casing, in a drawer near the very top of the high shelves, within the archive, behind lock and key. She had told me it would collect more on the open market than the nation spent to field some regiments.

My master made a great play to remind me of the importance, and that she was granting this trust to me.

It was the strangest thing, formed of a curious pattern of rising spirals. The material she presumed to be an extinct wood, from the oboc tree that was rumoured to once grow in the deep desert. The spirals were delicate, gossamer thin, and incredibly detailed in patterning. Each was impossibly inscribed with the tiny and elegant script of the Inchi peoples.

My hands were suddenly weak, too weak to hold the ladder any longer. My vision darkened. With a sickening lurch, my left hand slackened and slipped. As all my weight pulled on my right arm, my shoulder and then my wrist trembled violently and, before I could right myself, I was falling.

I tumbled to the tiles, my sleeve and ankle caught in the rungs of the ladder briefly before my elbow, hip and head struck the floor with a ringing crack.

The artefact was broken into a thousand pieces; I could feel them each digging into me, cutting, where they had fallen beneath my torso. What had taken a hundred years to obtain I had shattered in moments.

Chapter Ten

WAINWRIGHT'S
ENGINE OF MOTION

*It was a long time until I saw with my own eyes a game of Sentinel's
Gambit. Though I long before learnt of it from Rifleman Belfry who
attends often the admiralty below the archives. He frequently tells me it
is all the rage and that any officer of any decent rank, or any fellow of any
class, ought to be able to play the game and play it well. It is one of the only
subjects which loosens his usually well-tamed tongue.*

*The playing cards themselves are extremely valuable. For, when ren-
dered by a master inksman, they bind any who play to pay the stake pledged.
And woe betide any player who employs sleight of hand upon the green
baize, or has not the means he suggests to his fellow players. Nothing but
a painful death comes to a man who does not meet his debt or attempts to
cheat at Sentinel's Gambit.*

*Traded for great sums, incredibly rare, the substantial cards are also
supremely enchanting in appearance. Besides the inky blackness of the
frame, the monstrous Sentinel face cards, in particular, are so bound with
the special inks of the binders' ancient trade, that they shift and move in
the deployment of the game. Indeed, this element of chance is a key part*

of the appeal for players and onlookers both. Many are the gasps and exclamations when a card face first resolves from the swirling inks to view.

'Sentinel's Gambit' The Worldly Journal and Commonplace Book of
Shay BlueFaltlow
The Year Eight, Five Hundred Since the Signing of the Great
Concord of Westerbrook

I unfurled my arm as I had been instructed. The flintlock pistol was reassuringly heavy within my grip. The sun's brilliance beat down on my cheeks; ordinarily, I would have found the warmth a relief but this day it made me quite uncomfortable. I had sweated profusely, it seemed, from almost everywhere.

I sighed my irritation, to which the chief archivist replied, "You are still uncomfortable? Well. Your enemies will not wait for temperate weather to attack you, nor will they extend to you a comfort you ought not extend to yourself. So, all the better you feel discomfort. Now. Attend to your task."

The forest within which we stood was beautiful. It was a damnable shame I had managed to work myself into such a fluster. Had I not com-plained, of late, about being locked up within the confines of the archivist's offices? Around us, vast oaks and tall elms rustled in the gentle breeze, their moss-covered roots protruding from the earth like the most ancient of ribs. Water gurgled from a nearby stream and the breeze, when it came, was light and refreshing.

I wished, of course, to attend as I had been instructed. And yet it was especially hard to concentrate. For I knew, ultimately, the whole thing to be a bust. The simple truth was that I had failed, and it was simply a matter of time before this would be confirmed for all to know.

I nibbled upon my lip as I mulled the problem, drifting off to the arguments I had repeated to myself, the ones I had had a thousand times of late. The ones which held no answer, no way out, but my full disgrace.

"Prime the pan." Etherington's voice was brisk now, cutting into my daydreams. With a little toss of the head, I did as she suggested. I tipped my powder flask, careful of the slight shake of my grip, and tapped the measure of grains onto the dull patina of the priming pan as I had been taught.

"No; hold your arm straight, lock the elbow. As I've told you." I adjusted my stance as she admonished me. "There is something I must discuss with you. Something important."

I paused, waiting for her to continue, but my hesitation was met with nothing but impatience.

"Don't just stand there. Loose the charge, when you are satisfied!"

I did as I was instructed. With a fizz and a crack my arm kicked back, a now familiar stab of pain flaring deep within my shoulder. I might have complained, but I knew it would not serve me, so I held my tongue firm as firm can be. I coughed, despite myself, as a thick cloud of white powder smoke engulfed me. The pungent taste and odorous scent of rotten eggs was upon my tongue and in my nose. I plucked a handkerchief from my waistcoat pocket and dabbed at my eyes, which watered terribly, almost as much as they stung. My nostrils were afire, scalded by the foul reek and in the manner that was becoming far too routine. I imagined I would wake that night, freshly tormented by the smarting of that most tender tissue, unable to return to any form of restful slumber.

When the smoke had the decency to dissipate, I sniffed and looked to the warty old tree stump where my target — yesterday evening's wine bottle — stood. The brown glass was, disappointingly, intact. Though the very edge of the stump had been struck a glancing blow, resulting in a slight, near inconsequential splintering of bark.

I knew the pistol was wildly inaccurate at anything but the closest range, but still I frowned in displeasure. It irritated me inordinately, that I could not master what seemed so simple a challenge. One which the archivist despatched with effortless abandon. As with my other physical failings, they seemed to compound the more they were tested. This person I was supposed to be, nay, needed to be, was nothing more than an act.

This was my second such attempt that had failed this day alone. For three weeks now we had come to this spot regularly. For three weeks, I had toiled with nothing but the smallest hints of success. I was quite ready to declare that the pistol was not my weapon, nor the life of an archivist my business. My nerves, certainly, had no taste for the occupation, nor its smokes and its powders, for they were quite frayed enough to breaking from the administration of the fouler duties of the calling as it stood.

And yet, the intricacies of priming and preparation of ball and charge I believed I had, at least partially, won. I could, I feel confident to contend, prepare the charges with something approaching competency. I was adept enough at cleaning the ram rod, or wiping it down with oil. I understood the primary principle of the mechanical action, and its delivery of the requisite force. Yet in the physical act of discharge, I was quite stumped. I seemed singularly incapable of delivering a satisfactory shot. No matter how often I tried, nor how much I willed it. Indeed, it seemed that the more effort I expended, the worse the shot. And the greater the degree of my personal fluster.

But it barely seemed to concern the lieutenant, who made no comment about my lack of success, instead now intoning only, "You have always seemed eager to prove yourself, Shay. Well. You will be performing an act upon the field for our good office sooner than we had anticipated."

Again I waited for her to continue; again she did not further expand upon her meaning. Instead, she fiddled with her own priming pan, and assumed a confident pose: one arm extended perfectly, the other unfurled so her hand rested upon her hip, like the handle of a teapot. With a flash she loosed her own charge. The wine bottle shattered obediently.

She let out a full-bodied bark of laughter, which entirely startled me. When I turned to stare at her, a wolfish grin now lived upon her face.

"Oh. There's no need to scowl so, Shay, as if you've swallowed a wasp.

The skill you master in only a handful of days is the skill that is worthless. For any man may possess it."

She was full of energy this day. As sluggish and tired as I felt, she was as lively as a child at harvestfest. Her eyes shone, her cheeks were flushed pink; I recall thinking how much the outdoors and such work suited her.

"Come, try again. Patience is the virtue which will carry this day, and the next. You mustn't get frustrated so! Finish your task, and take aim, for then I must speak with you."

I very much wished to give up there and then, not least because I was keen to know what she wanted to discuss. Yet I recognised the limitations upon my choice. With as much of a childish sigh as I dared, I pushed the ball down the muzzle. With great concentration I jiggled the ramrod down the throat; she was suddenly close enough beside me that I felt the tickle of her breath as she whispered in my ear. Her voice was low and urgent.

"Aim for the gut." She pulled my arm down slowly but firmly, pausing at the height of her stomach to make her point. "Then toss your piece and close the distance, if you think tossing your weapon is likely to gift you favour. If not, wield it instead as a melee weapon. Turn it and grasp the barrel."

Here she gripped the barrel of her own pistol, demonstrating the action with a violent chopping motion. "Aim for the skull. Draw your small sword if you are lucky enough to have it about your person. Or your sabre. Either will serve you much more ably when you close to such a range."

She stepped adroitly away from me, and nodded curtly for me to continue in the manner she had shown. I grunted to her and mimicked her movement. The heavy weight of the walnut handle lolled about drunkenly in my hand, and I nearly lost my footing as I attempted an adjustment of my posture. I jealously wondered at the grace of Etherington's own action.

After many moments of shifting and fidgeting, I managed a very rough approximation of the movement, of the sort that no person could ever, truly, derive satisfaction. She smiled and nodded at me, as if I had performed for her a very fine trick.

"Enough, now," she said at last, clapping her hands together abruptly. Then, to answer my sulky frown, "You will have ample opportunity to practise this until you are heartily sick of it. This I promise you. Now," she said and I knew my curiosity was at last to be sated.

"You must attend a ball. A very fine one, indeed."

"A… ball? As in a… a ball?"

"Yes. A ball, an… evening rout. I have reason to believe that the hosts, the great house Grent, has acquired things they ought not. My agent in Quom informed me a rather large bid was placed for an artefact of interest, hidden behind another agent. But he is certain it was a mask. The bid came from this city. As it did not come from us, this is most unusual."

This caught me entirely off guard. I scarcely knew what to make of it. Yet I could not deny that a sharp pang of excitement, amidst the trepidation, blossomed within me. My palms were suddenly sweaty, and I ran my tongue along my bottom lip.

"Two pieces of evidence present themselves to me, and will lead us in this endeavour," she went on, but I was already speaking.

"Are… are you certain of this course?" I said. "I've never done such a thing. I'm not sure, with all respect, chief archivist, that it is… the wisest idea." When she did not reply, I went on hurriedly, "I have never attended such a thing. I don't think I know the steps of a single dance, nor do I have any clothing that… and least of all the bearing! Oh. I can scarcely imagine what I'd… the type of folk who must go there!"

I pulled nervously at my collar, acutely aware of the heat once again as I reported my concerns, of which there were many. Etherington allowed me to prattle on in this manner for several moments, waiting until I was quite finished fretting before she answered me.

"It would, yes, be advantageous to have another year to prepare. Damn, it would be better to have several! But existence seldom makes its plans around us or on our preferred schedule. And fate makes a fool of those who choose to ignore her whims. We must deal with the challenges that stand before us. As they are, rather than as we wish them to be."

I craved reassurance; yet having been met instead with the rugged practicality that was Etherington's particular gift, I merely nodded my head.

"In less than two months, the ball will be held. And you will attend. As one of the first of the season, it is a much anticipated event. I would not ask this of you if I did not think you capable. In three days, I will be departing the city upon an errand that cannot wait. And so, this responsibility falls to you." With a gentle pat she slipped her pistol into its leather.

"Do you mean to say that you will not be there? I cannot possi—"

"Most all fashionable society will be in attendance: government ministers, the more exclusive social sets, officers of navy and foot. I have acquired an invitation. A suitable story regarding your situation has been arranged and spread around such circles as play the games that matter to us. Duchess Hardy, who has been instrumental in the deliverance of this goal, will accompany you as a chaperone."

I longed for the details. Yet she would not offer them to me. Not yet, at least.

"Hardy will prepare you. You will go to her this week, where all shall be revealed. We have prepared a story for you. But this, as other details, I will save for Hardy to share with you."

I took a deep drink of water from my canteen, in an effort to still my mind. "But. Please. I must understand," I was bold enough to ask. "Why?"

She took a draught of her own water, wiping her lips with the back of her hand, and the answer came quickly. "Because I need to know what they know, and why they have purchased this artefact. We must have confirmation, and we must understand what they know. You will acquire evidences, documents, to confirm what we suspect.

"Upon the surface, at least, this will be the awaited presentation of the archivist's assistant to society: a small social debut. It has already been noted that you are amongst us. Why are you here? Who are you? It *is* strange behaviour, to hide such a bright, spirited young thing away. Tongues that are apt to wag are wagging; while those who don't indulge in such gossip surely listen on. Not to mention the sea lords and other such fools we are blighted to please, continue to nag endlessly at me.

"So. If we can put an end to that, all the better. We must hope our ploy sinks two concerns at once." I listened intently as she continued, everything else forgotten. I realised I had leaned forward upon my tip toes only when I nearly lost my balance. With an embarrassed cough, I steadied myself upon my feet, striking as confident a pose as I could summon.

"The Grent's are one of the most ancient and loyal of the old great houses. In theory, they ought to be sympathetic to our cause. And yet all indicators suggest elsewise; we must know why.

"But first, to present yourself you must learn much. Or our story shall fall to tatters the moment you arrive amongst society. To this end, your duties will be quite different than those to which you are used. But I'm sure you'll rise to the occasion; you're an adaptable young woman and I have every confidence in our plan."

***

"Come along, Patch," Fenton said to me, holding his gloved hand out of the phaeton's neat boxed seat. "If we are quick, we'll get there before the crowds are too thick. And we can get a proper look at it."

The *it* in question was Wainwright's Engine of Motion, a marvel of mechanics much discussed in journal and salon and common room. It was on display at the Commissioner's Central Office while both Ra and Guisi still stood in the night sky.

This was the third week in succession the young industrialist had called upon me, sought me out, or surprised me when about my business since I had come across him on the street as I made my way to post the letter that had, rather than precipitate my escape, not only asserted my position as Etherington's assistant, but quite expedited the process.

Our initial conversations, while awkward — on my part at the least — had, over repeated meetings, blossomed into something I came to think of at times unbidden. Quite how he had come to know the exact address of my lodgings I was not certain. For I had not given it to him that day, merely pointed out the general direction. But he had, somehow, and this fact had presented me with a most embarrassing predicament.

I had told him little that was true regarding my current station. First, his calling card had been passed to me by our sardonically smirking landlady. Who had aimed a knowing wink in my direction as I hid the card about my person before I could hurry out to the archival offices, my cheeks furiously burning.

To compound the problem, I had been given to understand that such a relationship would be most frowned upon. I suspected I was more than breaking any number of social conventions regarding the behaviour of a young lady of serious station which, with tiring exactitude, Ridley lectured me I ought, since my recent advancement, now consider myself.

Needless to say, this would not reflect badly simply on me, but also on the ancient office of the archivist, the royal palace, the navy to which that office showed allegiance, the good character of my guardian and superiors, and any one else who had offered any kindness to me in my short life thus far.

This knowledge had the combined effect of troubling me deeply and leading me to relish my new, imprudent friendship. How long I could hold off Ridley's discovery of my extended dalliance I was not certain. But I was certain that my impetuous behaviour would, more than likely, hasten that outcome. If I was not so distraught about the shortcomings I possessed — which I was sure would see me expelled from my position, sooner or later — I should likely have cared a great deal more. But as it was I was rash. In short, I gave close to not a fig.

As many a developing woman of tender years, I was brattishly high-minded to entertain a self-indulgence towards my own destruction. I considered that if I were to meet my downfall, I should do so head first and at pace.

Besides which, my new acquaintance had presented me with a novel view of the world which called out to me with its simplicity. Where Jemima offered me a glimpse of the, quite frankly, unsavoury side of the city, and the opera exhibited luxury until now unimagined, Fenton showed me something else entirely.

He favoured innovation, education and exhibition. His particular focus was on the mechanical arts, a subject for which he held endless enthusiasm and insight. It intrigued me, and offered a soothing distraction. For a short while, at least, I could lie to myself that all was well. I enjoyed our time greatly and I should be damned and damned twice if I were to give it up before someone expressly compelled me to.

But perhaps I have gotten ahead of myself, for I have not delivered a description of the fellow. Fenton had arrived in Fivedock a scant handful of years hence after, amidst a wave of many similar young industrialists and merchantmen who had then flooded the city and now crusted the tenements of Brook Street, and Parker's Row, and indeed all the upper quarter thicker than iced sugar on spiced wintercake. Replete, as they were, with new wealth.

Fenton's father had an interest in the Murmesseril and Kalchetti trade companies, no less, and had commissioned several offices and ships as well as lavishly investing in a number of other endeavours. From which he had turned, if rumour were to be believed — rumour knotted into such a thick matting I presumed there must be some truth to it — a healthily burgeoning fortune.

From the first time I accepted an invitation to meet with him, Fenton had provided me a pet name all his own: Patch. A reference to the conspicuous and tiresome birth markings I had all my life wished away. Which suddenly, somehow, seemed less of a blight. He had escorted me to the three moon parade, introduced me to a number of the more obscure libraries within the city bounds, and filled my head with a veritable trove of wondrous questions I was certain were but a fraction of that which filled his own.

His clothing was of the highest quality, and even of the latest mode, yet he wore the rich fabrics with a careless, dishevelled abandon. It was all unimportant, compared to the ire of his focus. Which was, invariably, the advancement of mechanics and anything related to it, as well as the development of our curious species, and the banishment of collective ignorance by the clear light of rationality. All of which was, to him, as assured as the morning sunrise.

His enthusiasm was waspishly infectious, and what little he lacked in grace or poise he made up for greatly in earnestness. His hair was a mop of dark curls, his cheeks often ruddy, and his green eyes were open and honest, ever wide to drink in all the sights around him. Small, round spectacles sat always a little off-kilter upon the bony crag of his thin nose. They were as much a part of him as his very legs or arms.

I knew Ridley would be angry with my behaviour, likewise Etherington. Still, I could not resist the temptation to indulge myself in the Fenton's company. The exhibition of the engine had been all he had talked of for some time now and his excitement had quite won me over. Indeed, I even had to admit that, by the end of the relentless barrage of his sharp enthusiasm, I did quite genuinely wish to witness the damnable thing for myself.

"Fenton!" I smiled up at him. Before I could protest, he wrapped his slim hand around my upper arm and hauled me up onto the box seat. "But I have so much work to finish!" I told him, adding a barrage of murmured, ineffectual protests, even as he made to drive off. My foot struck something heavy and I saw there was a case between us. I leant down to move it so I might sit more comfortably, but he rushed forward and pulled it from my grasp rather roughly. He quickly tucked it beneath his feet. I could see plainly that this was not the most comfortable way for him to sit, but his cheeks flushed pink and I decided to say no more about it. We all, I thought to myself, have our secrets.

He went on as though nothing untoward had happened. "Surely you can attend to your work later. Our opportunity won't last! Come along." He smiled back at me, turning to work the bridle. "Oh, do forget all that fiddle faddle. For the time being, at least." And we were away and out into the thronging multitudes of our city fair.

***

I hurried to the post master, carrying a large packet of missives for despatch, and a lightness in my heart at the prospect of the end of another rather dreary day's work. Little different had happened, but I felt excessively tired nonetheless, such was the relentless strangeness of the work.

Night had fallen over the city, the dark smothering the streets like a heavy blanket. I was craving a hot meal and keen to drop the packet off as quickly as possible so I might scurry home to the warmth of the fire and Peck's quiet doings as I prepared and ate a meal I could scarcely wait for. I was, dare I say it, feeling faintly positive for the first time in days; I realised I was relishing the first few moments I had had all to myself in quite some time. I could almost — almost! — crush down the pervasive dread that had taken to following me everywhere. My obsession with my failures I resolved to ignore, at least for a little while, even if I could not dispel it entirely.

And I was indeed distracted from my trepidation when presently I heard — and then saw — as fine a team of greys as I'd ever known thunder down the cobbles behind me.

I turned sharply on my heel, expecting some gamester to be holding the reins on an evening turn about town, before a night spent in some club or gaming hell, only to realise it had pulled up to collect someone. And that someone was in fact the good archivist.

I began to raise my hand, intending to call out and laugh with her about this strange coincidence. But then something stopped me; and I'm not sure what, exactly. Instead of alerting her to my presence, I grasped the railing beside me and watched as she climbed into the coach and four.

I stood on my tiptoes to peer inside, a safe enough distance from them that I could just see; I sincerely hoped she might not gain awareness of my spying for, although I had not intended to quietly watch my superior from the shadows, that was undoubtedly what I was now doing.

The man inside was dressed in a naval uniform, it seemed. He had the look of an admiral, perhaps, from the illustrations I had seen, though I could not be sure. His uniform was adorned with a preponderance of gold lace upon the shoulders of his unbuttoned coat, and his bicorne, which he patted to the seat beside him, was similarly decorated.

He and Etherington talked with a strong degree of familiarity. He was a slight fellow, though even Penelope seemed to defer to him, with a quick nod. Which was most unlike her.

I was pondering all of this, when they clattered away into the night, up the street past me as I turned and knelt down to pretend to consider something upon the buckle of my shoe.

Chapter Eleven

A DISCOVERY
OF SERIOUS MERIT

I had a look at the corpse of Madilow, the boy who sells the broadsides on Durrot Row, not three nights gone. I was alerted to his body by the dock officers.

I do not think we should inform the girl, nor Peck, it would only worry them unduly. Thus far they have not noticed the accounting in the papers. Perhaps our mutual acquaintance can work to keep further mentions out of the pages?

I suggest we aim to deal with this ourselves. I do believe it is related to our enemies. Yet you must promise to be more careful with her, if you wish for me to continue in my role as her guardian. I do not like at all how things are developing.

The initial terms of our agreement have been well exceeded. Not to mention that you will recall our history on such matters.

Ridley Fassinger, Surgeon of Fivedock

Peck beckoned me to follow him and down we went into a crooked, narrow alley. Where the old ironwork of Tatterley's Coachsmith was arranged; rusty springs as wide as my arm, and wheels twice the size of me squatting in the wet muck. Here the murmur of the street still reached us, though somewhat suppressed, and was supplemented with the muffled clangs and bangs and curses of industry in the buildings surrounding us.

Peck gingerly removed two loose bricks from the crumbling wall, working them with a practised shimmying, his tongue stuck out in the most serious of concentrations. Before he placed them as reverently upon a damp oak keg as if they were the finest jewels in all the plenty.

I watched his work with the great seriousness his actions demanded, forcing myself to suppress the giggle which welled up inside of me. Despite his complete deafness, Peck retained a curiously penetrating sense for mockery, a skill matched only by his capacity for sulking. When he beckoned me over I knelt down beside him, careful to aim for a half-sodden old plank, so as not to overly stain the white linen of my petticoat.

A draft of warm sweetness slapped into me; vanilla and cloves and sharp bitterness as unexpected as it was delightful. Now a rich golden light met my eye, warm and enchanting in contrast to the encroaching dusk beyond. My hand flexed instinctively on the brickwork, old soot and grime sticking to my palm and fingers, wet enough to send a fierce little shiver rattling down my spine. Yet I did not remove my hand, but instead gripped tighter as I leant in closer, settling and arranging myself to witness the provided display to the greatest advantage.

Peck nudged me in the rib, and pointed, his finger just fitting into the hole. Within was a bustle of activity. At a large bench two prentices toiled away at some unseen task. When one of them turned to wipe his forehead on his sleeve, I spotted a lick of flame and understood that the subtle smell of roasting emanated from their station. Another prentice worked at a large, flat stone, using another, crescent-shaped stone to crush and beat something; almost as I'd witnessed Jemima do in her store.

101

Following this, we replaced the bricks with great caution, and crept back out of the alley. Peck gestured to a neat little store around the front of the establishment. He gave particular attention to a low table, covered with a vast linen sheet. I recognised the front of the place, not having connected the industry we had looked upon through the wall: it was the cocoa nut millers.

Peck led me to the treasure and we watched as another prentice ventured out from the establishment to add to the hoard. And indeed, beneath the sheet was arranged a great quantity of chocolate tablets and powders, ready for the chocolate houses of the city, the coffee houses of Exchange Way and the private commissions of wealthier patrons.

Then we lurked, late, watching. When the street was as quiet as we hoped it might become, we each plucked out a tablet, slipping them under my shift and his shirt. We ran as fast as our legs would carry us. So fast I tripped and nearly fell, my breath coming in great gasps, looking back to ensure Peck followed, confused townspeople leaping out of the way.

For the rest of the days of that autumn, we took out our precious bounty from under the squeaking floorboard beneath the ramshackle dresser no one used, whenever Ridley was away. Here we grated the tablets into the heating skillet with water or milk, when we had it, and spice, where we beat it. Then we stretched out by the fire and sipped the frothing liquid until our young hearts were content.

Chapter Twelve

COUNTRY DANCE,
COTILLION & WALTZ

The figures, affectionately dubbed the Bennet Street Lurkers, have been on the boulevard ever since their mysterious appearance three weeks gone. Each day, it seems, the crowds around them grow larger. These figures stand curiously tall, perhaps twice the size of a tall man, though in most other aspects appear almost human.

They each point in a different direction. Superstitious midshipmen, sailors, and ships boys can be seen praying to them for safe voyage, as can the sappers and the musketment from the regiments of foot and shot. Bickering street children dare one another to touch them, pushing each other amongst them. The queerest thing is that one may pass a hand through them completely, as though they were made of mere vapour.

They shimmer, ghostly and translucent as the very clearest spring water. The sensation when doing so is not dissimilar to touching bledmettle. In short, something to be avoided at all costs. Still. I could not keep myself from the tentative attempt, despite being well versed in the hearsay. Once we had fought our way to the front of the mob, at the least.

It was three whole days before I felt entirely well again.

Etherington is certain these strange figures pertain to the return of the Sentinels. Indeed, she has upon yellowing paper a collection of reports from agents and broadsides as far away as Bodsprun, and as far back as the year eighty four, four hundred since the signing. This, amongst some other small evidences, she has long assembled as proof of the growing strangeness she believes is about to befall the land.

If what she presumes is correct — and I have found scant reason yet to doubt her — we can expect many more such curiosities.

'The Bennet Street Lurkers,' The Worldly Journal and Commonplace
Book of Shay BlueFaltlow
The Year Nine, Five Hundred Since the Signing of the Great Concord of
Westerbrook

The rest of the month of trimoon's fall was spent in preparation for the ball. I was given over to Hardy's keeping for the selection of my attire and development of the necessary skills — the particulars of which, I quickly realised, could not be found in any library. She was to be my tutor in the details of decorum, deportment, and demeanour; with only a handful of weeks to prepare, this proved to be a whirlwind of a task.

I still completed many of my usual responsibilities, but time was found for me to attend the duchess' grand abode on Pound Street. She even provided for my use her chaise and four, along with a liveried footman; I quickly became accustomed to being delivered across the city within its luxurious surround.

I asked, frequently, for the answers Etherington had promised to me. Each time Hardy, with great skill, turned me away. She assured me I should know all in the fullness of time and that I had more than enough tasks to contend with as it was. All of which was undoubtedly true. Yet it did not satiate my hunger for answers. Quite the opposite.

So I found myself standing stiffly, for several long afternoons, in an incredibly opulent dressing room. Hardy would tut over me as she held up bolts of silk or brocade, nattering, as if I were not standing before her, with her rosy-cheeked maid, or dour seamstress, or clamouring relatives. Or, sometimes, all of these rather penetrating presences at once.

Should the green crepe not set my eyes off most fantastically? Surely the tight waist and gentle drop would best suit my slight stature, and remind one of the ancient's noble bearing? Or might damask be the best material? Yes, it was clear as a summer's day! For to go against the current mode too far would surely be unfortunate?

Bountiful, soft ribbons were woven into my hair, veils lifted gently over my head. I tugged gloves of inordinate variety onto my hands and up my bare arms, and wiggled my toes into shimmering slippers. I was pinched and I was prodded, seated and forced to stand upon display. I pirouetted shyly for my small and variably appreciative audience without, it seemed, surcease.

The wise blackness of Hardy's discerning eyes appeared to take the greatest pleasure at my bewilderment, the crows feet of her perfectly powdered skin wrinkling merrily at my every wriggle of discomfort. Her voice — rich and melodic and deep — was entirely full of authority. She was, it seemed, as at peace within the general din of the address as she was in the rampant tea and subscription rooms of Upperton Row, and I could not imagine what might fluster her. Save that I did not wish ever to meet it.

Matters which were the source of the greatest consternation and shame to me, she took in her stride with nary a thought. Upon the most sweltering afternoon I had run through the street not to be late for our appointment and arrived breathless and dizzy. Soon I felt myself wavering unsteadily on slippered feet, struggling to breathe in the latest costume I modelled with the vexatious weakness that so plagued me. Hardy, endlessly practical and not the least bit anxious, gently but firmly directed me to an exquisite chaise longue before I fainted.

I awoke shortly thereafter to find one of her hands employed in fanning me absent-mindedly with a quarterly; the other held a dinner invitation she had received that morning, which she consulted carefully. My spluttered apology was met with nothing but a snort and the assurance that,

"You are not, my dear, the first and nor should I imagine you will be the last young lady to be temporarily incapacitated by her attire. Worry not, Shay; you are quite becoming when you flush."

It seemed I should never run out of garments to try on, or details to remember. We sat sipping tea on the soft sofas of her pastel drawing room and nibbled on divine, crumbly ginger cake, and spiced almonds and soft bread spread lavishly with golden butter. We inspected the pages and plates of *The Lady's Quarterly Mode* and *The Woman's Magazine* and *The Five Dock Gazette* and every other society periodical or journal I imagined could possibly be in circulation.

I recounted my lessons to her until my throat was hoarse and my mind numb with the weary repetition of it. Three of the things one should never do: snap one's fingers in a country dance; conduct oneself in a 'fast manner'; pour one's own drink. Five of the things one must never forget: to deliver one's ticket at the outset of the event; to wait to be presented by the master of ceremonies; how to address a duke, though not a baron; when it was appropriate to approach a man standing alone and when it was one's duty to stay the tongue.

And then, just when it all seemed too much, her dancing master was loaned to me. A severe, punctilious gentleman named Godfrey, with badger-like eyebrows, who inspected me down a long and crooked nose with all the imperious indifference of an absolute master of his craft. A master who was as neatly attired as any dandy I had set eyes upon, although his mode was of some older, more abiding style. One which was somehow more refined, more elegant, than all those others.

Even duchess Hardy seemed a little daunted by him, or at least quietly respectful. And I came to learn that he and his own line had been within the family for a very long time, so long that no one could quite recall the exact period, save to say that they were certain it was a great time indeed.

I was cheerfully terrified to be so inspected, and my first steps were as doddering as a newborn doe. But in time I found his manner to be reassuring, in a way, for it was a constant which was never in any doubt. I did not have to second guess it, only meet it upon its own terms. Though I never grew fond of his scoldings, nor of my spotty progress which seemed to be won in the measure of the tiniest increments. This drove me to fluster and high irritation; my feet seemed always to tangle beneath me, and the simplest step or movement was incomprehensibly more difficult than it appeared upon display.

The young, tittering cousins of the household Hardy — Meredith and Fortune — were enlisted to practise their fiddle and piano and flute while I bashfully learnt the steps of any number of dances within the echoing majesty of the ballroom. My slight hands grasped in Godfrey's long and elegant white gloves; my soft, chalked slippers sighed gently against the polished pine, and my breath came in hurried gasps.

When he pulled me close, or turned me out at the length of his arm, I felt colour flush my cheeks, the aroma of his sandalwood scent lively in my nose. We danced by watery stormlight, and by the flickering glow of beeswax candles. We stepped under the midday sun, and in near darkness. We practised the lines of country dance, the square of cotillion, and the heady indecency of the waltz.

Hardy sometimes stepped in to join us — or clapped along while she observed. Even Hendric the footman, Barnaby — Hardy's oft-drunken son — and Jasper the labrador joined the revelry upon occasion.

I struggle to say whether I should have preferred to conduct these particular lessons in privacy. Certainly, that was my first opinion. Which I do not doubt was readily apparent upon my features, as I cast sour glances at the gathered witnesses from tired, bleary eyes. But I think, with the clear vision of hindsight, that I am glad they were in attendance. For otherwise I would have missed the sense of camaraderie and mirth which developed at the most unlikely moments. Such as when we all, every one of us, broke into an exuberant dance quite of our own design; and we clapped and laughed so very gaily, Jasper prancing and barking amongst us all, until we were too breathless to continue.

By the time those most intense of months were up, I was not an accomplished dancer. No; and I should certainly blush to begin to describe myself as such. But we had agreed I should at least not overly embarrass myself, nor draw undue attention to our cause. Some of the steps had come to me, and I had begun to enjoy them. I was, I should also say, inordinately exhausted. But I was also, deep down, more than a little proud. I felt pleased to be acting as an archivist, even in the secrecy of our subterfuge, and unduly keen to prove myself.

And the diversion, though initially unwelcome, had allowed me almost to forget the twin failings I had not yet revealed. The weakness of my constitution, and the terrible mess I had made within the archives.

***

While preparations for our plan occupied almost every waking moment, I had not seen Fenton for some time. This had become a problem I simply had to rectify; I had come to rely upon him to support me in all of my endeavours, and his absence drove me to distraction.

His knowledge was not limited to the subject of the mechanical arts, but was as wide ranging as you might expect of such a well-educated fellow. He had taken his foundational studies in the classical thinking, natural philosophy, logic, and political economy. I was not, nor did I think I would ever be, so brave as to ask him for advice on dancing, lest he offered to practise with me. But where others similarly accomplished might make me feel like a bumbling simpleton with their wealth of knowledge, Fenton's ready curiosity and eager mind seemed always to include me.

Eventually I entrusted to him knowledge of my true role and he swore to keep my secret. His fascination quite bettered the man, often. And on this subject more than usual. Upon one occasion, I discussed some small details of my activities with the archivist, in which he was always interested. When I confided in him that it was amongst my duties to administer and care for a number of items, such as the archivist's astrolabe, he became incredibly excited, and told me greatly wished to gain a proper look at that particular mechanism. Whereupon he could ascertain its properties within his workshop. Would I be able to take it for him so he might borrow it for just a little while? Although I knew this to be an impossibility, I told him I would try.

He made me feel braver, more committed, and full of belief for the possibilities of my life and work. In truth, he made me trust my own burgeoning capabilities. And what could be more beguiling for a child who craves to make their mark, a girl both unsure of her place in the world and thirsty for acceptance, than a dose of self-belief?

So I was keen and keen twice to see him. I hoped to share some details of my current struggles; I had begun to share with him an increasingly dangerous amount of information, but felt the benefit I gained from his worldly knowledge was worth any risk I might be taking.

So sharp was my desire for his company that I arranged, upon the first evening in many Hardy had an engagement she could not miss, to invite Fenton to share an evening at an exhibition he had long talked of. The running of a locomotive upon a track of five hundred yards. The vouchers cost me most of my meagre savings but I gave the money gladly, sure he would be unable to resist the outing.

As I had feared, Ridley and Etherington had begun to suspect the growing closeness of my relationship with Fenton and felt it necessary to intervene. Indeed, Ridley had reported to Etherington that I had, on occasion, not attended to my tasks, and instead had taken Peck out, against his express direction. The reporting of my relationship with Fenton, I was convinced, was delivered purely from malice for my actions with Peck. Whether this was true or not, my feelings on the matter certainly matched my mood.

Ridley had begun to bore me with his constant monitoring of my whereabouts — as had his continued scepticism regarding Peck and his other tiresome ways, and I was growing livid with him.

I lied to him, telling him I planned to attend Hardy's upon the evening of the exhibition. And he had discovered me, most probably by directly asking her. He had brusquely shredded my most difficulty-won vouchers and tossed them into the smouldering hearth, before plucking up the poker and wickedly stabbing at the coals until the card was most certainly consumed.

The tears that formed at the corner of my eye I am proud to say that I stayed from becoming a torrent. The quiver within upon my bottom lip and within my voice I forced myself to mask. To make matters worse, Ridley had the audacity to instruct me to sit down, whereupon he proceeded to pace the room while delivering a lecture on the subject of his most frequent obsession; the vital importance of self-discipline, patience and respect.

To enforce this lesson within my young mind, he bade me spend the evening in study. Brushing aside the clutter upon the table, he took out my previous notes upon the subject of Sentinel anatomy; these I was made to retranscribe until I had memorised them completely. For an interminable time both that evening, and the next.

I became certain that his sole purpose was to humiliate me. As I could not leave to even inform Fenton of my absence, I became increasingly flustered. I filled pages and pages with the foolish notes as I seethed, quill clutched so tightly between my fingers it dug white tracts in my tender skin, marks that remained for many hours. Even the drumming sound of the rain upon the windowpanes, or the crackle of the coals within the heart, which so often soothed me, failed to dissipate my hot anger.

When Peck approached around supper time, bucket and brush in hand, he had wit enough to sense the atmosphere of the room and about-face to some more accommodating place. I missed his presence and, upon reflection, felt his company might have helped to disarm my mood. But I did and do not blame him for retreating.

I recited the insult over and over in my mind, becoming more and more agitated with every round. Oh, I came so close to challenging the dull man! But I had gained enough experience to know that when he sat in that particular way — his back erect, in his old wingback chair, tapping his pipe upon the desk as he attended to his paperwork — that it was only with the greatest rashness that one should seek to interrupt him. If I ever again wished to be permitted to attend such an evening as that which we had planned this night, I knew I must remain docile. For now at least.

Still, I had summoned the gumption to refuse the supper of coarse bread and mutton stew he brandished at me hours later, no matter how my stomach clenched at the smell of it. Instead I sat stiffly and continued to scratch away at my task, my lips pursed, until I heard his grunt and felt his presence leave from over my shoulder.

He placed my bowl on the stones of the hearth with a very gentle clink, as though he were trying not to disturb me. Which somehow stirred in me a greater aggravation than if he'd slammed it.

***

Soon, I had almost forgotten this slight. The ball was upon us, and at last the details of our plan and purpose were to be laid out to me. Hardy had summoned me to the subscription room at Ballad's, by the loveliest engraved calling card sent that morning to the offices.

So pretty was the card, I had put it into my box with all the others I kept; a little collection of effects I might have to remember this strange time, were my new life suddenly snatched from me. Which I was increasingly sure should happen at any moment. I had even hurried home to stash it at the end of the day's work, daring to steal the time to ensure the success of my little habit before I met with her — and only arrived in time that evening at the greatest stretch.

She described the exact details of my duties as she leaned over the table and patted my hand. I nervously listened. I was still unused to attending such places and it was an effort to focus all my attention on the Duchess, resplendent as she was in a pink taffeta dress which looked, somehow, perfectly suitable for the occasion. Hardy's residence was one matter; this was something else entirely.

Across from us, two young fellows were deep in discussion on whether Hazard or Sentinel's Gambit was the superior diversion, a debate which had developed a heated edge. To the rear, old parliamentarians snoozed in deep armchairs by the well-stoked hearth, long tired of any sort of debate beyond where to take dinner.

She smiled at the serving fellow. "Yes, another pot of tea, if you please." Then she continued to address me.

"So. You are a distant niece of mine, from Quom. The Concordian place and custom, in all its sophistication, is new to you. No lie there!" She let out a small, incredibly genuine burst of laughter. I was proud that I did not show how much it scalded me, instead taking a large draught of the truly delightful tea the place served. I permitted myself to squeeze my eyes shut as a little quiver of pleasure ran the length of me at the taste; I was glad she had ordered more.

"You are recently orphaned, from moderately high-born parents. They were... strange. Too long out of society. Your father caught the red pox, in the year eighty three, with the result that is common amongst those who took that affliction; his mind soured in constitution and proclivity. Alongside this, they mixed too long with the wild people of that vulgar place. So. They did not raise you in the appropriate ways."

I conjured these parents in my mind, sympathised with their plight. I was beginning to wonder which of them I looked most similar to when Hardy rapped her knuckles upon the table to retrieve my attention. For all her rebukes

112

of my manners and bearing, she had a habit of behaving in a way one could almost describe as erratic, at times. A manner of being, I was quickly realising, only those of the best breeding could pass off with any merit.

"My dear? Do you think you could carry such a story?" she asked impatiently. As though I had a choice in the matter. Her eyes were keen and bright as they appraised me. She had leaned forward, over her tea cup.

I thought about it for a moment. "I– well, yes. I suppose I might." I said. I was surprised but also a little intrigued. "At least I hope I can."

"Good. For you must practise the details until they are as familiar to you as your fingers. So, remember: orphaned; parents estranged from good society; father mad with the pox; any little… peculiarities you might possess can be explained by good breeding corrupted by living… well, like the savages who masquerade as society in Quom."

Now she fished around in her reticule, and placed her hand flat upon the table cloth before she slid it across to me. With a wink, she raised her hand, and nodded to me. "You will permit me not to share with you where this came from. Do not misplace it."

I took the small object and laid my hand on my knee, beneath the table, before I looked upon it: it was a key.

"The fact that matters to us is that I am assured it will work." She sipped her tea and placed her cup back into her saucer with a clink. "The room is to be found upon the second floor; it is to the left of a painting of the family's forefathers, at the battle of Crow's Breach. I have a plan and shall show it to you later. This you will also memorise. It is the second youngest Grent you will be focusing upon, Anton."

I nodded; though understanding the plan in detail was not as comforting to me as I'd been certain it might be.

"We suspect our targets to be engaged in tasks of far wider concern than they admit. It will be your job to find out exactly what. At the height of the ball, you will slip inside. Once there, you must find and take the items that the archivist has specified."

The reality of the situation suddenly occurred to me; not only would I have to sip wine and dance the cotillion and use the correct eating implements at dinner as though this was all well known to me, but I had to sneak into the private chamber of a man of high standing and *steal* something from him. Hardy did not notice my panic.

"I will remain in the ballroom, to ensure our mark does not leave while you are away. And now," she said, as she leaned forward and gave my shoulder a little squeeze. "I must go. Member Arksthrotle is pressuring for the hardening of slave owner rights in the Murmesseril colonies. He'd see the poor things brutalised and dead and simply purchase more, for all he cares. I am certain they suppressed the scandal of two months gone. Though I cannot prove it to the other members. The damned man is more than a nuisance. We are close to losing the vote. I must shore up support as best I can."

Chapter Thirteen

AN INFAMOUS ROUT

There is, surely, no finer rout in all of the Whispering Coast, and even the realms beyond, than the Grent's first ball of the social season. You may travel to the Yellow Palaces of Kalchetti, or the Subterranean Gardens of Bodsprun, and while each no doubt has its own charm, there is something uniquely invigorating about the Concord's endless society occasions that is almost impossibly delicious. I suggest to you that it is sweeter than the sweetest dessert, and just as decadent.

The Fivedock Gazette Mirror of Fashion

How to describe that night to you? How to recount the sights and sounds and tastes which assailed me? I had thought myself prepared for the splendour which was to be on display, but in this regard I had very much been a fool. For it was an event of such grace, of such gravity, of such wealth and indulgence but also such unbridled gaiety that I scarcely knew how to comport myself from the moment I took the soft white cotton of the footman's hand to alight from the duchess' carriage — most opulently bedecked for the occasion.

Were I simply attending my first such occasion, it would have been too much. Had I been concerned merely with the fulfilment of my secret task, I should have been overwhelmed. If my pure goal was to put into practice the varied and exacting skills so required to present myself satisfactorily, it should have consumed me. But, in combination, each of these experiences took on an intractable weight for which I was not prepared, suddenly striking me. And that nearly clear bowled me over.

We proceeded beneath the deep, ochre-burning glow of a thousand beeswax candles suspended above us, of a thousand more arranged around the room and guttering gently from the most tastefully arranged mirrors. And yet, and yet! The light stole almost as much as it offered. The soft shadows of its glow suggesting more than it illuminated, feeding one's imagination. And dispensing to the many and most distinguished guests a mysterious, regal quality. Indeed, improving the bearing of those whom, to my inexperienced judgement, needed no improvement.

That I found myself in a situation far above my station that night is a statement of patent truth. The announcement of our entrance by the master of ceremonies served to offer me a thrill of both fear and excitement which did not, from that point forward, let up. I felt the heat of scores of eyes upon me. Yet just as greedily I drank in the details of those around me, and I stole surreptitious glances of my own whenever I felt it was possible to do so.

For such an array of people!

When the fiddles started up with such warmth and richness that I felt the reverberations deep within my bones, they were closely followed by an exhilarating swell in my chest. When the clapping of hands and the tapping of oh so many feet subsumed the great and thronged chambers, I was quite moved. Almost beyond myself. When the sets performed the figures so prettily, my delicately slippered feet itched to show off their new knowledge. I gave not a fig for the hard calluses and tender blisters my lessons had recently rendered so cruelly into them.

And it was from that moment forward, that time flowed both slow as treacle and fast as lead shot from the muzzle. For all I understand that such a thing sounds impossible, I assure you that upon this night, it was true.

On and on we danced, and on and on people arrived and milled and promenaded in a great clatter and hum of activity that wound into the depths of the night. Duchess Hardy took her role most seriously, presenting me to a great number of people. The endless array of whom would have served to steal my breath and flush my pale cheeks with pink spots had the dancing not already done so, which it surely had. I bobbed and I curtsied and I nodded to these members of the upper ten thousand until I was dizzy and quite at a loss as to who was who.

Earlier in the day I had worried that tiredness might dog me into the night. I had fretted about it from the restless night to the excessive preparations which had filled the whole afternoon. On that account I need not have worried. For to think that I should be anything but wide awake now seemed most foolish, nay, the silliest trifle imaginable.

On and on they went. The smart brigadier general from the regiments of foot, in the crisp uniform that clung to his rotund belly, whose hawk-like eyebrows quivered when he kissed my fingers so politely, and moved with a clipped motion like the regiments he commanded. The eccentric lordling with the wan fingers, who tilted his head only the barest fraction of a degree and spoke with the faintest voice, but whose eyes smiled with such lively expression and merriment that our meeting quite exceeded all the folk I had met the last hour combined, in my estimation.

I did my best to log them all within my imperfect memory, but it was of course quite impossible to do so. The duchess kept up a steady stream of commentary in the small of my ear. With exquisite subtlety, she brandished her fan in the direction of a lady who had scandalised the city not this last season gone.

"Surely born with no shame, that one. And like to die the same." Or delicately lifting a finger from her glass to point at the three brothers mur-

muring together quietly by the great roaring fireplace, who had squandered their entire fortune. "A shocking loose screw, each and every one!"

She offered me criticism of my own countenance, too. "Your jaw is hanging open, my girl. Be a dear and close it." Or the gentle admonishment, "Take care not to stare. And certainly not at the first secretary's beau!"

One figure in particular stands out in my memory, however. She took me, by the hand and quite deliberately, to be introduced to a peculiar navy admiral, named Russell. After I nodded politely for the hundredth time that evening, they fell deep into easy conversation; I realised with a start he was the very same man I had seen Etherington join in his carriage, that night outside the postal office.

He was dressed in half, rather than a state of full dress, yet he was still remarkably put out. He was slimmer than I might have imagined and also somewhat awkward, though in a slightly endearing way, if such a thing were possible. What's more, as we talked, it became clear he was somewhat popular. For not one but two individuals of significant station approached him.

I badgered Hardy for answers, but we were busy. She waved my questions away and I stored them for later, determined to learn whatever I could about this interlocutor in our life.

***

The time quite left me. I was lost in the sweep of the music, when Hardy took hold of my sleeve, and hissed, "Now, my girl. If you are to act, now would be an opportune moment. Much longer and supper will be served, and you shall be missed!"

I nodded nervously. I had known this moment would come, yet at some level had allowed myself to forget it. Just as I was about to slip away for my most important duty, my attention was robbed by yet another woman I recognised, and her companions. Who constituted together a solid gaggle of the most well turned out folk in the entire Circular Room. In the middle of the throng was one Felicity Hapeworth-Arksthrotle, and the fellow she had been with at the opera. Now I realised, with a little gasp, that this was in fact the same person who was our target tonight, the one Hardy had quietly pointed out to me, and briefed me upon tirelessly. The host of the fair party, and most infamous member of the ton: Lord Anton Grent. They looked like an illustration from *The Lady's Monthly*, so perfect were they.

His waistcoat was the most resplendent shade of green imaginable, his starched shirt points perfectly set, cradling the snowy silk of his bountiful neckcloth. All combined to present to the greatest aspect a jaw as neatly chiselled and perfectly square as a chunk of granite. He held a pocket watch with a fine gold chain; and in his other hand, a meticulously carved cane upon which he lounged with animalistic intent. This is how I recall him, and how one suspects he always wished to be recalled.

Pale, sharp eyes lazily drank in the surroundings, beneath an imperious brow. He looked up, and his gaze met mine for just a moment. And when it did I felt colour flush my cheeks, fast and searing. I thought for a fleeting moment that he might beckon me over. My eyes betrayed me, falling to the floor. Then they betrayed me twice by darting back up. But he did not beckon me over, or anything like it.

Instead, the back of his hand rose, and he gestured towards me to his companions. Where with the growing certainty of a tumble down the stairs, his true intention became clear to me.

Hapeworth-Arksthrotle fanned her face, then let out a giggle of cruellest mirth, squeezing her eyes shut in delight at what I knew in my heart to be some slight. She was every bit as radiant as he, more so. Her teeth were dazzlingly white, her golden hair set high above her head in the most perfect arrangement.

The laughing — which I could do longer deny was at my expense — was immediately taken up by the rest of the small set. Quickly, relentlessly, I felt each attack rake across me. Indeed. If each had drawn a small sword and probed my defences with the piercing tip they could scarce have discovered their mark so completely.

Despite every effort to maintain my composure, I could not control my instinct to flinch. And I turned my face away from them in burning shame. I felt embarrassment rise up my chest and neck, hot and prickly in its sudden intensity. That beastly habit with which I was increasingly cursed.

I turned on my heel almost immediately, and pushed as politely as I could manage into the throngs. Throngs which at that moment took it upon themselves to thicken to a consistency of tar. I wished to flee. I wished to flee the whole damnable place there and then.

It was only with the most direct enforcement of my will that I managed to hold my chin up. When the crowd thinned suddenly before me and I stepped too quickly into the breach I almost fell. I blundered, stumbling into one of the servants, who adroitly stepped around me, avoiding spilling the expensive bottle he carried with a neat, practised side step. My apology caught in my throat and then I did flee.

I lurched into the hallway, and leant upon the picture window looking onto the vast garden. I stood breathing in the dust from the huge velvet curtains, watching those of the ton who had ventured outside to take air or mutter privately to one another. The dark little groups of friends and couples wavered into spectres before my eyes, then suddenly became solid once more as I blinked away the sudden rush of tears. My task could wait no longer.

Inspired by my ill mood, I stomped rather than slipped away from the revelry, certain any onlooker would regard me dissatisfied with a friend or lover, and pay me no mind. I wiped my hand across my eyes to clear already dry tears from my skin and fled up the stairs. I was almost disappointed my performance went unnoticed; I passed no one.

I found the room more quickly than I had expected, the precision of my habits serving me well. As we had expected, a quick rattle of the handle revealed that the double door was locked. I reached my hand up my sleeve, and produced the small key Hardy had entrusted to me. I inserted it into the gleaming lock and fiddled with the mechanism.

Just as I felt the barrel begin to turn beneath my fingers, I heard the sound of a bickering pair from down the corridor. I was preparing excuses in my mind for my presence. Poor ones, I quickly realised. I muttered curses under my breath. The moment they rounded the corner, just as I was certain I was to be apprehended, and had flattened myself into the doorway, the mechanism completed its rotation. The lock sprung open.

I burst in and clicked the door closed behind me in as measured a fashion as I could force upon myself. It was all I could do to stop myself from slamming the door behind me and propelling myself over the threshold and beneath the furniture like a frightened jackrabbit.

I leant the back of my skull against the heavy wood, my eyes squeezed shut, heart hammering, drawing deep breaths. I heard the couple pad past, their inebriated argument now pleasingly muffled. I waited for them to gain further distance, though I knew time was not with me. When I could no longer hear their feet or their quarrel, I whirled around upon the tips of my toes, and opened my eyes all at once.

Well. There was certainly much for me to see.

It was a bedchamber. A room of vast proportions, and significant station, decorated in bold colours, in keeping with the rest of the imperious abode. White walls accented by gold leaf, with rich fabrics of red and purple.

An intimidatingly large, posted bed was unmade, scattered with silk pillows and finely embroidered sheets bunched up in soft, plump little pools. In another corner was a great and gleaming dressing table, with a matching stool, beside a huge chest of drawers. A ruffled shirt was draped over the corner of an ornately carved chair, pulled away from the dresser as though recently used.

I stepped across the thick pile of a luxurious rug to the table, and inspected the dressing table. It was a curious mixture of order and disorder.

The ephemera of day-to-day living was mixed amongst other items which spoke to the character of my target; a well-thumbed copy of *The Concordian Colonialist* being one such item. With a sharply indrawn breath, I opened the ornately gilded drawers.

In one, nothing but the accoutrements of a particular sort of gentleman resided: an ivory and lacquer snuff box; a pungent greased packet of Hardshaw's 42 tobacco mixture, its obvious fellow; a tidy little collection of gold and brass pocket watches. In another, many sumptuous neck cloths were nestled among several pairs of snow white stockings and what, at a quick glance, appeared to be love letters, in a variety of hands, and emitting a variety of powerful fragrances. Slowly, at first, I rifled through the drawers, and then with increasing pace as I began to doubt my task.

Concern grew in me. Had we made a mistake? Had I? Was I somehow in the wrong room? None of the missives between the bidding agents Etherington had been sure should be there were apparent. Nor anything like it. I yanked on handles, and ran my hand through an endless array of soft fabrics and useless scraps. The bottom drawer would not budge; I could not tell whether it was locked or merely stuck. I picked up a boot, and thumped it into the drawer, but it only gave a hollow thud.

The reality of my failure sank into my stomach like a terrible stone. I inspected all the drawers I could open once again, from top to bottom. I ran my hand around the sides, and under the bottom lips. I looked around the room again, even lying down on the rug to look under the bedframe, but there was nothing. Contrary to the clutter on the dressing table, the wardrobe was rather neatly organised.

All the while I strained my hearing to detect anyone approaching. Such that I began to imagine things; upon more than one occasion I made myself startle. Whether from a sudden cry of elation above the general hubbub, or a door slamming, or one or another of the oh so many sounds a rout inspired in the full heat of its pomp.

Etherington would not be happy. I could not shake the thought. I would not redeem myself and she would think me unworthy of her instruction.

Well. Even if I were doomed to fail, I would still do as I had been instructed. She would wish for me to report to her what I had discovered, exactly. Even if she were still bound to cast me out.

I drew out my reticule, popped the brass clasp, and pulled out the paper I had secreted within, and a stub of pencil. I shocked myself by hugging them tight to my chest, like a child with a favourite toy. I was so nervous I was afraid I might faint. I straightened out a page with a slightly quivering hand, and scratched a quick, frantic accounting of what I had discovered. The deliverance of such a controlled, familiar act gave my mind a pleasing little pulse of surety, one that I guiltily relished. I even permitted myself the luxury of the moments required to sketch the table top, albeit very roughly.

With a deep sigh of disappointment, I folded and stored away my notes and prepared myself to return to the ball. I was crushed not to have found what I needed. Clearly, Hardy and Etherington had been mistaken. Yet it was so unlike them.

The sight of myself in the mirror displeased me; no longer did I enjoy the finery Hardy had insisted showed me to the best of my advantage. Instead I saw only my failure. The flush of excitement that had carried me so far drained out of me. The silly exuberance of a child. I shook my head at my reflection, feeling defeated, and that was when I saw it: a small silver key, hanging from a ribbon upon the mirror.

I leapt over to it, and snatched it up.

I pushed the key in the lock of the bottom-most drawer. It took a few seconds of wriggling to convince the mechanism to turn, as though it were not opened often. I held my breath when I finally pulled the handle towards me, expecting it to hold nothing.

The first thing that I saw within the drawer surprised me most strongly: a field Golspek harmoniser. I had little time to examine this but permitted myself a brief glimpse.

There were only a handful of harmonisers in existence, and I knew well the characteristics of each, for I had studied them all. They were so closely

guarded by the remaining offices across the lands that each was accounted
for to this day. Though it was rumoured that, once upon a time, others had
existed. Was this one of those? Where had they found it? I hesitated, nearly
taking it. Then I set it back down softly; I had no way to hide it.

I turned back to the drawer. I could see no ledgers or missives. Other than
the harmoniser, it was as empty as the others. I pushed my hand in, sliding
it to the very back, my elbow jamming painfully. My fingers brushed against
something thick and soft. Paper. As I finally slid the little pile out with a
grunt, the side of my hand touched something cold and glassy.

I seized the notebook, and slapped it on top of the dresser. A single
missive slipped out of it. It was the details of the auction — less than we had
expected, but something.

Then I turned my attention to the glass objects. There were two vials, both
of them small: one contained a milky substance, the other an oily brownness.
Both were labelled, and I ran my finger along the ancient symbols. I whispered the strange sounds to myself, forming my tongue around their rasping
quality, as I had seen Penelope do.

It was marked in ancient runes. The large and eerie glyphs of the forgotten
language of Golspek.

I turned back to the notebook. Within were plans of some variety. There
were many pages of them. I rifled quickly through a few leaves. On one side
of the page, quantities of substances had been written out. Studying them,
I realised they were formulations. Were they what resided in either of the
vials? Were the vials used to make the final substance? I recognised some of
the substances.

Further on, I found something quite different. Inscribed upon some of
the pages was scent song notation.

I withheld a gasp; it was worse, even, than Penelope had suspected. To
render the notation outwith the sanctity of the national archival offices was
a treasonous crime. And had been ever since wars long forgotten. A binding
agreement against this very act had been signed by and in the presence of

each of the nations of the Whispering Coast: the Treaty of Hawksbay, as my recent, extended instruction in history had taught me. Bound in ink that should curse those who broke them, to death or worse. Whoever our targets were, they were happy to gamble with the highest of stakes.

When I heard a crash, and quickening footsteps, I hastily folded the pages, and stashed them within my bodice, stuffing them down, wishing not for the first time that rigid whims of decorum would have permitted me to carry a case.

The small vial of brown oiliness, I slipped into my reticule, realising it held a substance which was listed in many of the formulations I had found. It was excessive rare, and valuable.

The other puzzled me more. Was it the result of the preparation? As I plucked it up better to see it in the light, with a barely restrained yelp, it slipped from my grasp, and shattered upon the corner of the dresser, shards and milky mess tumbling to the resplendent rug.

I took up an empty perfume bottle, from the clutter atop the dresser, and crouched down beside the mess I had made. With one hand I pinched my nostrils to stay the worst of an acrid scent which forced my eyes to stream. With the edge of my small blade, I scraped a goodly helping of the viscous stuff into it, smearing as much of it against the clear crystal as I could, as quickly as I could. I jammed it closed as soon as I was able, then thrust it, too, into my reticule, which now bulged unhappily.

I plucked up a handkerchief from the dresser, and haphazardly arranged it upon the spillage upon the rug. For all the good it should do.

I let out a loud tut and a hiss, when I accidentally brushed the delicate crepe of my evening gloves, leaving a greasy, ugly stain upon the pale surface. It seemed almost to sizzle. I took two hurried breaths, then forced myself to take another from my belly, counting to five in my mind.

Willing myself to slowness, I turned the glove's lip over, from above the elbow, then repeated the manoeuvre two, three times, hiding the stain. None of which was entirely satisfactory. On the fourth I creased it down with an

125

excess of force and a wince. The rest I covered by crossing my arms, and resting my other hand around it. I knew that neither of my efforts would pass more than a cursory examination. Yet it would have to suffice.

As I turned to leave, I realised I had never expected to win, so far. Yet I had done it! I had the auction missive. Though only one, it was something. These other items I had found were sure to be useful to us. A queer thrill passed through me, from nose to slipper tip. What had seemed, until now, almost entirely impossible was done. That which I had denied myself grew within me: I dared to think I might redeem myself.

***

I hurried down the hall and towards the main staircase, a warm glow of success blooming within my chest. Almost, I had to stay myself from skipping. The smile tugging at my lips could not be suppressed, however. I had done it. I surveyed all below me with the warm glow of possibility. The party was the most welcoming sight I could imagine.

I envisioned the archivist's delight, and I basked in the thought. Yes, she would be pleased with me. Yes. I had it within me to prove my capabilities, no matter how I may have felt earlier, or whatever anyone may say or, indeed, how they may look at me. Perhaps, when she discovered all my other failures, which she surely must, she would not cast me out. Now. This hope bloomed in my chest and I clung to it.

When a serving fellow appeared, I ducked my head to stare at the rich red carpets and strode forward, pausing only to nod my head at his muttered, "M'lady."

For a moment my mind faltered as I tried to think of some excuse for passing alone down the hallway, wondering how hard he might press me if he were to do so. Then a shriek came from the ballroom; the servant and I both stopped in our tracks, staring at one another for a heartbeat in utter bewilderment, each looking to the other for something: an explanation or merely reassurance. Then it seemed every single person was talking all at once and none listening to each other and I fled down the stairs to be met by chaos.

A melee of musketmen and palace guards surged into the Circular Room and through the double doors. Of such patent difference to the finery within that they brought to mind filthy canal water, bursting from a broken dam into a clear and perfect spring. A clamour of confusion followed them; though at first glance, the music played on, and a number of folk continued to dance. Others stopped and turned to take in the commotion. Cries of genuine revelry mixed with discordant yelps of confusion.

With a sharp intake of breath to brace myself, I pushed amongst the throng, my eyes seeking desperately for the duchess as I was buffeted around. Selfishly — foolishly — I did not wish to lose any quantity of my triumph. I wished to share it with her, quickly. Before this other commotion, whatever it might be, robbed it of its power. So it was slowly that the words broke into my mind, collected reluctantly from the half-heard conversations of those I squeezed past.

Amongst the elbows and shoulders that jabbed at me, I heard someone mutter, "The Rose Palace and the barracks have been attacked. The second lost completely." This voice was frightened and insistent.

"No. Esmerelda. Not that. I said the Rose Palace has supposedly been attacked!"

"Yes! Truly!"

"It doesn't matter that she's the worst gossip…"

"No? Of course we must lea–"

"Whatever is all this fuss?" spat one drunken gentleman, thoroughly displeased to be interrupted in his pouring from the sweet snifter of brandy he waved expressively. "I see no reason at all for us to leave. Utter poppycock! The night is yo–"

I stopped and grabbed at the arm of one of the men Hardy had introduced me to earlier in the evening.

"Please," I said. "Have you seen the duchess?"

"I have not," he answered. I pushed further into the crowd, starting to panic a little. And then I felt a hand grasp my wrist, and tug insistently.

"Hardy!" I shrieked, the sound far higher than I had intended. I leant in close to her, and hissed at her, almost spat. "I have done it!"

"Good, my girl. Good. That gives me hope. But there's no time for that, Shay. Oh. I shan't say I do not feel glad. But listen. You must leave. Now. Take the carriage; Stepton will return for me. I have things I must attend to before I follow you." She slipped a note into my palm. I immediately recognised Etherington's hand.

I pray this finds you in time. Leave immediately.

I have detected the greatest signature imaginable, from even my station here. By the gods it is deafening!

I believe Archivist Jannic was right. Of that we can now be all but certain. The very essence of the realm may be changing, as I have long predicted. And worse, much worse.
It is happening now. Far faster than I had envisaged. We must record it. The fools at the palace and the parliamentary houses have no concept of what we will face. We must know as much as we can. Discover what is happening. Take the notations, Shay.

Do not fail us. I return as quickly as I am able.

Without another word to Hardy I hurried out into the frigidity of the evening, looking up as I did so to a night sky as vast as it was clear, in which the stars burned cold and bright. I was not the only person leaving; it was as chaotic outside as it had become within. Folk ran both towards the waiting coaches and away from them in the most disordered fashion imaginable, whirling like eddies of breakwater.

I was still exulting from my success. What had happened since had scarcely sunk beneath the surface of my consideration and so I was somewhat distracted as I walked toward the waiting coach and footman. Or would have, if I could locate them. I struggled to make out the fresh, gay yellow paint of Hardy's colours in the intermittent pools of buttery light which weaved or glowed gently in the darkness.

A pale debutante and her brusque governess brushed past me, whispering together fiercely. Startled, I stumbled on the uneven gravel and into a passing link boy, inhaling a deep lungful of the acrid smoke of his torch. I waved away his sincere apologies, coughing foul blackness into the white cotton kerchief from my reticule. I squeezed my eyes shut, tears streaming down my cheeks, for they stung most fiercely.

And then, amongst it all, I heard a familiar voice. "My Lady Bluefaltlow? Here. If you please."

I squinted and saw it was indeed Stepton before me. Through some great strength of spirit, I forced a weak smile upon my face while he guided me to the carriage.

I took a further moment to gather myself as he opened the door. I waved him away when he held out a hand to assist me, begging him to hurry and he acquiesced with perfect grace, hopping onto the driver's perch with a nod. As I moved to enter, I was startled by the sound of an unfamiliar voice, low and insistent.

I turned to see a man approaching. I took a moment to appraise him; he was not dressed for the ball, that I saw immediately. His lower face was muffled with a dark material, yet I could tell that his nose had been broken, at least once; potentially several times more. He held up his hand, to stay my question. There was a tattoo upon it. It was familiar, and I could not say why. A name. Ludlow.

"Yes?" I answered, more from surprise than intent. I began to vaguely wonder if Etherington had sent him.

"Good," he bit off gruffly. And here I recall being startled at the wildness of his eyes. The sense of my gut was moving faster than that of my mind and I wondered somewhat absently why my heart rate rose as he said, "A little message, for that witch you call master, and any wot choose to follow 'er."

Then he jabbed his hand forward. I cannot say why, perhaps an ancient instinct awoke in me, but my own hand flashed upwards; in a blink, I had encircled his wrist. We wrestled like base sailors for some moments, lurching forwards, and then back on unsteady feet until, with a grunt, he slammed me against the door.

Any remaining breath driven from my lungs, he pinned me there with capable arms. Then his face was suddenly close to mine, far too close; a stench of sour wine and rotting teeth and stale sweat assailed me as I stared into bloodshot eyes not three fingers breadth from mine. I knew then with a startling certainty that it was the fellow from the backstreet. His eyes were cruel, wide and, far more frightening than either of those things, they were very much assured. There was no doubt in them at all. His greater strength was certain to prevail, easily, were we to continue our skirmish much longer and, despite myself, I uttered a whimper. Then Stepton gave a barked cry and leapt from his perch. In his hand was the stave that sat beside him, and he rapped it against a panel with a loud crack.

With an animal snarl my assailant broke free of my grip. His arm snapped out, quick as quick can be. With a dull thud and a brisk rap, he punched my shoulder against the woodwork.

I stood in silence. I wondered if he might follow up with a more deadly blow but he turned and stumbled, almost falling, carrying the motion into a crablike run, and then he was gone into the milling masses. It was only in response to the tender words of the normally so punctilious Stepton that I raised my hand to pat the dull ache of my shoulder.

With a lurching wave of nausea, I realised the rough green crepe of my gown was stained dark and sticky, the heavy material clinging to my skin. I reached around my other hand and touched it gingerly. There was a hot wetness there, a slippery warmth that was entirely disconcerting. Before I could draw to mind even a modicum of the truth of the incident, and in the deliverance of that most mortifying habit that was becoming my hallmark, the dizziness grew until it subsumed me, and it is here that my memory fails me.

Chapter Fourteen

A DISCORDANT CHORUS

I have begun fresh communication with the curious fellow from the principality, the Brigadier-General Lice. It seems he has rediscovered a strange substance much fabled amongst our order, once I believed lost to the world. A substance which can be used to lure the great Sentinels.

This may be the thing that saves our desperate position.

I am considering sharing this information with my new assistant, as I have widened her responsibilities elsewhere, for it is surely time that I lean into the resources available to us, whether she is ready or no...

In time, I hope to court the eccentric diplomat, and win what we must from him. Though it shall be anything but easy.

Chief Archivist Etherington

My memory of the end of that evening is as addled as the closing of the ball was fraught. The next thing I remember was peering around blearily and, through the haze of my confusion, sluggishly taking an inventory of my surroundings: I had been deposited, I realised, in the cluttered old lodgings that were our home.

Old woollens were bunched up beneath my behind, pleasant and familiar. The room was dimly lit, mostly by the red light of the low fire, and shadows danced upon the walls. Peering at it, I realised it was choked terribly with ash. I made a promise to myself to sweep it in the morning, mindful that the task made Peck cough so. I should also fetch a bucket of water, to keep Ridley happy.

Despite the struggling flame, a small iron pot bubbled gently above the fire. Still, a little more wood was required to take the chill from the air. I leant forward and tried to stand; everything lurched before me as though I were drunk. Then I felt a strong hand on my shoulder, pushing me firmly back down into the seat.

"But I'm fine. I can manage just fine," I said, even as I realised the words for the lie they were. They came out strangely, my voice sounding thick. I was disorientated enough not to know whose hand gripped me. Yet, of course, it was Ridley. For who had such great paws but him? A hundred other details of his countenance suddenly occurred to me — his breathing, his scent, his stature and many other things — and I relaxed into the chair. I was, truly, home.

Ridley himself took up two small logs and placed them on the fire. He set water to boiling before he tended to the wound in my shoulder as my mind whirled with the truth of real danger. Something, I now came to realise, I had never faced before coming to Fivedock. I had listened, albeit absentmindedly, to Penelope's warnings. But I had not, I offer, truly understood the stakes. They had not seemed real to me, somehow. Well. That naivety was very much at an end.

"Sit still," Ridley barked suddenly, his brow furrowed. "Don't wriggle so."

He cleaned the wound gently, with something that stung and then something that soothed, before he packed it with clean linen and wrapped it. As he wound the rough material under my arm and over my shoulder, I realised the sleeve of my dress had been hacked away so he might access the injury without undressing me.

Ridley did not meet my eyes as he worked, focusing on his task, but he continually asked me questions, his gaze sharp and his mouth an angry line. His tone was displeased, almost resentful, but I found I could not separate the sounds into words and I struggled to understand his interrogation. I was, of course, in shock; I sat mutely watching him as he scowled and tended to my wound.

I was more saddened that my gown was comprehensively ruined than I should have cared to admit. I appraised the damage with my good hand clasped around a scrap of bloodstained fabric. It would, at the very least, have been a surprise to me that I should feel such a way only a scant few months beforehand. I think Ridley became at least somewhat aware of my heartache, because he tempered his scoldings. Or perhaps he realised I was quite insensible.

He worked in the quiet, methodical way that was his nature, yet with the intensity of focus that I had seen him dispense when the cause was serious, such as when he believed the patient might pass. By the time he wrapped the final linen strips around my upper arm, his touch was as tender as if he handled a newborn.

I was excessively grateful and would no doubt have expressed this to him, were it not for my inability to render my thoughts into vocal expressions of any merit. On another level, I was certain his manner was ill, and could not fathom why. A charge coursed through every part of me; harsh judders periodically racked my torso and my arms, so that I bucked and danced. At least I had no audience to find mirth in my predicament. With gladness, I noted Peck must be abed. I did not want to frighten him with my condition.

I tried to gather my thoughts to myself, to string them together in a coherent chain. But they were ethereal, agitated things, never quite forming enough substance to put forward my emotions, or my musings, or anything at all. It was as though my mind had been blasted blank, and I was now nothing but an empty vessel. One which, sadly, retained no control over its actions.

I sat, mute and awkward, while Ridley tidied away his basin and ewer, his blade and his ream of canvas. He stoppered bottles with a little glassy pop before tidying these, and all the accoutrement of his macabre trade, into his leathers.

Once he had finished, he busied himself at the hearth. Occasionally a dull thud reached me, or the slight crackle of coals freshly awakened. Until a scent of stewed tunny and pease wafted suddenly over me. I had not thought of hunger at all. But now it gripped me with a strength that was startling. And along with it a fresh wave of dizziness fell over me. When I finally made to speak, Ridley interrupted me sharply.

"No. You needn't say anything to me." He did not look up from his task. With a screech he manoeuvred the old table with the wonky legs before my person. Then he placed down a spoon and a steaming bowl. Besides these he put a hunk of bread, a small knob of butter and a pewter mug containing the restorative brew he had given to me the first night I had arrived in the city, which I had later realised was so popular in Fivedock.

"You just eat up and drink down all I've left you. Rally your strength, for you will need it. We shall speak when you are recovered." I smiled my thanks and hoped he understood me. When he spoke again, his voice was stern once more. "Do no work, for a week at least. Do you understand me? And if anyone has a problem with that, they can take up the issue with me." He jabbed his thumb at his chest.

Without another word to me he went to tend to the struggling fire, and then to the study, and after that I cannot be sure. For, once I had eaten, my eyes became very heavy indeed, and I fell into a deep and dreamless slumber.

***

I awoke in the old chair, the burst stuffing soft beneath my elbow. My eyes were gritted shut, my left refusing to open at all until curled my finger over and burrowed it in with an irritable wiggle.

135

My arm still throbbed, and I winced the first time I moved more than the slightest amount. But the bleeding seemed to have been staunched. I worked my fingers, one by one, and they moved stiffly. Well. It should have to suffice.

Something was digging awkwardly into my hip. I reached around and, with a sigh, pulled out the message from the evening before. I read the words with a keen fear. All was not lost quite, though almost an entire night had passed already.

With a curse and several extremely awkward attempts to rise before I managed to stand, I bustled through to my bedchamber. I performed my ablutions as best as I could manage with one arm that functioned, and another that I daren't use excessively.

The shaky sickness of shock had passed, but in its wake was a deep weariness. One which infected my bones, and I suspected should taint the rest of my day. This was no early morning sluggishness, to be set aside with the bracing stimulation of a quick cup, but something much more essential.

It was a chill spring morning, though a bright one. The sun's glare was strong indeed and cast a harsh glow over the mess within my room. Normally, I should have exalted at the coming of the spring. But not this morning. The bright glare hurt my eyes, and I shielded them as I went about my business.

It was still early morning when I arrived at the admiralty. I hurried through the navy office, avoiding any and all gazes. When I noticed Rifleman Belfry, deep in conversation with a young clerk, I purposefully made sure to walk in a different direction, lest he try to engage me in discussion or worse.

Not only was I feeling pensive and in no mood to prattle, but I expected a fierce and tiring day ahead of me, judging by Etherington's hastily-written missive to me. Though I did pause long enough to notice that the office itself was working in a merry furore. It seemed news of the attack upon the city had reached them now, too.

In the coming days I would come to learn that our generals had opted to retaliate with gusto. The press gangs were despatched back to the streets, a bounty was put out for any mercenary company who should meet it, and every part of the city fell to the fevered preparation of wartime.

Determined not to allow my exhaustion to hinder me any more than strictly necessary, I quickly swallowed down a few drops of tincture from a vial, with nothing more than a little water to try and render the vile stuff palatable.

I hurried directly to the empty apparatus workroom where we performed the harmonic measurement. I took several moments to prepare the harmoniser and the hydrographometer for any secondary measurements. What I knew in my bones already to be true — what Penelope had told me of — was much in evidence.

While I awaited the sickening layers of ague to descend upon me, I held the murky glass of the jar and the stolen sample in my hand, my thumb rubbing the label absent mindedly as I mused on all that had happened the previous night. I occasionally winced when a burning pain flared within my arm and wondered vaguely if I should have checked the wound or changed the dressing before I left.

Then I sat, for several hours, with nothing but the large Golspek harmoniser and some paper before me for companionship, frantically scratching out the new truth of our world.

The strength of the signatures was so strong, so multifarious, that at first I though the contraption must be malfunctioning. I quickly realised, however, that this could not be; a broken device might fail to take a reading but there was no way for it to fabricate scent song. Despite her urgent note, I had not fully understood what Penelope was telling me. Something monumental was happening.

I pushed my head under the heavy hood when, finally, I felt ready. With my teeth clenched, I wound the cranking mechanism myself, with no assistance available to me. Though I was using the opposite arm, my wound was stretched taut and by the old gods did it pain me. The crunching of the crank was audible to me, strangely discordant, raking painfully against my tender senses. Yet I bit my lip and continued.

If I had considered the scent song strange before, I was to find it queerer than ever; impossible, as always, to put the sensation into words but also difficult for me to comprehend, despite my practise. Loud, is one insufficient term, many times louder than anything I had experienced. This was full of vigour and colour, stinking as rancid milk, sharp as vinegar. The very air pulsed with it, and it infected everything. There were several signatures, several songs, overlaying each other.

I had heard nothing like this before and was confident enough in my ability to read and render notation that I was sure Penelope had not, either. What Sentinel was this?

Wavering and unsteady on my legs, I lurched drunkenly along the empty corridor to the library, careening off the walls. Once I fell harshly upon my wounded arm. Even the yelp that left my lips seemed distant, delivered not by myself, but rather from whatever force it was that controlled my body as I drifted.

Instead, with a grunt of effort, I pushed open the heavy door; my energy almost entirely spent. I made my way to the desk and used the very last of my power not to sit at the desk but to duck my head beneath it and curl up on the faded rug. I felt simultaneously afraid to be alone and relieved that there was no other person present to witness my plight. Not even Chief Archivist Penelope Etherington's hard stare could have inspired vitality in me at that moment.

I lay there for a long while, perhaps even slept. When I began to feel merely tired rather than exhausted in my very bones, I forced myself to sit at the desk and attempted to make sense of this unprecedented scent song. I hefted the vast register of scent onto the table. Then with all the reverence I could muster, I opened it, and leafed through the heavy pages. They quivered slightly in my grip.

The signature matched none I could find; in fact, none were even remotely similar. With dusty old pages swimming in my vision, and a deep nausea worming its way through the pit of my belly, I carefully forced myself to take the notation once more. The effort took every ounce of concentration that yet resided within me, and more; I resisted the urge to hide beneath the desk only because I knew the task would grow ever more difficult with time.

To worsen the situation, the hydrographometer, which it was my duty to maintain, with a great crashing creak ceased to function, exactly at the moment I most required its capacities. For I had skimped in these duties, afraid of the strange sounds of the great beast of a contraption.

While I desperately attempted to complete my task I wished vehemently for the archivist's return. Then I cursed her for having gifted me the task at all, for having introduced me to the very notion of scent song. When I began to wish I'd never been taken from Quom I found I could think of no desirable alternative to the current situation, despite the throbbing in my mind and the acute pain in my shoulder. And so I attended once more to my work.

***

The rest of the week continued in a similarly fraught fashion. There was not one day where I was to be found without the Golspek harmoniser, whether I was perched awkwardly in the slurry of the alley behind the Kalchetti Trade Company warehouses or ducked under the bridge, or leaned over the railings of the Slips. I even considered heading to Netson Island for its favourable harmonics, but the weather was too foul for rowing. Instead, on another day I used my connection to Fassinger to gain entry and climb the many steps to the top of the Consort's Hospital for Foundlings. There and only there was it possible to separate the signatures out, and isolate the largest sufficient to take the notation.

I arrived home late each evening; while scent song notation may be made outwith the office, the sacred documents must be safely ensconced within the archives as soon as possible. The register must be kept, ready for the palace at a moment's notice, as was our noble duty. This added an hour or more to the end of each of my days.

Ridley was, perhaps understandably, truly livid at my disobedience. It says much about my appearance at the end of that long, weary day after the ball that, rather than deliver the lecture he had likely prepared for me, he simply ushered me into a chair and bade me take tea, then food, followed by a little laudanum. The relief from the pain was exquisite; I told myself I would take no more, lest I succumb entirely to convalescence. There was, I was beginning to understand, much work to be done.

My injury made every action almost impossibly difficult. One might imagine the partial loss of a single arm to be nothing but an inconvenience; certainly, in my youthful ignorance, this was how I had assumed it would be. The challenge was simply not an even division, as would seem to make sense to a mind of my mathematical countenance. But I assure, in the event, it rendered even the most base task a momentous, dreary problem of awkward juggling and angles and tumbles and curses.

I should attempt to brace my back against the flaking plaster of a wall, my legs straight as ram rods, the resonator sat upon the palm of my good hand while I slowly passed it through the air, and every other measure of configuration I thought might aid me in my most important task. Such that I found myself thinking that I would have been better served, perhaps, to have joined the troupe of mummers and acrobats who inhabited the market in the months of the single moon's full light. Suffice to say, I learnt a newfound and lifelong respect for any cripple.

But I persevered, even while it became increasingly clear to me that I was unlikely to succeed. For what other choice did I have?

The great pile of notations I had prepared by the end of that particular week was denser than whole collections of records spanning years and years.

Chapter Fifteen

TINCTURE

The Sentinels are material creatures in many ways, much like you or I. That is to say that they walk the same earth, and drink of the same water. Though in other configurations of their character, both material and spiritual, we must presume they draw from a much wider, more enchanted pool.

Beasts, then. But beasts imbued with some other property. Beasts so precious a single one might move nations.

My knowledge of the great beings comes from the accountings, reports and other representations it has been my duty to study. The pictorial markings of the early Quom tribesmen, and the illustrations of Sentinel archivists long dead.

I shall describe one here, as I have seen him rendered. His hide is thicker than the largest whale of the deepest ocean, mottled red and brown. He is scaled upon the shoulders and neck, as a flatfish. Though the density and thickness of the scaling is much thicker. Indeed, it is much more in the manner of the mane of a lion. If you have seen such a creature, putting it in mind will be more instructive as an aid to one's imagination, when attempting to picture the great brute. Though I have not myself witnessed a lion in the flesh, the illustrations of 'The Newdock Statesman' in the heady summer of the year six, five hundred, where the news of the great Jameson expedition was, it seemed, recorded absolutely everywhere, answers winfully.

As is common for a Sentinel, many pores run down the hide of all four of his limbs. Our ancient office suspects, though has never confirmed, that these most peculiar appendages are used to dispense the scent song which we use as perhaps the primary lead in their tracking.

I grow increasingly restless and, though I would scarcely admit it out-with these pages, also frightened, to find this, or indeed any, Sentinel. That I might be amongst the first to do so in over a hundred and fifty years… why, I struggle to state how that makes me feel. Save to say that if it is to happen at all, and it has to happen, I would rather steel myself and have it done and done now. Better to face the foe today you'd wish for tomorrow, or fear him twice when tomorrow comes. So goes the wise old saying of many a Fivedock fishwife. In this matter, as in many others, I am cursed to find no cause to disagree.

'A Sentinel's Earthly Appearance,' from The Worldly Journal and
Commonplace Book of Shay Bluefaltlow
Fourth of Trimoon's Fall, the Year Seven, Five Hundred Since the Signing
of the Great Concord of Westerbrook

Within the greens of the parks, pale butterflies glistened with dew as they zig zagged drunkenly between the daffodils, the late snowdrops and the early lilacs. It had become clear to me that I must show myself to be capable, were I to win back the favour and position that was, if not due to me, then at least something I now was certain I wished to attain.

My earlier rejection of it only stoked the flame of my desire to succeed and that fire burned brighter within me than ever. A display of dazzling capacity that Etherington could not ignore was the only thing which should answer. Since I had proved — to myself, at least — to be incapable and since I had not managed to perform the tasks to a satisfactory level, I should seek out assistance where it had been most obviously waiting.

The solution was as clear to me as clear can be, and I wondered at myself for not having seen it sooner. Fenton. Fenton would help me. Fenton, with his strange obsessions and his sharp eye for detail and his understanding of anything and everything that resided in the strange world of mechanics he seemed to consider home.

The sky was a brilliant blue, the air still and warm and lovely, and the sun's bronze cast beat down with all the sweet favour of deepest summer. Despite myself, it brought a smile to my face as I hurriedly prepared myself for the day. And if I had not been so preoccupied with the malfunctioning hydrographometer, not to mention what had happened at the ball — a matter which I was increasingly sure Penelope would regard as due to my own lack of diligence — I should have very much allowed the beauty and splendour of the season to quite carry me away. But my recent problems had occurred, and I could not ignore them.

The news and outbreak of hostilities, which had stirred the city up like an ants' nest, had in some regard settled with the breaking of the ominous winter. As if the rising temperature had lulled the tumultuous denizens of the teeming place into a soporific slumber, though not necessarily a restful one.

I was extremely eager to find Fenton and did what I had not dared before: I went all the way to the intimidating curve of Upperton Row to seek him out at his abode. I took up the gleaming knocker and rapped neatly upon the enormous door. With more force than I truly wished, from which I winced and peered twice around me.

I was, luckily, in control of my faculties enough to show an outward façade of normalcy when Bryne — the butler — informed me that he was most sorry, but Master Fenton was not at home. He had gone to attend the races at Stockworth. Neither was the full master in residence, but I was welcome to go through to the morning room to take tea. It would not be any type of trouble. No, he could not, unfortunately, recommend that the young man was likely to return soon. He believed, following the entertainment at the tracks, a soiree was planned, though he knew not the exact address. I waved away the rest of his enthusiastic and earnest apologies and bid him farewell. My mind more than made up.

I made my way to Silton Street and, with a frown, glanced up at the gilded clock outside the jeweller's. I did not have time for this diversion. Firstly, Ridley would be expecting me to be working within the office; secondly, word of the attack would soon likely work its way back to my master; and thirdly, if was to have any chance of improving my desperate situation I absolutely needed to repair the blasted hydrographometer, amongst more things than I dared to consider.

I was, clearly, not dressed appropriately for the races. But when had I ever let a little thing like that stop me? I could not think of a single occasion. And nor, upon this day of all days, was I likely to begin now.

When I reached Stockworth there was such a commotion I scarcely knew where to look. And I very much regretted my earlier decision to arrive in the attire I had upon my back. I drew a certain quantity of attention, attention that I neither desired nor assisted me in the task I had set myself.

The heat of the day, which should normally be so welcome to one who had lived most of their life in Quom, felt relentless, suffocating. I felt sticky and close within the stained archivist attire and wished I was the type of young woman to carry around a fan.

Furthermore, I remembered upon my arrival that I had never before attended a meet. Regardless of the most pressing time, I still managed to find a few moments to pause in the thick crowds and peer at the great thoroughbreds as they thundered by.

And then, I recognised a face in the crowd. A very beautiful face. A perfect chin turned, and perfect lips formed words to a perfect companion. It was Hapeworth-Arksthrotle who spoke; I could not be sure if I had seen her friend before. Both were utterly resplendent, in delightful bonnets, and shimmering gowns.

My staring roused Felicity's attention and she looked over her shoulder. Too late to pretend I had not noticed her, I nodded and smiled. She aimed a cruel squint my way. Then unfurled her fan and yawned behind it. She darted quickly to whisper into the ear of her companion once again, who broke into peals of giggles. I approached them regardless.

"I... excuse me? I need to speak with Fenton, have you perhaps...?" I began. She very deliberately turned her attention to me.

"Shan. Isn't it?"

I could not believe how beautiful she was. In person, and so close, even more dazzling than she had been from a distance, or in the journal. It stole the very breath. I inclined my head a little, and offered her a small curtsy. Though inside I broiled with annoyance. My own eyes having briefly narrowed until I, through some incredibly material effort, gained a measure of control of them. I forced my lips into a polite smile.

"I've heard such an awful lot about you," she went on. Her voice was not the rich, appealing sound it had been in my imagination, but a thin, girlish thing. She lisped ever so slightly, too. "You are quite the talk of the town. How interesting it must be to be in such an... *unconventional* arrangement! But, I suppose, with your sort of background, you have the... freedom to pursue that sort of amusement. I myself could never begin to do such a thing, sadly. But we are each called to the station that suits us, Mamma always says!"

She paused to tug an errant strand of golden hair behind her delicate, doll-like ear. It sucked the power of my conviction from me and I am ashamed to say I actually nodded in acknowledgement of her words. She blinked at me as her friend giggled ever so softly. When I made no reply, she spoke to me slowly, as though I were dimwitted.

"Fenton is not here, I am afraid, Shan."

"I was informed not many moments ago that he... was," I said through my tightly clenched jaw. The utterance lost all power as I spoke it. I felt very foolish.

She aimed a radiant smile my way, all brilliant white teeth. "And I do believe he was. A scant moment ago. And yet," she feigned a glance here and there for him in the crowd, "He is not here now, is he?"

"I believe I will wait for him," I said.

"Oh, I'm terribly sorry, Shan. That won't be possible today. Much as it would be so very… refreshing, to have you join us. We have things to discuss that just wouldn't be suitable for — oh but I just know you won't mind me saying this — someone of your station. I'm sure you'd find it incredibly boring, anyway."

Her friend's giggle was louder this time and she raised a gloved hand to cover her mouth. Before I could respond, Felicity continued.

"Esme," she said to her companion. "Do you recall the time that Cassandra… Oh. No, never mind. This is not so bad as that!" She turned back to me. "Why don't you come along tomorrow, perhaps? I'll be sure and tell him you were here, of course. Whenever he returns. Or maybe send him off to find you? But, Shan. Dear."

She stepped closer to me and I could smell the sweet violet of her perfume. It reminded me, absurdly, of a cake shop and I could not help but wrinkle my nose slightly, though I'm sure I myself smelled of the hard walk I'd taken.

"I so wish I wasn't the one who had to… But you're not accustomed to… Oh, Shan. Perhaps you'd be better off leaving Fenton alone. It's not really… You see, we each have our own furrow, as the gods intended. Some are for the ballroom, and some are for the… well. For the street."

Now she gave her most dazzling smile, the one I had admired from a distance outside the theatre all those months ago. But it was not for me; she gave a pretty, weak little wave to a passing admirer, a young man decked out finer than a prince.

I felt embarrassment fill me, rising up in that horrible way that was so familiar. I felt I was back in the schoolroom, or the dormitory, surrounded by the other girls and without a single friend. My cheeks burned and every part of me seemed to freeze exactly where it was. But beneath it lurked something new, something I had found in Fivedock: an incandescent rage.

A wicked little part of me considered loudly feigning ignorance, pushing her further until I drew attention to her speaking to me. But I resisted the temptation. For it was clear that nothing but my abject humiliation would serve her. Her companion now had a hand clamped over her mouth in faux shock; Felicity herself had already turned away to look back at the track, though no race was currently underway.

I forced my limbs to move, through some great force of will. I turned upon my heel, and marched into the thick crowd. I felt their eyes upon the back of my skull, fierce and true and hot, and it was only with the greatest act of concentration that I managed not to turn.

As I walked, I considered my options. It was clear to me that Hapeworth-Arksthrotle would not permit me to speak with Fenton were she in the vicinity.

I lurked until the sun was low in the sky. I gave up on the tasks I knew I must complete later that day. I wandered around the crowds, and watched the races. Until, at last, I spotted him; I darted out quick as you like, and whispered in his ear, "Fenton?"

He snapped his head around. "Shay?"

"I need your help, Fenton. I know you wanted to see the archives. I should have agreed before but... Oh, there are incredible things I need to show you! You were right. When no one else was. I don't know how you were, but you were. I'm involved in all kinds of things. Things I should have told you about."

I wanted to reach out and take his hand in mine, but I didn't. Instead I stood there feeling foolish.

He looked at me with the queerest expression on his face. He glanced away, and there was something hidden in his eyes. Almost, he seemed like he steeled himself. It was quite curiously unlike him. His usual infectious enthusiasm was gone, and I wondered where. Its absence made me cling after it, like a pathetic little child. I knew it and I knew how stupid it made

147

me appear and I didn't care. I watched his face intently, for signs that he would agree. Varying emotions flashed across his features. He looked into the distance, and screwed his eyes up in consternation.

"I don't know, Patch. Maybe it's best if we don't spend so much time together any more. I've been… I've been thinking about it."

My stomach lurched as if I'd tripped and fallen from a cliff. That, of course, was the last thing I wanted to hear. I couldn't bear to lose Fenton as well as let down Penelope, all at once. Which was now certain to happen. I couldn't bear it at all.

My thoughts ran away from me, narrating my bleak future in that wicked way they could. My breath caught within my throat and came in hurried little gasps. I squeezed my eyes shut to try and silence the many thoughts. It made me bold. Bold enough to say something I surely never would have said before.

"Is it… Are you ashamed to be seen talking to someone… not of your station?" I whispered fiercely. "You think I don't… I don't belong–"

"What? No. I — I… Listen, Shay. It's for your own good. There are things I have going on I haven't told you about. It's not only you who has your secrets. I can't explain it now. Alright? But you ought to listen to me on this."

He turned to leave and I could not bear the slight. I lurched forward suddenly and grabbed his arm, forcing him to look me directly in the eye. His surprise was evident in his expression.

"Please," I said. "Please, Fenton. I need you. Here, look!" I said, fishing the astrolabe out of my bag. I thrust it at him. "I brought it for you." I hissed, my eyes darting this way and that. "Here, I took it."

And then he lost his temper. All of a sudden. It was a thing I had never seen before. He pushed my hand aside in the most forcible action I had ever seen him display.

"I've told you, alright? Listen to me for once! You are such a stubborn ass!" His cheeks were flushed red; his eyes blazed at me. "I didn't want it to get to this point. I didn't want to have to hurt you. But you haven't listened to me.

You never listen to me! Not really, not properly."

"Fenton," I gasped, the very breath exiting my chest. "I. I'm sorry." My face crumpled as I forced the astrolabe into his hands.

"Oh damn it all to blazes," he shouted suddenly, "I don't want it. I never wanted it, don't you understand? Not from you! Don't you understand? Damn you! I don't want it and I don't... I don't want anything to do with you!" He dashed it from my hands to the perfectly manicured grass; his ring scraped the skin on the back of my hand and it stung me. "I want it all to... I wish I'd never met you!"

I turned on my heel, and ran through the crowd, not turning back to hear if he had shouted out, not turning back for anything at all. I ran and I ran all the way back to Biltern Road. I ran long past the point the light fell and my feet blistered and bled, and my legs burned with fatigue. Yet I did not slow. Nothing could have made me. I ran all the way to my inevitable defeat.

***

With no one left to turn to, I knew only the largest action would suffice. Despondent and broken as I was, I felt I had little to lose. When my master returned she would discover the destruction of the artefact, the spoiled notations, the malfunctioning hydrographometer, the missing astrolabe, and every other of my failures, and it would be too much. These, together, I would no longer be able to hide.

The next morning I hurried to the archives, and took up the plans I had discovered at the ball; I would not show these to Penelope. As I studied them, I banished from my mind the many warnings scrawled upon them, those that matched the warnings in the accounts within the archives I had read with Penelope, as I had earlier acquired the substances for our experimentations. So too Etherington's stern admonishment never to alter the tincture formulation alone. And to bring what I found directly to her. This was no time to lack conviction.

What better situation than the one fate had presented to me? I even had, I hoped, enough money in my possession: the last two dram bills Etherington had entrusted to me for any essential expenses with the stern warning that no more would be forthcoming, not for a long time. With a twist of my lips I tucked it into the leather pocket book that had been given to me with the rest of my archivist uniform.

I travelled down to the arcade which had recently opened to great fanfare on Brook Street. Here, amongst the dizzying array of stores, amidst the bandboxes and the ornaments, the cookware and the combs, I purchased almost everything I thought I might need for my coming task.

The streets around the arcade were all afluster, for a duel had been fought there, to the death, that very morning — for the honour of a lady's hand, I gathered from the chatter. I passed two young masters of prodigious upbringing and immaculate dress, playing out the events, as their governess looked on in weary bewilderment.

From what I could understand of the notes I had taken, the plan was simple. It proposed a unique formulation of ague tincture, one that should exact some excessively powerful effect. One entry suggested it had been acquired at great cost from the distant lands of Kalchetti, and the site of the ancient city of Drakratha.

What exactly this effect might be I could not be certain, for the record had been damaged in my desperate flight that night. In addition to this, it was also incomplete. I guessed by studying it that there were at least a further five, maybe six pages.

And yet they were enchanting to me nonetheless, for they seemed to offer an alluring possibility of saving our fate; it was clear from the excited notes upon the material I had that the authors believed the concoction more reliable — and far more potent — than that which we currently used. The note talked of surpassing the archivist! Of usurping her. Of great power, lost for generations. I would not just save my own situation, but improve things for Etherington and for our work. Or so I hoped.

I was pleased to find it was indeed Jemima behind the counter at the apothecary. She waved to me through the window, where she carefully weighed out a measure of ambergris for a neatly dressed and heavily perfumed dressmaker. And she grimaced to me as she set down the bottle of laudanum for the Foundling Hospital nursemaid who complained of a terribly teething charge. She agreed to meet me, an hour hence, near the haberdashers on Brook's Row and seemed pleased at the prospect of a little respite.

I walked briskly through the streets to bide my time until our meeting, nervous energy propelling me along quickly. Five minutes before we were due to meet, knowing she would not be punctual, I purchased two of the sticky ginger cakes I knew she particularly enjoyed.

She was wrapped tightly in a woollen shawl, her kerchief nestled round her neck. The skin on one hand was burnt and puckered from recent handling of her wares and her voice croaked from a just-passed malady. She looked bright and cheerful nonetheless, her easy smile soothing my worried mind.

She stood nibbling her lip, and tapping her sturdy leather shoes upon the street while she listened to my predicament. As I wittered on, she smiled at a passing purser, who tipped his hat to her in recognition.

"It does not come cheap, but I know where one may acquire it," she said, turning back to me. "I'd like to know what you need it for, though. Before I agree to help you. What business have you gotten yourself involved in, Shay?"

***

That evening I went straight to work as soon as Ridley and Peck had retired for the night. After we had shared a simple and welcome meal of coarse bread toasted over the fire with sweet Addington cheese, salted pork rind, and sharp, green apples.

I was deadly tired, and had nearly fallen asleep at the table. Yet I knew well the importance of my task. All the while we cleared the table and washed the few dishes, I thought of how I should proceed.

I changed quickly into my plainest dress and pulled on my old redingote. I gathered together the supplies and folded them together in a woollen blanket. Suitably wrapped and equipped, I crept quietly out into the night air.

When I arrived at the archival offices, I took my key from my pocket, and quietly let myself in. Every so often, I massaged my wounded arm; the brisk walk in the cold had caused my shoulder to cease slightly and, as I warmed up, the puncture wound began to smart abominably.

I measured out the foul substances. The first two attempts were wildly unsatisfactory; the mixture did not blend together into a fluid but rather separated, and clumped together like earth floating on pond water. With a mildly quivering hand, I took a measure of the stolen essence, and dropped it carefully into the mortar. Then, with a wet pop, I unstoppered the cork from the gunscwert that Jemima had sold me. It had cost almost all of the remaining blunt I possessed, despite the fact that I knew she sold it to me at a reduced price. My nose wrinkled at the overwhelming scent.

Finally, I succeeded: the substance took on the milky white hue the formulation described. It looked exactly as it had in the vial I had dropped in Anton's chamber. To ensure I had not erred, I carefully compared it with the tiny smear I retained in the perfume bottle. It seemed almost exactly alike!

At last, I measured out a few drops of the tincture onto my tongue.

Chapter Sixteen

AN ACQUAINTANCE
OF SERIOUS MERIT

It was I myself who first discovered the scent song Etherington suspected may belong to the great Sentinel Velspritt.

She studied my notation for a long time before asking me exactly where I had discovered the harmonics, and under what precise conditions. She donned the delicate kid gloves used for the most precious of our records, repinning the loose material above the missing part of her finger so it would not slow her down. Then we moved deep into the archives, finally withdrawing one of the most ancient of registers: composed by Chief Archivist Burrow, in a time before even the forming of the Great Concord.

The following morning, in the piercing glare of dawn and beneath a vast and empty sky, we choked down a few drops of ague tincture each with a sip of brackish water from our canteens. Penelope mentioning that it tasted fouler and more unusual than ever, dragging the back of her hand across her lips with a grimace, from which response I did not meet her eye. Then we mounted her charger, Bolt, and rode quickly to the height of Hangman's Hill, which had offered the clearest harmonics within the city for our recent activities. With the dull clanging of the merchantman shipbells in the distance, and the kiss of the morning's briskness upon our

*cheeks, here we confirmed what we feared, Penelope transcribing the scent
song notation with her own experienced hand.*

*It appears perhaps the greatest Sentinel of them all moves once again
upon our mortal plane, and mighty close to us at that.*

*In the hoarse words of my master that bracing morning, may we find
gods, old or new, to protect us from what is coming.*

'The Greatest Sentinel,' from The Worldly Journal and Commonplace
Book of Shay BlueFaltlow
The Year Eight, Five Hundred Since the Signing of the Great Concord of
Westerbrook

When Penelope returned, she was keen to immediately see my notations.
So too the items I had acquired that fateful night of the ball. In fact, she
knocked upon the door of Ridley's abode before dawn, waking us all with
a start.

With the lightest of apologies, she explained she had arrived in the city
during the night and, unable to find my notation in the workshop, had
sought me and my records out.

I had, of course, filed them appropriately within the archive; despite my
many and varied shortcomings, even I was not so impetuous as to err in
that regard. Ridley sent a bleary-eyed Peck back to bed and joined us on our
journey to the offices. While at first he tried to prevent me from leaving,
eventually he recognised the futility in trying to reason with both Penelope
and I together.

From the moment we entered the carriage Penelope had waiting for
us until our arrival at the office, he described the injury I had received at
the closing of the ball in great detail. My face burned with shame, sure she
would admonish me. But Penelope merely pursed her lips and listened to
his remonstration without comment; though her eyes flicked occasionally my way, I was struck by how calm she seemed. Almost, she seemed

unsurprised by the news of my attack.

***

We were subsumed in a hive of activity from the moment of her return and I allowed myself to be pulled along by the tide of our work. So much so that I also did not find the occasion to inform her of my experimentations with the powerful tincture, though I'd promised myself I would. For what reason I cannot say. I also held back the discovered formulations, only showing her the missive.

Instead, I kept quiet, and hoped that ingesting the tincture should quietly aid both of us, and improve her consideration of all matters, if and when a time came to reveal the initiative I had taken. In truth, I was devastated by Fenton's rejection and more than a little hurt at Etherington's indifference to the injury I'd sustained at the closing of the ball.

The destruction of the artefact, and the other spoiled documents, remained hidden, though came very close to being discovered on several heart-raising occasions. When Etherington asked about the measurements of the hydrographometer I assured her all was in order, and when she made movements to take fresh measurements I hurriedly assumed the task myself. Quite despite the obvious fact that I could do no such thing. I promised myself that I should tell her all. Soon. Perhaps tomorrow, or the next day, or maybe the day after that. And yet, whenever the day arrived, I watched my brusque master complete her work, serious and powerful and oh so assured. And my bravery always left me.

When I saw her, in the same study, arguing vociferously with a member of parliament, and slamming her fist on her great desk, it did little to embolden me. When I timorously asked Ridley about the developments in that place, he was almost as irritated.

"All the games of those chambers are for the greatest fools. We'd all be better off if every man of them resigned, and sought an honest profession. If they choose not to listen to as good and true an individual as Penelope Etherington? Whatever is delivered to this blasted city is deserved and more."

***

This day we were about a task that was favoured by neither I nor Penelope: a trip to the mixed Amari district to negotiate the purchase of some of the rare items of our noble profession. And as we learnt the good freeman who was to be our trade contact had been held up indefinitely, we had several hours to while away. Never one to spend time in the wicked diversion of idle leisure, Archivist Etherington had been quick to suggest we peruse the curious artificer stores of magical repute lining Ivy Row.

These long-standing establishments drew a diverse array of clients from who knew where, exactly; a rarefied combination of lordly dilettantes, and foreign merchants, and tinkering mechanists, and the soldierly professions. We, of course, were there so we might engender the acquisition of the more exacting supplies required for the deliverance of our duty, and upkeep of our ancient office.

The war situation had forced the paranoid palace — staunchly backed by the sea lords and parliamentarians, naturally — to place strict limitations upon who may do business with the Ivy Row traders. The grumbles of the artificers themselves suggested they were bold to do so. Most of the artificers were of colonial stock, and from the Plenty. Either of Marathi bloodlines, tall and foreboding with curious ash-white hair, or of the stockier, cheerful Annai lineage.

Penelope told me much trading still continued, and that the palace wouldn't truly clamp down upon it. For the artificers were too valuable, and all knew it. Of course, as officials of the archivist's office, we had the requisite paperwork anyway. Most recognised Etherington by face, yet there was a tense mood regardless, and I keenly felt the presence of the surly Murmes-seril Trade Company officers

It was a strangely cold summer's day. The faltering blue of the sky had been in retreat the last week and only viewed as a rare, welcomed sight glimpsed between billowing, ominous clouds. Now even that disappeared from view, and instead we were enveloped in a thick soup of dreary grey-ness, a fog which one's eyes could barely penetrate more than a few yards. With the miasma came a deep chill which permeated the very bones, complemented by a foul storm that had blown in that morning.

The rain drove against the store shutters in great shuddering, rattling gusts. When we scuttled from one doorway to another, the heavy cloaks that we clung tightly to ourselves danced as if alive, and did little to protect us from the assault. We held onto them most gratefully nonetheless; our shirts sodden, our boot leather glistening with wet.

We walked silently together for some moments. I felt the pressure with-in me, to speak, build up and up and up. Questions broiled inside me, and accusations. Hurt. The hurt that I was dispensable, that in her material focus on her task she cared little for my safety. I had known that she was thus, so driven it was frightening, yet I had still presumed that she cared for me at least a little. And then I could hold my hurt no longer.

"But who are they?" I asked, as we ducked out of a further flurry of rain, and into a large Etched Emporium. Once I had dared to breach the topic which had so consumed me, I was determined I would have my answer.

"Who are who, child?" she replied, without turning to look at me. Instead she strode into a large store, filled with an abundant assortment of wonders.

I swallowed down my indignation, and my fear. "You know who I mean." I spoke to her back, my voice almost a whisper.

A darting glance over her shoulder told me my arrow had made its mark. "Hmmm. You are bold today. I told you we had many enemies, did I not? We now know that we may include the Grents, amongst their numbers, not to mention–"

"I think I have done enough to deserve answers! Why would they attack *me*?" I spat out suddenly, surprised by my own venom. For I surely could gain nothing from angering her.

Penelope seemed quite taken aback herself. Rather than continuing to argue with me, she stopped stock still exactly where she stood. Then with a little laugh and shake of her head, she continued to peruse the items before her. She waved her arm towards the counter. "Please, storekeep? I would like to inspect the Gobli beads. Is this your entire collection?"

She turned and negotiated with the man.

With a sigh and a knowing glance towards me, she hurriedly placed the glowing objects on the greased cloth, and folded them into a neat bundle.

***

The following morning Ridley checked my wound and professed himself incredibly surprised at the pace of my recovery. He ran his thumb over the spot, badgering me incessantly over what I had eaten, and how I had rested. Just when I was certain he was finished, he remarked upon strange black spots upon the top of my shoulders, and down my arm. I grew tired of his mithering. I assured him it was all quite usual I wascertain. When I finally broke free from his probing, his eyes were puzzled as he considered me.

I visited again with Bamcroft, a habit I had found myself repeating once every week or so. For I discovered I very much enjoyed his company, though upon this occasion I was tired, and he preoccupied. He told me of the new press upon his capabilities, and those of the rest of the companies of the great navy yards. And indeed, while he had been showing me his latest compositions, men from the inspectorate had arrived.

He was to design a ship of entirely new rank, a 114-gun brute, the greatest ship of the line ever sailed. The excessive press of the war had been all around us. The yard, never anything but a hive of activity, had taken on an almighty reverberating hum. One which I was informed ceased at no hours of the day, a murmur broken only with the clatter and bang of a thousand hammers at work.

But it was not in those moments that we formed our friendship, bracing and interesting as they were, but in others that we began to share. He often used my visits to take a break from the busy work of the dockyard. From an old canvas sack he would pluck out a rather worn set of numbered cylinders, hewn from ivory or bone, and arrange these on a spherical, tufted mat, ringed like a tree stump. With this apparatus he taught me a game that seemed simple upon first glance, but which was, in actuality, devilishly complicated and extremely absorbing.

While we did this he produced a bottle of aged brandy, from the Plenty, and poured a small measure into our coffee cups. This became our habit. For hours we would sit, in the soft old seats arranged within his ramshackle dockyard quarters. It became something of a sanctuary to me, this place, my mind distracted by the strange game and stimulating company, as it was pleasantly warmed by the fiery drink.

I found our discussions on technical matters fascinating, just as I found his cramped offices a perfect escape from my daily duties. When I was there, it was possible to set aside the truth of my abject failures, the tangled heats of my relationships. In short, I permitted myself to concentrate only on our discussions, insulated as they were from most of my other concerns, least of all Fenton's rejection.

It did not matter that I was exhausted, nor that my mind seemed ready to burst; when I was there, things were simple. We talked of tunnage, and of square yards, of mizzens and of forecastles, or of games and other inconsequential matters, and it was pure. I could believe, for a short time, that I had no other concerns.

Bamcroft's quality of speaking was never condescending, despite the great qualifications of his station. He spoke as if I was capable of understanding all he said and, when I occasionally interrupted to confess I was ignorant of some thing or other, he gave clear, concise definitions and then continued on as before.

It was obvious he enjoyed enormously our conversations and, at first, I was shy with the attention. But time emboldened me and I came to think I could speak freely with him. Perhaps freer than with any person but Peck. I enjoyed spending time with him for no reason other than the simple pleasure of it, and his simple enthusiasm for life was a most pleasant trait to witness.

Beyond, in the yard's dry dock, cursing, burly men and women crawled all over the bare skeleton of the great naval beasts of the sea, that would set sail and into battle before the year was out.

While he was always enthusiastic in the matter of his work, the various games of this land and others, it was clear to me that the strains of his situation had rendered him terribly weary. In the few short years since I had first met him, his hair had taken on fresh grey, both in his voluminous side whiskers and upon his head, and his skin sat sallow upon his craggy features. His old eyes were reddened. Yet he did not permit himself one inch of respite. Diligence being a quality of character that came to him as easily as the breath in his lungs.

The sea lords and navy board, he told me, drove him harder than at any point since the Clove Wars. He added that they were much more concerned than public statements would have one believe.

That this sentiment, and others, matched Archivist Etherington's I left unspoken.

Chapter Seventeen

AN ARCHIVIST'S BUSINESS

The Grand Republic's assault of that summer in the year seven, vicious as it was unprovoked, came as a terrible surprise to many. Though our nations had known much war in the past, having been forever in an almost constant state of skirmish and manoeuvre, it still clashed firmly with the current relations between the power centres. Indeed, it was hard to see how any should profit.

So it was that rumour ran farther than fact, as it is ever likely to do, thick and fevered and relentless.

It was only in time that we were to discover anything like their motive. And what a discovery it would prove to be.

'War Comes,' The Worldly Journal and Commonplace Book of Shay
Bluefaltlow
The Year Eight, Five Hundred Since the Signing of the Great
Concord of Westerbrook

Lieutenant Etherington was preparing for a short visit to Burror for a hurriedly convened planning committee with the sea lords and as many of the list as could be summoned. She was always irritable when she had to deal with the officious fellows of the admiralty. She was likewise distracted with the news of the great Sentinel, distracted enough that she did not press me about my sullen mood and I moped around the office for the next two days.

On the morning Penelope departed, I slept unusually late. Lack of supervision sapped all motivation to work and I decided to walk through the draper's district, to peruse the clothing stores, for the placating quality such a visit sometimes delivered.

I chose the longer route — winding past the milliners and the cobblers as well as the stores selling fabric and garments — in an attempt to clear my head from the muddle that had plagued it. Heartsore as I was, I did nothing of the kind, but rather dwelt on the embarrassment and disappointment I had suffered at Stockworth races. Part of me wished I'd left the damn city that morning with Etherington.

And it was then, as I stood outside a dressmaker's considering the delights within and wishing myself away, that I was jolted from my reverie by a hand lightly tapping my shoulder.

Dreading that this was the moment I was to be assaulted — as Ridley had so often promised would happen if I were to walk the city alone absent of my wits about me — I was more than shocked to find, when I turned, it was not an arch rogue who stood before me. But Fenton.

"Take me to it then. Damn you," was all he said as I gawped at him like a featherhead. I forced down the strongest of urges to throw my arms around him and whoop for joy, merely nodding as I beckoned for him to follow me. My heart felt so light I fancied my feet might leave the ground at any moment as we made our way through the busy streets together. I did not ask him why he'd changed his mind nor how he had found me; I simply did not care.

Finally, I showed it all to him, just as I had promised. With a gentle sigh I reverently unlocked the heavy archive door, and we crossed the threshold together.

He surveyed the archives with wide eyes, his arms raised up as he turned around on the spot with a somewhat foolish smile across his face. His hair was tousled, the capes of his greatcoat spread wide in a fashion I could have found most humorous, were it not for the gravity of our situation.

"Oh, geeze, Patch. This is something and a half, ain't it?" His enthusiasm was infectious, and I nearly laughed aloud at his joy. "But won't she be coming back soon?"

He had stopped spinning, and had opened his eyes. Now he bent clean at the waist, his quizzing glass appearing miraculously within his clever fingers, and he used it to peer at the drawer labels before him. The tail of his expensive Murmesseril twill shirt had come untucked unevenly, one side flaring out untidily, the other not to be seen. The gay, gold-threaded buttons and emerald damask of his waistcoat sat likewise rakishly. So that I had to resist the urge to step forward and pull it tight as if he were a wayward schoolboy.

The resplendent nature of the garments suggested that Jenny, his long suffering housekeeper, had been attempting to uprate the young master's outward appearance once again. With, I guessed, nothing but the mixed satisfaction I feared she was ever likely to face.

"No," I replied, my voice instinctively low. As if someone, perhaps Penelope herself, might hear us. I forced myself to speak louder, but it came out awkwardly, my voice wavering at the end of the utterance. "At least I don't think so. She's to return from Burror tomorrow, at the earliest. Most likely later. It's not a short ride. I'm here alone."

He didn't seem to notice the weakness in my voice, thankfully. Indeed, he noticed me very little at all. It almost made me quite cross, and any other day I might have upbraided him. But I was too overcome with relief.

"What about those navy chaps downstairs?" he said.

I waved away his concern — over-vigorously truthfully, to conceal my own. For in reality I was a little worried about them. I was certain I had it in hand though. Belfry, I liked to think, was a friend of a kind, and most of the rest were too busy with their own work or knew better than to interfere in archivist business. Besides which, it was a busy office, always full of clamour and din, with so many ships and men to maintain. And since the surprise military action, and the coming naval campaign, it was a wonder they considered anyone's business besides their own. I massaged one sweaty palm with the other, realised what I was doing, and dropped both to my sides.

"Don't worry about them," I said. "Just make sure you leave the way I told you. If you don't mind?" he looked up long enough from the pre-Great Concord registers to frown at me with irritation he couldn't mask and I was suddenly reminded of his words at the racecourse. I glanced down at the hand his ring had cut before we'd last parted, but the mark was almost invisible already.

I could tell that his mind wasn't with me from the vacant look behind his eyes. So I snapped my fingers before his face and he was there, again, suddenly. "I said don't worry about them. But make sure you leave the back way, like we discussed. Alright?"

To which I won a quick nod. Then he clapped his hands together, and rubbed them. "Very well." he said to me. "Show it to me, and we will see what we can muster." At that moment a wave of the queerest feeling washed through me and I flinched, for I felt I was entirely in another place. Then I had returned. "What was that?" he asked, his eyes shot up, surprised, though in a lazy, empty way.

"Nothing," I said, shaking my head. "Well. Are you going to help me, or not?"

"So…" he answered, wandering over to the contraption. "A hydrographo-meter? Ah, yes. Yes, I think I understand the reckoning of it."

Fenton ran his hand across the curve of the wood, and the three glass flutes that rose from the central arms so high, so queerly, like bulbous onion heads. With a frown he fiddled with the mechanisms, then popped out a brass stopper. He crouched down and inspected the gear teeth closely.

"One of the best I've ever seen," he confided in me, everything else forgotten in the heat of his consideration. "Wonder where the devil it came from?" He seemed to think better than continuing, but then struggled to contain himself. Reticence was most unlike him.

"You can't get anything like this from smiths at Buckerton. Oh, They try hard enough, I'm sure! But the only blighters who make anything of this sort of quality are in Kalchetti. And they don't let them leave their sight! Not that I blame them."

Fenton stuck his tongue out in concentration as he gradually turned a crank, before it came to an abrupt halt, his arm stretched as far as it would go, his head barely still visible from the guts of the blasted contraption. "I wouldn't either. Do you have another bottle of that oil?" He nodded almost imperceptibly, only his eyebrows visible above the mechanical beast. "I say. Be a good fellow and pass it over, would you?"

I did as I had been instructed, wiping a cool slickness from my hands on a rag afterwards, for it had leaked somewhat. I continued to watch nervously, as Fenton disappeared down lower. A dull clang, a shrill squeaking, and then a curse emanated from within, and all of a sudden the main shaft turned, as I'd never believed it would again.

I thanked him half a hundred times, but he was distracted, admiring the contraption. I offered to make us tea, perhaps the licorice root he so favoured, or fetch some brandy, but he shrugged on his greatcoat without acknowledging my offerings.

"Shay," he said. And there was something in his eyes once more, that thing I didn't like the look of. He licked his top lip. His gaze met mine, but then skittered away. It was the strangest thing. As if he didn't know me. As if he had suddenly retreated. The boy who almost always acted without self-consciousness or hesitation suddenly seemed... bashful? No, it was something else. Something more like shame.

His eyes roved over the archives a final time as he gave his head a little shake. There was something ailing him, for a certainty; he had never acted this way with me before. I wanted to put it to him, to gain the measure of his distemper. But I understood well that I could not risk upsetting him any further. This was more important than our friendship, more important than anything. I needed to start putting archivist business before myself. If one thing had become clear to me, it was that. I would save my questions for another day.

"Yes. What is it?" I said. I took his hand in mine. But he said nothing more and would not meet my eye. As if the sudden closeness, the vulnerability, made him uncomfortable.

"You must promise me," I said, "that you will tell no one of this, that you have been here. Or I will be in the most terrible trouble."

He shook his head vigorously, as if to dislodge something from it. But still he said nothing.

***

To say I was as pleased as punch to have so neatly repaired the contraption would be an understatement. I felt only a small tinge of guilt at having used Fenton to help me. To salve myself I contended that it was an excellent display of initiative. Why, it was both Penelope and Ridley – and, in honesty, any person of responsibility who had been in control of me since my youth – who had endlessly told me to use the tools available to me. To attain a bit of backbone. One could not very well say that I had not done that.

I impatiently awaited Etherington's return, gloating over my new achievement. With the hydrographometer repaired, the missive acquired, and the formulation of the tonic, perhaps I had begun, now, to offset the columns that went against me in the tally. And oh. It felt wonderful. I was so elated I could scarcely bring myself to leave and go home. When I did, eventually – worried Peck would await me when he should seek his own bed – it was very late and with the silent promise to myself that I'd return early the next morning.

166

Peck had indeed attempted to do so. Though he had failed, and fallen into a deep sleep, burrowed into the hole in the stuffing of the chair by the heat of the hearth. His breathy snores barely broke when I wrapped a woollen blanket around his small frame and carried him through to his pallet. He felt as light and warm and alive as a starling as I covered him well and, not for the first time, felt enormous gladness to have him.

I gnawed on an old husk of knotty bread and sipped some cold tea left over in the pot without bothering to sit down or light a single candle. Then I myself slept soundly and awoke before dawn feeling perfectly rested for the first time in many, many days.

***

I rushed to the office the following morning before Peck or Ridley were awake, barely pausing to wash my face. There were no carts available that early, so I ran through the backstreets, exhilarated by the cool morning air.

I turned the door handle to witness the worst devastation I could conceive. As I looked on, the most horrendous lurch descended upon my stomach. Fenton. No. No. That surely couldn't be right. And yet. How else could this have ever happened?

It had been ransacked. Ransacked with a wild, vindictive abandon. Shards of broken glass littered the ancient tiles, browns and greens and blues glinting dully in the soft yellow light of the lamp which I quickly set down. The drawers had been dragged out. I ran into the mess, with no care if I tripped or cut myself. And then I stood there, still as a statue.

The apparatus of our unique and curious profession had been smashed with a brutality that stunned me to silence. The many and varied Sentinel samples: those for which we had paid such tidy sums; the one I had myself stolen; the many, many others that had been stored here for aeons, stretching back beyond all possible imagining. Each and every one, impossibly precious, perhaps beyond all human value. All were incredibly conspicuous by their complete and stupefying absence. They were gone, completely gone.

I ran down to the, my breath hitching in my throat, the hollow *huh huh huh* catching strangely in my attention. My only companion on that terrible journey through the perfectly proportioned corridors of the archivist's offices to what I knew I must surely discover.

The larger apparatus of our profession, the Golspek harmoniser, lay mangled in the corner; the leather hood had been torn off and flung across the chamber. The crank sat, splintered, surrounded by glass and spilled ink.

One of the vast registers had had its pages pulled out and shredded. It was worth an incredible amount, even to our enemies. Especially to them. To see it destroyed in such a manner shook me to the absolute centre of my very core. It spoke to the lengths they would go. It sent a terrifying message.

Sickened, I went to it, picking up the torn remnants of a scent song rendition many thousands of years old, perhaps more. I pushed the shredded scraps together, limply, as if that might somehow undo the terrible ruination all around me. What a fool I had been. What an incorrigible fool.

"No. No. No," I whispered to myself. And yet, despite it all, my imagination seemed almost incapable of accepting what had happened. It stalled at the very concept; it told me it could not be. It told me it was not. But whenever I brought my head up to consider the evidence afresh with a startling jolt the truth of the situation jarred against me again and again, finding new ways to wound me.

I felt entirely violated. And if I felt such, it required little thought to form an understanding of Etherington's likely mood at the discovery. It took every ounce of my conviction to sit in the study, and not to simply flee to anywhere but there. It took me hours to begin to tidy anything; the destruction was so complete that I could do little more than hold broken objects in my hand for a moment before returning them to where I'd found them. Once I had done my best to restore some form of cursed order to the chambers, I wrapped my arms around myself, and I rocked backwards and forwards. Occasionally, I sobbed quietly — or compulsively ran my hands through my hair.

I had not eaten at all that long day, and my stomach growled and cramped at me. I ignored it. The sun had just risen as I left home that morning and it had long set by the time I returned to our lodgings. I feigned moon sickness, signing to Peck that I wished to be alone, and went immediately to bed.

All of it was ruined. Near nothing had been spared.

***

I awoke early the next morning to Ridley shaking me. "Wake up, Shay," he said. "You must wake up."

My last memory had been of the evening before, as I lay in my bed-chamber with my eyes closed. The window had been open, and I had listened to the burp and splash of the rain as it trickled from the roof-top gutters.

I stared up at him, bleary-eyed. My mind was blank, but in my soul I knew. The most terrible sinking sensation struck my stomach as I looked at him.

"Dress yourself quickly, and come."

I did as I had been instructed in silence. A silence which continued as we made our way to the office together. Though I was not in such a hurry to follow him. I dragged my breeches and shirt on, and pulled up my half boots, with little enthusiasm. The dependable, regular beats of the activity of preparing myself did nothing to soothe me as it frequently did. Instead I felt empty as I tidily drew and crossed the laces, as I tightened and tucked my halfboots. Almost as if it were not I who performed the action, but rather some apparition which had assumed my worldly form.

As we rocked along in a hired chaise, I watched Ridley ever so carefully from the corner of my eye. He did not elaborate on our hasty trip to the offices, and I did not ask. I watched him for any clue that he might speak out about my actions. Yet none was forthcoming. He seemed nearly as flustered as I.

He peered from the window while he fiddled with the buttons upon the sleeve of his old tailcoat. Or he coughed into his kerchief, and massaged his brow. We clattered and bounced along the cobbled street. I could not bring myself to eat but held in my hands an apple Peck had pressed upon me as I had passed him upon leaving.

Outside the lamps glowed dully in the burgeoning light of the day before us; soon the link boys would repeat their round of the previous evening, to extinguish them. In the thick atmosphere of predawn we rushed to Etherington. The huge courtyard of the Navy Offices was as great a melee of carriages, horsemen, and navy folk as I had ever seen. It was clear that some important action was afoot, though what it could be I could not be sure. Surely they could not be there because of what I had done? But no, I told myself; they would not be gathered outside, were it so. Regardless, it further enhanced the sense of foreboding which had taken up a growing residence within me.

With a creak the door was opened, and we stepped out. I rested my palm against the flaking paint of the panel, and took in more seriously our surroundings. Woodsmoke was in the air, air which sat deathly still, a stark contrast to the action around us, and the turmoil of my sentiment.

With a grunt Ridley paid the jarvey. I stood with my hands crossed, listening to the discussion from the carriage closest to us. A young midshipman spoke to his fellow, a naval clerk, in a hurried fashion, his voice high, cheeks ruddy with cold. He was every bit the eager youth, this one.

"Immediately," he said. "For the straits of Erlang. About time we set a hand to them, by jove."

"Sailing under whom?" his companion said, leaning in.

"Russell!" came the reply.

"We knew it must come to this, or like it," Ridley said to me, crouching down to straighten my lapels with a firm tug; I realised he too had overheard.

Two captains from the Regimental Foot clattered past us on huge steaming bays, in a great hurry, backs as straight as ram rods, heads held as high as bloodhounds upon the scent. The wind of their passage swept into us, tugging at our clothing.

"Come along." Ridley pushed his hand into the small of my back.

In the distance, a firecracker popped and a flash lit up the predawn sky.

***

Penelope met us at the foot of the stairs leading up to the archival offices. "Thank you for coming."

"You are back, then?" Ridley asked, giving her a quick nod of greeting. "Sooner than I expected."

"Aye, but not for long. I've been ordered to the front." For a horrible moment, I thought the Lieutenant was yet to visit the archives, was unaware of the terrible truth. Yet I saw her eyes were swollen from more than tiredness, that tiny broken blood vessels adorned the skin high on her cheeks. Almost, it appeared that she had been crying. Or perhaps shouting.

"You'll go?" he said. Ridley seemed not to notice the signs of anguish in his old companion, but he himself was close to collapse from exhaustion.

"Of course. No choice left to me," she said, turning to watch over the great hubbub of the courtyard.

"On whose orders? To what end?"

"Come, both of you." she said. "I will tell all in good time. But first there is something you must see. We must take care of… a damn terrible business. Our time is short."

Chief Archivist Etherington led the way, first through the admiralty offices, her weariness evident in the heaviness of her footsteps upon the stairs. Though she was tall and strong she was usually light of foot.

Before she opened the door she turned to Ridley and I and addressed us. But I knew her words were for me.

171

"I have something to show you. But first. Could you think of any reason…? No, of course you cannot know. Come inside."

She passed into the workshop and I found I was rooted to the spot. Ridley pushed past me; the tiny exhalation he gave upon seeing the room was worse than hearing him rant and rave. As a surgeon of many years, his constitution was incredibly sound, and very little drew shock from him.

When I did not enter behind him, Penelope came out to me. I spoke without meeting her eyes. It was time.

"I have something I must tell you."

"And what would that be?"

"Archivist. I have… That is, I've done something. Oh, I… I…" I fought back the urge to sob.

"Explain yourself," she said but I shook my head. "Speak!" she thundered, sudden and loud. I could not bring myself to confess that I was responsible for the destruction of her life's work, and many others besides. But I knew, I knew deep down inside, that I must confess everything. I could hold back no longer. I nipped at my leg, and held my chin up.

"Well. I… I made an ague formulation." I heard myself say. "A new… a different one, that is. I used a… I used information from papers I found. At the rout. I was going to tell you about them, I was. But then I realised what they were and…"

I was answered by utter silence; Penelope may have been holding her breath. "I found the substances they referred to. I recalled a mention from… from Chief Archivist Marwell, in the records. I thought that… I have not been… all you wanted me to be. And so, I thought. I thought… if I could redeem myself. I thought. I only wanted…"

I looked into her face but it was expressionless. Framed in the doorway as she was, she resembled something fierce, an apparition from an oil painting, perhaps. When still she did not reply, I realised she was waiting for me to continue.

"The last time I prepared the tincture, I used the directions I found. I made… especially potent samples, when you were last absent. I made them as strong as they could be. They spoke with great excitement. I thought. I thought, why, if I could do it once, maybe I could do it again. That we needed every advantage that we could find. I knew how much we needed to…"

"You did what?" she said. Her consideration was icy cold. She stared at me with such intensity that I flinched back. I heard Ridley move within the room beyond but he did not come to my aid. "Shay. Is this to mean? The tincture we have both taken. The tincture we have been using in these last days. Where are the papers? I must see them!"

"There is more. I must tell you. I've-"

"There is no time for that!" she snapped. "This exceeds everything!" She placed her hand in the crook of her elbow. "When it first began. When I first saw it. I wondered. Just a fleeting thing. But I thought…" Her eyes had gone very still. She put a hand to her mouth. "No."

"Not only this, but… the… I-"

"You have no idea what you have unleashed, girl! Show me your arm!" she hissed at me, suddenly. She rolled her own sleeve to her elbow, in decisive folds, snapping down the fabric, and held it out for me to inspect.

I did as she instructed. Under her fierce consideration, I dare do nothing but comply with her exactly. Upon both her flesh and mine was a pattern of black blotches, an almost identical patina of ruptured skin

"By the blood of the old gods! *Seekers*, Shay. *Seekers!*"

Part Three

FORBIDDEN
FORMULATIONS

Chapter Eighteen

SIGNIFICANT REPAIR

I submit the following contentions to reasonable folk of all hues. It is abundantly clear that the Concordian archivist's office has outlived its usefulness. Chief Archivist Etherington has provided nothing but poppycock and fiction these last years.

There are no Sentinels under her control any longer; the beasts that we once knew are gone, and her accountings are exaggerated if not entirely fabricated. Her suggestion that a brute places our own city under danger, in this very moment, is the greatest nonsense. Nonsense, I humbly submit, we can no longer afford to entertain.

We must assume she acts to protect her own position and character. Understandable as this may be, no person is above the needs of our noble nation, and there is no honour in such behaviour.

The solemn requirements of the office must be achieved in some other fashion.

Guest Letter from Member Arksthrotle to *The Newdock Statesman*

I would not have the pleasure of Fenton's company again that summer. It took a long time for me to piece together what, exactly, had happened between us. Or, rather, what he had done.

No lie could I convincingly tell myself to balm my sensibility, try as I might: my dear friend had betrayed me. This inalienable fact wounded me in the most penetrating way imaginable. Was he ever an ally, truly? Dwelling on the matter caused me enormous pain and so, naturally, I did so almost every night before I slept, and in the quiet, still moments that plagued the coming days.

In the end I sought out Etherington, and recounted everything to her — all that I had done. But not before Ridley forced me to march to the gallows of my humiliation. I should like to say that I would have done so independently, but I shall not attempt to deceive. Were it not for the acid rebuke delivered to me and the stern admonishment that I might do my best to mend the damage I had caused, I may be hiding in my bedchamber to this very day.

When I entered her study she was sitting at the desk, absorbed in some task from which she did not raise her eyes. She seemed oblivious to my presence, though I had knocked.

I stood before her, wishing I had rehearsed what I might say to her, and saw what had so captured her attention. In her hand she held the crushed base of one of the glass bulbs from the hydrographometer. She had placed it flat upon the polished wood, and picked up the tiniest pieces of glass with tweezers, one at a time. She did this repeatedly, tiny shard by tiny shard, as though she could somehow will the smashed artefact back to wholeness once more.

I jumped when she spoke. "Yes, Shay?"

Her distant, quiet consideration was more unnerving than if she had screamed at me to leave her office.

I cleared my throat quietly before I said, "I know."

"You know? And what is it that you know?"

She listened soberly to my confession, setting down her current splinter and sitting back in her chair to regard me coolly. At first she spoke not a word. Then she began to ask the odd question.

I told her about Fenton, how he had befriended me. How I'd been frightened that my poor constitution, and other failings, might result in failure to meet my duties. I let her know how desperate I had been to win her favour, and to defend the office; that I understood the great import of the work we did. To this I added the simple truth that I had allowed myself to be beguiled.

No. I did not know why he had been sent, nor by who. I was unaware of any affiliations. I confessed that, yes, I had taken him within the archives, but only once and only after I had known him for some time and thought him trustworthy. And had become increasingly desperate. I told her all.

Then she rose and left.

***

"The order went out for all that night. Practically the entire fleet. I'm to advise on the pathway through the bled. If we sight any Sentinels — which some accept is now a possibility, I haven't lost them all yet — I'll be needed."

An evening later, Lieutenant Etherington quickly recounted to us the details before she departed. A fresh front had developed in the low sea, raking attacks against our merchant vessels. Sentinel sightings had been made and intelligence had been received which suggested that the Grand Republic intended to take and hold the entire colony. This was of great strategic importance to the Thirteenth Fleet of Admiral Russell.

It was vital that our deteriorating position be braced, and in this no expense of man or coin could possibly be spared. The sea lords had long debated it, and their decision had come on down in the officious manner with which they usually comported themselves. All distant and nebulous in nature to me.

That the deliberations and decisions of the very state which I now named home revolved around our own actions was a strangeness pure. And one which suffered no loss of impact in the fractured degree with which it became clear to me.

Penelope looked more weary than I could recall seeing her. Her features were drawn, her skin newly papery over the bold angles of her cheekbones. Her shirt cotton was spotted and yellowed with the marks of travel and toil. Her eyes glanced to mine. Yet I found I could not meet them, such was my cowardice. I instead inspected my half boot tips upon the rug; one of the laces had already come untied despite my particular attentions. It was entirely unusual.

"Damn terrible set of events," Ridley had said, listlessly, as he took his pipe.

"We must continue to track Velspritt, as best we can, insufficient as it may be. I'm increasingly pressed by parliament, the fools have never been so bold. The key will be the arrival of the curious Brigadier General Lice to our fair city, from the Principality as we discussed. I must, somehow, use his discovery — this lure — to lead the great Sentinel so that we might learn all that we need from him, and take him from the city. I will return in time to meet with him. He seems… potentially open to our advances. It is the last hope that I cling to."

***

As to the news itself, it continued to pass through the city. Arksthrotle's faction — in alliance with several others, including the Tanithites — in parliament had at last drawn sufficient support between the parliamentary houses for the military action. And indeed I heard reports from a variety of sources, with varying levels of truth and embellishment. Each time it made me feel entirely queer, to be a part, however small and unknown, inside this matter of such public interest.

I caught the news from the salacious lips of the housemaids scurrying past me down Fishbinder's Way, wicker baskets full of apples and plums clutched tight as they teased and pinched and gossiped with one another in the dying daylight; from the lurid accountings and staid debates raging within *The Newdock Statesman* and *Gentleman's Monthly Magazine*; in the sudden, raised voices and slamming drinking vessels from the men below the archival offices; and, finally, in the official packet which arrived early one morning.

I received it from the messenger and delivered it to Etherington word-lessly. She had paced with it for hours on end, muttering to herself upon occasion, while I worked, head bowed and chewing upon my lip, daring to take the odd glimpse, within the draughty study that was the shared chamber of our work.

Chief Archivist Etherington was to travel with the fleet and offer all assistance possible to the Admiral. Penelope had time to expand upon the situation only simply. That the timing was atrocious for our personal stakes was obvious, yet there was little she could do. The press of the admiralty was strong and nor could she, in any reasonable manner, refuse the request. Both because of the power of the admiralty, and the weakness of our current position with every faction with which rested control over our fate.

The news carried with it a storm of activity which subsumed my master, never one to idle at the most favoured of times, as she prepared everything for her extended travel and ambiguous task.

Penelope planned to complete her duties as quickly as was possible. She would, all going well, return speedily so we might resume our activities. She did not have to say that our situation was desperate. She did not have to remind me of all we had lost. For it was such a patent example of unspoken truth that it coated our every action like rancid pig oil and I could not rid myself of the taint no matter what I tried.

This, and more, I received through a general haze of self loathing. Such that I could scarcely meet her eye when she recounted these details to me in the brisk neatness of her study, staring instead at my fingers, or the window, or the floor. Before I hurriedly retreated back to my chores.

I should like to say that I assisted her preparations in the spirit of our unified success. But I did not. Oh. I helped to prepare her voyage, while avoiding her actual company as much as was possible. Yet it was not for the mutual success of our shared endeavour, nor for my responsibility to the office to which I now owed allegiance. Rather it was for my own selfish purpose. Because I knew not what else to do.

***

And then, as suddenly as it all had seemed to begin, she was gone. I longed to retreat deep into the fitful, anxious slumber which had become my insufficient refuge. When I awoke each morning, for the briefest moment, I possessed the fresh naivety of a newborn babe. Until, with a curse, my memories came flooding back to me, and the startling reality of the situation rose to meet me.

I tugged the sweaty linens back around my tangled limbs, and I tossed left and right. Some mornings I squeezed my eyes shut once more, trying to force sleep to return. And yet all that awaited me was the pounding of my head, and the fitful torment of the most lurid half-dreams. For my body knew well that I needed no more rest, and if all my dreams were an ocean, I could barely break the surface to sink my head beneath the very top most handspan. And yet, that still seemed pleasanter than what otherwise awaited me.

In the immediate days after Penelope's retreat abroad, I seized the opportunity her absence offered me with a vigour that shames me. I did not use the freedom with which I was presented to burnish my responsibility; instead, for the first time in my short life I did the minimum for a given task and sometimes not even that. The act made me feel strangely awful. It nagged me and followed me wherever I went, and yet I turned that perversion of my spirit ever inwards, using the potent fuel to power my immolation.

I sought solace in whatever place I might find it, with a reckless abandon I had only really experienced in others, so unlike me it was impossible to recognise myself. I wandered the city with a restless energy that never seemed to leave me, telling myself such a pretty pocket of little fibs as ever there was that I might permit my indulgence. Almost, I dared the city to spite me.

When no harm or tragedy immediately befell me, I began visiting increasingly inappropriate locales. I spent an embarrassing and raucous evening in a dingy alehouse with a sinister sort of patron, and a bracing night in a gaming hell.

Foul weather rolled in from the broiling ocean to match my mood, and buffeted Fivedock with thick fog and howling winds and stinging rain. One blustery morning, I attended the launch of a thousand-ton merchantman of the South Murmesseril Company, my shirt fluttering about my bones and my jaw set purposefully. I wore no cloak or topcoat, perhaps to spite myself. Instead I winced against the bitter cold and drove myself onwards.

I did not avail myself of the rarefied company watching on from the fine vantage of the box, where behatted ladies dabbed at the sea spray kissing their faces with pretty handkerchiefs, and oohed and ahhed at the display. Instead I elected to observe the great spectacle from the depths of the dockside, pressed close to the seething mass of porters with billhooks, and watermen puffing upon cheap tabac. The dockhands, hands and cheeks grimy with labour, smelt of the sweat of their skin and the rot of their breath as they jostled and japed with one another. I let the risk of their closeness thrum through me a charged sense of fear, and did not allow myself to turn away from its fierceness. Instead I told myself the truth I was certain of: I deserved anything that came for me. Almost, I welcomed it.

I had never favoured spirits, finding the tartness of the foul liquid disagreed with my palate, and the loss of control they inflicted entirely uncomfortable. Still, following a misspent evening at a shambolic alehouse near the docks after the launch, I found they called out to me, and discovered their merits were singularly matched to my current needs. First sour wine, then blue ruin, became my companions.

I pushed my indulgences further each time. Until I walked the Slips, daring, almost wishing, to fall. For the pickpockets and sailors and hucksters who inhabited the ruinous streets to attack me. Yet they did not. Perhaps sensing the reckless energy with which I radiated and choosing to avoid the crossing of it.

When, one evening, I was hounded down and followed by a persistent stranger, I lashed out with my arm, ready to do combat. Only to realise the stranger was in fact Jemima, wrapped in a thick woollen cloak, leaning in to pinch my cheek. So drunk was I that I struggled to recognise the concern upon her face. Until she shook me, and brought me to a step where she sat me down and forced me to take a steaming restorative. Then escorted me out of the Slips, where she would not leave my side until I promised her I should return directly to my lodgings and take myself to bed.

So inebriated was I that I might have clear forgotten our encounter altogether, had I not awoken the next morning with the distinctive taste of the brew in my mouth and the stain of it upon my shirt, to go with a thundering headache and the driest of throats.

Chapter Nineteen

BLUE RUIN

The three moons are Ra, Guisi, and Aises. Each resplendent in its own right. What follows are the movements of each.

Benton's Whispering Coast Astronomical Diary or 'Almanack', wherein are contained the lunations, eclipse of the luminaries, aspects, times of high water, and judgements of the weather

I stuck my head into Peck's chamber to find him abed, as he more and more frequently had been in these last days. He looked up from the book he was reading — he favoured adventure novels — and smiled weakly at me before he broke into a coughing fit.

His eyes had gone frightened, which they sometimes did when he struggled to find his breath. I had been ill-mannered and short with him of late. But he seemed pleased to see me, all the same.

I pushed down my guilt, a thing I was becoming increasingly skilled at.

In bed again?

He dropped the book to his knees so his tiny hands might sign to me.

Tell me what is happening. I can help. I'm your friend. I want to help you.

I smiled. He was so determined. *Fine. Tomorrow. We'll talk tomorrow.*

You promised me powder. When?

Soon.

I left the boy. For I had purchased a bottle of cheapest ruin from a local hell two days before. Now, despite the illness it had last rendered in me — almost because of it, in truth — I sought out its torment once more.

I warmed my palms from the low coals in the hearth every so often as I sloshed the acrid-smelling stuff into an old chipped mug, and sipped at it periodically. It was a foul night, the window panes rattling in their frames, gusts of rain incessantly driving against the glass. I found it matched my mood quite neatly.

My head had begun to pound in the strangest, most intimidating fashion. One worse than any liquor had ever offered me before. It was almost as if the archivist's ague now bled into the rest of my life. To make matters worse, my senses had begun to perform fearsome tricks upon me.

Sometimes I felt suddenly vast, somehow, distant and entirely out of harmony with my own limbs. Dizziness frequently overcame me, so that I nearly fell; this was something different from the weakness I had always harboured, as though the earth itself were pulling me down.

At other times, an eerie chanting seemed to suddenly taint my hearing, a ghostly echoing from whichever sound I had last heard. Such as when I passed the furious clacking of the looms down Draper's Way, falling to my knees and clasping my palms over my ears, so the passing muffin man and his patrons stopped their dealings to ask me as to my wellness.

The black marks on the insides of my arms had increased all the length of those limbs and had now grown small, furred extremities. They reminded me of pine needles around a branch. They itched abominably.

At some level I was aware of Etherington's foul warnings; at another, I pushed my concern downward, along with the rest of my worries. For I knew of nothing else that could be done. As I drank the blue ruin, the awful truth began to rise within me, persistent and intractable as the tide.

I sipped the nasty drink more and more frequently, desperate to escape the horror within, until I drank near as often as I drew breath.

It was Fassinger who found me and who took me to task. Four days after Lieutenant Etherington had departed for the front. I had continued to bank the fireplace and had filled the water kettle and set it to heat several times, but had otherwise entirely avoided both my master and my household chores. When I heard him at the door I was too despondent to hide my shame.

With a creak and blast of frigid air the door came open, and the surgeon bustled in, brandishing a broadside.

"Shay? I've been looking for you. This damn city is all a kerfuffle. It's hard to complete any normal business. At the admiralty they told me that you had not–"

He took in the scene with surprise. His hair, never the neatest aspect of his appearance, was particularly unruly. His shirt was not just damp, but sodden. It was also dirty, stained around the sleeves with dirt or maybe blood. That, I knew, could mean any number of things. It meant he could have been at the Foundling Hospital, though for some reason, and I cannot say why, I did not receive that sense from him.

I had enough gumption to dart my eyes across his face, bleary as they were. He looked paler than I recalled. Thinner, too.

I should like to say that I was concerned for him, this respectable man who served those around us with no complaint, who had been so kind to me, and had done so much. And while it was true that, yes, a lurch of guilt did pass through me to have added to his woes, it had little true bearing upon my mood. For I was selfishly sure that my own pain was of far greater import at that moment.

Indeed, a deeper part of me, a part I am loath to own, was affronted that its own moment might be usurped. So that I felt a strong flash of irritation that must, surely, have been apparent upon my features. Though I nervously eyed the mess I had made: a smattering of dirty ashes where I had stumbled into the fire trying, too late, to rekindle the dying flames; my shoes, caked with mud from my latest wanderings, kicked off in the middle of the room; the bundle of threads and needles tipped from the sewing box and strewn across the table as I tried, vainly, to mend a tear I had made in my sleeve.

But he seemed not to notice the disarray, his eyes alighting on me instead. With a delicate sniff of his nostrils, he cast me a concerned glance.

"Spirits?" A puzzled frown coloured his weary features. He placed the broadside on the table, slowly, as though he were trying not to startle a wild animal. "This is most unlike you." His eyes were tired and bloodshot, and by his look I guessed he had had little sleep. My curiosity wondered briefly what trouble he had lately faced. But, selfishly, my own heartache won out.

"Is it?" I spat at him, petulant as a spoiled child. Then, as if to further compound my point, I tossed back the remaining liquid in the bottle. Like an idiot, I had gravely misjudged its quantity. It splashed over my face, and some of the foul stuff worked its way up my nose. It burnt, all of it, my throat, my tongue, my nose. And I gagged. I followed this with an almighty cough, then a most undignified splutter, gin streaming wetly down my chin and my front.

And then it all caught up with me. I lurched forward in an attempt to clear my throat. My ankle, wrapped around the leg of my chair, tangled and I tripped.

The whole lot came crashing down, the chair still half attached to my back. My knees slammed painfully onto the hard planking of the floor. Before my outstretched palm had time to awkwardly arrest my fall with its jarring blow, I retched violently and emptied my stomach all over everything: myself, the rug and the hearth.

Tears streamed down my cheeks, mingling with all the foulness below. I retched and retched and retched, long past the point there was anything left to pass. I was sick until my ribs and my stomach ached. Until, in some form of mangled common tongue befitting a resident of the asylum rather than an officer of the state, I begged for my body to cease its torment of me. I cried and I cried until my chest heaved and my nose ran.

And then there were strong hands upon my back, rubbing and patting me. "Here, now," Ridley said. "Here now."

He heated a basin of water before the fire and, with a wadded cloth, helped me clean the filth from my face. The water was warm and soothing, yet it stung. He swept his long arm across the clutter of dead candles and needles and thread and papers upon the table, clearing us room.

"Sit there." He placed a warm cup in my hand, and wrapped my fingers around it. "And drink that." It was simply a weak tea sweetened with honey. My throat was tender, yet my body sang to be offered proper sustenance. I gulped at it greedily, very nearly choking myself once more.

"When did you last eat a proper meal?" Ridley asked me with a quizzical raise of his eyebrow. To which I managed barely a shrug of my hunched shoulders. And then he went away and busied himself with the dull thuds and dings and the occasional mutter of his culinary endeavour.

When he returned he placed down a plate of food for me; he had a large helping of his own. I realised it had indeed been days since I ate properly and, despite the recent emptying of my stomach, I was quite famished. There was a hunk of bread, and a bowl of steaming stew. The smell of both slapped into me, as bracing as the sea's swell, and I struggled not to fall immediately about it.

I ripped off and slowly chewed a corner of the bread, wincing occasionally when it rubbed against the stinging sores within my gums. And I took increasingly large spoonfuls of the thick stew, picking out the softer lumps of carrot and potato first. Before working my way towards the gristly lamb. It tasted heavenly, despite the pain. The rich gravy coated the roof of my mouth and my tongue in a pleasing manner.

"Now, tell me what the devil has been going on here, since last I saw you?" He leaned back in his chair. He had already finished his own meal and picked up a stained old piece of linen from the table, with which he began to clean the small frame glass of his spectacles in small but vigorous circles. "Tell me and leave nothing out. For I shall know, if you do. Make no mistake about that."

And so I told him, suddenly tired and weary of all the lies and the struggle and the subterfuge. Out it came, and each word of it as bitter as bitter can be. Yet it also felt better to have said them.

They tumbled out, slowly at first, and then quickly, and then I couldn't stop them, so that they came in a frantic flurry, over and over like a tumble down the stairs. Until the whole thing was out. Or at least all the parts I felt so ashamed of: that Fenton had betrayed me; that I had ruined artefacts and documents; that when Etherington most needed me I had failed; that, even now, when I ought be tracking the great brute Velspritt, I had turned to drink. And I realised my voice was hoarse and I had nearly been shouting.

And I fell back on to the old chair, and lay there as if I had run a race, feeling strangely empty. The food had now done its work on me, melting my heavy limbs and infecting my mind with a ponderous sluggishness.

Ridley had tossed a woollen blanket over my body during my ravings and delivered to me a steady supply of sweet, hot tea. I burrowed further into the blanket, a warmth I had not felt in days suffusing through me. My eartips tingled hot from the heat of the fire. Almost, I could have curled up into a little ball and sought my slumber.

For his own measure, Ridley considered me sternly. By now the fire was almost out entirely, the coals nothing but glowing red embers from which the odd crackle and hiss reached us. I remember thinking that the cosiness of the moment was strangely at odds with the pain of my loneliness and my shame. Then I recalled my first nights here. Oh, and how I wished to go back to such simpler days. My thoughts drifted in the hodgepodge manner that precedes sleep, overlapping and dancing upon one another without ever snagging truly on one thing. But I caught myself in the act and ceased the reverie with all the strength I could muster, which was not much. Just enough. I wriggled upright, and forced my weary eyelids open to meet his gaze and the discussion I knew I must face.

"The boy has consumption," he began. I opened my mouth to answer but was so disarmed by this change in the direction of the conversation that

I said nothing. "I don't expect you to understand, not exactly," he went on. "But he is… frail. His lungs are terribly weak." His words were direct but not unkind. He sounded very, very weary.

We sat looking into the fire for many moments before Ridley turned his attention to me again. "You are acting like a bird-witted child, which we both know you are not. Be a woman, and leave this self-indulgent moping behind."

"Penelope… she has been too good to take me to task," I said. His expression turned stern but I spoke before he could reply. "I know I have been the most terrible simpleton."

He took down the sandalwood case which contained the surgical instruments of his trade. He undid the clasp, opened the lid, and gently set upon his lap. Now he set a large jar of vinegar upon the floorboard by his foot with a gentle thud. He uncorked the bottle, and took up a bundle of threadbare rags. Then with a weary sigh he extracted a cannula and began to clean it, slowly and carefully, in the manner I knew he believed cleared his thoughts. And I knew better than to interrupt him. If he was in a decent mood, he would talk fondly of his sea days, or complain of the price of ale or grain. When he was like this, no good came of interrupting him.

"Well. That's as may be," he eventually replied. "But don't you think perhaps it's time to do something about it?" I nodded into the blanket but he did not glance my way. "You have a decision to make," he said to me. "That's what you'll be judged on. Ultimately." He raised the metal object to the light before he began cleaning it once more. "Each of us faces setbacks in our life. Each of us makes mistakes."

"Why would she want me?" I spoke the words that nearly choked in my throat. "I've ruined everything. Why would anyone…?" I gritted my teeth and squeezed my eyes shut to stay the urge to break down.

"You've been taken in. You wouldn't be the first. And you won't be the last. Now. I don't doubt that you've acted foolishly. And I can't say that I understand every part of it." He spread his huge hands wide. "But I do know that you are capable of more, oh so much more, than you seem to realise. So let us put an end to this weeping, and this drinking."

"I have betrayed her trust so terribly, I… I fear she may never forgive me. I can hardly forgive myself."

"Show yourself worthy of her forgiveness, then!" There was icy steel in his voice now, despite his clear exhaustion. "When we make a mistake, any person who is worth a damn makes amends for it. You, Shay, have made a mistake. And you are the only one who can set it right."

Chapter Twenty

VERACITY
OF SUBMISSION

Member Arksthrotle hereby proposes motion 3,874, taken into the public record and hereafter known as The Dissolution of the Archivist's Office Act of Five Hundred and Eight.

The dissolution and replacement of the ancient Concordian office of the Sentinel archivist shall be put into order forthwith, at the earliest possible time, while accounting for the mind and vote of the members of each of our noble parliamentary houses, common or otherwise.

All responsibilities heretofore held by that ancient office shall be passed to a committee of this house, before the end of this current year. It is proposed this committee be formed of the Freemen and Lords who reside in the house and shall, hereafter, represent her best endeavours.

From 'The Dissolution of The Archivist's Office
Act of Five Hundred and Eight'

I had arisen that morning with fresh vigour driving me on. But I beheld the broadside Ridley had brought home the previous evening with a sinking terror.

Chief Archivist Lieutenant Etherington to be Stripped of Office:
Questioned on Veracity of Archival Submissions

The attacks on Etherington had intensified far further than we had known, further than I had imagined possible. So this was why Ridley had sought me out so desperately. It was time for action, indeed.

I briskly attended the postal office to collect the archivist's mail, yet this proved to be a difficult endeavour. There was much chatter amongst clerks and patrons alike. The poison had been unleashed by the Arksthrotles and Grents, and any number of others who opposed us, a figure which — to my mind — was growing ever larger with each passing moment. I imagined danger all around me. It was in the looks and the glances, and the whispered asides. One fellow even timidly questioned me on the whereabouts of Etherington, and whether she would answer in parliament for her supposed crimes.

When, at last, the clerk handed over the letters, I fled from the place as quickly as I could manage without breaking into a run.

Breaking open the seal of one of a great bundle of missives with a gasp, I was further shocked: the Brigadier General Lice from the Principality Glisk, the man who we held out hope we may bring to our aid, was to be in attendance in our fair city this coming week. Etherington had been absolutely certain he would not arrive for several months. The man was critical to our plan to deal with Velspritt, whose existence we now needed to prove more than ever before.

***

"The lady is not available," Sekington, Hardy's butler, told me as I bustled past him through the main door of her townhouse and into the entrance hall without greeting. "She is entertaining. Would you care to—"

I turned to give him an apologetic look, unable to actually voice my defiance, as I made my way to the foot of the main staircase. His hands reached out to me, imploring, as though he wished to physically stay me, but dared not. I hastened my step regardless.

"Miss Bluefaltlow. Please! This is quite unconscionable. It won't do at all." In all my many visits to Hardy's home, I had never heard Sekington raise his voice before now.

This time I did ignore him, though somewhat guiltily, and carried on up the grand marble of the staircase. I burst into one of several drawing rooms — the Lavender Parlour, Hardy called this one — through the great and heavy double doors, with no consideration for whosoever was inside might think.

It was a vast, impeccably decorated chamber, and one I knew reasonably well. Hardy and I had taken tea there on more than one occasion during my intense instruction; those whirlwind weeks spent in anticipation of the rout. This afternoon the light was somewhat different, though the many oil paintings which looked down upon us were no less imposing for it. Indeed, if anything they were now more dramatic.

The patterns upon the wallpaper were as resplendent, bold, and as undoubtedly in keeping with current mode as they had ever been. The scent in the air spoke of autumn coals and evening wines, and the distant chatter of deliberations of import far above my station.

It was in the very far corner of the large room from which those deliberations came; disembodied voices floated from behind a triple screen. One with warm oak panels of exotic origin. Painted upon the panels were a variety of foreign fruits and spices, each unknown to me, and all the more intriguing for it. The colours were as richly evocative as one imagined those foods might taste, all blood reds and emerald greens and midnight blues.

With a hitch of my breath I stepped quickly across the room and around the pretty panel before I could lose my nerve entirely. The duchess sat at her morning table, holding court with the small group before her. She herself was seated upon an ornate sofa. Across and to the side of her, in velvet upholstered, wingback chairs, four guests lounged in varied states of ease or interest.

I quickly assessed their features, one by one. I found I did not know them, not personally, though from reputation and my instruction I could ascertain their identities. One was a member of parliament and a popular lord, Eppinglow. The two ladies, in green and custard ensembles respectively, I believed to be heiresses. With a scarcely concealed gasp I realised the consort's younger brother, Elfron, was in attendance, too.

His long legs were crossed above the knee. He plucked strands of tabac from his ornate snuff box, and sniffed them delicately as his perfectly manicured eyebrow arched at my disruption. The ladies exchanged knowing glances from behind the soft silk of their fans.

Fear flashed ever so briefly upon Hardy's face and then, in a moment, she had concealed the emotion with the considerable skill that was her calling card.

"Shay," she said, clapping her hands together. "What a wondrous surprise! Treasured guests, this is my niece, from Quom!"

An interminable number of moments began, where I was firmly directed to sit beside Hardy and encouraged to make polite but pointless talk with these titans of the ton. Until, at last, the duchess leant in front of me enthusiastically to hear the last of an anecdote delivered by Elfron, tiny milk jug in hand; indeed, his story was so fabulously charming that she tossed her hands — and the milk jug — into the air. Pouring the creamy stuff all down my shirt. Nary a drop landed on either her chair or the rug, I couldn't help but notice.

"Oh, oh I *am* clumpish! You must all forgive me. And you especially Shay. Come with me at once, and we shall remedy. Fortune has a similar frame to yours, I am certain she will have something suitable in her wardrobe. Now, now. You musn't resist. It is the very least I must do. I cannot have any niece of mine sitting around all the afternoon in a such a sodden state. Oh, *what a clutter brain I can be sometimes!"*

***

"Have you news from the front?" Hardy closed the door to her dressing suite, having sent her maid to fetch a choice of suitable garments for me to choose from. I had never seen her look so discomposed. "And those fools who've gone blundering off with them?"

"No, no, nothing like that. I didn't know who else to come to." I said. "So, I—"

She relaxed a little. "I have seen the papers. Tell me what you know. Save none of it."

I pulled out the broadsides I had brought. The ones slandering the archivist, that suggested the sea lords and the upper house were likely to act. And that she should lose her ancient office.

"These are from the last three days. Every one worse than the last!"

Hardy wrinkled her nose in distaste. "Odious."

"We have been tracking a Sentinel, one particularly. A vast one. Penelope believes he may be the greatest brute ever known."

The maid — Jenny — came in with several garments folded over her arm. Hardy waved her over, and promptly swept them from her before sending her away with the request that she serve further refreshments to her guests, and invite them to stay for dinner, where her fantastic chef would delight them as never before with a rare but incredible dish.

"Oh, and do tell my man in the kitchens!" she added.

"The Brigadier General wasn't supposed to come until Penelope had returned," I whispered as Jenny bustled away, tutting. I leant over and handed the letter to Hardy. "She... he has access to something we need. A lure, Etherington called it. If we could use it... the Sentinel, Velspritt. He's coming now. His song is incredible! It is everywhere, all around us. I... I almost

feel that I can sense it without any equipment, though that is clearly madness, or…" Hardy looked at me with something akin to horror in her eyes.
"It would be… beyond dangerous — devastating! — if he were to approach
the city."

Hardy furrowed her brow, nodding. "Yes. Whatever we do. We must
show that Penelope is truthful! Perhaps there is something that can be
done."

"We know Lice will arrive by tomorrow," I said. "With no Etherington… we need to win the substance from him. Someone must represent
the archival office, and that someone must be me."

"The Brigadier General Lice, of the Principality of Glisk. Something
of an infamous gentleman… a most curious creature, by all accounts. I
have met him twice, I believe. A long time member of the court, and
trusted implicitly by the Prince Royal of Glisk. He has long held a keen
interest in the natural history of the Sentinels. Are you certain he has it,
this… lure?"

I nodded. "Yes. Every report the archivist has received suggests both
that he has it, and that it functions. She was quite sure."

Hardy bit her lip and stared out of the window before she remembered
what we were about and gestured for me to change my soiled clothing.
She tutted as I slipped behind her dressing screen – its brightly coloured
paper inlays glowing in the dying afternoon light – and threw a seemingly
random array of garments over the screen.

"No. It is too much of a risk," she said, at last. "Even if we decided
it was a winsome strategy. This is diplomacy, Shay. If we lose access to
the stuff, if the man turns away… Penelope may not be able to undo our
handiwork."

"I'm ready for this," I said. Perhaps the obdurate steel my tutors once
admonished me for, long ago, entered my eye. I surely couldn't say. "I want
to help. Have you no shirts, or–?"

"Choose one of the gowns, whichever you prefer, and the stockings. The fact you wish to help does your character credit. But, Shay, this is a dirty business. One you aren't ready for."

"It's only a little milk, I can head straight home to change, it's–"

"I understand the need of the archivist to wear base clothing. But it would serve us well here for you to dress more to the occasion and station, at least a little. You dine with the ruler's brother tonight, Shay!"

I began to stutter out a refusal but she gave me a look so withering I hurriedly ran my hand through the gowns, holding them up to the light, pressing them against my torso.

"An archivist's duties are quite one thing. And all too much alone for one to take, especially one so young. This is something else. Child, you must attend to me." Her tone had become very stern; she leant on a great dresser as she considered me. A colourful assortment of pomanders and lotions was arranged upon it. "The situation is dangerous enough. Sometimes, the best move is no move. And you are staying for dinner; it would look queer for you to leave now."

"No one else can do it. We must!" I said.

"I need not negotiate with you, Shay. Do not forget to whom it is you speak."

"What are we to do? Let the Sentinel loose on the city? Let them take the office from Etherington? We cannot let this chance slip away. Etherington, she would–"

"This must wait, for now. Until after dinner, once everyone leaves. We've been gone long enough. Now come."

***

The meal, though apparently impromptu, was a lavish affair. I had chosen the gown which covered the most skin; Hardy raised her expressive eyebrows at my unfashionable choice, but did not push me to change.

Sekington gave me a rather reproachful look when he entered the dining room to announce the first course: chestnut and chicken soup, thick and creamy and savoury. There was a pile of warm bread rolls and a huge slab of yellow butter served alongside. I found I was quite satiated once I had finished.

As our plates were cleared with a flourish, I noticed that mine was the only one that was entirely empty. Sekington announced the next course: trout, stuffed with egg balls and pickled turnip. It swiftly arrived and I found my appetite had returned. As I ate heartily, all the other dinner guests were engaged deeply in conversation. Once again I found I was the only one who finished the food.

I was becoming increasingly anxious to speak to Hardy alone once more and hoped that soon we might retire to the drawing room for brandy — or whatsoever might be the modish refreshment of the current season.

To my surprise, Sekington returned and, while several servants ran to and from the kitchen laden with heavy plates, yet another course was served. There was beef pie, mutton with gooseberry jam, fried oysters and roasted squab; butter mushroom sauce, meat jelly and onion gravy; herbed peas, pickled figs and boiled red cabbage. More bread and butter arrived, too, and I felt quite incapable of eating another mouthful.

Sekington served us sparkling wine throughout the meal; I sipped at mine while wishing for weak ale and a bowl of stew. The other guests, regulars at Hardy's table, served themselves from the dishes and continued their chatter.

One of the heiresses, the one in the custard ensemble, turned to me and pouted. "Say. Bluefaltlow, aren't you hungry? You've barely touched the main course!"

Before I could reply, Hardy laughed like a bell. "Oh, someone must have *known* my darling niece would arrive this afternoon; I've served her very most favourite foods for the first two courses! Now Bella, do tell me.

Has your lovely Alicia planned what she'll serve at her name day recital this year? Always such an *exquisite* spread!"

***

When the last guest finally left that evening, I sat down heavily on the sofas and Hardy joined me. To my surprise, she pulled off her pretty little shoes and began to massage her feet.

"Etherington won't return in time," I said. "She's like to be gone for weeks. That much we know for certain. We can't waste the opportunity. We simply can't."

"No." She tapped her fingernail against her teeth. "No, indeed." She stared long into the hearth.

"Please. I must do this thing." I said at last, to the silence. "We cannot let them make the discovery before we do."

"What do we know of him?" she asked me, with a long drawn out sigh, leaning forward at last.

"You know more than I," I said, taken suddenly aback that she had entertained me.

"Perhaps. Still, tell me what you know. It serves you well to so apportion your thoughts."

"I know only this: he has not reached out to our office of late, despite Etherington's considerable courting; he will be here within the day; he has something we desperately need. What do you know, duchess?"

"What I know and do not know are not—"

"What choice do we have?"

Hardy let out a deep sigh. "Yes. Quite," She offered me a probing glance, "We shall perhaps make a diplomat of you yet." She laughed wearily before she continued. "I know he is an infamous gambler." I gulped; for I knew I had won, though it did not feel like a victory.

"Then might that be the key to our success?"

***

He was in the city for only these ten days, and so we had little time within which we could strike.

I was to continue our courting of his interest. As that same office should represent the state in all matters related to the Sentinels. He was no fool, though. My knowledge was scarcely sufficient, and yet it was not completely barren. Somehow, I should extract from him the good favour we required, namely the lure.

His taste for the game, and the unparalleled suite of such gaming hells as Fivedock owned, we would exploit to the maximum advantage. Once I had fully won his trust, I would deliver him an invitation to the most renowned of them all — Hoodle's — to witness the most infamous game of them all: Sentinel's Gambit.

Meanwhile, I would continue to track Velspritt. We would convince Lice to lend to us the use of the luring substance — with the offer of collaboration between our nations or whatever bribes we deemed necessary to sway him. These Hardy would secure for us, with her diplomatic and political graces.

As soon as the opportunity revealed itself, I would put the substance to use. This we would use to lure Velspritt out from one of the locations we had strong evidence to suspect he resided.

Concurrently, we would petition all we might, and hope to stay the hand of the sea lords and the members until Penelope returned. Hardy would utilise her powers to win what time we could. She would arrange a number of social occasions, some intimate, others elaborate. Each would be tuned to the particular proclivities of those who might influence our fate. To which the duchess kept immaculate notes, which were drilled into me whenever the opportunity arose. No expense, nor charm, would be spared.

As the days ran ever past us with a frightening pace, I felt emboldened to have Hardy's considerable capacities upon my side, and yet we were under no illusions as to the difficulty of the task before us.

Chapter Twenty-One

BLACKPOWDER & MISCHIEF

The Concord's social season, currently in full flow, seems in no way limited by the reality of the live war the nation finds itself in. No. Rather, the outbreak of hostilities lends a fevered, almost festive air to proceedings.

Talk of war is everywhere. But, from a simple perusal of the periodicals, one would think that the social events might never end. There is a bewildering number of soirées: horse races at Grantsop; promenades at Wellspring Gardens or St Gilda's Park; scores of assemblies at Mellberry's assembly rooms and a great array of lesser halls; not to mention what seems to me to be every type of gaming event possible. All laced with the most substantial measure of chicanery and pomp, fashion and rambunction.

And if one were to grow tired of this tidy little lot, there are fireworks at the palace, regimental marches, hunts, theatrical and operatic offerings, prize or cock fighting. Every young blueblood can be seen to display themselves to their very best advantage, puffed up as the most resplendent peacock, each partaking in a subtle, unspoken competition of the greatest importance. The periodicals breathlessly report each and every move of the rarified participants as if tracking their every action were as vital as reporting on the progress of the war.

It is an eye-opening experience for me, a social season in Fivedock. It infects everything, spilling over onto the general mood of the city which can be tasted on every street, and upon every tongue. More than once, I have overheard discussion — between patrician beauties, dandies, huntsmen and young bluebloods alike — about the many and bracing merits of the season and war with equal aplomb.

From these observations, it seems to me the general consensus is that any war will be won easily, and enhance the natural good standing of our most noble nation. Fortunes are to be made, land acquired, glory won. Oftentimes, it is difficult not to be swept along with the enthusiasm and energy, despite my knowledge that the situation is far more dire than the citizenry believe.

'A Time of War & Strife,' from The Worldly Journal and Commonplace
Book of Shay Bluefaltlow
The Year Eight, Five Hundred Since the Signing of the Great
Concord of Westerbrook

As Peck skipped and giggled away from me, I found I could not help but join him in his laughter. His joy was infectious and I ruthlessly pushed aside any remaining doubt I had about our outing; to see the boy so happy made my heart soar. Though not for purely unselfish reasons. No. For the child that resided deep within me, who had so spent many years playing in mortifying seclusion, delighted to have a playmate in the mischievous boy. This was as new and fascinating a delight as anything Hardy or Bamcroft or Etherington had shown me.

Fassinger and his endless warnings be damned, I would give the boy his pleasures. Besides which, had I not given him my word? If I could not meet a promise to the boy, then there was little left in my life that mattered. Not in spite of everything else that was occurring, but because of it.

I flashed my hands up, communicating the sign, in the clearest terms. *Ignore him. You are strong enough.*

The segment of the city we ventured into now was older, more crooked, than much of the rest and a sense of adventure accompanied us. The wattle and daub buildings lurched over us as though mocking the drunks who wandered among them on unsteady feet.

Despite having sustained such a long convalescence, and sheltered experience of a life, Peck still somehow knew which way was quickest, cutting through Draper's Ward to come down to the ever-lively dock district. I followed him down the narrow stone steps beside the cartwright's and Mason's Cacao Nut Millers, picking my way carefully through the cramped, foetid alleys. Before we burst out at the dense melee of the lower Slips, running now though careful not to lose our footing on the loose cobbles, slick as they were with river water and slime.

Here the sounds of commerce and mercantilism never ceased, no matter the hour. The thud of kegs, the clop of hooves, and the squeal of fat sows ready for slaughter suddenly subsumed us. The bark and curse of sweating workmen alongside the dull clang of shipbells was an endless hymn to the ascendant gods of industry. We jinked and dived past two bickering vagrants, a waft of knock-me-down reaching our nostrils, cutting through the tang of salt and iodine.

Under Hangman's Bridge, I grabbed Peck by the waist; he was so light I hauled him upwards with ease and he clambered onto my shoulders, agile as a monkey breaking out of a menagerie. He wiggled and bucked like a belligerent puppy, and I grasped his legs as firmly as I was able, the better to stop his muddy boots from streaking the good wool of my redingote, which would be most displeasing to both myself and Ridley.

Finally, Peck acquired a sufficiently firm grasp on the beam, riddled with rot and damp, hanging just above his head. I pushed up onto my toes to assist this final hazard of his climb then winced as he dangled there, squeezing my eyes shut to cease the horrifying consideration of myself in his place.

From the vantage of my limited experience, it seemed certain that the rather pathetically structured joist should surely come down upon any moment. Though such mundane concerns seemed not to occur to Peck at all.

He rummaged around in his pocket before producing our blackpowder wrapping with relish. He carefully pushed the little bundle into a dank old brickwork hole nearest him, as if he were born to it; pausing only to grin at me over his shoulder as I hopped from bootheel to bootheel in agitation.

Now was my time to provide the source of fire for our experiment. I produced Etherington's best tinderbox from my pocket and popped the clasp with my thumb. I fished about the contents for the jute cord and flint. Crouching down, I cupped my hand to protect the thing from the thin drizzle that soaked us sodden, in that persistent, unavoidable way.

Following a number of curses, I acquired sufficient flame for our purpose. I carefully passed the jute up to Peck; who could just reach it at full stretch. He moved slowly, carefully, so as to protect the flame from the frequent gusts of wind. His long years of work at hearth and stove and pot fortifying his action.

He finished his task, then dropped down, clinging to my outstretched arms to break his fall. I was struck again by just how little he weighed, for he landed as lightly and gracefully as an acrobat of serious merit.

Together we retreated a safe distance to witness the result of our long plotting, in firm hope that the endeavour might not be thwarted by the heavy drizzle that had been our constant companion that morning.

Just as I had begun to doubt the effectiveness of our workmanship — concerned that I had ill prepared the fuse, or misjudged the quantity of grains, or that the mixture had indeed been spoiled by moisture — our little explosives detonated with a ferocity of incredible proportions.

A great cracking bang rang out, from which we leapt back into a huddle. The grimy panes of the warehouse beside us shattered, tinkling to the ground. My ears rung, shrill and disorientating, but amidst the shrieking I could hear jubilant giggling.

A crowd of baying seamen, musketmen, and porters had appeared at the railings above us.

"What devilry goes on there?"

"Them there've got something to do with it, I'm sure!"

We sprang up. I seized Peck by the flannel of his shirt and hauled him to his feet, already moving myself. But then he was away.

He ran with wild abandon. He raced like a hare through the streets, he darted and he bolted and he streaked away from me, under arms and around legs and over puddles, so quickly I could scarcely keep up with him.

Full of fret was I that he might slip and fall, or that I might, and that we should be caught. My own breath came in ragged gasps, my lungs burned, my legs ached. And yet, he was flying and his laughter, ringing out loud and clear as a church bell, echoed from the old stonework all around us, in a way that will live forever in my memory.

***

The opera season was in full swing, and the streets were seldom quiet now. Sometimes, I closed my eyes and thought of Sentinel's Gambit, and took little greedy sips of the last of our stolen chocolate. Other times my mind strayed to the future. My thoughts never ceased.

I was finding it increasingly difficult to hide the secret I shared with Penelope. The strange marks we had discovered upon our arms had quickly spread and worsened in character. Upon several balmy mornings, I sat crossed-legged upon the bare floorboards and, with the chipped ewer of freshly heated water from the hearth, tried to scrub them clean away. They had resisted the strongest exuberances of a washcloth, soap and water that I could bear. If anything, it had only made them worse.

They more than itched now. They had become incredibly sore; when I studied them beneath the optic glass in the archives, under the gentle glow of candlelight, they appeared almost puckered up from my skin in little rings, each somewhat indented in the centre.

Despite my very best efforts I could not stay my fingers from seeking them out, often through the linen of my shirt, and absentmindedly tracing out their boundaries. As it is possible to do with one's tongue when a canker appears within the mouth, or as surely every child has done when it comes time to lose their milk teeth.

They now circled my entire upper arm, with the strongest density beneath the flesh near my underarms. I had taken to wearing only the most modest of clothing, and certainly to covering my arms at all times. I had also become extremely self-conscious; never one bold in such matters, this new truth now near-paralysed me upon occasion, so afraid was I that someone might discover the secret I so meticulously hid.

***

I had sought out Bamcroft at the shipyard, and the raucous coffee houses of Exchange Way, yet struggled to locate him.

Before I could give any more thought to the matter, I had to deposit a bundle of victual remits for Etherington, submitted every quarter as part of our records, in exchange for the docket of future supplies.

I had been to the Victualling Board on Hedges Way only once before and did not recognise the man behind the desk, nor he I. When I told that I was from the archivist's office, he looked surprised. He was certain someone had already been about the matter. A man, he claimed, which was so obviously impossible it scarcely deserved a response.

While Penelope could have been mistaken, or completed the errand herself — though such oversight would be wildly out of character — there was no man who would have come to represent us. And, besides, I held the very records in my own two hands! He persisted in his confusion for far too long and I, in my frustration, spoke increasingly frankly. Almost to the point of rudeness.

It was only when Belfry — the musket squadron sergeant who worked below us at the admiralty — appeared and supported my case that my mind was put at ease. He confirmed that I was the only one to be found at the Navy Admiralty at Bingham Square, with Chief Sentinel Archivist Etherington, and that I was well known to be her nominal assistant by all who had business at that place.

He merrily said how lucky he was to be reporting their victuals at the time. I pretended to take it all in good jest for his benefit, but the truth was I was more than a little concerned.

The officious gentlemen acquiesced, but told me he could not give me what he did not have, and that I should have to wait another two days for him to replicate the papers. This he most certainly did not have time for, but he was a man of kindness and duty. For which we were most lucky, indeed.

Chapter Twenty-Two

THE AERONAUT'S BALLOON

Many are the tools deployed in the primary pursuits of a Sentinel archivist, outnumbered only, maychance, by the skills required to wield them.

The capacity to track Sentinels is, unsurprisingly, at the core of the profession, accomplished primarily by following the trail of scent song. Yet, as Archivist Etherington endlessly reminds me, other capabilities are of equal import and must not be neglected. Indeed, so imperative was the deliverance to me of such knowledge that my preparations began as soon as I had landed in Fivedock — before I knew of the archive at all.

Navigation, shipmanship, and a deep knowledge of the bledland and all its creatures are the bedrock upon which the education must be founded. To this we may add weapons training and survival, as well as the practical capabilities required for effective curation. Politics and the discipline of manners must also be mastered. Languages, too, are essential, both for carrying out the primary archival activities of our trade and for the secondary duty of passing through such places as are required to enact them.

I could write far more extensively upon the subject, and this list should not be considered exhaustive. As Ridley is fond of saying, "Skills of character are perhaps harder to inculcate in a person, than other matters, for it can go against the nature found within." In this regard, patience and fortitude are virtues expected in an archivist of any reasonable capability. For long can be the hunt, in the measure of months and days, or decades and centuries.

The sighting of a Sentinel is itself a rare event, when compared to the frequency of logged notations, even in the regular activities of archivists in all but the most abundant — though, sadly, largely forgotten — days. A decent perusal of records is a simple enough method that I have myself affirmed this contention. It is an event for which an apprenticed archivist might train for years and seldom if ever witness, despite the unique and extended lifespan of almost all who commit themselves to the trade.

In this regard, the tale of Chief Archivist Saldwent is instructional. He being one who, during the First Great Quiet, sighted not a single Sentinel, nor notated but one scent song — despite the devotion of his entire life of one hundred and fifty-six years to the feat.

'The Skills of a Sentinel Archivist's Education,' from The Worldly
Journal and Commonplace Book of Shay Bluefaltlow
The Year Nine, Five Hundred Since the Signing of the Great Concord
of Westerbrook

I prepared to meet Duchess Hardy on the rich greens of the meadows of St Hilda's Park. Here we were to lose ourselves in the great crowds of parasols and curricles gathered to witness the expeditious raising of Aeronaut Merton's balloon.

It had grown impossible to avoid the boarded walkers who flocked the streets, the large bills pressed thick upon the walls, or the handbills thrust so frequently upon one by a link boy. Not that the advertisement was much needed; the event had been the talk of the town for several weeks.

In the distance, small figures could be seen upon every available surface, in the vast oak and elm, on buildings and monuments and towers. I had to strain my eyes to make out the gaggle of rowdy school boys ringed around the entire circle of the park's stone observatory, their bare and dangling legs kicking gaily in anticipation of the event.

I wondered if we ought to have met elsewhere to discuss our progress. But at least the thick crowd would assure us the anonymity we craved. Hardy had grown concerned that someone might be watching her abode these last days, and had taken to conducting all counsels in public.

That morning I had penned seven letters, in my most careful hand, each requesting patronage for the good office to which I owed allegiance, having already sent nearly thirty over the past few days. Though I could not find the binding ring to stamp them appropriately, no matter where I looked for it. I found this most troubling, indeed. I could only hope that it did not damage our efforts too extensively, or cause undue questions. I scarce liked to consider what Etherington should say to it.

I also received a number of missives, though few if any bore good news. One struck me as particularly strange, for it stated it was in reply to my own query. No matter that I was absolutely certain I had penned no such letter. What is more, I had no note of the sender, and nor had Etherington made mention of them upon her departure, and she was most fastidious in these matters. Neither did I recognise the foreign address, nor did I understand what the blast they were talking about. No matter how many times I read it. In the end, I stored it away, safely, with a frown, promising myself I should attend to it properly later, when time was available to me. I concluded that my mind was too befuddled, and time's passing should gift me clarity.

Seeing to this correspondence came before I performed what remained of my weekly chores amidst the wreckage: I meticulously calibrated and polished the optic lenses of the telescope and the microscopes and logged the daily barometric, celestial and navigational measurements within the brittle pages of the old ledger. While I sadly looked on to the place where the hydrographometer and harmoniser had stood.

Then, with displeasure, I dressed as quickly as was possible, slipping into a simple mustard gown in the current style, which I did not favour. It was one of the many the duchess had ordered be delivered to me in the oh-so-pretty bandboxes, overflowing with ribbons. For I understood that today was no day to draw either eye nor attention to my strange and eccentric proclivities. I followed this by the performance of my ablutions, working my wild snarls of hair into something approaching an acceptably modish style. Finally, I donned the simplest bonnet I could find, an item that was still, to my unrefined eyes at least, unfortunately conspicuous. Thus – equal parts flustered and refreshed – I walked briskly to the jarvey collection spot. Where I waited some half an hour for a driver to arrive and take me in his hire carriage to the park.

Once safely ensconced from the heat of the day within, I rehearsed the details of our plan, and the most vital developments I should have to relay to Hardy. I was acutely aware that I was now all but alone in the administration of our endeavour, and of the weight of responsibility that lay with that position.

I was keen to ensure I used every advantage to its fullest; I felt my mind was becoming more agitated with every passing day. Equally, I was concerned that any questions I might put forward would disquiet her. I was beginning to see that her unflappable façade was precisely that: a mask which concealed her true feelings from the world. Not to mention that I was, even now, still more than a little intimidated by the forthright noblewoman, despite our growing closeness.

And, if that were not sufficient reason to fret, I could not shake loose the unmistakable sensation that I had missed some essential element of preparation. There were so many details to retain control of. So many duties, each more important than the last. Worse, was that the lady had agreed to *my* plan. An obvious one, which could very well expose me for the simpleton I truly was. Never, had I been trusted with so much. It made me nervous in a way I had not experienced before, but I was also flushed with a restless excitement.

It was with these thoughts I was distracted when I arrived at the park and dismounted the creaking step of the coach. So much so that I was entirely unaware that the duchess herself had approached me on light feet, until she placed her slender hand upon my arm. She leant so close to me that I could almost taste the spicy cloves of her pomander. The close touch and broken etiquette startled me.

"Your grace," I said, unfurling an awkward curtsey. One which I was entirely grateful to make, for it allowed me a brief moment to attempt to hide my loss of composure.

Yet laughter greeted my alarm, a sound as rich and full as a strummed harp. And when I glanced up I saw that her presentation and bearing was likewise. She was as immaculately bedecked as always, but her garments were also playful.

She wore a neat yellow redingote, adorned with an abundance of matching ribbons. Her imperious face was powdered pale, in the old style, and she wore two taffeta beauty marks, one above her rosed cheek, a balloon, and the other below her neat lips, a fleeing horseman. Her smile was wide and full and gay, her expression a picture of delighted contentment. But her black eyes shone with the purpose of our meeting, and her gaze was steady.

She grasped my arm firmly again, and this time looped her own through it as if I were a wayward child. One who was to be given a tour of a fantastical exhibition, whether she willed it or not. Then she popped open a parasol, hitched it over her shoulder, and set off into the fuss and furore of the mustered many. The clamour of which provided a curious sense of both privacy and exposure.

"What a wonderful occasion," she said, glancing each way. "Don't you agree, dear niece?"

She spoke low and her eyes searched the throngs knowingly, but never did she alter her step, or let falter the perfect presentation of enjoyment from her face. She gently patted my hand with hers as she went. On occasion, she would raise it to point out a detail in the distance, or stop and gape in wonder and delight at a small side performance which had itself drawn a clapping crowd.

But our real discussion was conducted in whispered asides. I leant in as if we were exchanging gossip, and felt the heat of her breath tickle my inner ear.

"Have you received any reply?" she asked gently. "From the letters, I mean."

"From eight and twenty, twelve replies. Eight expressing deep sorrow, but in the negative. One tentative request for a report of future findings. Four outright rejections with requests not to solicit further. I sent more this morning."

"Oh. Damn and damnation," she said, and stretched her delighted smile further to mask her displeasure. "I do believe our fellow patriots, those noble representatives of our state with whom we find ourselves opposed, are more influential than we believed! And have grown bold. Perhaps there are a greater quantity of them than I suspected. This is something I shall have to ponder. I must confess my expectation was for a far fuller tally in our favour. Still, no matter. I am only sorry, child, that I have exposed you to such a fruitless scheme. Will you be able to forgive me?"

"Of course." I bowed my head. "I am only grateful to help."

"Good. Good. For not only do we need you to continue, we will need you to work even harder."

"Harder?" A murmur broke across the crowd, and I turned my head to blink away the dark shadows crowding my vision. The bright sun was quite at odds with the chaos of my mind.

"The truth is, the court is not as it was. Nor is the city. Sometimes I scarcely recognise either. Repeatedly, I have sensed my efforts being blocked. Our enemies are better resourced, and connected, than I had known. There was a time when I knew the tune of every piper. The gods know I paid a few to play! But things are shifting and they are shifting quickly, much more quickly than I had envisaged they might. Plans are put into place, daggers and pistols drawn. Something is mounting; I can sense it. If I've developed a sense all these years. And I certainly have."

Hardy paused to twinkle her fingers at some acquaintance before encouraging me to keep walking with a subtle nip of my arm. I jumped, afraid she might somehow feel or sense my changed flesh. Yet she was too distracted for any such thing.

"Every advantage we can win, we must. If we are to win outright. And we surely must win outright. The old gods only know how all of this will end. I feel they would have little mercy for us, were we to fail."

"What else can we do?" I practised smiling as I spoke but only managed to clench my teeth. I imagine I looked as peculiar as I sounded.

"We must be seen to be pressing, my girl. They must think us desperate, lost even. And in this way we must hope they stay from striking further, while we do all we must. Until we've won all we must."

A cheer from the crowd gathered around the fence suggested the main event may soon be under way; I could just see the top of the balloon as it was slowly inflated.

"Upon that important matter," Hardy continued, "What of our... mutual friend? Our curious brigadier who marshals no men?"

"I did as you suggested. Three letters have I written. We have entered into a correspondence," I said. "Yesterday; he replied almost immediately, though he seemed... somewhat preoccupied. Yet I know he craves attendance at the game; I'm sure of it. If I were to guess, I should say the invitation you have organised might suffice to draw him in."

Hardy nodded. I could tell that she was both pleased and making an effort to restrain herself from excitement, lest our ruse fail.

"Whether he will give it to me rather than Penelope, I surely couldn't say. That is entirely another question. Even Etherington wasn't completely sure she would be able to extract it from the peculiar man. And she holds near two hundred years of service to the office, the thing he is rumoured to respect perhaps the most."

"Yes. Quite. Well. We shall have to follow through with the details of our plan. Control the parts we can control. And hope the rest falls into place. For what else can we do?"

It seemed so wildly speculative to me, now we spoke of it plain. Surely it could not succeed? "So. I think he will meet us three days hence, if we continue to press him." I carried on, to break my mind from its tangle of despair.

"Good," she said trailing off. Her eyes grew suddenly distant, and we walked in silence for several steps. The heat of the sun beat down upon me.

Until I prompted her. "My grace?"

"Good." Hardy said, again, and was suddenly back. "We must move carefully, now. Another interloper was discovered at the estate. Crossing the Yin river. Barker, my groundsman, spotted him. He took shots at the man, as he fled. Yet the scoundrel's bag split, and his papers were recovered, sodden, from the stream. Though not sodden enough to prevent us taking the measure of some of them. They had been taking copies of my ledger, and more. We must assume our enemies have eyes upon us at all times."

"Have you heard any further word of the archivist?" I asked. Though I thought I perhaps knew the answer.

"No. Not a single damn thing. My man in Quom is silent, the tropics have fallen to foul storms and not a whisper has made it out to anyone." She let out a barely audible sigh. "There is more. My son may be good for little, but in this his service is impeccable. I had him ask around his usual haunts. If he is to waste away his hours with frippery, then we may as well put him to good use. Not a man at the exchange or any of the clubs has heard a single thing, from anyone at the front. Nor do they expect to."

Hardy's smile took on a pained quality for the briefest of moments, before she asked, "And what of the rest? How are your other preparations?"

I placed one gloved hand upon the cast iron railing — for we had circled to the edge of the park to gain a decent view and a little quiet — with the other I shielded my eyes from the bright glare of the sun to peer up at Merton's balloon, which had begun its ascent. The yellow and green fabric rippled gaily in the light breeze. Various rounds of sporadic applause and gasps had begun to emanate from the crowd around us.

"Did you know it contains four thousand gallons of inflammable air?" I heard from one erudite gentleman, dressed impeccably in as tidy a morning coat as I had ever seen, leaning on his cane. He brandished his eyeglass and spoke to a young pair of not-long-weds, judging by the bashfulness of their interactions with one another. They stretched up upon their toes to better take it in, heat rushing through their pale faces in excitement, rosing their cheeks.

As I watched them, Fenton appeared unbidden within my mind. Within the fancy of my imagination, his hand was proudly working his pumping contraption, a long hose linked to a varnished globe suspended for own his balloon experiment in the centre of his ample and transitory workshop, resplendent with gleaming mahogany. A workshop which had otherwise, until that most recent moment, been the Yellow Saloon of Banbury House. I recalled his father and maid's growing apathy and bewilderment at his antics. I wondered if he were on the meadow, in the throngs somewhere. I shook the thought free and turned my attention back to the duchess.

"Passably," I answered. "But it's scarce a secret I'm not an archivist's first yet. I'm barely even an assistant. Oh, I feel like nothing but a terrible charlatan, truth be told. I don't see how I can ever become such a thing. I so wish Archivist Etherington were here. Or even that there was someone else who understood what we were trying to do."

Hardy murmured sympathetically. We stood side by side, among the crowd whose cries of delight and wonder quite drowned out my worries.

"My training was not approaching complete," I continued. "My knowledge is so limited. I find myself ignorant often. I just know she would know what to do. And save me the endless visits to the libraries, or the archives. And there's so much that neither of us understand." I suddenly felt close to tears.

"D-do you really think it will work? If we can prove it, that Sentinels *have* returned, that she's been truthful all along... Do you think it will stay their hand? They seem so vicious, the attacks so coordinated..."

"Oh. They are interested, and watching." Hardy said to me. "Even if they don't show it. Whether they want to do away with the office or not. It's been a long time since Sentinels have walked among us. That's valuable information. Any fool can see that. For all their protestations to the contrary, they'll be intrigued, at the very least. If only to steal a march on the other legion of plotters and prospectors. Fortunes will be won and lost, not to mention reputations. Any that show disinterest, are lying. Or dunces."

We stopped briefly to converse with the Marques Lynch and his niece, on the subject of Allsop's extended closure for repairs, and to pet her small, curious lap hound. Everyone roundly agreed that Allsop's closure was a thoroughly disagreeable affair; in contrast, the hound was the most delightful creature imaginable. I found the young lady to be clutter-brained, but in a likeable fashion. And found myself wishing I could be friends with her. Though my mind was so full with our other concerns that my own chatter was more stilted and halting than ever.

When they disappeared into the thick crowds, Hardy continued as if we had never been interrupted. "At the least, it will buy us time. At the best? Draw out an enhanced settlement we can really work with. The rest we can plan for when it is in front of us."

We went over and over again each of the members that we expected to attend the parliamentary debate for the terrible bill, and would stand in our judgement. As well as those who held influence, but would likely not be present. Until I was dizzy with the memory of them.

Many I knew from my studies and Etherington's patient instruction, as well as chatter and journal. Others, I knew not at all.

Hardy instructed me who to greet, and who to ignore at the upcoming occasions she had arranged to press our case. She forced me to recite their names, and their predilections as the gathered crowd watched the balloon float higher and higher and travel further and further away.

The day's light faded. Then, just as I was beginning to feel as though I may faint from sheer exhaustion — not to mention hunger — she plucked up her pocket watch and inspected it closely.

"Drat," she said. "I am expected at the palace tonight. This will have to suffice. But come along. I will have my man take you home."

With that I was deposited at our lodgings where a long night of consternation awaited me.

Long after I had retired to my bedchamber, I found it impossible to sleep as my mind whirled with all I must know and do and remember. I rose when the moon was high, and quietly lit a solitary candle. I drew out my make-shift, sham Sentinel's Gambit cards, and my commonplace book. With my lips silently working, I memorised the movements of the game, as Sergeant Belfry had patiently instructed me.

Chapter Twenty-Three

SENTINEL'S GAMBIT

'Hacktonsfield': Man-o-War, fourth rate, 423 men, 50 guns
Bound for the front upon the thirteenth
'Victorious': frigate, third rate, 504 men, 64 guns
Bound for the front upon the eighteenth
'Foxglove Hill': packetship, unrated, privateer, 50 men, 6 guns
Bound for Glice then onward to Murmesseril upon the twenty-first
'Sallow Fall': sloop, unrated, 96 men, 16 guns
Bound for Melt Island upon the twenty-second

'Of Ships, Manifests, & Destinations,' Shay Bluefaltlow

The day itself arrived.

That morning I checked and double checked the atmosphere for the taint of scent song with the sole field resonator that remained to us; the oldest and most arcane had been left unmolested, perhaps presumed defunct by our adversaries. For that we had to count ourselves grateful, Etherington had reminded me before she left.

I slathered the bledmettle needle with the amplifying fluid, pressed my thumb to the brass harmonic plate, and rendered the harmonics in notation half a dozen times. I walked from the dockyards to the Foundling Hospital, from beneath Hangman's Bridge to Upperton Row, hoping the physical exertion might distract my disquiet mind.

I did as much as I could without taking a full draught of the tincture; I dare not risk falling deep into the ague, given the gravity of my task the coming evening. I had begun to feel quite strange enough; now a constant chattering followed me, whereether I went. It was not unlike the foul taint of the ague tincture, in certain ways, except, increasingly concerningly, it did not fade.

The black blemishes upon my upper arms had continued to grow in size and quantity. The strangest pattern was emerging among them, reminiscent of a whirling forest.

I wondered if Etherington was experiencing the same, and wished very much to speak directly to her on the subject. Since the peculiarities had begun, I had taken some moments to consult the varied old tomes in our libraries on the subject of the Seekers. Yet the simple truth was that I could understand little of what I read; and what I could understand left me more confused and frightened than if I had read nothing at all.

At strange times I also fell into what I could only describe as some form of waking and stupefying dream. Similar to the occasion when I had stood with Fenton within the archive. All sounds would fade around me, and the purest note of the strangest sensation, one I have never felt before and have no words for, overcame me. Yet it was not unpleasant, only excessively, excessively strong. So strong it left no room for other thoughts, or sensations, of any variety. Indeed, it was so peculiarly calm that I almost craved it, and found myself pondering it, often.

Aside from this, there was enough of the essence of the tincture within me from my frequent indulgences that I could taste what was clear. Such words are not wholly appropriate, I hasten to add, for I did not *taste* it quite in the way one might understand. But the scent song was deafening, though without sound, and of incredible intensity; more disorientating than ever, though also conflicting. It took me much time to transcribe in notation my findings; the vast, spidery glyphs filled ever more pages, and grew ever larger and darker to register the strength of their harmonics, such was the manner of the notation.

Amongst all these, the incredible trail of our particular bounty filled the spaces such that one would think there was no room for any other. And yet it *had* faded somewhat from our earlier and first discovery. What this might mean for our desperate requirement to take evidence of the beast, I dare not guess. Yet it concerned me as I continued my preparations for the gaming hell. The other signatures remained as shrill and numerous as they had been these recent days.

I had to hope we would acquire the necessary luring substance, whatever it was, that evening, in time to attempt the sighting myself. While difficult, I was grateful that the possibility was still somewhat alive. It was hard to believe we had brought the plan to this stage. For that, I could hold my head high. Even amongst my now constant terror.

I thought of Penelope, and her anger, often. But when I did, I reminded myself of Ridley's words: I was, indeed, determined to do whatever I may to redeem our situation, and her favour. And if I did not? Why, I believed I was doing everything in my power and, at the least, could rest easy on that mark, no matter how I might be cast out. So I soothed myself, at least.

I tried not to think of any climbing that might be required in the coming pursuit of the great Sentinel. Whether it be upon the roof of a building, or atop a cliff-face, or some other as-yet-unimagined structure. Despite my determination to do whatever I must, I knew that would be a measure that may unman the entire endeavour.

I spent an inordinate amount of time in the shipyard district. Once more, I had frequented the shipping offices, and the great exchange, and the coffee shops of Pound Street. I had talked to the shipping agents, bribed the cabin boys and eavesdropped on the pursers. I returned to the methods I had employed so many months ago while planning my escape, acquiring a comprehensive knowledge of perhaps each and every ship due to sail to any place, within six leagues, where I believed the great Sentinel Velspritt could, potentially, be located. Finding the creature would not be a simple task, for even an experienced archivist, but it had to be done. With or without the lure.

I had scratched every detail in the rag paper of my commonplace book, in my neatest hand, and studied them until my eyes were dry and bleary. Indeed, my fingers were long chapped with the descending cold and the combined efforts of our ploy. The great map of the Whispering Coast had been my companion those lengthening summer nights and days; the log boards and traverse tables and moon charts once more my assistants.

To each route, I had developed a plan sufficient to win aboard the ship. Some included what small quantity of coin I had stored within my drawer. Others a gentleman's agreement with an agent with whom I was familiar. When I ran out of money, I considered approaching Hardy for more, but time was too short; I was mindful that she had warned me to be wary of watchers and to limit our contact as much as possible. I wished to do nothing that should risk our plan.

Near all potential shipping routes, alas, were more speculative than I was comfortable with. They each required some element of chance. Not to speak of ignorance of our scheme or any interference from our enemies. Or, indeed, lack of disruption of the type the war had rendered most frequent. None of these things I could reasonably bank upon. But it was the best I could do, and I was grateful that a passage to success still seemed a possibility. I was determined that, if any such possibility remained, I should find a way to achieve it, somehow. This much I owed to Etherington, to Peck, and Ridley. To everyone who had offered me their trust.

As for the gaming hell itself? Well, I would never feel truly comfortable in such an environment. But at least Brigadier General Lice had agreed to meet there. That much, at least, we had won.

These considerations ran through my mind as I greedily added another scoop of coals to the fire and sat, warming my hands and pinching my leg in turns. My archivist's supplies had been packed and repacked three times. And the urge to repack a third or fourth time I pressed down with all the strength I could muster. Instead, the afternoon before the event, I took on some of the usual tasks of the office. Or at least I had attempted to, for I struggled to make myself concentrate on anything so mundane.

Bitter sips of boiled coffee grounds did little to settle my stomach, or my nerves, and my mind was muddled. Such that, when the timepiece began its dull clanging of two in the afternoon, I had clear forgotten one of my most important duties. Thirskton, the palace's courier, had attended upon this day, twice per lunar cycle, for all of forty years, to take the chief archivist's accountancy of Sentinel activities to the palace.

Thirkston nodded and bent himself into our office, rubbing his small hands together in his nervous manner. That I was not concerned with the base task of submitting the accountancy, but rather too flustered to handle the task regardless, spoke well to the fevered state of my constitution.

I scarcely could offer the regular courtesies which he was assuredly owed. Muttering incoherently, I gingerly plucked the documents together into a pile to pass to him. Before they tumbled from my grasp as I dropped them with a great thudding flutter.

I wished to speak with Peck, to take a moment from my troubles and share simply in his company. Yet he was entirely absent in a manner which was most unlike him. I wondered, briefly, at his absence — his shoes were missing from the hearth, a sure sign he was out of doors — but could scarcely spare the moments to work myself into a real fret. Still, I spent the little time I had spare in checking his most favoured spaces.

He was not to be found on the rooftop of the gunsmiths, or in the alley next to his favoured costermonger. Neither was he spying on the refiners of that most delightful cocoa, or wandering by the playhouses, seeking out the oyster carts.

I resigned myself to his non-appearance; he often became poorly in the cooler days and, as I knew Ridley would not have sent him on an errand in such weather, considered it possible the surgeon had taken him with him in pursuit of some remedy or other.

I made a promise to myself that, when all was said and done, I would lavish a suitable amount of attention upon my little and most dear friend.

***

The gaming tables were full, the evening's most anticipated showing of Sentinel's Gambit soon to be underway.

I keenly observed those around me. All the while ignoring the itching under the restricting embrace of the excessive fabric of my shift, my stays and my dinner gown. In combination, the garments I had used to cover up my shame. I refused to think of the strange protrusions, beyond the practicalities of covering them from sight.

The dealer wore black silk gloves. He was brisk and efficient in the deposition of his duty. He picked up both genuine decks, worth the value of some Fivedock streets, and dealt four cards from each. In a fluid and well-practised motion, he drew each in turn. He turned them over to the players and onlookers with exaggerated slowness. So that each partici- pant and onlooker could confirm the veracity of the deck. Before, with a delightfully deft flick of the hand that drew a gasp, he turned and then shuffled them together.

To my left, a dashing sharp leant in close to whisper in his companion's ear. To my right, the other player stayed fastidiously still. A large group had gathered around the table, pressed in close; the game was about to begin. I noticed the young dodderbrain from the park, the marquis' niece, who nodded to me. She took neat little sips of some jewel-bright con- coction from a heavy crystal glass, and I permitted myself a little wave to her.

Periodically, the Brigadier General plucked up his quizzing glass from its hanging cord, and peered at the cards happily. He appeared as comfortable and content as if he were in his own parlour, while I did my best to disguise my wriggles of discomfort as the bristlings of excitement.

Which was when I spotted him across the room, Anton Grent; I had known it was a possibility one of their set could attend, and interfere. I bit off a curse under my breath, and aimed a wayward smile at our enemy who I found met my eyes. His cane was tucked under one arm, the elegantly carved bronze head gleaming in the honeyed candlelight. His waistcoat set him off to the very best advantage, two golden fobs hanging from it.

He lingered to chatter quickly with an excessively pretty, plump little thing well known about town and society. And then he kept coming, and stopped when he was before us. I briefly considered ignoring him.

He gave both of us a formal bow, and then gestured to take my hand, which I reluctantly proffered to him. He touched it to his perfect lips, brushing them across my fingers. I shook off a little shiver.

"Assistant archivist," he said, his voice thrumming, silky and rich as velvet. And then he turned to my guest. "Brigadier Lice. A pleasure, again. I trust the office has been taking care of you?"

On his third finger was something from which I could not take my eyes. Something which forced me to suppress a gasp. A dull beast glowing faintly in the amber light. It was the signet of the archival offices, the one Etherington only removed when she left the city.

"Oh yes," Lice said.

"Well. I believe the main game is about to begin. If you will excuse me?" Lord Grent continued.

I inclined my head to him politely as he strode confidently away to his own seat, and his awaiting gaggle of hangers on.

"I have been meaning to say to you... I was, really, more than pleased to help once I received the communication from your office." Lice slipped a letter from the inside pocket of his topcoat and waved it merrily in my direction. The seal upon it I knew immediately. As well as I knew the empty spot where it once had lived, within the archivist's study. Just as I had recognised it upon the man's finger. The script upon the letter, though, was neither Etherington's solid hand, nor my own.

The complete truth of Fenton's betrayal was clear to me.

"Your request was one with which I was most happy to comply and, though I am of course very grateful and appreciative, the gifts were quite unnecessary. Indeed, I could not understand why you were so very… formal in your invitation to meet me this evening, when we had already agreed to help you. And then it became clear to me. It is a matter of decorum. The old Concordian charm, eh? Well. It would please me if you would, henceforth, consider us friends."

I tried to mask my bafflement as best as I was able, as fear took icy control of me. "Of course," I said, thinking as quickly as I possibly could. "And who was it from our office who communicated with you? Only, there has been some confusion of late. We have had an awfully disruptive season."

"Oh. Why, but you should have said!" He inclined his head. "Yes. Certainly you knew that your compatriot had been in touch with us for many weeks now. A most charming gentleman, and truly a credit to your office and state. I'm sure you will agree with me. I – I thought he had told you. Certainly he indicated that he had. When I received your invitation. Or. Perhaps. Why? If I am mistaken…" Now he dabbed at his watery eyes, and neatened out his little waistcoat.

"He has?" I whispered, with a terrible sinking sensation descending through my gut. Horror coursed through me. Horror at my stupidity. Horror at the obviousness of the folly.

"We delivered the substance to him three weeks gone," he hissed out of the corner of his mouth. "I presumed that you would speak amongst yourselves. It *is* a terribly fascinating development. Really, we are only too happy to share it. Between ourselves, I quite relish finding others who would appreciate the discovery appropriately. The large ones you speak of will already have been lured away, as your office requested.

"When we discovered the capacity we put it to use immediately. As much as we respect the old ones, they were causing significant expense and disruption in our most far flung interests. At the worst time of year, what with the trader's bounty being due.

"It is a truly incredible sight. I implore you to experience it yourself as soon as the opportunity permits.

"Tell me. Is it common amongst you Concord folk. Perhaps a cultural difference? A specialisation, if you will? I find I am forever misunderstanding your forward ways. I hope you will forgive me. One does not like to pry."

I waved him away. "Why. Yes. Our ways often confuse guests. I myself was once—" for the deciding round was about to proceed.

"Well. Tonight truly has been marvellous," were the last words he muttered to me, as he took a long cigarillo, placed it into his lips and allowed a club man to light it. Then he leaned back in his seat, happily expelling little puffs of the earthy tabac. His eyes were intent upon the game.

"Quiet all. If you please," the dealer said clearly.

The excited chatter fell to a low and insistent hum, a buzzing of palpable tension from every possible direction. One that forced the hairs upon the back of my neck to stand on end.

"Stakes at quadruple, Pikes and Muskets trump, all Sentinels in, all loose," said the dealer, knocking once and twice upon the green baize of the gaming table. "Bound now, bound then, bound forever."

The dealer met the eye of each remaining player, waiting until a firm nod of assent was delivered, before he clearly enunciated the final words to start the round:

"Sudden death."

Chapter Twenty-Four

ALL IN

I record here what I unfortunately understand of the demise of the boy who was my charge for the ten summers of his short life.

He was beaten, relentlessly. His little face pallid beneath the ugly yellow, greens and browns of the bruises inflicted during the assault. On Bickham Place, I found his small body, curled up, swollen, and sodden from the extended summer rains.

From these truths I feel it is safe to presume that he lay in the elements for a number of days.

That he was outside at all in the storm went against my very strictest counselling. I believe he gained wind, somehow, of the difficulties of my master and other charge, and decided he should attempt to help. For the location in which he was discovered, two streets on from member Arksthrotle's office, was certainly far farther than he would be expected to roam.

It is my belief that someone — or several individuals — attempted to gain answers from him as to the whereabouts and business of the archivist and that, when no answer was forthcoming thanks to his deafness, they set about him with a great ferocity. It is my hope that the boy's consumption stole the last of his breath, before the more brutish injuries were visited upon him.

The next morning I carefully cleansed and dressed the child and laid him to rest, in the manner of Ra and the old gods, as is proper.

I record his name here, and elsewhere, so that he may be remembered.

Master Peck Fassinger.

Ridley Fassinger, Surgeon of Fivedock

I found Ridley on a call, having asked for him at the Foundling Hospital. It was a small home, of one Freeman Baker; a very successful, though somewhat taciturn, buckram stiffener. His home was located in the old town of the Draper's district. His ailment was blood poisoning, of the finger, possibly hand and perhaps even, the gods forbid, his arm. A nervous shrew of what I presumed was a wife, wrapped so heavily in shawls that she almost disappeared beneath the fabric, answered the door to me and reluctantly led me into a modest room. As though she had no other choice.

The ceiling was low, the plaster flaking from the walls. Yet the chairs were good, the table stout and a tea set of significant quality lay in readiness beside a well-polished candelabra. A fine walnut bureau sat in a corner, crowned with an elegant vase of dried flowers.

She bade me sit at the table and offered me tea. When I refused she apologised for leaving me but said she had much to do. I sprang to my feet as soon as I was left alone and paced the room until Ridley appeared.

The place was so quiet that, when he began to descend, Ridley's steps were thunderous as he climbed down the narrow staircase.

"Better to lose a single finger, good woman, than his life," he said to Mrs Baker brusquely when she scurried out from wherever she had been. He placed down two little bottles on the table, while talking over his shoulder. "Laudanum, and tincture of white willow bark. Be sure he takes both, morning and night. And that he rests, as well as he is able. He may take supper. The best you can manage."

She nodded and I suddenly realised she was upset; what I had taken for rudeness had merely been fear. I cursed myself for not offering to make the poor woman a drink of some variety.

"His fever may break, if the old gods will it. If it does not, you must seek me out before the sun sets three days hence." She nodded, sniffing, and sprang to the stairs to see the convalescent for herself.

"Shay," Ridley said, wiping the sweat from his brow with an old rag. His hands were darkened with blood. The stench reached me. "Speak, then. Why do you find me today where I've asked you never to?"

He packed away his surgeon's wear and snapped closed the lid of his apothecary case. He had his old steel flask of rank brandy, which he carried for his patients, in his hand. The battered thing that had been with him from his service days. He surprised me then by bringing it to his lips and taking a long slug. I had never seen him act in such a manner. There was something new in his deep brown eyes. Something dangerous.

I had returned from the disaster at Hoodle's, shocked and disconsolate, to empty lodgings. As the final games played out, I had felt the heat of Grent's eyes upon me. All the while my mind had run rampant. If they had breached the trust of Lice, what else had they achieved? Lice had said the Sentinels were likely to be sent to the front. Was Penelope in a much greater danger than we had envisaged? There was more here, I was certain of it. More that I absolutely must discover.

"Where's Peck? And what of you? Where were you last night?"

"I was needed at the hospital; I am sorry I could not leave word, it—"

"And Peck? I haven't seen him in what must be days, almost; I know he has been out. It is so strange. Have you sent him off on an errand? Where is he?"

Ridley shrugged on his topcoat and called out his farewell. He opened the front door and ushered me into the street. I raised my voice.

"Well? Is he unwell?"

"No, Shay. No, he's not unwell." Ridley walked briskly away, his long strides eating up the ground as they had so long ago, that day I had met him. I struggled to keep up with him.

"Then where is he? Have you… have you sent him away? Did… if he has done wrong, then you should know that it was at *my* behest, or at least by my influence. I never did understand why… I don't think that you—"

"Shay." Ridley whirled around to face me, his eyes forbidding. "Please. You know that… I was honest with you, about his… Oh, Shay." Suddenly a deep foreboding awoke within me, and I shook my head, *no*, to a question I had not been asked.

"I cannot be certain but I think that perhaps his… his breath failed him. He… Peck is no longer with us, Shay. He's dead."

***

For the price of three Concord pennies, I rowed a cheap dory out to the gritty shore of Netson Island. To the location I had most suspected to be a starting point for our search. Here, amongst the jagged granite of the cliffs, and the wheeling gulls, I performed the duty I knew I must.

With the harmoniser held aloft and my thumb pressed firmly to it, I confirmed all that I had feared; the distinctive signature was now almost completely absent. The great Sentinel had indeed been lured away. I slowly lowered myself down to the pebbly sand, not caring for the wetness that met my behind. My chest gently shook as I allowed myself to sob.

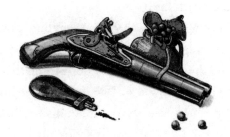

Part Four

FURIOUS
ENDEAVOUR

Chapter Twenty-Five

BLUE'S CHOCOLATE
& COFFEE HOUSE

The harvesting of the Groves is a violent, deadly business, best suited to violent, vulgar men.

I propose you round up undesirables, as many as might be easily located. Empty the cells, the gaols, and the gutters if need be. Despatch them promptly with a commission from the fellow whom I introduced upon my last visit to the colonies. He can be trusted. He knows well the routes and his rates reflect his capacity to limit unnecessary expenditure.

One of those beastly natives will no doubt prove an apt guide for the business you must attend to. I can provide a contact familiar with their ways if you so wish.

As for what wonders and strangeness the brutes may find at their journey's end, and have so scandalised the palace: I say that they are welcome to them, sir. And may the old gods deliver them their succour.

Letter from the Count Agraham, First Son of the Ivy Line, to Goodman Bransin, Free Gentleman of Murmesseril. The Year Two, Five Hundred Since the Signing of the Great Concord of Westerbrook

I felt Peck's absence in our lodgings so acutely that the place became unbearable to me. I also felt I could not face Ridley. It did not seem that this reality could be the truth. Indeed, I angrily denied it. I cycled quickly between the fiercest anger, the greatest despondency, and the jarring sense of an awful reality that simply could not be, but somehow was. Striking, sudden and implacable.

I penned Ridley a simple missive, reassuring him that I was well. I did not tell him that I had gone to the archives, for I did not wish to be pursued. I promised myself I should deal with him properly in good time, and yet how I should do that, I held no real plan for, nor did I truly believe I ever would. Such were the contradictions of my outlook, on this matter and many others.

I took a small collection of garments, ill thought out and hurriedly collected.

Once I arrived at the offices, I realised there was little for me to do. I tried to bury myself in work, to bathe myself in it, in the hope it might wash away my thoughts. Yet it did not. It only made them clearer.

I ate scarcely, with little relish, purchasing food only from the street vendors closest to the building.

Occasionally, I considered going somewhere else, or speaking with my friends. Yet I soon discarded the idea. Belfry had long set sail for the front with the rest of the fleet and his squadron. The other clerks and officers of the admiralty either sensed my need for solitude or were unaware I had ensconced myself within the archives. They left me to my peace.

I was interrupted while I worked at the old field harmoniser on my third morning by a heavy knock at the door; I jumped in surprise. A footman bowed politely when I opened the door and proffered a card he insisted must be delivered into my hand. I opened the thick cream paper and read:

I require your attendance this evening to discuss a most important matter. There are things I must tell you. Six o'clock, Blue's Chocolate and Coffee House off Foxglove Lane.

235

You will be expected. I shall await you with anticipation in the
subscription room.

The card has been sealed with red wax imprinted with the letter H. I wondered at the formality of the invitation and what it might mean. Almost, I shrugged it off, and did not attend. Almost.

That afternoon I washed my face with lukewarm water and dressed myself as well as I could from the modest collection of clothing I had brought with me. I decided to don the uniform I'd adopted for daily wear to the office, a sort of lesser version of the full dress I would wear if I ever became an archivist proper. My best white shirt, black breeches and tall boots, with the foxglove pin Hardy had gifted me on the breast. I spent several moments brushing my tiresome hair, regarding my reflection in the glass for the longest time since the evening of the ball.

Blue's was not a place I had ever visited; it was an extremely exclusive club, one where I imagined every patron would be dressed in the very latest mode and in the finest fabrics. This fact only served to further unsettle me. Not only was I troubled by the terrible news I had received, but also by the physical discomfort I felt.

The searingly hot day, one in a long series of searingly hot days, possessed a heat of a particularly savage variety, and the streets were particularly thronged. To this crowd of people another may be added: fat flies hovered everywhere, in great clusters upon the jarvey's coach panels, upon the horse dung, and upon the beasts themselves. Yet even these seemed rendered lazy by the heat.

If one hoped to find relief in the falling of the evening's coolness, then one was set to be disappointed. For it seemed the cobbles and the tiles and the oaks of Fivedock had soaked up the heat with the capacity of a sea sponge, and now released it into the miasmic air leaving no place where one might hide.

236

To all of this was added the rich, yeasty scent of hops, for two large merchantmen had just returned to the city, laden from hold to deck with the crop, which had been despatched to the great brewing houses. Now the scent permeated everywhere, at every hour. The mail coaches rattled by, to the great bother of the mailmen, their horses, and the folk who wandered before them.

Within the club, my mood was not to be improved. For I discovered it was not merely Hardy I was due to meet; I had been invited to a small conference. Across from the duchess sat Bamcroft, as well as Fassinger. These details I noticed with a steadily sinking stomach, Ridley's presence in particular. I did not know that they were even known to one another, let alone that they might all appear here together.

They were seated at a table within a large and well appointed room of immaculate, precise proportions, and the classical styling of the ancients. Such was the calling card of this most exclusive establishment, with the great rugs, enormous chandeliers, and vast curtains of its subscription rooms.

Ridley had done his absolute best to improve his demeanour, dressed as well as I had ever seen him. And yet he sat awkwardly in all the finery, and I found myself considering that his regular attire was much more to his advantage. He peered downward, a long-stemmed pipe gripped tightly within his teeth, puffing pensively as he worked his substantial lips around the stem. The tabac, different from his usual, smelled similar to the varieties a certain set of dandies and sharps had taken to — imported from Ertrie or some such of the newer colonies — and was richly pungent with a spicy tang that lingered. This, I attributed as a gift from Hardy. Her knowing smirk and nod as I sat furnished me with confirmation of my suspicion.

Bamcroft was, likewise, dressed in a manner unusual for him. His cream pantalooned legs were spread akimbo, tall top boots planted firmly so as to ground his important endeavour, his softly upholstered seat thrust back from the table. Within his grasp, upon the bulging and worsted fabric of the waistcoat which contained his ample midriff, sat a small notation book.

I snatched a glance at it as I seated myself across from him. Though it was partially obscured by his carefully working paw, I could make out several curious diagrams, and a number of tallies in a large, angular hand. I was ever so tempted to attempt a second glimpse, possibilities wheeling away from me. Instead I seated myself and he grunted an acknowledgement to me. Then he gently folded the book closed, pulled his chair to the table, and raised his hand to wave over a club man.

With a raised eyebrow and a wry smile, Hardy promptly made to acquire the promised supper. She ordered for me, clearly familiar with both man and option. He awaited my brief nod of assent, but I uttered not a word.

Questions writhed within me, but I controlled myself as best as I was able. The rest of the members in the club made a gentle hubbub in the background, soft and regular as the rise and fall of the harbour waves.

The meal arrived quickly and tasted exquisite. None spoke while we ate and I was glad I could focus on the food; I realised that Hardy, Ridley and Bamcroft were as famished as I, and that the past days had been difficult for all of us. Despite my hunger I felt unable to manage more than a few mouthfuls and caught Ridley glancing at my plate with suspicion.

I felt the sudden intensity of Hardy's inspection, and I questioned my choice of dress for not the first time. As was wont to happen at the most inopportune moments, I felt a flush suffuse my cheeks. And I took a larger than intended quaff of the dry wine to hide my embarrassment. Then spluttered as my throat spasmed awkwardly.

As our plates were cleared away with a flourish, Hardy summoned brandy for Ridley and Bamcroft and tea for ourselves.

"And cake, too. The selection, if you'd be so kind."

Ridley created a wall of smoke between himself and the rest of us, his pipe hardly leaving his lips. Bamcroft consulted his notebook, a soporific look in his eyes. When the club man returned it was with a trolley carrying many small, china dishes piled high with cake of every kind: fruit cake with marzipan; apple and cherry sponge; spiced gingerbread studded with dried cranberries; honey cakes; lemon sponge; plum cake. There were even slices of raspberry tart.

Before I could decline, Hardy herself served me a small piece of lemon sponge as the club man poured our tea and the men helped themselves to the decanter of brandy. She waited until he retreated before she spoke in a low, clear voice.

"I have received grave information. Dire news. I am awaiting confirmation on some of... the details. In the meantime, I would have you all provide everything you know." She turned to Bamcroft first.

"I thank you for attending my summons at such short notice. Please, tell the others what you told me earlier." He looked up, nervously, and nodded to the duchess; he clearly held her in the greatest awe.

"Well. They started coming down the shipyard. Months back, truth be told. At first we didn't know what to make of it, if anything."

"Who did?"

"Well, that's the thing; I didn't know, at first. I sent Bennet, my yard man, out to speak to them. He's a good man. Sharp eyes. They said they were acting under the watch of Member Arksthrotle and the sea lords. It was always the same inspectors, from house Grent. They were not in their livery, which struck me as strange. But they travelled in their coaches, which I recognised. Quite often with the young master Grent, the right handsome one, at the head. Him I knew regardless. They demanded, each time, to know everything. How many ships, and when they should be ready."

I was temporarily distracted from my discomfort while I leaned in to listen. I had not been aware of this but it explained Bamcroft's increasing weariness of late.

"We began to hear whispers of the plan to beat the republican boys and that we should prepare the fleet. They arrived at dawn and demanded this time to see the plans we held for each ship, as well as a list of victuals. The young master Grent looked foxed, as if he'd been up drinking into the night. Everyone knows he's got a taste for the hells, and the liquor. He berated his man outside with a particular savagery. We've all heard he has a fierce tongue. This was my first time to witness it. The man's beyond cruel."

Ridley spoke for the first time. "What did you do?"

"We handed over the plans. What else could we do? Russell's ship, they wished to know most about. The day before the fleet set sail. They came aboard. I watched them as well as I was able."

"You could do nothing other," Hardy said encouragingly.

"Two didn't leave. They stowed aboard, I am certain of it."

Hardy tutted at this but no one spoke for some moments. Then she turned to me. "Now. Shay. Tell us what you can of the great Sentinel your office has warned the city of."

I did as I was instructed. I leant my elbows on the table, massaging my temples as I spoke. The small amount of food I had eaten had done little to revive me. Instead, it sat heavily. All of me felt heavy and I wished I could lie down.

"I rowed out to Netson Island, four days ago. We've seen… I mean, we've been tracking him for months. The harmonics should have been incredibly strong there. We are certain he was nearby. And that was always the strong-est point outside the city. But… no. It was faint, the song. Almost gone altogether."

A page bustled through the door. With a nod to the club man he hur-ried up to our table. He gave a deep bow to Hardy as he proffered her a missive. She thanked him warmly, and dismissed him. No, he should not wait for her reply. She opened it and read, but did not otherwise interrupt me. She nodded, encouraging me to continue, but I was quite spent. I shook my head.

"So we begin to piece together the puzzle," Hardy said quietly. "There is worse," she went on, her voice rising suddenly and sharply above the increasing din of the subscription room. "I have lost my seat on the trade rights committee. I was informed this morning. I need remind no one that I have been chair for thirty-six years."

Bamcroft, gave a whistle. The decanter of brandy had depleted considerably and his eyes were increasingly reddened. Ridley only shook his head sadly, his fingers massaging his temples.

"It appears our enemies make their move." Hardy said. Now she waved the letter in her hand. "I have confirmation of it, now. The blackest actions. Treachery of such variety it steals the breath. They must be certain of victory, to act so."

I began to shiver; Bamcroft raised an eyebrow at me and I worked my hand beneath my legs to stay the shakes.

"Member Arksthrotle intends that the Thirteenth and Eleventh fleets should fail. I have a... whiddler, I suppose. A woman on his staff. I only acquired her services recently, and at considerable cost. I am almost certain of the veracity of this knowledge."

Hardy looked as discomposed as ever I had seen her. Beneath the smooth powder she favoured, she was blotched. The merry bell of her voice faltered and she spoke almost in a whisper.

"They are in league with the Grand Republic. Your Sentinel, Shay, has been lured away, for not one purpose, but two. Not only shall they seal the fate of the archivist's office — suggesting that Etherington's warning of danger was a mistake, or a lie — it shall also seal the fate of our fair navy."

"What do you mean?" Bamcroft served himself and Ridley more brandy before sloshing some into Hardy's teacup. I waited for her admonishment of this flagrant breaching of decorum, but she tossed back the drink smartly, before she went on, tapping her cup for another serving.

"It is to be used in battle. Amongst other such creatures. Though exactly *how* I struggle to say. Penelo— our good archivist, is waltzing directly into our combined downfall."

"How can it be so?" Bamcroft said. His eyes had grown wide, "It is rank treachery. Treason! We must take it to the highest office!"

"No," Hardy interjected. Her voice was calm, but her expression had grown awfully fierce. She looked at each of us in turn. "I do not trust that we would

241

survive if we did so. I leave no limit to the allies they have rallied to their cause. No limit. My removal from the counsel teaches us this lesson, most plainly. We would be poor students were we to fail to learn it."

"So. They plan to do away with our boys? But why damage our own standing? To what purpose?" Ridley interjected.

"So they may seem to rescue us." Hardy said. "Or something of that fashion. It is nothing short of a coup." She turned to me. "Now. Shay. You have been hiding other... details, have you not? I have spoken with Etherington. You need mask your torment no longer. Ever since I saw you that day, a few months ago when we met for tea, I pressed the lieutenant. She never could tell a lie to me, that woman. Now. Don't be concerned. You stand with friends, here."

"I... I don't know."

"Yes, you do," Ridley said. His voice was full of kindness. Kindness so unexpected I nearly choked. I did not want it. And that made it worse.

"What can we do for Penelope?" I asked. "A letter will never get there in time and even if it did, it would probably be intercepted. What will they do to her?"

"I don't know, Shay," Hardy answered steadily. "She's leagues away."

"We have no way to reach her — no ship, nothing!"

"Bamcroft." Hardy said. "Is it possible?"

The shivering now became unbearable. It started in my head, a sharp jolt, which worked its way down my limbs. I shook far worse than I ever had from simple cold, no matter how extreme. I wrapped my arms around myself to stop the judders.

Ridley looked up. "There must be a way. We must be able to reach them, somehow. They would find a way. Russell and Penelope both."

"Yes. Quite. Russell's a good man. No one braver or more proper that I know. However peculiar he might be sometimes."

"Through the bled is the only route that should in any way answer," Bamcroft said. He looked up at me suddenly, his eyes pinning me to my seat. I didn't understand at first, but the look was a question.

"No!" I said. "I'm no archivist! I could not get us through the bled!"

"Well." Hardy said. "Is it possible?"

Bamcroft spoke slowly, took a deep draught of his brandy. "It can be done. But it's awful risky."

I realised they were all looking at me now. It was Hardy who spoke. Ridley was scowling at her.

"Will you be able to hold yourself together for the journey, Shay?"

I could scarcely hear what she said, the ringing was so fierce. I felt the strangest sensation from within the flesh of my shoulders, then my arms. A writhing as if worms were burrowing out of me. At that moment a wave of the fiercest sickness washed over me, and I vomited onto the table.

Chapter Twenty-Six

A DESPERATE FLIGHT

There is no known cure for saddle sore. Though for the desperate, fellwort —
having an affinity for foulness — may be employed. A pound of which should
be had for no more than two Concord pennies at any good market across the
Great House territories, particularly the eastern counties. Alongside this,
one may pummel herringbark until the tough fibres break down, leaving a
pungent and viscous substance. Once the fibrous tangles have been carefully
removed, this must be mixed with two parts of the former. The resulting poul-
tice should be used before two nights have passed. The application will draw
a fraction of the ill humour through the skin, providing a modicum of relief.

The better cure is time, practice and humility. A prescription that I have
found nearly all youngsters to be lacking.

Smool's Compendium of Leech & Miasma

Once we had agreed upon the outcome, we set about making it happen with
all the promptness we could muster. More than once I cursed myself for the
time already wasted, time I had squandered. Though Barncroft, Fassinger, and
Hardy made me focus on what we could change, rather than that which we
could not.

The very same day my shaking somehow subsided. I was well enough to walk, and I was escorted to Jemima's apothecary. I shared an intolerable coach ride with Ridley, in complete silence, which Jemima, though very surprised to see us, happily broke when we arrived.

Once she had overcome the considerable shock our request incited, she listened to Ridley's instructions and questions, chewing upon her lip as we described the challenge. She locked the front door before disappearing into her workshop and was gone for several minutes, the rustling and banging of her endeavour the only sounds in the apothecary.

When she returned to us, she carefully measured out a number of different substances into delicate glass receptacles. When she strained the dried pepperbark, pungent and familiar — though I knew not from where — with a tight muslin, finally she handed the bottle of resulting liquid to me.

She stated what was abundantly clear to all of us: the formulation would do little but temporarily brace my weakening constitution and offer a modicum of strength. It would, for the time being, keep me upright and, potentially, dampen the stranger effects of my extended ailments. Or, at least, my perception of them. This would come at a cost, and could not be extended for an overly long period without the most serious of consequences.

In my case, the particular humours afflicted — and, indeed, the rules acting on them — were of an unknown and perhaps unknowable variety. This rendered the likely effects especially volatile. The surgeon concurred; Jemima's advice matched his assessment exactly. I nodded solemnly as she explained, pretending to consider her words. As though anything so luxurious as a choice was available to me.

I took a brisk two drops upon my tongue immediately, as soon as she pressed the vial into my palm.

She raised her eyebrows as I slipped the small bottle carefully into my pocket and thanked her. As we bid her goodbye, she rushed around the counter to briskly shake Ridley's hand. To me, she did not deliver the fierce embrace which was her usual method of greeting or farewell, but stood quickly on her toetips, to set her lips upon my forehead. Then she hurried back into the cluttered confines of her inner workshop, leaving us to unlock the door and let ourselves out into the street.

***

Our final deliberations were made at Bamcroft's temporary lodgings, or at the coffee houses and subscription rooms Hardy recommended for the purpose. So that I might watch the fellow stuffing clothing inside his trunk, or listing victuals, as he tersely discussed the coming challenge with me. Or sweeping his arms up into the air, eyes serious, as he made his point. Other times he set down his teacup and saucer with the precise firmness the seriousness of his endeavour demanded, so that a loud clink rang out, and a slosh of bright tea slipped over the edge. I had never seen him so overcome. It was clear he took this responsibility most seriously.

His impressive side whiskers began to take on an increasingly dishevelled air, his cheeks flushed redder even than usual and, with the more tea he consumed, the more quickly he began to speak. For he was clearly braced by the stimulating properties of the leaves, until there was a somewhat fevered quality to his demeanour. If it were not for the startling efficiency with which he rendered the completion of his many tasks, the truth that I knew him rather well, or the obvious esteem to which he was held by Hardy, society, and Fassinger from their recent collaborations, I should have likely begun to doubt him and worry more than I already were for our immediate future.

Our final plan from this point came together quite quickly: though there were clear weaknesses inherent to many elements of it, for the time to act was now.

***

The day we were due to leave, I woke early after a poor half a night's sleep. I was keen to be under way regardless, enthused as I was with a fresh and vital vigour to be finally taking action. A much more than welcome visitation upon my constitution.

I tried as well as I might not to think of Peck, and threw myself into all the practicalities of our new endeavour to aid that purpose. Our plan was simple, if such a thing could ever be thought of as simple.

First, we would hire ourselves aboard a ship heading to the bled. Bamcroft had put to good use his position and acquired us passage. It was a fast packetship, nominally part of the Concord navy, but in actuality infamously independent minded. Her master had a strong taste for the bonus bounty the navy offered for a speedy delivery. What with a lively front developing out in the tropics, he was confident he could best the most aggressive transit times recorded, and Bamcroft assured me the man's reputation meant we would be fools to doubt him. This, needless to say, suited our requirements rather well.

Once positioned on the edge of the bled, we would take a simple dory commissioned from a Quom shipping agent and awaiting pick up by the packetship. We would then attempt a short but difficult dash across the shifting bled to the front proper. In the bled, we would lean on my somewhat questionable skills as an archivist, relying on my capacity to dosomething I had never done in anything but the most rudimentary, dry practice. Such that, for all my skills, I may as well be reading about the matter in a school book. From there, somehow as yet unknown to us, we would get ourselves to the Erlang straits. Where, all being well, we should catch up to Admiral Russell's Thirteenth Fleet, and the Eleventh Fleet, before the deadly trap had been sprung.

Anyone could see the many limitations and difficulties facing us. And I was high minded to pester anyone who would listen on the issue. But any details beyond the absolute essentials all parties declined to discuss further. A matter I felt, upon reflection, strangely sanguine about. Better, I thought, to concentrate on my simple tasks. To pack my things, and plot our course once we reached the shifting bled.

And then the flurry of tasks were over, and we were ready to depart. At the harbour, in the dark before dawn, I offered Ridley a stiff little wave, and Hardy a more invigorating embrace. And then we were aboard the packetship, soon to be underway.

***

The initial packetship was both terrifying, which I had expected it to be, and exhilarating, which I had not. My journey from Quom to Fivedock with Ridley — which seemed to have occurred so long ago — had passed in a haze of fear and nausea; now, I felt the wind in my hair and the seaspray on my face.

Salt-kissed, my skin felt clean, invigorated. The low queasiness which hung in my belly was something akin to excitement rather than pure dread, and I wondered vaguely whether the girl I had been in Quom was all too timid, or if the young woman I was becoming was, instead, much too reckless.

All too soon, however, we left the sea to enter into a territory with which I was wholly unfamiliar. We left the packetship and were lowered down into the ocean in our little dory. And I found myself in a new world, too entranced to allow fear to overcome me completely. We were delivered, as the master had promised, in a rapid and breathless fashion to the edge of the bled.

And from there, oh, what a journey. Perhaps, one day, I shall write in greater detail of the sights we witnessed. I can tell you that there are colours among the bled that I have never seen repeated, and that the air shimmers with the dancing selites, the strange glowing phantasms of that place, in the strangest way. It is both a frightening and incredible thing to witness.

The nights and days, if that is what one should still call them, blend together as one. I recall that as much as the corporeal sensations. The gentle sloshing of the oars as we grasped them in hand, and pulled and tugged at them again and again. The ripple and snap of sailcloth in the brisk sea breeze. The chill touch of the sextant's brass upon my palm and the curious scent of stale coffee that we carefully apportioned out from the twists of paper in our precious possession, bitter and earthy and true.

Bamcroft proved to be a reassuring companion. But here, in this terrifying place, even his experience counted for very little. A terrible truth we gave the ultimate respect by denying it the attention which would undoubtedly present it before us.

When I was not rowing, Bamcroft had me perform maintenance upon my pistol, my blade and every other part of equipment we carried that would bear the consideration.

I carefully unscrewed the wrought iron of both the pieces I carried. Then I took out a stained old rag, squeezed out two drops of the gun oil upon the frizzen, pan and other parts, and carefully worked it into the mechanisms. Such that the corrosive force of the sea air should be resisted, and the full working order of the parts be maintained. So that they might perform ably when called upon.

I was ever mindful that a build up of powder residue in bore, or pan, did not unman me at the most awkward of moments, previous misfires being visceral, jarring recollections, felt as deep as my deepest memories, as much a part of me now as my fainting fits and love of numbers.

My knife and sabre I set against the whetstone Bamcroft carried for the purpose, the repetitive whisper of metal on jasper as hypnotic as the gentle motion of the sea beneath us.

Our supplies of shot and powder we guarded carefully from our single lamp and the abundant water, both. As I observed this duty I thought often of Peck; of how we'd shielded the spark of flame from the damp air before igniting our stolen powder, the memory precious to me. And though it somewhat blackened my mood, I clenched my jaw tight and the pain set within my bones a new and serious will to see through our shared endeavour.

The more furious the focus with which Bamcroft gave these regularities, the more I sensed his fear. At first I found it irritating, yet in time I came to understand. The exact order of our simple duties became the structure to which our sanity clung in that dayless, nightless, endless time.

At some point on that long, long journey, I fell into the strange waking dream again, with no warning. The note, the emotion, was as pure as the last occasion. Perhaps purer. When I came around it was to discover that I was lying down awkwardly and had salivated all over my face and neck in my semi-consciousness; my limbs were curiously cold, so cold it was several minutes before they responded to my commands. Bamcroft had bunched up sail canvas and used it to pillow my head as best he could. He had also wrapped me tenderly in a rough blanket.

I sat up slowly, shaking my head and wiping at my wet face. Bamcroft simply nodded to me, and did not cease his pulling of the oars. As before, once I resumed my work, I struggled to shake the strongest urge to know the sensation again, and for many hours I pondered how I should name it. It seemed the language of the common tongue entirely lacked the most fundamental capacity, a chasm so vast that it spoke terribly to the utility of the parlance. Could one even name such a thing in mere language? It astounded me.

Frequently, we checked our calculations and corrected our course.

Through at least three days and nights worth of shadow we rowed further and further into that darkness, with no dawn apparent. Nothing but an eternal gloom that spread beyond us in every direction to the very horizon. Itself barely visible and almost impossibly far away.

One night, the gently lapping swell gave way to vast waves of such incredible proportions that they might as well have been mountains. Our little dory felt almost foolishly feeble, a child's brittle toy. One I was entirely certain should be consumed by the walls of towering water.

All the while the waters stayed warm.

I had questions aplenty for Bamcroft. Though I tried to leave him to his musings, and the scratching of his pen within his papers, I found it impossible to stay quiet and asked him one of the countless things I was desperate to know as often as I dared. But he was not forthcoming with answers.

"Think little on it. Let the work soothe your mind."

After what felt like several weeks — but could only have been a few days — of travelling beneath a dark sky devoid of the usual celestial bodies, my throat raw from thirst, my palm and fingers aching from the relentless bite of the dull oar, I became absolutely convinced that we had failed, and should die where we were. Our rotting remains nothing but a monument to the folly of man.

It was difficult to believe we could possibly survive such a journey. In such a situation, which so mocked our nascent and hereto proclaimed triumphant understanding of the natural world. And if we were mistaken about this understanding, which the evidence of my senses suggested we very well may be, in what other areas did our understanding fall short? Where did the natural laws begin? What made them and for which realms or places were they consistent?

In that endless, strange blackness, or in the sudden and violent bursts of luminous colour, I thought of the archivist's workshop, and our limited experiments of natural philosophy. Did the plogiston, that caused the explosive action within blackpowder, work dependably or was it also open to change? Were there many such lands as this one, as yet undiscovered and, if so, what was the configuration of their undulations? Was the realm of the gods so made, and where did that meet the lands of man? It seemed that at the edge of every area of investigation lay a thousand secrets. My mind unfolded a thousand times, my imagination as expansive as the ever changing bledland sky.

I promised myself I should seek out the answers to these intoxicating secrets, were we to make it through our current ordeal. Then, with a grimace and a keen pang of pain, I found myself thinking of Penelope. I cursed myself for a damn fool; I had taken her counsel, her guidance, and her tentative fellowship for granted. Now I craved her understanding and experience, the keenness of her intellect and reason. I realised with a start that thinking of her made me feel homesick, an affliction I had never before experienced. The slight tears, which I smothered with my sleeve before Bamcroft witnessed them, were as warm and salty as the never-ending ocean that spread around us farther than our eyes could ever see.

Chapter Twenty-Seven

A FIVEDOCK CREW

A Sentinel's name is his song.

Transcription from an Unknown Artefact

Our time traversing the bled ended at long, long last. When we reached the small Antiglian ocean, it was with a sigh of disappointment that we noted the distinct absence of masts upon the horizon; neither the Thirteenth nor the Eleventh Fleet were anywhere to be seen.

Invigorated by the returning of day and moon light and the blessedly familiar, we pressed on with a new and furious endeavour. When at last we first witnessed the smoking ships of the line fleeing — several leagues off the starboard — and when, on the following afternoon, the boom of shot and climbing clouds of acrid smoke became apparent in the distance, a sinking feeling descended upon me. A dread which I dare not voice.

In silence we rebent our backs to the hard, base labour of rowing. I should like to tell you that I found solace within it, that the work provided me sufficient succour to balm my terror. But I did not. No. Our every thought was laced with a rising fear. Yet they were at least subsumed in a sense of action, a visceral task with which to aim the ire. The smooth softwood of the oar was reassuringly real and familiar in my palm; the sharp pain of my many weeping blisters acted to awaken in me a vigour which helped focus my efforts.

For the last day we had rescinded the strict schedule of our rest, whereupon we had taken turns to burrow into the dank stern, a damp woollen cloak wrapped tight around us, and fall to a grateful, bone-weary sleep. It had been a hard pattern to follow; it seemed scarcely sufficient, and it was with deep regret that I cracked my bloodshot, crusty eyes open, and forced aching limbs to further work they had no taste for. That once I had been roused enough to understand even where we were, or what we were about.

Now we jettisoned even that ballast to aid the swiftness of our most desperate flight. The only rest offered or accepted a quick sip of brackish water, or a quiet moment to massage aching limbs, nibble upon the dry and ill-flavoured tack and press dry eyes closed for the briefest of moments.

Talk was mostly short, and I was grateful for it. Bamcroft occasionally raised an arm and shouted to point out a sighting, or I suggested a slight change of course. He studied the traverse tables in our log books often and frequently pulled out the chronometer and the bled-marked sextant to squint at them in the blinding sunlight. Sometimes I assisted him, cased pencil lead held tightly within my stiff fingers, cloak wrapped protectively around the papers to shield them from spray and spitting rain. So together we might strike as true a course as we could muster.

What felt like the deadening truth of scent song, but more acute, was huge within me now, a raging torrent that near deafened, choked, paralysed me. When we first set sail I suspected it might be the purest reckoning of my addled mind that I could sense it in the air without the use of the ague or a harmoniser; now, I came to believe it. While it might be my delusions, it accompanied me constantly, whether I was awake or asleep.

Every moment was tainted with it, and it frequently broke in upon the simplest of actions, rendering them incredibly challenging. I began to question myself; was I truly pulling the oars in the steady rhythm of rowing, or was I somewhere else? My notations seemed untidy, then illegible, and suddenly were in a language entirely foreign to me, made up of the most peculiar glyphs, ones I'd surely never seen before. The tops of my arms, where the protrusions had sprouted, tingled constantly. How much Bamcroft knew of my disposition and how much he attributed to exhaustion or fear I do not know. I do not doubt that it was written plain upon my face. He was kind enough not to bother me over it; his way of assisting me was not to give it voice. For that I was grateful. I hid where I could from it, tried to partition out a small part of my mind. The horizon danced and juddered wickedly in my senses as I repeated the mantras under my breath, and envisaged the imaginings in the manner the cryptic old accounting suggested. But I was almost certain I had misunderstood some vital element of the translation, rendered as it was into the common tongue through no less than two separate languages. Neither of which I held anything but a passing skill for. My attempt could only ever have limited success. Though I did not let that hold back its vigour. Every ounce of control available to me I plunged at it.

And then — finally — we sighted land. And all in a rush, what had seemed to last forever, was over.

***

We drew in under the eerie half-light of dawn, the ocean's swell slapping gently against the keel. Here I ascended the limestone steps of a harbour, long worn into bowed grooves, slick with the boots of generations. I caught the frayed rope Bamcroft tossed to me upon the second attempt; with what reserve of strength I cannot say, I ran it around the mooring, securing us to the dock with a deep and heartfelt sigh.

We collected most of our baggage and covered the rest with oilcloth. Then we made our way into the wakening town. My legs were as heavy as if filled with lead. But I forced them to move, one after the other in a shuffling gait. Somehow I stayed upright. As we laboured up a steep hill, the sudden wink and glow of lamplight became apparent in a number of the rugged houses squatting low against the hillside.

The earliest fishing boats cast off silently as a handful of gulls broke up into the air, their caws ringing out loudly in the stillness of the dawn, the only acknowledgement of our quiet arrival. A queer stillness hung heavy over the town, one I was certain was not supplied solely by the peculiarities of my own imagination. As well it might; news of Sentinels, and all that entailed, had likely spread here. One door was daubed with a thick stroke of red paint, a superstition I found I did not grudge the household.

The air reminded me of that within the bled. It carried a metallic thickness that was more than palpable, that invaded one's sensibility. It felt as if it seeped into my body, and I wondered how anyone could live within it for any length of time. I was certain that even if the senses of the poor denizens of Gullsrack were unaware of it, as it seemed they might be, that it should surely leach into and oppress their very souls all the same.

I found myself realising it might indeed be so once we arrived at a reasonably sized and — I assumed — once well attended coaching house. It was three stories tall. Anyone of sense knows well that such an establishment trades at dawn as well as nightfall. As such it was reasonable to expect at this time a hustle and bustle that was entirely absent.

Instead, here, the only activity upon the dusty coachway was a pitiful commotion. A young woman wrapped in a faded purple pelisse leant her bony hand listlessly against an equally bedraggled chaise. The green paint on one of the panels had long peeled and flaked, and the gilt of the lamps had been almost bleached away to nothing by the relentless beating of the sun. Despite myself, I turned my head upon my neck to observe the scene.

Her face was gaunt, her eyes haunted as if she had seen the spirit of her forefathers, her lips pressed thin in displeasure. As she berated her maid-servant waspishly, it seemed patently obvious to me that she had once held a high station, of one form or another. I threw my mind back to my studies, to recall what little I knew of the islands. Not as much as I ought, truthfully enough. But enough to know that, since the Clove Wars, the richest groves and ranches had been gifted out to favoured families. Those who were loyal to the Perpetuals, Concordian and Peninsulan alike. Perhaps her kin had licensed one of the plantations. I wondered what had caused her downfall, and to where she now fled. Likely we were portents of her doom with our warships and our Sentinels.

When, with a creak, the door to the establishment swung heavily shut behind us, I heard the jingle of harness and the clatter of wheel tread on stone and scree as they departed with the poor haste left to them.

We were soon bundled inside the large common room. A sparse assortment of folk were dotted throughout, some breaking their fast, some preparing for the day's work, still others who inhabit such places for talk, gossip, camaraderie or the want of anywhere else to call home.

While my own appearance might not mark me out as one of the Concord — the mistreated breeches, the now stained and heavily crumpled shirt, my dishevelled hair and dirty face — Bamcroft's Concordian manner and accent certainly did.

I was incredibly grateful to find myself wrapped in thick, dry woollen blankets in front of a good wood fire. Where I was left to burnish my keen appetite with nothing but a rough coffee, served to us by a softly spoken and scrupulously clean fellow while we awaited the owner. I curled my hands around the metallic cup to hide my filthy fingernails as I tossed back its lukewarm bitterness with business-like relish, and awaited its invigorating action more in hope than any true belief.

Three ships of the Concord fleet had taken damage at the latest exchange, and were docked for repairs. They were scheduled to leave and meet up with the rest of the Thirteenth Fleet, and soon after the Eleventh. Vice Admiral Russell was a master manoeuvrer and tactician, yet even he had been harried by the Grand Republic's fleet, far sooner than expected, and with heavy damage taken. Full battle was surely not far off now. The Eleventh Fleet racing to arrive in time. Though rumour said they had found trouble.

Did they know where the crew were? The mistrustful eyes of the denizens of the coaching house spoke of their unease around the citizenry of the Concord. Yes, some were aboard; they were expected to depart soon.

The complaints of the longshoremen had been loud and vociferous within the common room. Well, I could understand that. There was little to be won by the attentions of the two great powers, and much to lose.

And this was not to speak of the locals; the peoples of the Concord had perhaps never been well liked, for the mistrust was deep rooted. Pervasive. You did not have to go far in Fivedock, or indeed any of the provinces of the Concord, to find a family with one or many relatives from the edge of the Plenty.

Those who live closest most often hate the brightest. And who cares for those who come to seize their land and all its bounty? Not that I was aware of such truths at my tender age. No. Instead I considered their disdain with a curious sadness, and I should be lying were I not to recount to you that I felt the barb of their attentions with the tender sensitivity that served to unman me so frequently.

Though my sensibility was not enough to keep me awake, as the fire's warmth reached out and washed over our weary limbs. I realised I had nodded off when Bamcroft's elbow jostled me in the ribs. My eyes came open to find the innkeeper leaning over us.

"Why, the purser of the *Spirit Breaker* was in 'ere only yes'erday," he told us, frowning down at us. "Though you din't 'ear it from me, you understan'? Say. She's a Fivedock ship, with most a Fivedock crew, far as I know." His fingers were curiously long, clever things, and they toyed absent-mindedly with a piece of harness. Sometimes he drummed them in a merry rhythm against the dark leather.

"Las' thing I need's more bother. Your coin's good as any, and I don' 'ave anythin' 'gainst you Concordians. Never 'ave. But this war ain't good for any o'us. Sooner it's over the better. Whoever wins it." He pushed a thin strand of his long, greying hair behind his ear and darted a challenging glance at us, as if we might chastise him for his treason. He seemed pleased when we offered no such difficulty; Bamcroft nodded his agreement. Catching on slowly, I offered my own, with a somewhat wayward grin. Then Bamcroft pulled out his pocketbook, produced a bill and, with a significant thud, slapped it to the table.

The innkeeper nodded to himself, pleased enough. Now he truly warmed to the exchange. "'Ead down the docks an' ask for Poppington. Tell 'im Shaw sent you. He'll see you righ'. See if he doesn'. Eat 'smuch as you will." He said, gesturing to a bubbling pot. "But go soon, if you are of a mind to catch 'em. Rumour is they'll leave before day's out. And I offer you the ol' god's speed. If they will it." With that he slipped the bill into his pocketbook, folded it closed, and was gone.

Chapter Twenty-Eight

A SHIP MASTER'S
PREROGATIVE

An optic glass should assuredly be one of the most vital tools acquired for the work of any natural philosopher, purchased from a glass smith of no little skill. Be stringent with the fellow whom you choose; precision is paramount.

Undertakings of The New Princely Society for the Advancement of
Natural Philosophy — Roger Fellgood

And so we found ourselves once more at the harbour, approaching the good ship *Spirit Breaker* with the hope of convincing the captain to deliver us post-haste to the front. And the knowledge that we must do so, whatever the cost. I chewed one of several bread rolls I'd taken from the breakfast table in the coaching house and stuffed into my pockets as Bamcroft pleaded our case.

The master did not agree that he would take us to the front and Lieutenant Etherington, making it plain he did not favour our strange

260

interruption. He did tell us, hand held to brow as he peered out to sea, that they were due to set sail imminently, and that we could discuss the matter further once we were underway.

I was certain that he should deny us. Until it was made known to him that Bamcroft was a shipwright from Fivedock, and he immediately grasped the man by the hand, and shook it vigorously. As they exchanged pleasantries, I felt a soft tap on my shoulder. I turned warily upon my heel, to find none other than Sergeant Belfry standing before me.

I smiled wide to see him, truly pleased to have an ally aboard, though he asked if I were quite well with concern upon his face. Then he promised to find out what exactly I was doing aboard such a fine ship as the *Spirit Breaker* as soon as possible; for now he had his wayward squadron of musketmen to keep in some manner of order.

Muttering about the luck of the sea, the ship master said that, for now, he could provide us with a station. As it was unlikely we would be of much help with the launch — this he ascertained with a glance at what I imagine was my rather sickly pallor — it would be far better if we were out of the way. Bamcroft, rather than take offence to this slight, seemed relieved to be off-duty, for the time being. It was growing abundantly clear he would be pressed most frequently for the rest of our voyage. The ship's carpenter nodded as we passed, his eyes already full of questions.

The captain's tone, on the other hand, spoke much; he was worried by the coming responsibilities and hostilities, yet also excited. He was a young man to have gained his step, a young man indeed. And I found myself piecing together what information I could of his history from the little evidence provided to me.

His skin was pale, his hair bright red. His elocution and bearing set him out as a man of breeding as much as his relative youth. Yet he also seemed experienced and, beneath the steel of his watery blue eyes, there was, perhaps, a generosity of spirit somewhere to be found. By the way he carried himself and gave out orders to his men, he struck me as a likeable man — he was forthright and direct without sounding harsh or brusque.

I quickly ascertained, by the speed of their actions, his crew both liked and respected him. They sprung to action in an entirely impressive manner which, to one as naive to the workings of a Man-o-War as I, offered deep enchantment. They buzzed and hollered and busied themselves, with all the industry and coherent poise of a nest of ants.

Bamcroft echoed my internal assessment. "Well. He seems a good man, at the least. I have heard decent things about him, to boot. Upon that we must pray we might depend."

I almost permitted his words to soothe my spirit. Enough, at least, to stay the rejoinder that I had lost faith in whatever gods were watching over us. For I dare not hope.

Our cramped quarters filled barely a few squared yards and smelled strongly of vinegar. Yet we ducked our backs down gratefully into them. Bamcroft thumped the hull with pleasure. But we exchanged not a word, both climbing straight into hammocks nailed to the thick oak of the beams. And before the gentle creaking of the hull against the swelling tides had indicated to me we were under way, I had fallen into fitful slumber, my hands tangled in the coarse fibres of my rest place.

***

We sailed on for an odious day before we dropped anchor and awaited the signal to approach the front. The master had secreted himself away with his most trusted men where they had, I assume, debated our request amongst themselves. Now the mate had approached us with the final promise that it had been agreed we were to be taken to the front, where the admiral and the other masters could decide best what was to be done with us. If we survived the battle, he glibly cackled, as he hurried to join the thunderous preparation of the vessel.

And the truth of the impending battle had niggled away at me all the hours of the two days we had spent waiting. A strange mix of building excitement and terror blended with the jabbering of the more incorporeal internal torments which had been my companions for so much longer.

Upon the rough paper of my now tattered and stained commonplace book, I had written out calculations and lists over and over again. The tons burthen of ships we were like to face — or to ally — and the rank of the same. The names of the Sentinels, known to the past, and those not yet seen or witnessed. The sea battles won, and lost, in known history. I wrote snatches of random song notation, in what seemed the most patent sense to me, whispers and fragments that came from where I do not know. But would have to others surely been the purest sign of my impending madness. The mantras, too, I whispered increasingly frantically beneath my breath, nearly every moment I set the watchers of the old forms, that they might stay the terror that seemed sure to swallow me. Over and over and over again with a furious and exacting concentration. My head ached, and my muscles cramped, and a cold sweat slicked my brow. I did not feel like one person, but many, and none. I did not think with five senses, but ten, which leaked and bled between one another. Though I could not name them, nor really speak.

I wrote and wrote untill my fingertips were so sore they nearly bled. I had not realised I held the pen so tight it nearly snapped until Bamcroft swept up beside me and, with great kindness, braced his arms around me, and gently massaged it from my grip with the soothing sounds reserved for children, and animals, and the mad. Then took me up to the Orlop Deck, where I stared all around me with barely seeing eyes, raw to the world.

My clothes were filthy now. The fabric torn and crusted stiff. I stank, I think. And yet I found I could no longer bring myself to care.

I permitted Bamcroft to take me amongst the second watch for a simple meal of pease and dry tack, and a little stewed tunny. Once I had taken a few sips of the proffered rum to rinse it down, I was struck with a sudden urge to take more. Much more. And my previous memories of my drunken shame could not stop me from allowing the foul stuff to melt the tension from my throbbing limbs, the fear from my heart.

Bamcroft did not stop me, but with a grunt joined me, and so, to my great surprise and gladness, did Belfry and his squadron. Until we drank ourselves insensible.

When Baker the midshipman and Marric the cabin boy sang *The Song of the Mermaid's Daughter*, I clapped along with the rest of the second watch under nothing but the cold burning stars and the vast stillness of the night, with the scent of the holystoned decks deep in my lungs, the burning fire of rum in my throat.

***

A hand — hot and salty — was pressed firmly over my mouth. As my eyes snapped open, I bucked and squirmed instinctively, trying to free myself from my attacker. But my assailant's arms were strong, perhaps thrice the size of mine, and enveloped me completely with all the ease of a man lazily swatting an insect. My fingers scrabbled uselessly against his bulging bicep.

Panic flooded through me. I did my very best to temper it, and to take an accounting of the situation. The glare of the light hurt my eyes, and I had to force them open against their proclivities. My view lurched before me, but when the oil lamp swung sickeningly into view, I realised I was still within that same tiny cabin aboard *Spirit Breaker*.

Still incredibly muddled in my mind from the strong exuberances of drink, and my ailments, and sleep, I had to strain to hear my assailant's words over the sound of the crashing waves. They doubled up, and echoed, and then I could taste them. They were the colour of violet, and I wondered if we were under way finally.

There was something familiar about the scent of the man. Something terribly familiar.

"'ello. Shay," he spat. "You'd'ave done better to take my las' warnin'." The sound of his voice woke a deep, primal fear within me. I bucked against him once again; this time the top of my skull met his jaw with a crack. He rearranged his grip and held me down painfully but I felt the tiniest burst of triumph in my chest.

"You are too late. That master o'yours will soon be gone." His whisper was sharp and rasping in my ear. I was certain I should vomit. "As will all rest o' you. You chose to plot and ploy against them rightful powers of our good nation."

I attempted to crane my head around, to gain a glimpse of the other hammock. But I could not manage. With a grunt, the fellow acknowledged my attempt.

"Oh? That one who was wiv you 'as been dealt with! He will sleep most deeply and surely, til we've done wot we must, 'ere. I promise you that."

The insistent roar of my madness and my nausea met the panic rising in my chest; I bucked again against the figure who held me so tightly, heat prickling along my flesh.

"Now, now. Be easy. Now. You maintain wot strength you 'av for wha's to come." He let out a nasty little laugh. "Maybe now recognise them error of your ways?" He continued his merriment, a snuffling, huffing sound. "But it is too late." His excitement became almost too much for him. His final words he purred. "Yes it is. They always finds out, at the end."

Suddenly a knife appeared before my eyes, a dirty, short thing. It was chipped, too, yet I was under no illusions as to its effectiveness.

I was released but the blade danced assuredly, in a confident little figure of eight before my eyes. I am ashamed to say that I cowered before it.

"Dress," he spat. "We must speak wiv the good master, now, 'im who 'as sailed us to our goal so ably." Under my tormentor's watchful gaze, I did as I was instructed. And all the while my mind raced. How far had we travelled? How long had I been asleep? The rum and my worsening hysteria muddled my mind.

I wondered if I might gain the opportunity to grab my blade or pistol. I studied the man as well as I might. He had changed, now, from how I had known him at our previous meetings. He wore a musketman's uniform,

265

dark green, dull silver tassels across his chest. Yet the wool was torn at the shoulder, poorly maintained. His hat sat awkwardly upon his greasy hair. It was spotted and dirty, and he was every bit as intimidating as he had been that day. He stank the same, and his beady, cruel eyes watched me greedily. A dull fear, deep within, recalled all he had done to me, and I struggled not to flinch from his consideration.

As he led me up onto the deck, my suspicion was confirmed: we were indeed under way once more. The previous night's stillness had given way to bracing wind which rippled through my thin clothing. My woolen shawl was still in my hammock and I shivered as seaspray spattered at my face. Above our head, the vast mainsails snapped and billowed in the wind.

"Five knotts, captain!"

"Steady as she goes there, if you please, Mr Dedley." I just managed to make out his voice above the squall, from the forecastle.

"Your attentions, Master, should you be so kind!" My captor raised his voice just as the captain slid the overlapping layers of his eyeglass down his eye. "This interloper," he hawked and spat upon the deck, "is 'ere under the command of that false archivist, 'er wot is shortly to be relieved of 'er duties! Now we know for certain she is a traitor to the houses. You will do right best to take both of the traitors wot you 'av aboard your ship into your keeping, right away," he said. "For surely you won't 'av it spoke that you 'arboured 'em?"

"What are you speaking of? I am the master of this ship. This passenger is my guest, and enjoys my protection. To what end do you presume to challenge my authority, man? You may have noticed that we approach battle. Whatever mischief this is can surely wait?"

I hoped beyond any hope that my initial assessment of the captain's character had not been misguided. His imperious gaze swept over my gaoler, and rested upon him, still and intractable. I felt the ice within, and the steel.

Suddenly there was a familiar voice, breaking clear in the silence. "I know this woman, and I vouch for her!" It was Sergeant Belfry. I offered him a

266

most grateful smile, but he did not meet my gaze. Instead he stood, perfectly at attention, hands folded behind his back.

"Thank you, sergeant. That will be all," was all the captain said.

Despite this, he seemed, somehow, not entirely ill-disposed toward my assailant. He had simply not apportioned his judgement as yet, and awaited the evidence to be presented by the parties. He stood considering him, arm resting upon his hip as he continued.

"If you don't know of 'em now. You will surely learn of it soon enough. Them wot wants to do well, in the service, keep abreast of what goes on in the capital. If they are worth much.

"So. Master. Commander. I would not tarry, were I you," he drawled. The deck lurched beneath our feet as he went on, impatience barely contained, "You can be certain the sea lords will hear o' it. We know you 'av only just made the list? It would be a big shame, were you struck from it, so soon. Would it not?"

The master considered us for the longest moment, his eyes glancing from my assailant, to me, then to his officers. Eventually he spoke.

"Your general holds no rank here, musketman. This is a naval action. Much as I respect the good general and all our brethren of foot and gun. No. I think not. It will not do. I must ask you to untie your prisoner. Mr Dedley, please escort the infantry man, and his captive, from the deck."

I watched my enemy lick his lips, and his eyes quickly danced across the officers aboard the deck, from the two midshipmen, to the coxswain, and then the captain. "I offer my apologies. But there are things wot trump even your duty! You understand command, and rank. So I tell you I am 'ere for a far higher power. It is the consort himself, and the counsel! He wot is head of our nation! He who now follows the wisdom of those of great purpose. Members of our parliamentary houses. Them wot offer wise advice, so that the consort and the counsel are all now in sure agreement. This is a power higher than both the General or Admiral Russell."

He licked his stained lips. "It is *your duty* to obey them exact governors, wot are masters of us both. Is it not? Master?"

The distaste rode clear upon the captain's face, and the surprise, but he spoke no words. Instead he stared into the far distance, incredibly still. A low muttering broke out amongst some of the working sailors who had strayed close enough to hear.

"On the other 'and, act out your clear duty right and proper. And perhaps your lapses of thinking might be forgot. In that case. I am told we sense a right good career a'ead of you."

One midshipman placed his palm softly to his pistol handle. Hope briefly flared within my chest.

"Wait," I said. "Wait, please. I beg of you. I speak the truth. You must listen to me. The entire fleet is at risk. I have important information. I must be allowed to reach the front."

I do not believe Bamcroft and I had been mistaken about his character. Nor that his evil was any great thing. Instead it was that worse wickedness, the normal, simple little evil we all commit each day. Precipitated by the doubts of the strictures our society heap upon us, and that build up an unbearable weight.

His furrowed young eyes met mine, and I read the guilt within them. He did not appear to relish what he had to do, he was merely a serving officer dispensing the more unpleasant duties of his command. His nod to the marine behind me was nearly imperceptible.

The blow to my head was sudden, hard as possible. And I knew no more.

Chapter Twenty-Nine

A CONSIDERABLE HEIGHT

Such is the immense power a Seeker is cursed to gain that there are but two emotions one might feel in their regard: total pity and abject fear.
Once the transformation has begun, nothing will stop it. Nothing.

Hendrik's Accounting of the Ancient Peoples

Such a din to awake to, cannon fire rumbling like the thunder of the gods. A deep roar, a boom that reverberated through the stained oak below my cheek, sending a terrible vibration rattling through my skull. A pain both sharp and dull followed, splitting my tender forehead. I squeezed my eyelids tight in a vain attempt to lessen the ill taint.

With a deep grunt, I rolled onto my back, awakening a litany of stings and stabs within my battered torso. I reached a wavering hand to my forehead and felt wetness and searing warmth against my fingertips — an open wound. My mouth was impossibly dry, my tongue thick and clumsy. I worked it along the inside of my gums, and was answered with further pain and an unfamiliar configuration. Several of my teeth had worked loose. When I sucked in a muffled grunt of air my scent came with it. I stank of stale sweat and vomit.

There was nothing else for it. With a sigh, I attempted to force my throbbing eyelids open. My left eye resisted completely, swollen firmly shut. The other answered, of a certain measure at least. It was gummy, and the crust broke painfully, tearing out several eyelashes.

My thoughts came to me in a confused morass, blending and shifting. I could not recall what had occurred, where I had been, or the order of my actions. Nor exactly where I was now. Perhaps in the hold? I strained but my sluggish thoughts responded barely at all. They were slow, pondering things, scarcely worthy of the name — near incapable of forming such a thing as cogent or complete concepts, no matter how much energy I expended in the pursuit.

And then it all came to me at once, in a great rush, clearer and brighter than dazzling sunlight as a rusted shutter catch suddenly bursts open: I had failed. We had failed. I was tied up in the hold, after Ludlow had delivered me a vicious beating. I lay in silence listening to the pounding of cannon, feeling the rock and lurch of the Man-o-War under my shoulder blades, as that terrible truth settled over me. The dread of the realisation was heavy and deadening, complete in its terrible truth.

I almost chuckled at the absurdity of the situation. All those months of worry, and it seemed I was destined to miss the very action we had so strived for. And how close we had come, only to fall at the last! Likely we would be sent to the bottom, with me trapped right where I was. And all the fleet alongside me.

Perhaps it was a fitting fate. Perhaps my expectations all along had been too much. I supposed I had always known that to be the truth, deep within: that, when the moment of reckoning arrived, I was like to fail. My attempts, to prove my worth, at control, my obsessive nature, were nothing but the most foolish graspings.

It was at that instant I heard perhaps the last thing I might have expected: a light cough. It was polite and so strangely out of place that I sat up suddenly, with no mind to the ails of my condition, nor the shooting pains that ran down my arms and my legs. The one eye which remained within my power came as close to snapping open as it was capable, which is to say it came painfully unstuck, and burnt terribly while I blindly tried to make sense of the wavering shapes and colours before me.

But then a dark mound resolved into a crouching figure. I studied my new, lurking companion in the murky darkness. A lantern swinging from a low beam, cast dirty red light and long shadows over his features, which danced as it swung.

Still I recognised him, almost immediately. Fenton.

He was hunched low, on his haunches. Even while he crouched in the dark — and through one injured eye — I could see he was taller than I recalled. His features had lengthened. Both changes suited him.

The expensive twill cuffs of his shirt were more stained than usual. The emerald cut of his waistcoat sat a little queerly and its fat gold buttons were scuffed, loose threads fuzzed upon them. His topboots had lost their shine. He had acquired a small cut upon his cheek, and his face was intermittently smudged with soot or dirt or powder. His eyeglasses were quite bent, as if he had done his best to repair them himself. They sat upon his features at a more excessively jaunty angle than they had naturally. But apart from all these details, I could be meeting with him in his makeshift workshop.

As he rose, his lips pressed into a firm line. His green eyes, always fair and alive, now carried seriousness as they considered me. The suggestion of tears glistened in the corner of them. He did not blink.

Fenton slowly raised his chin and, abruptly, presented his slight hand to me, stiffly. After a moment's consideration, I reached out and took it in mine. And there his fingers coiled around my palm like an adder. I felt a slight tremble in his grasp. He belied the slightness of his frame by hauling me to my trembling feet. I stood for a moment, before they fell out beneath me. The world whirled and wheeled with a sickening lurch of nausea and blackness.

But he pressed his other hand to my shoulder, bracing me upright. Then, from nowhere, he wrapped both hands around me and hugged me firmly to him. I pulled a great gasp of air into my lungs in surprise and his scent came along with it: he smelled of coal soot and whale oil, just as he always had. And it was wonderful.

And oh, it felt good to be held. So good that I hugged him back, fiercely. Not caring what had happened, not caring for any of it. I craved a simpler time, an old friend and the person I had once been. Any recriminations I might have held washed away in the warmth of that embrace.

I was sick of all of it. Sick to the very death.

Then all at once it was over. He stepped back and peered down into my face.

"Here," he said, as he staunched the wound on my brow with a wadded mound of sailcloth. It was a curiously tender act, and it made me feel strange. I did my very best not to probe those feelings too closely.

"My thanks," I whispered, barely a sound from my cracked lips.

"You have to come," he hissed at me, suddenly intent. "We still have time."

"We…? I don't believe I can," I said and with that I coughed and sputtered blood onto the floor. I was so weak I almost shook with it. "Fenton. I'm glad you've come. Truly I am." I forced the words from my quivering lips, and they came out as the hoarsest little whisper. My throat was devilish sore. It was almost too much to swallow. I winced as I did so. The effort took much from me; I paused when even the arm which braced me buckled beneath me.

"Shay. I'm so… Can you ever forgive me?"

I almost laughed; his apology seemed absurd to me, in the situation. I spoke quietly, my mouth too sore to open properly. "Forget it, now. It is done. And you—"

"I swear I didn't know. About Peck. I would never have… And I tried to stop them. When they… when they… did that to him. I could carry on with them no longer. I should never have started with them. They said it was for the city. For all of us. I never thought they'd — I thought they'd merely close the office! Or… or, take it over. Oh, Shay. The poor boy. I didn't…" I realised he was crying as he spoke, tears running down both of his cheeks entirely unchecked. As if he wasn't aware they were there.

"What do you mean, about Peck?" I asked.

"You don't…? He… he died, Shay."

"Yes, he was ill for many years, he died of—" Horror flooded through me as the truth dawned on me. But I knew it was too late.

"There is nothing to be done, Fenton. You don't know, I… I'm… unfit. And even if I were able. It isn't possible. There isn't time. I wouldn't even know what to do."

I wasn't sure how to share my weakness with him, or what had befallen me. What I had become. I grinned a grim smile as one of the evil little appendages that were now part of me spasmed. We had walked the most foolish of paths. I suddenly felt glad I wouldn't die here all alone.

And then he was supporting me, trying to coax me to walk. "I do know," he whispered gently as he proffered a bottle to me, one I recognised. "Here. Bamcroft gave me this. I woke him. Though he has seen much better days. Drink that."

When I simply closed my eyelids with a weary little shake of my head, he pushed it to my lips, seized my neck with his other hand, and forced me to take a spluttering skinful. I coughed, liquid running from my nostrils and down my chin, bubbling at the corners of my mouth. I fought him with what strength I could muster. But he was relentless. He pursued me as I shook my head from side to side.

He was saying something to me, but I was too agitated to listen. Then bodily weariness overcame me once again. As opposite as all that surrounded us, and I felt, as it was possible to be. A sudden rush of vitality washed across my body, in strangest tension with the crushing exhaustion beneath.

"I said it will help, damn you Shay. Listen to me! It will give you strength."

"For what? I don't understand."

"There is no time for all that needs to be said." I felt my eyes open wider, my lungs taking in more air. Then Fenton grasped my hand once again; this time he jerked my arm painfully as he pulled me out of the darkness and into a pool of light. Not quite daylight, something deeper. He ushered me forwards, up the ladder towards the rolling deck above our heads.

"You have to come. I wish I could explain, but I don't... You... I," he faltered and looked more lost than I'd ever seen him. I looked away; his grief was, somehow, too much for me to bear. "I'm sorry, Patch." We stood in silence, for a moment more, staring at each other as the weight of his words settled upon us.

"We must hurry," he repeated at last. At my weak nod of assent, he turned and moved. And so I followed him. I find I cannot say why, simply that I did.

He led me to the maindeck. All around us voices cried out, men bellowing to one another. Drums beat a steady rhythm. It truly was the most impossible clamour, with not a hint of the romance I might have assigned it were I to rely solely on the stories so readily exchanged in the ale and tea houses of Brook Street or in the little novels Peck had steadily collected.

One ship had come alongside us. And all around others were doing battle. There seemed to be a forest of Grand Republic vessels. How could it be that we were so outnumbered?

Whistles shrieked, shrill and tormenting. Marines and seamen bellowed and muskets crackled. Sea spray drove at us. With a crunching crash that vibrated through the soles of my boots, the hull downwind of us exploded into a lacerating mist of splinters as a thirty-two pounder ripped through the first deck.

A half dozen marines still stood, bodies littered at their feet, priming their pans to repel a boarding action.

"Hold your position. Steady now lads. Steady!" I recognised Belfry. He nodded briefly to me as we moved past him.

"If you've any special archivist ways, now'd be the time to deploy 'em, if ye'll forgive me for saying, young mistress," he shouted as we hurried past. I turned back briefly, for I wished to speak with him. But his eyes were steely concentration. "On my mark, gentlemen, if you would be so kind!" His knee had buckled beneath him. It was roughly bandaged, bleeding, the fabric stained almost black.

With a great creak, the yore mast came crashing down, smashing the purser's chest like a hammer through a rotten apple, and taking the bowsprit with it to the waves.

As the deck rocked and hummed beneath my feet, I paused to look up and out to the horizon, and that was when I saw them. I stopped and stared, awestruck. I raised my hand to my brow. In the distance, amongst a thick and rolling fog, towered Sentinels. One had five heads, each wavering on a thin, serpentine neck. Another, excessively broad shoulders, mottled in greens and reds and browns, hide tough as a cliff face.

Their heads loomed out above the fog. They were impossibly vast, huge colossi. Full taller than the tallest flagship laid upon itself a score of times, they blotted out the very sky. To see so many of the great ones, gathered together, to see the beasts, finally, that it had been my duty to pursue... I could not contain the rush of excitement that burnt through me. A smile burst over my face, even while the scent song that emanated from them threatened to blast my very essence to tatters.

"Look!" I shouted to Fenton, raising my arm to point, heedless of the jolt of pain that answered.

As I studied the Sentinels, I realised a strange temper was upon them. Why I should understand their natural movements I could not say, save to say that I assuredly did. Yet these were wrong, somehow. Languid, docile... uncharacteristically inexact. They lurched into one another, inelegant and aimless, like herded cattle. And then it struck me. They had been lured. They had been lured, as Velspritt had been. As we had known they would be.

We were trapped.

"The Eleventh Fleet are close. The Thirteenth held, here beyond the strait. The two are cut off! We have to find a way to release them!" said Fenton.

"We must go to them!" I said, not taking my gaze from the great beasts. I turned back to Fenton. "Where is the archivist?" I screamed at him.

"They have her!" he shouted back at me. He raised his hand to shield his eyes from spray and shrapnel. Then we both crouched instinctively as a volley of muzzlefire crackled and popped around us. "She was captured. Aboard the *Updike*. They plan to kill her. They seized the ship, and others! They are in league with the Grand Republic.

"But Shay. You must listen to me. There's no time," Fenton seized me and cupped his hand to my ear, shouting at the top of his lungs. I could just make him out above the sudden roar of our thirty-two pounders, as they barked into the latest great ship of the line that had come alongside the starboard. A boarding action from both sides seemed our fate, sure to sweep us away. If we were even afloat by such a time. And still some of his desperate words were lost. "I should have helped you a long time ago. I should have been honest from the start."

He pressed something firmly into my grasp and I thought I understood. It was cold and round and familiar. "I didn't give it to them!" he said, as I stood staring at him like a simpleton. "I knew. I knew I shouldn't."

***

It was the bledmarked astrolabe. A silly trinket, really. One that mattered little, now. Yet I clung to it nonetheless.

"I don't know what to do!"

"You have to do it. Do it now!" he bellowed. As we stumbled forwards, I wrapped an arm around myself. I ran my sore finger along the fleshy pores that had formed beneath my armpit. "I don't understand either. Not truly.

But Etherington told me you would." He continued in my ear, dropping to a knee as we mounted the steps to the quarterdeck. "I spoke with her. I confessed all. I came along with Grent when I heard the plan. Then I sought out the archivist. You do, Patch. You do. I know you do," he reached out his arm and gently laid his hand upon my back.

"But I'm afraid. And I don't. We just came to give the warning!" I spoke those words and knew them for the horrible truth that they were. I began to cry at the realisation of my weakness. Tears tracked down the grime upon my face. It was all so out of my control. Every effort I had expended, my will to contain this truth, had failed. It had all been useless, all of it. Every silly little game I'd played. Every diagram and chart and list. A child's most patent foolishness. "What else could we do? I'm too afraid," I whispered.

We crested a wave, then plunged into a surging torrent. A chill deluge swept across the deck and slammed into me, knocking me prostrate. The wind was driven from my chest, hard, in a great distressing gasp. I pushed my hand out in front of me to break my fall, and my finger snapped backwards, bent completely over in the reverse. Broken. The cloth of my shirt and breeches clung to my skin all over my body, slimy and horribly frigid — inescapably chilling. I struggled to stand. I nearly blacked out from the pain.

And then there was a cry from behind us. I turned in time to see and hear a hail of fire from Belfry's musketmen; in return, another peppered them. With a fierce cry, a second boarding party swept over the bannister of the larger ship that had come alongside us. They charged into the few remaining Concord marines, in a clash of sword and dagger and smoke. I choked on it, and coughed to clear my chest. When I looked up, it was to see, at their head, stood Ludlow. Dagger in hand, fingers scarlet. Belfry was slumped at his feet. They outnumbered our boys, and were finishing the last of them. Ahead of him, looming suddenly from the smoke, came Lord Anton Grent.

He was as handsome as ever, more handsome. His skin was radiant, his eyes glowing with malice and glee. He was breathing hard. One of his men had stumbled from the melee, a hand clutching a gaping wound in his gut, the other grabbing hold of Grent's breeches, reaching for him.

"Please. Sir," the soldier said, wild panic in his dying eyes. "Your aid."

Grent recoiled. "Unhand me, man," he said. Now he pulled back one shining boot, and stamped upon the man's face, twisting his heel. In unison he glanced down at his bloodied hand in distaste, as if he had been soiled with dog mess. With a sniff, he plucked a snowy kerchief from his pocket with delicate little tugs, and fastidiously cleaned his hands upon it. His stature, his imperious bearing, suggested he might have been stood in Allsop's ballroom, rather than upon the Orlop deck of a second rank ship of the line in the centre of a raging battle.

He drew the most exquisite dress pistol, worked in gleaming wrought gold, and silver, and white. He waved it languidly at me.

"Assistant archivist!" he said, his voice somehow carrying clearly to me. "So pleasant to meet your acquaintance once more!"

He took a step closer to us, and I lifted my chin; I would not die cowering from him.

"Has your transformation begun?" he asked as he yanked up his sleeve. He pointed to familiar blemishes on the inside of his arm, though his were far smaller and less dense than my own. "I am afraid we cannot allow it to go on any further! Too much power, I should say. You would not know how to wield it."

He shouted, arms raised to the sky. "We stand at the dawn of a new day. A new glory. One we shall guide! We of the Grent line are survivors. My greatest grandfather stood at the battle of Crow's Breach, did you know? And we shall stand at many more. We have served for over seven hundred years. Bold action is required, for the good of our Great Concord! Indeed, for the good of the civilised nations of the Whispering Coast, above the savages and other muck that surrounds us. And damn any who lack the vision to think otherwise."

He shook his head at me. "It would have been better were you to stay below, girl, for your end. No matter, though. Here will do just as well. We shall be leaving, in a moment. You won't be able to come along, I'm afraid.

"And you, Fenton? You never fail to disappoint. You could have done something proper with yourself, you know. Could have been useful. But, alas."

With incredible grace and fluidity, Grent drew an immaculate small sword from the scabbard at his waist. He turned to Ludlow, and nodded to him.

He had been considering me with his head cocked to the side. "I said I should 'av done 'er proper, when we 'ad chance."

A little twist of distaste sat upon Grent's lips, but he inclined his head ever so slightly, in assent. "You may fulfil your desire now." He looked around. And waved to the Grand Republican boarding party, who swarmed it seemed everywhere.

"Now let us be gone. While the opportunity remains."

Ludlow sprang forwards, an animal snarl leaving his lips. But it was Fenton who moved quicker. He jinked past Ludlow, and was upon Grent, thrusting a hand into the man's stomach to stop him. They wrestled with each other, unsteady on their feet, backwards and forwards. I lurched forward myself, but the rocking of the ship forced me from my feet once more. With a sharp crack Grent clipped Fenton's brow with the pommel of his sword. Then Ludlow neatly stepped up behind him, wrapped one arm around his chest to still him and, with a curiously gentle caress, touched his flintlock to Fenton's mass of dark curls.

I stepped forward to stop him.

Powder flared, white smoke and a flash. And a mess of bone and blood and hair burst over the cruel grimace of Grent's face. I recall noting the strangest thing, the most peculiar detail of the glowing whiteness of his teeth in the horrific mask of human matter. Dark filth dripped from his chin, and sticky pools of it clung to the immaculate bright snowy silk of his neckcloth.

I watched, wordlessly. Fenton. His body was dropped, tossed to the deck. His head lolled unnaturally on his neck like a jack in the box. Fenton. His eyes glassy and empty. And then Grent stepped in, and with a satisfied grunt punched his glimmering blade into his chest. One. Two. Three times. Fenton.

"So long, old fellow," he said as he stepped over the body.

Then he languidly stretched back, to consider me, his imperious chin rising in challenge and triumph. His pistol's barrel followed in a fluid arc, to face me.

One hand tightly clutched the astrolabe, and I shrieked in wordless pain. With sudden clarity, I ripped the tattered and sodden shirt from my back, bearing my arms, my chest, my stomach to the air. And I did not deny the sensation I had fought for so long. Nor did I care, any longer, who saw me. What I had become, or was becoming.

I flexed the musculature of the small, peculiar structures which were now a part of my torso, the new organs which nestled beneath my armpit, down the side of my body. Like the fins of a fish or the bract of a flower, the apertures were a part of me. They were me.

Perhaps my assailants frowned, and gestured to one another, each waiting for the other to strike — I cannot say, for their enterprise no longer mattered to me a whit. Only one thing did I have in my sights: the vast behemoths in the distance, towering above us and into the heavens. Blotting out the very sun.

"Damn it all to hell," I said, though none could hear me.

I tangled my mangled hand in the rigging, with a shriek of pain so severe I nearly vomited. I forced myself to look up. At the sight of the mizzenmast lurching sickeningly above me I squeezed my eyes shut. Then I yanked myself up and into the mess of ropes and cables, catching my flailing leg on a rung as it slammed around with the violent rocking motion of the hull. I climbed the rigging and it danced in the wind.

A shot fizzled past my face, grazing my ear with searing heat.

I felt, with a dry grimace, the musculature of the gill-like appendages. I flexed the filaments, timorously, for they were tender as any new flesh. Or as hairs raise upon cold skin. And as my nose scented the salt and the sweat and the fear so too did the fronds, now exposed to the atmosphere, bristle at the scent of the Sentinels. I felt a strange slither of blood or mucus or who knew what; I winced and ignored it. Instead, like a snuffling hound, I opened them wider. Sensing. Tasting. Feeling. I flexed queer muscles no person was meant to have, and huffed in the strange scent music of our most alien bounty. And I *tasted* it. I *knew* it. I *was* it.

And the song of the Sentinels was all around us as it, now obviously, had always been. It was as much of nature as the air or the water. And the torrent which had been my internal companion for what seemed so long rose in pitch and pace until it was dizzying. I grasped the rigging with everything I had, scarcely clinging to the thick rope with the little strength left to me. My fingers were so battered and numb I struggled to understand if they even responded. Words in languages I half knew, and a thousand I did not, babbled in my ear, in my thoughts, along my limbs, threatening to drown me.

It was more than the archivist's ague. Much more. As if that were the tiniest glimmer. It span so quickly in my mind, in all my senses, that I was certain I should fall. It was the sound of the gutter, a discordant hymn. It was within me and beyond me, high pitched enough to make me wish to cover my ears and cry out, and impossibly low, deep enough to rattle my bones. I might say that it was like the screech and pop of bird chatter, but that would not be accurate. I should describe it as the foreboding chants of a hundred monks. Though neither does that come close. Perhaps it will have to do. For how to relay such a thing?

Grent and Ludlow had closed the distance to rigging, so at least is my understanding, surely eager to finish their work. But they were also fearful, for the strangeness of the queer young commoner before them. Ludlow threw himself into that ropework and started to climb methodically after me, and

Grent readied another shot. Though little conception of my surroundings did I retain.

Suddenly, I gasped out a huge breath, and, with all the strength within me, I *expelled*. I flexed the fronds, *my* fronds, and I shook them and I *sang my scent*. The only way to hold myself together was to centre everything within me, and sing it. I vibrated with the sense of *me*.

First, they responded timorously, and then with a deeper vigour than the weak and regular motions my slight body had ever known. I sang and I sang, not through my voice, but through my being. I shook and I shrieked and I puffed until my new appendages were beaten and sore.

And the world as I knew it stopped. Then I understood, suddenly, how limited and foolish my simple human senses were. Even the idea of senses and how we conceive of such things! In this moment other powers suggested themselves to me — other controls, and understandings of the true nature of the mortal realm we consider home. They were tantalising and nebulous. Yet from these I turned aside. For I had one goal, and I knew what I must do.

I could not control the Sentinels, not in the way one may understand it. Nor could I really communicate with them in the way a man converses with his peers, or even with an animal. It was the most impossibly disorientating experience.

So, I didn't try. I simply made them aware of me.

In some way I touched them. One brushed against me suddenly, impossibly vast, a whale past a minnow. And its presence was familiar. An overwhelming sensation of clarity flooded through me, an amplification of all those times in the recent days it had visited me. I was certain, incredibly certain in that moment, that I had known him before. I detected a tinge of... *humour?* I felt, for a heart beat, amusement, and curiosity. And then it was gone.

And then the understanding grew too much, too strange, too heavy to contain. I was back within my body. And that, too, was too much to contain, or understand. So that I did not witness the result of my visitation, but tumbled heavily to that salt-stained oak, blood tracking from my tear ducts, flecks of frothing spittle thick upon my lips.

I am told, by those survivors who were there to witness the event, that each vast Sentinel stopped at once, and swept their impossibly large heads to look in the direction of the *Spirit Breaker*. Then they bellowed out in unison, so that the bones of unlucky seamen cracked, and others never drew a single, solitary breath, nor ever heard another sound.

Chapter Thirty

CURIOUS GODS

Dearest Patch,

I called for you this afternoon, but you were absent.
It is my honour to cordially invite you to attend a most exciting event: luncheon at the Yellow Saloon, upon your earliest convenience, for a fantastic exhibition of the like you have never seen!

Your friend,
Fenton

I did not gain a full wakefulness of wit and sense for many days. When I did it was to learn that the infamy of my action had been greatly curtailed. Survivors were bribed, sham accountings submitted to the broadsides. This at the pressing of the Etherington and Hardy. For that, I was grateful. And when we determined that we should keep my actions that way as long as we may be able, for the advantage of all our situations, I was far more than grateful: I was indebted. No, I returned, instead, to a quiet convalescence that was as long as it was blessedly dull.

For a time, at least.

Many were the tales told of the battle of the Erlang Strait. Of the men who lost their lives, and of the great Sentinels who turned aside and cast the luck of their ancient power upon the Concord forces.

Vice Admiral Russell won a famous victory that secured our position that day. Oh, we lost many ships, and the list of men lost is a longer one. The official tally is written in blood, blood to compare with historical battles that to me were nothing but legend. This I know. For I have studied them within the dour, imposing military library at the admiralty. Thirteen ships of the third rank were sent to the bottom, ten of the second, and three of the first. More than a score would see not see battle for many a season, and the unranked are too many to list. Three would only be hauled back, to be broken up in harbour. But the tide was turned, by my action. The Sentinels turned aside.

With the coming of the Eleventh Fleet, Admiral Russell swept the remaining Grand Republic forces into a direct and daring action, which swiftly fell to a rout. His good flagship, *Indomitable Spirit*, holed below the line, limped bravely on with less than half her hands still standing. It was he who commanded the broadside fire that sank two third rank ships of sixty-nine guns, and one first of one hundred. He who sank the Grand Republic flagship, and convinced the remaining enemy forces to flee the field of battle.

Three ancient Sentinels turned back towards the bled and I list their names here, rendered in the closest approximation I can muster in my hand and our common tongue: majestic Slithrinl of the five heads, svelte Epthphilaas, the great lurker; draconic Velspritt, rumoured amongst our ancient order to have lived ten thousand years. I wish that I could record their scent song signature here, or try to explain it in a fashion one might understand. For that is the far better measure of their character than mere name or moniker. And yet it is surely an impossibility. Better to tell a blind man the colour of the third moon, or a deaf woman the sound of a stranger's voice.

Know this, then. They boom out, large as large can be, larger than the world is big, and the sun is bright. As different from each other as wind and flame, yet also oh so similar. It staggered me, and surely always will, that the taste we had once experienced, the curious ague, was less than a quart of it. It humbles me. We are small, indeed. Far smaller than we would tell ourselves. The true scale of existence operates on a level beyond our reckoning. On this any man must know my word, and know it true.

I knew them, as they knew themselves. In bewildering senses that mere men do not possess.

Once one has experienced such a thing, the world is never the same.

Archivist Etherington continued to press the admiralty for the return of a ship of suitable tonnage and rank, with a full compliment such as was traditional for the ancient position, and in that endeavour she began to win a fulsome measure of favour. For, now Russell had returned from the front, he applied his significant station to our situation.

Fresh from his undoubted victory, he formed within society, and those sets whom wield power, the most influential faction that could simply not be ignored. Indeed, I should run out of paper were I to attempt to tally the endeavours to which society honoured him: courtiers flocked to him, dandies mimicked his style, and ministers courted him. Plays were written of his exploits, poets gushed, and the broadsides ran endless conjecture on his every move.

To stand against such was the greatest folly.

I was impossibly shy when I first gained a more proper introduction. But his was a winsome manner, and once I had seen with mine own eyes on the quiet evenings when he sat with Penelope and opened her up in such a way as I had never witnessed did I warm to him. While I did not grow bold in his company in the year that followed the battle, I came to favour his presence in our lives.

Our enemy did not disappear, and we would know greater tussles. The bill that was set to doom the archivist's office, did not pass the vote in the second house. Member Arksthrotle took an extended trade mission to the distant colonies. In the face of the power of Russell's and Hardy's faction he had little choice. Anton Grent joined him, then found excuse to tour the capitals of the grand tour.

While he did return to Fivedock on occasion, he was circumspect and remained distant. Though of a certainty we suspected they continued the transformation we had begun, and manoeuvred, and it spurred on our own actions. Felicity Hapeworth-Arksthrotle remained within Fivedock, and was as present as ever amongst the ton. But when I saw her her torments were muted, her venom I assumed saved to strike more keenly at us in future days. Absence, I was certain, that did little but increase its potency.

Sponsored by the Houses, Penelope and Ridley won my guardianship proper in both royal and common court. When the thick creamy paper of the courts, with the missive with the Lord Adjudicator's seal, to confirm the act was delivered to our door. What had once terrified me, now filled me instead with a sense of awe and joy.

In time, all would fall to flux once more. Sentinels would rise. Nations would crumble. We and all we knew was set to fall. The great conflagration that had settled over our world was but paused, or at least in our corner of it it might seem so. We knew a small moment of peace, and by Ra and Gussi did we relish in it.

My days of convalescence, and they were long, were spent in between bewilderment and the regimented workshop which I now called home.

And when even that, at last, began to pass, I subsumed myself in the reassuring measure of work and it rose to meet me. When I learnt, once more, to walk upon my shaking legs as man does, I took the opportunity to learn more of my adopted city. I took pleasures where before I had took none, and noticed things with a startling newness that can only have been rendered by the extremity of my most recent and unusual experience.

Freed from the watchful shackles of a malicious admiralty, our research continued at pace. We studied more intently than ever. We used our hard won influence to deploy our resources afresh. Beguiling and terrifying findings poured in to us, from every corner of the known world, and more beyond. We chased them down like bloodhounds.

Ludlow's body was never found. But rumours of a wild man, ears bleeding and deafened by the Sentinel's roar, who had been carried from the deck near where I was found aboard the *Spirit Breaker*, abounded. Hardy's agents received many a suggestion that such a man wandered the colonies, raving about the power of the Sentinels, then faded.

Was it him, and was it true? I am not so sure.

But I like to believe that it was.

War would return, and on a scale that would rend the very world asunder. But in those impossibly long summer days, and indeed in the brutal winter that followed upon its heels, it felt so very far away, indeed.

I like to think of many things from those days, strange things and wonderful things: I think of a dance of bled selites impossibly bright against a shimmering ocean, of the kiss of frigid sea water against my palm as my hand cuts through the waves, the tang of iodine and salt raw in my lungs.

Others come, more fleetingly, but no less alive. The touch of cotton against my breast, a sudden bark of the purest laughter, powder smoke thick and cloying. I think too of the pealing glee of a surgeon's mute as he runs with the wild abandon of the free, who was friends with a foolish slip of a girl, and the boy with the dark mop of curls who would be a Master of Mechanics.

That I was a Sentinel archivist's first now was a simple statement of inalienable truth, and one I spoke with pride at the barrage of social engagements that became increasingly difficult for us to ignore. Though I am sad to report that I developed no great taste for them through the familiarity of my new duties.

As to my relationship with the master archivist herself — I should not dare to say that I was immune to Etherington's set downs, and we argued still. My impetuous nature and her relentless manner must surely ensure our clashes. Yet still, despite all of this, we agreed one thing beyond all dispute: we would learn, together, what it meant to become a Seeker.

We would know who they were, and how they lived. We would come to reckon with an intimidating magic that tainted my dreams and living moments with an impossible sense of awe. The die was cast, the bargain made. We must surely follow it to the end. Whether because there was, truly, no choice left to us, or because we craved it or because it should consume us I believe mattered little. For within our breast and heart and soul now whispered the very words of gods.

And I was the woman who whispered back.

THANK YOU
FROM SAMUEL

Thank you so much for reading *Seeker*. I sincerely hope you enjoyed the story, and will join us for the rest of our journey into *The Sentinel Archives*. Reviews are the lifeblood of an author. So if you enjoyed this book, now is a great time to go and leave yours, on Amazon, Goodreads, social media, a retailer platform, or any other place you favour. I'd personally love for you to join the conversation.

If you'd like to sign up to the Samuel Griffin newsletter, or browse the Samuel Griffin website, you would be just as welcome! You may do so at www.samuel-griffin.com. Soon you will be able to sign up as an advanced reviewer, receive special editions, access early chapters, acquire discounts, and more. I hope to see you there.